Pascal Garnier

Pascal Garnier was born in Paris in 1949. The prize-winning author of over sixty books, he remains a leading figure in contemporary French literature, in the tradition of Georges Simenon. He died in 2010.

Melanie Florence

Melanie Florence teaches at The University of Oxford and translates from the French.

Emily Boyce

Emily Boyce is in-house translator and editor at Gallic Books.

The A26

How's the Pain?

The Panda Theory

'Small but perfectly formed darkest noir fiction told in spare, mordant prose ... Recounted with disconcerting matter of-factness, Garnier's work is surreal and horrific in equal measure' *Guardian*

'Tense, strange, disconcerting and slyly funny' *Sunday Times*

'Combines a sense of the surreal with a ruthless wit' *The Observer*

'Devastating and brilliant' *Sunday Times*

'Bleak, often funny and never predictable' *The Observer*

'Reminiscent of Joe Orton and the more impish films of Alfred Hitchcock and Claude Chabrol' *Sunday Times*

'A guaranteed grisly thriller' *ShortList*

'Brief, brisk, ruthlessly entertaining ... Garnier makes bleakness pleasurable' **John Powers, NPR**

'This is tough, bloody stuff, but put together with a cunning intelligence' *Sunday Times*

'Garnier's world exists in the cracks and margins of ours; just off-key, often teetering on the surreal, yet all too plausible. His mordant literary edge makes these succinct novels stimulating and rewarding' *Sunday Times*

The A26

How's the Pain?

The Panda Theory

by Pascal Garnier

Gallic Books
London

A Gallic Book

The A26

First published in France as *L'A26* by Zulma, 1999
Copyright © Zulma, 1999
English translation copyright © Gallic Books 2013
Translation supported by the French Ministry of Foreign Affairs as part of
the Burgess programme run by the Department of the French Embassy in
London. www.frenchbooknews.com
First published in Great Britain in 2013 by Gallic Books

How's the Pain?

First published in France as *Comment va la douleur?* by Zulma, 2006
Copyright © Zulma, 2006
English translation copyright © Gallic Books 2012
First published in Great Britain in 2012 by Gallic Books

The Panda Theory

First published in France as *La Théorie du panda* by Zulma, 2008
Copyright © Zulma, 2008
English translation copyright © Gallic Books 2012
First published in Great Britain in 2012 by Gallic Books

Typeset in Fournier MT by Gallic Books
Printed in the UK by CPI (CR0 4YY)

The A26

by Pascal Garnier

translated from the French by Melanie Florence

For Isa and Chantal

The third streetlamp at the end of the road had suddenly gone out. Yolande closed her eye, which was pressed up to the shutter. The echo of the white light went on pulsing on her retina for a few seconds. When she opened her eye again there was only a black hole in the sky over the dead streetlamp.

'I've stared at it for too long, and the bulb's gone.' Yolande shuddered and left the window. She had been watching the street not through a gap in the shutter but through a hole made specially. In the entire house this was the only opening on the outside world. Depending on her mood, she called it the 'bellybutton' or the 'world's arsehole'.

Yolande could have been anywhere from twenty to seventy. She had the blurry texture and outlines of an old photograph. As if she were covered in a fine dust. Inside this wreck of an old woman there was a young girl. You would catch a glimpse of her sometimes in a way she had of sitting down, tugging her skirt over her knees, of running a hand through her hair, a surprisingly graceful movement in that wrinkled skin glove.

She had sat down at a table, an empty plate in front of her. Across the table another place was set. The ceiling lamp hung quite low, and was not strong enough to light up the rest of the dining room, which remained shrouded in darkness. You could sense, however, that it was cluttered with objects and pieces of furniture. All the air in the room seemed to be concentrated around the table, held within the cone of light shed by the lampshade. Yolande waited, bolt upright in her chair.

'I saw the school bus this morning. The children were wearing every colour imaginable. Getting off the bus, they were like sweets spilling out of a bag. No, it wasn't this morning, it was yesterday, or maybe the day before. They really did look like sweets. It brightened up just then, a streak of blue between the clouds. In my day children weren't dressed like that. You didn't get all those fluorescent colours then, not anywhere. What else did I see? Any cars? Not many. Oh yes, there was the butcher this morning. I'm sure it was this morning. He comes every Sunday morning. I saw him parking, the old bastard. He's always trying to see in. He's been at it for years. He never sees anything, and he knows he never will.'

Beef, some stringy, some covered in fat, with a marrow bone to boil up for a *pot-au-feu*. It was ready, had been cooking away all day. *Bub, bub, bubble*. The pan lid was lifting, dribbling out greyish froth, a powerful smell, strong like sweat. 'What else did I see?'

Yolande showed no surprise at hearing the three quick taps at the door and the key turning in the lock. Her brother had always knocked three times to let her know it was him. There was no point, since no one ever came. But he did it anyway.

Yolande was still sitting with an empty plate. The room was cold, the cooker was off. Bernard hung up his wet coat. Underneath he was wearing an SNCF uniform; he worked for the railways. He was around fifty, and looked like the sort of person you would ask for some small change, the time or directions in the street. He greeted his sister with a kiss on the back of the neck as he went round to take his place opposite her. Locking his fingers, he cracked his knuckles before unfolding his napkin. He had a yellowish complexion and big dark shadows under his eyes. His flattened hair showed the circular imprint of his cap.

'Haven't you started? You should have, it's late.'

'No, I was waiting for you. I was wondering when the school bus last went by.'

'Saturday morning, I expect.'

'You've got mud all over you. Is it raining?'

'Yes.'

'Oh.'

They were both equally still, sitting upright in their chairs. They looked at each other without really seeing, asked questions without waiting for an answer.

'I had a puncture coming home from the station, near the building site. It's all churned up round there. You'd think the earth was spewing up mud. That's their machinery, excavators, rollers, all that stuff. The work's coming along quickly, but it's creating havoc.'

'Have you still got a temperature?'

'Sometimes, but it passes. I'm taking the tablets the doctor gave me. I'm a bit tired, that's all.'

'Shall I serve up?'

'If you like.'

Yolande took his plate and disappeared into the shadows. The ladle clanged against the side of the pot, and there was a sound of trickling juices. Yolande came back and handed the plate to Bernard. He took it, Yolande held on.

'Have you been scared?'

Bernard looked away and gave the plate a gentle tug. 'Yes, but it didn't last. Give it here, I'm feeling better now.'

Yolande went back for her own food. From the shadows she said, without knowing whether it was a question or a statement, 'You'll get more and more scared.'

Bernard began to eat, mechanically.

'That may be, I don't know. Machon's given me some new pills.'

Yolande ate in the same way, as if scooping water out of a boat.

'I saw the butcher this morning. He tried to see in again.'

Bernard shrugged. 'He can't see anything.'

'No, he can't see anything.'

Then they stopped talking and finished their lukewarm *pot-au-feu*.

Through the closed shutters, shafts of light came in from the street, illuminating the chaos cluttering the dining room. A network of narrow passages tunnelled through the heaped-up jumble of furniture, books, clothing, all kinds of things, made it possible to get from one room to another provided you walked like an Egyptian. Stacks of newspapers and magazines just about managed to prop up this rubbish tip, which threatened to collapse at any moment.

At the table, Yolande had swept the used plates, cutlery and glasses from the evening before over to one corner. She was busy cutting pictures out of a magazine and sticking them on to pieces of cardboard to make a kind of jigsaw puzzle. By day the pendant lamp still oozed the same dead light as it did by night.

'Bernard's not gone to work today, he wasn't up to it. He's getting tireder and tireder, thinner and thinner. His body's like this house, coming apart at the seams. Where am I going to put him when he's dead? There's not a bit of space left anywhere. We'll get by, we've always got by, ever since I can remember. Nothing has ever left this house, even the toilet's blocked up. We keep everything. Some day, we won't need anything else, it'll all be here, for ever.'

Yolande hummed to herself, to the accompaniment of mice scrabbling and Bernard's laboured breathing in the room next door.

He was asleep or pretending to be. He was fiddling with a sparkling pendant on a gilt chain: 'More than yesterday and much less than tomorrow.' He wouldn't be going back to the doctor's. Even before setting foot in the consulting room he had known it was his final visit, almost a matter of courtesy. As usual, Machon had adopted specially for him the jovial manner which he found so irritating. But yesterday evening he'd struck more false notes than usual, stumbling over his words while looking in vain for the prompt. In short, when he'd sent Bernard away, his eyes had belied what his lips were saying.

'It's a question of attitude, Monsieur Bonnet, and of willpower. You've got to fight, and keep on fighting. In any case, you'll see, two or three days from now and you'll be feeling much better. Don't forget now, take three in the morning, three at lunch time and three in the evening.'

It was true, on leaving Bernard had felt relief, but that had had nothing to do with the medication. These regular appointments with the doctor, for months now, had been eating away at him as much as his illness, a never-ending chore. He who had never been ill in his life had experienced something like profound humiliation at handing himself over body and soul to Dr Machon, despite knowing him well. Every Wednesday for years now, the doctor had caught the train to Lille to see his mother. They had ended up exchanging greetings and passing the time of day until there had grown up between them not a friendship exactly, but a very pleasant acquaintanceship. As soon as he'd begun to feel ill Bernard had quite naturally turned to him. He'd soon regretted it, he had become his patient. In front of the large Empire-style desk he'd always felt like a suspect stripped for questioning, one of life's miscreants. These days whenever he met the doctor at the station he felt naked in front of him, completely at a loss.

Bernard had crumpled up the prescription and got behind the

wheel of his car. There had been no puncture beside the building site.

Spurts of water added whiskers to each side of his Renault 5. Bernard was discovering life in its tiniest forms. It was there, rounding out with yellow light each of the droplets of rain starring the windscreen, million upon million of miniature light bulbs to illuminate so long a night. It was there too in the vibrations of the steering wheel in his hands, and in the dance of the windscreen wipers, which reminded him of the finale of a musical comedy. The anguish of doubt gave way to the strange nirvana of certainty. It was a matter of weeks, days, then. He had known for ages that he was dying, of course, but this evening he felt he had crossed a line. Deep down, these last months, it was hope which had made him suffer the most. 'Bernard Bonnet, your appeal has been refused.' He felt liberated, he had nothing more to lose.

Then in the beam of the headlamps, he had seen the redhead, thumbing a lift, caught in a mesh of rain and dark.

'What an awful night!'

'Three months at the most,' he had thought. She smelt of wet dog. She wasn't even twenty, surely.

'I've missed the bus to Brissy. Are you going that way?'

'I'm going nearby, I can drop you off there.' She had a big nose, big bust and big thighs and smelt of wide open spaces, the impetuousness of youth. Bernard's uniform must have made her feel safe, as she was making herself at home, undoing her parka and shaking out her mop of red hair.

'The next one's not for half an hour, and I don't want to wait. I'll be eighteen in a month, and sitting my test. I've been saving up, and for a car as well. My brother-in-law's going to sell me his – it's a Renault 5, like yours.'

'That's nice.'

'Don't I know you? D'you work at the station?'

'Yes.'

The stripes on her trousers looked like scratches. She had sturdy thighs, and the same smell as Yolande when she came home late from the factory. Their father would thump his fist on the table.

'Have you seen the time?'

'Well, how d'you expect me to get home? There isn't a bus any more. There's a war on, haven't you heard? What are we having to eat?'

They always had the same, and she would always have some boyfriend waiting in the wings.

'Why are you smiling?'

'Because you remind me of my sister when she was your age.'

'Oh. What's she called, your sister?'

'Yolande.'

'I'm Maryse. And what about you, what's your name?'

'Bernard.'

'Like my brother-in-law!' She was practically family. Nothing for it but ... He had stopped thinking about his death. This girl was like his life, a huge gift which he hadn't dared even begin to unwrap.

'What does your sister do?'

'Nothing.'

'Housewife and mother, then?'

'Something like that.'

On each side of the road the houses dissolved in a wash of brown ink. A triangular yellow sign had appeared right in the middle of the road, forcing a diversion.

'The fucking motorway, it's driving me mad! We don't need it, do we?'

'The march of progress. If you'll excuse me, I just have to stop for a few minutes, a call of —'

'Got it!'

20

The girl's laughter had sounded in his ear like the tinkling of the doorbell when you're not expecting a visitor. The rain had eased off and was now little more than a drizzle, the tears of a star freshening his face. Standing squarely in the mud, he had urinated against a concrete block bristling with metal rods. Work on the motorway had begun at the same time as his pain. With a wry smile, he noted how fast it was progressing. The arched back of the unfinished A26 soared like a diving board into the violet sky. A star had appeared between two banks of cloud. His hard-on was so big that he hadn't been able to do up his flies again. On the way back to the car his feet made a squelching sound with every step.

'I'm sorry, I've dropped my watch. There's a torch in the glove compartment.'

'Would you like some help?'

'That would be good. Thank you.'

The pair of them had waded about in the mud, Maryse's backside just a few centimetres from Bernard's nose. A whole life right in front of him. The girl had made a sound like a deflating balloon when he had jumped on her. Lying on top of her wildly flailing body, he held her head down in a puddle. It had gone on for quite some time, the girl was sturdy. But the grip of Bernard's hand on the back of her neck had finally proved too much for Maryse's 'nearly' eighteen years. 'Strong as death! I'm as strong as death!' His eyes were like a hound's when it bays at the moon. The water in the puddle became calm again. Soon it reflected nothing but a sky empty save for one quivering star. Bernard had loosened his grip. A slender gilt chain had got twisted round his wrist, at its end a small disc inscribed 'More than yesterday and much less than tomorrow'.

The hardest part had been dragging her to the far side of the building site. There he had heaved the body into one of the holes which would be filled in with vast quantities of concrete the next day, and covered her with earth. Maryse no longer existed, had never existed perhaps.

Bernard let the chain drop back on to his belly. It was unbelievably heavy. He thought he would give it to Yolande as a present. What would become of her without him? Nothing. She had stopped 'becoming' the best part of fifty years ago.

She would go on, every morning knitting the little scrap of life which she then unravelled every night, tirelessly, without ever thinking there might be an end.

'Bernard, there's the grocer's van!'

'I'm tired, Yoyo. Do you really need something?'

'Yes! Those little chocolate biscuits with the animals on. Please ...'

'OK. Give me my coat, will you?'

'Get a few packets, just in case.'

Since Monday evening there has been no news of young Maryse L., born on 4 April 1975 in Brissy. The young woman was last seen close to the Jean-Jaurès bus stop. She is described as one metre sixty-four centimetres tall, of medium build, etc. Anyone with information should contact the police in ...

Bernard did not think the photo was a good likeness.

Newspaper photos never looked like anything, or rather they all looked alike, sharing a family resemblance, hangdog and miserable. The papers said any old thing. They never had anything very interesting to report, so they told lies. There wasn't so much as two lines to be said about the girl. Apart from a handful of individuals, no one knew Maryse existed. Her death made no difference. What album had they dug that photo out of? She couldn't be more than twelve in it. The silly smile of the young girl turned his stomach.

'Oh Bernard, you haven't eaten a thing! That's no good, and you know you like shepherd's pie.'

'I have, Jacqueline, I've had some. I'm just a bit out of sorts, that's all.'

'I can see that. You haven't touched your food. Have you seen Machon again?'

'Yes, on Monday. Everything's fine.'

'Everything's fine, my foot!'

Jacqueline put her pile of plates down on the corner of the table and ran her hand over her face as if removing an invisible spider's web. She had had this habit ever since they'd been at primary school together. Jacqueline was his best friend. They might have got married, had children, a dog, a caravan, the most modest of lives but a life even so. But there was Yolande. Jacqueline had waited for a long time, and then married Roland. They had the restaurant across from the station.

'Are you coming on Sunday, for Serge's First Communion?'

'I don't know, maybe.'

'But you've got to. He'd be hurt ... I suppose you're fretting about Yolande, is that it?'

'Of course not.'

'Of course you are! She'll take advantage of you for your whole life, that one! Why don't you put her in a home? It's about time you started taking care of yourself. Have you looked in a mirror recently?'

'You know perfectly well that's impossible. She's not capable of —'

'Give me a light, will you? Yes, Roland, I'm coming, just a second! He's a bloody nuisance, that one. Can't do a damn thing for himself. It's a mess, isn't it?'

'Please don't start, Jacqueline.'

'What? What would we have left if we no longer had our regrets?'

'Remorse, perhaps.'

'Sometimes I think I might prefer that. At least it would mean we'd done things.'

'Things? They don't leave much of a trace behind them.'

'Well, did you want to leave pyramids behind you? Things aren't just stuff made of stone, your churches, castles, monuments! It's the little things, like when you used to go fishing in bomb craters, smoking your first cheap cigarette round the back of the bike sheds, all the things we said we were going to do even if we already knew we'd never do them ... I'll be right there, I said! Please come on Sunday, just for me.'

'All right, I'll be there.'

Jacqueline got up with a sigh. She could almost have supported the tray on her ample bosom, leaving her hands free to carry other plates, other dishes. It must feel good to lie sleeping on those breasts, like being on a cloud. A long time past, down by the canal, the weather was hot. You could smell fresh grass. He had laid his cheek on Jacqueline's white breast. Beneath the thin stuff of her blouse he could feel her quivering, giving off a fragrant dew. Fish were jumping, snapping at dragonflies. The air was alive with a thousand tiny things. One of them had said, 'This is nice, isn't it?'

The small fluorescent green letters on the screen were no longer making proper words. They were now just long wiggly caterpillars, line upon line of them.

'Is something wrong, Bernard?'

'No, a spot of dizziness, that's all. It must be the new pills. Take over from me, François. I'm just nipping out for a breath of air.'

'Of course. Why don't you take some time off?'

'I'll think about it.'

Where did those rails along the platforms go? Not all that far. They joined up again over there, behind the warehouses, the end of the world was within arm's reach. Everything was rusty here, down to the ballast stones, even the grass clinging to life beside the track. The railway had left its mark, a lengthy scar with dried blood at the edges. Sitting on a trolley, Bernard ran his fingers over his face, feeling the rows of teeth, the angle of the jaw. Beneath the pallid, soft skin a death's head was hiding, like the one on a pirate flag or the labels of particular bottles at the pharmacy, with two crossbones behind. So what if it was ugly here, it was still the richest landscape on earth. You could make a life here. It was all there ahead of him, rails leading to more rails, on and on to infinity. François was right, he would take some leave. Actually, he would leave. Like old Fernand the year before. But he'd been retiring. He was old. He had gone off with a fishing rod under his arm, a cuckoo clock and a return ticket to Arcachon, first class. Bernard would never go to Arcachon. To tell the truth, he didn't give two hoots about Arcachon, there were so many places in the world where one would never set foot. What was there, anyway? A dune, a big Dune of Pilat which looked just like the desert, they said. It was people who'd never been there who said that. Everything looked like everything else, people couldn't help comparing the things they knew to the things they didn't know, so they could say they did know, that they'd been round the world without leaving their armchair. Six of one and half a dozen of the other, no cause for regrets. No gifts for sick employees, they'd prefer them just to clear off, preferably without a trace. Illness really annoyed them, it was bad for business, and they took a dim view of it. It lowered the troops' morale.

'Oh my poor Bonnet, and with your poor sister too! How much time off do you want?'

Taking his cap between thumb and forefinger, Bernard sent it flying somewhere over the containers, like a frisbee. He had another one in the locker room. No harm done. The wind caressed his baldness. In the early days, when Yolande's hair had begun to grow back he'd loved running his hand over her head. All the little hairs standing upright had given him a feeling like electricity in his palm. Her hair had grown back pure white. Yet she was only twenty. The shock of it, no doubt. Before that it was blonde, red blonde, Titian she used to call it.

WITH SEVEN CENTIMETRES OF HAIR

I have already told you how hard-working the Germans are. They make clothes and chocolate out of wood, and make lots of things from all sorts of materials which have not been used until now. They have now discovered it is possible to make felt hats out of the hair cut off by the hairdresser. It is likewise possible to make rugs from these hair clippings. Since hair has to be a certain length for this, however, people are not allowed to have it cut before it reaches this length. If the hairdressers are diligent and collect up the hair carefully, in one year almost 300,000 kilos of hair will be obtained. That sounds like a lot of hats and quite a few rugs.

There it was in black and white, in the girls' own annual *La Semaine de Suzette*, under the heading 'Suzette across the world', an old copy from 1932, worn to a shine, stained and yellowing, like everything from that era. Despite knowing it by heart, Yolande loved to spend hours leafing through it. She had done all the crosswords, every rebus and sewn the entire wardrobe for Bleuette (a 29-centimetre doll with real curled hair, eyes that shut, and unbreakable posable head). She loved the smell it gave off when the pages were opened, a musty smell of old biscuits. The Germans would be back. She wasn't especially waiting for them but she knew they'd be back.

It was the drop of water falling on her newly shaven head which had hurt her the most, a deafening sound like the stroke of a gong which had stayed with her ever since. As for everything else, she had let them get on with it, like a sheep, there was nothing else to be done with morons like that. For as long as they kept her in the café, amidst their yelling, she had been outside her body. She was a past master at switching off, what with her bastard of a father who would bawl her out for the slightest thing. She'd had enough time to practise. But on leaving the Café de la Gare, after

27

they'd let her go, *plop!*, a large drop filled with all the absurdities of the past four years. It was as though the sky had been holding itself back ever since they'd dragged her out of her house, so as to fall in on her with all its might in that drop.

Yolande didn't even remember the Boche's name. To tell the truth, it wasn't so much for what she'd done with him that they'd shaved her head, more for what she'd refused to do with some of her 'barbers'.

What did it matter anyway? She had never liked them, they had never liked her. It had let her get shot of the damned lot of them once and for all. Besides, they must all be dead by now. But what had he been playing at in the lav for the past hour?

'Bernard, what are you doing in there?'

'Trying to unblock the toilet. How many times have I told you not to use newspaper!'

'I didn't have anything else. You forgot to get bog roll when you were at Auchan.'

'There's tissues.'

'They're no use to me, there's nothing to read on them.'

The sound of the flush drowned out Bernard's reply. He emerged from the toilet, wiping his hands. He was wearing a white shirt, the collar gaping wide round his thin neck.

'What are you dressed up like that for? Are you going to a wedding?'

'No, it's Jacqueline's nephew's First Communion. I told you that last night.'

'You didn't tell me a thing. You're always up to something behind my back.'

'For one thing, I did tell you, and for another, I'm not up to anything. I'm going to the Communion, that's all.'

'So basically you're going to get sloshed and let her sucker of a husband foot the bill.'

'Yoyo, that's enough. I won't be staying long. I'm done in but

I've got no choice. I won't be late back. The toilet's unblocked and I'm begging you, please don't put any more newspaper in there.'

Yolande shrugged and buried herself in *La Semaine de Suzette* again. Bernard rolled down his sleeves, slipped on his jacket and planted a kiss on his sister's neck.

'Come on now, don't sulk – I've got a present for you.'

The pendant on its gilt chain was dangling over the annual like a pendulum. Catlike, Yolande caught at it.

'What does that mean, "More than yesterday and much less than tomorrow"? Is it about the blocked toilet?'

'No, it means I love you more than yesterday and much less than tomorrow.'

'You're going to love me less tomorrow?'

'No, it's the other way round.'

'It's beyond me. Can you put it on for me?'

Bernard's fingers fumbled with the clasp. Strange, the skin on Yolande's neck wasn't an old lady's but a baby's, all soft, warm little folds.

'You're very beautiful.'

Yolande put the pendant into her mouth. 'I used to have one with the Virgin Mary, a blue one, it tasted of electric wire. At school when you went for an X-ray, you had to put it in your mouth so they didn't see the Virgin Mary in your bones. This one doesn't taste of anything.'

'See you later, Yolande.'

The countryside, accustomed to low skies and drizzle, looked ill at ease in its Sunday best in the sunlight. The bricks were too red, the sky too blue, the grass too green. It was as if Nature felt embarrassed at being so extravagantly made up. She was quite still, as if for the camera, except for the occasional crow hopping about in the middle of a field. At the wheel of his car Bernard was feeling good, for the first time in a long while. He loved these expanses of brown stretching as far as the eye could see, you could almost fancy you were by the sea. He passed a motorcyclist at the roadside, leaning against his bike. He was smoking a cigarette, at right angles to the line of the horizon. There was no house nearby. Here was a chap who had simply said to himself, 'I know what, I'll stop here for a cigarette because this is absolutely the best place in the world for that.' It was over in seconds, just the time it took for the motorcyclist's image to disappear in the rear-view mirror, but Bernard felt every bit of that man's happiness in his own body: 'I feel good.'

'And what about me? What will become of me while Yolande's still here?' He realised he had never asked himself that question before. He would very much have liked to be a biker stopped at the roadside for eternity. No doubt Yolande had never asked herself that question either.

She didn't care, had never cared about anything but herself. It couldn't really be called egotism, she had simply never been aware of other people. They were bit parts, at most, even her brother. When she had come home with her head shaven, never to leave the house again, she had appeared relieved, her face serene like that of a young nun. They didn't want her any more, and she had never wanted them. At last things were clear, ordered, everyone in their place. She had never wanted anything but this cat's life of cosseting and food.

Bernard slowed down as he passed the works on the A26. The pillars supporting the slip road had advanced a few steps. RIP Maryse.

'Now, Bernard, that's not an empty glass, is it?'

'Yes, but I'm fine, thanks.'

Roland's eyes looked like two blobs of phlegm, pastis yellow shot through with red.

'It's lovely to see the young ones having fun, so full of life!' In the back room of the café, where the tables had been arranged in a horseshoe, the young ones were jigging to one of the summer's hits. The acrylic of the girls' little skirts was stretched out of shape over their bulging thighs. The boys, a glint in their eye, were blowing themselves a smoke screen to hide their acne and drinking out of cans. Jacqueline, hair dishevelled, was zigzagging amongst the dancers with a tray in her outstretched hand. She looked like a statue carrying its upturned plinth.

'She's not bad, even now, huh?'

'No.'

'Even with a few miles on the clock she's still a catch, don't you think?'

'Yes.'

'I'm telling you, Bernard, not only am I not angry with you, I feel sorry for you. Yes, I do, don't argue. What's more, out of all the men who've come sniffing around after her, you're the one I

31

like best. You are! Because you're going to kick the bucket soon – before me. Not by much maybe, but before me.'

Roland's brow was dripping with sweat. The few hairs he had left were plastered to his temples. He'd been a very good footballer, the best goalkeeper Subligny had ever had, and had inherited the café-restaurant from his parents.

'I had to tell you, Bernard – it may not seem like it but I respect you. Look, if you want to, you can have her right here and now, before my very eyes, and I won't say a thing. Scout's honour.'

'You're talking rubbish, Roland. You're drunk.'

'Not at all! You'll see. Jacqueline! Hey, Jacqueline!'

'What's the matter with you? You must be out of your mind, yelling like that!'

'He won't believe I respect him! Do your business, you two, and I won't so much as raise my little finger. Go on!'

'You must be mad! There are children present!'

'So, there's children. They've got to learn the facts of life, haven't they? Like on the farm, the pigs with the sows, and the mares with the ... I don't know what, but that's nature's way, isn't it, shit!'

'Be quiet! It's you who's the pig – clear off, you're ruining it all.'

The music had stopped, and so had the dancers. Some of them were sniggering behind their hands, others rolled their eyes. Only Serge, whose Communion they were celebrating, still moved around between them on his brand-new Rollerblades.

'I've got to go, Jacqueline.'

'No, you don't, that's stupid.'

'It doesn't matter. It's not because of him, I'm just tired. I was leaving anyway. Say goodbye to Serge from me.'

Out in the car park Bernard rubbed his eyes. The red sphere of the setting sun was pulsing on his retina.

Someone knocked on the window.

'Hello. Which direction are you going?'

The girl was made up like someone from a silent film, hair all over the place, black and red, like a kid disguised as a witch.

'Towards Arras, but I'm turning off in six kilometres.'

'That'll still be a help. Could you give me a lift?'

'If you like.'

She was wearing such a lot of heavy perfume, she needn't have bothered getting dressed.

'On Sundays, the buses ... Is it all right if I smoke?'

'Of course.'

The girl lit a cigarette. The smoke lingered above their heads. They weren't saying anything. Bernard was driving slowly. The sky took on streaks of purple and mauve.

'It's pretty. All this silence does you good.'

'Yes, it's like staring into a fire in the grate.'

'Wasn't there a war here?'

'That's right. The Great War and the other one. It's taken a while for it to look alive again.'

'Do you remember the war?'

'Just a little. I was young then.'

'All our lives we've heard people talking about it on TV, all over the world, but we can't really take it in. We're not quite sure it exists. It's like fairytale monsters, and ogres and death. We know it exists but we don't believe in it. We doubt everything, even ourselves. We're never quite sure we're not in a video game.'

'Does that bother you?'

'No, you just have to get used to it. I spotted you just now during the shouting match. You were different from the others. Me too. I'd come with a mate of the boyfriend of ... well, whatever, it's a shame, he was cute. You look so sad ... it's nice.'

'I'm not sad.'

'You look it.'

The sound the girl's stockings made as she crossed her legs caused him to jerk the wheel. But he was very swiftly back in control. She had noticed. He could just imagine the smile on her face as she crushed her cigarette end in the ashtray.

'What do you do for a living?'

'I'm going to drop you off here.'

'Really?'

'Really.'

Bernard parked on the verge. A car hooted as it went by. The lower part of the sky was turquoise with a tinge of gold right at the top.

'OK, well, thanks a lot anyway.'

'What's your name?'

'Vanessa.'

'Goodbye, Vanessa. Very nice to have met you.'

Vanessa, the motorcyclist, Jacqueline, all of them in the rear-view mirror, in one small piece of mirror which saw things back to front. A life wasn't very much, not much at all. Giving, taking away. It was so easy. Sometimes death spares people.

Yolande was making pancakes, dozens of them, building them up into an enormous stack. There were enough to feed at least fifty. It was her only way of combating the successive waves of 'outside' which had been beating against the walls of the house non-stop since the morning. For almost two hours now she had been busy, frying pan in hand at the stove. To begin with, she had counted them, as people count sheep to fall asleep, but then it had become mechanical, like breathing: a ladle of batter, turn the pan, wait, toss the pancake, wait, put it on the pile, a ladle of batter, turn the pan ... They were like the skin of faces, faces she could put names to: Lyse, Fernand, Camille ... She saw them go past one after the other, the way they used to lean over her cradle, gigantic, stinking of beer or cheap perfume, and belching out their slobbering coochie-coos, disgusting. Even then she had hated them, was nothing to do with them. She had only had to look at her father's face or her mother's belly to know for certain that she did not come from 'that'. Each time she tossed a pancake bubbling with dark craters, she said, 'Nice one.'

An hour after Bernard had gone out, the clock-radio in his room had come on by itself: 'Stock market news now, and all week the CAC 40 has been on a continual ...' Yolande had jumped in her chair. She had been in the middle of copying a map of France, concentrating, tongue sticking out, on making a good job of the shades of blue along the coast with a coloured pencil.

'Who's that? Who's there?'

She had taken the poker from where it hung on the handle of the stove and burst into Bernard's room, brandishing it aloft. The metallic voice coming from the small plastic box by the unmade bed had metamorphosed into an unbearable loud rasping with the first blow of the poker. But the creature was not dead and Yolande had had to finish it off with her heel to silence it for good. It had been some time before her nerves recovered and she was able to pick up her pencil again to draw the outline of Finistère.

The 'nose of France' was so hard to manage, with all the little ins and outs of the coastline from Saint-Brieuc to Vannes. She had always got ten out of ten for her maps; they would be pinned up in the classroom they were so beautiful. For that she'd needed to sharpen her coloured pencils really well and wet their points with spit. It was Brittany Yolande took the greatest pains over, because of the holidays. There were cousins in Pénerf, a little village near Vannes. Yolande used to have a thin frock in embroidered muslin from St Gallen, with tulle trim at the shoulders and waist, and a sky-blue straw cloche hat. But most of the time she would be in her bathing suit, barefoot, spattered with sand up to her knees. Every day, crowds of workers would pour out of excursion trains for their first visit to the seaside. Only the villa residents held themselves aloof from this display of overwhelming joy. It seemed as if the holidays would never end, like the Paradise they learnt about at First Communion classes. Yolande had a constant humming in her head. Perhaps it was from pressing seashells to her ear, or maybe the water from all the swimming. Yannick had white-blond hair, dry as straw. They would have play fights with sticky seaweed, and, squealing wildly, feel for each other with outstretched arms, under cover of the foam. That was the first time she had kissed using her tongue. For everything it was the first time.

A thudding at the door had ripped through the iridescent haze of her holidays at Pénerf. Her pencil point had snapped clean off on the south of Brittany. Yolande had pressed her eye up to the world's arsehole; two women, one stout and the other small, were rummaging in the letter box. They had waited, while Yolande held her breath. She had rumbled them, they were Boches disguised as French. Unless they were the girls from the Resistance done up to look like Boches ... You could never tell, there was no difference. Either way, playing dead was the thing if you wanted to stay alive. The two women had taken a step back and then moved off. Yolande had waited for a long time before retrieving the piece of paper from the letter box: 'Do you know the Bible?' Yolande hadn't read to the end of the text because it was obviously written in code, the proof being that it was signed 'The Jehovah's Witnesses'. What a bunch of losers! There would never be witnesses at her trial, because there would never be a trial. Bernard had promised her that. But they kept on trying all the same; they needed guilty people, even guilty people who were innocent, to fuel their morbid obsession with stamping out clandestine goings-on. That being so, she had to be on her guard; they would be back, they always were. That was her day shot to pieces. The only way to ward off the misfortune was to make pancakes, pancakes and more pancakes.

'You mustn't upset yourself, Bonnet. We are all ...' His boss had searched for the appropriate word – 'Mortal? Alike?' – but held back, from embarrassment, perhaps, or fear. 'OK. Have some rest and come back to us soon.'

Right, that was sorted, indefinite sick leave. It seemed just like any other day, however. Bernard felt no worse than the day before. Decidedly better in fact. The two days after Serge's First Communion had been a veritable agony: vomiting, migraines, an intense feeling of malaise. Then, on making this decision, a sort of respite. 'It's a question of attitude, Monsieur Bonnet,' Machon said. Perhaps he was right; they were mysterious, the body and the mind. Of those two days spent at the mercy of Yolande's whims and the vagaries of his physical condition, all he had left was 'room' in his life, 'room' like in a garment which is too big. Someone who knew about such things had once told him you shouldn't be able to see any light between two good dancers. His dancing days were over, and that was that, except with Yolande, of course, for the light had never been visible between them. As for his boss and his colleagues, he knew he wouldn't be seeing them again. It was no sadder than casting off an old pair of slippers. In taking leave, he had married death, and death fitted him like a glove. Sorrow came from denial – that was why life had so often made him suffer. Now he would say 'yes' to everything, good and bad, sunshine and grey skies alike; this

November afternoon it was the latter.

Sitting behind the wheel of his car in the station car park, he felt desperately free. Doubtless this was how someone felt on the first day of unemployment: 'I could go here, or there, do nothing, go home and be bored stiff, go mad ...' The excess of freedom knocked him sideways. Maybe he should start collecting stamps, or keep pigeons like the retired men in these parts? Or build model ships? It was too much, too ...

An urgent rapping on the window made him jump. Roland's face, squashed up against the glass, looked strangely distorted, like a portrait by Bacon, streaming with rain.

'Bernard, help me! Féfé's just been run over by a lorry.'

'Who?'

'Féfé, my gun dog. Let me in.'

A smell of frying came off Roland as he got in beside Bernard. His eyes were glassy from tears and the rain.

'Shit, shit, shit!'

Bernard let him drum his fingers on the dashboard.

'He's one of a kind, that dog!'

'Calm down. What's going on?'

'My parents just phoned. I left Féfé with them for the weekend. I told them to keep him tied up! He always goes chasing after lorries!'

'Is he dead?'

'If only! I have to go and finish him off. I'm not brave enough. I saw you getting into your car and thought you ...'

'I'd what?'

'Well ... that you'd be able to ... Don't make me do this on my own.'

Roland was leaking all over, from his eyes, nose and hair. He was the last of that ridiculous breed, the Sunday huntsmen who shoot at anything that moves, or not, as the case might be (he was the one to thank for the shot-riddled 'Caution. Children' sign on the way into the village), and now he was crying over his Féfé, half flattened by a lorry. A man who would swear on his deathbed that he loved animals. His own. He was a stupid, sad bastard, but at this moment Bernard could not bring himself to treat him as such. He knew he was a stupid bastard, a stupid bastard who hated him, but a stupid bastard who was weeping, the way the sky weeps, sometimes.

'Why me?'

'I couldn't bring myself to pull the trigger. Féfé and I ... I just couldn't. But you know death.'

'Not yet, I don't.'

'You've seen it. I can tell you've seen it!'

'You're still drunk, Roland.'

'True, but it's because I'm suffering. You're the only one who can do it. Bernard, please ...'

'Where d'your parents live?'

'Over by Brissy.'

Black and white like an old Chaplin film, minus the laughs. The sky could not decide whether to be bright or not. Most annoying. They parked outside Roland's parents' place, a once elegant house, which had been revamped with garden gnomes and fake wells made from tyres, like something out of a bad novel. Roland emerged, carrying a .22 rifle.

'Over there, by the bridge.'

Bernard parked. As they got out, Roland handed him the gun. They walked along the verge, the grass green against a backdrop of grey sky. It was a little slippery. In a dip in the bank, the tan and white dog, with a vacant look and his tongue lolling, was lying stretched out on his side. His back legs were now just a wet mush of hair and blood.

'Oh damn! Kill him, kill him!'

Bernard aimed the barrel at the back of the animal's ear, as it looked up at him, eyes growing dim. *Why me?*

It was a small rifle and the noise it made going off was no louder than a fart under the bedclothes. One click – and lights out. The dog's head fell back on to the soft grass. *A gully of green ... foaming trough of light ...*

Behind Bernard, Roland was busy throwing up.

'What do we do now?'

'Bin bag. In the car ...'

Bernard took charge of everything. The dog was nothing but a piece of rubbish.

'What next?'

'How should I know? Better dig a hole.'

'Go on then.'

'Bloody hell, you're cruel!'

'I'm a killer not a gravedigger. There's a spade in the boot – off you go.' Nowhere, here was nowhere. Unconsciously, while Roland was digging a hole for his dog, Bernard adopted the stance of the motorcyclist at the roadside. He smoked a cigarette; the sun was not there, however, and nor was the serenity which had made that moment special. At best, there was the complicity between two killers, one of them too cowardly to do the deed. The cigarette butt he flicked down on the wet tarmac was out in less than three seconds.

'I'm done. We can go.'

Roland was green, the colour of goose shit. 'That's another reason you'll have to be angry with me.'

'What?'

'I'm the person who killed your dog. Who will you have to complain about once I'm gone?'

'There's always someone. Do you think you're the only man who's screwed Jacqueline?'

Bernard smiled. If nothing else, humans were marvellously resourceful.

Getting out of the car outside the restaurant, Roland did not say thank you. He ran off, jacket up over his head, a hunched figure. People never said thank you to those who did their dirty work for them.

He already knew which dog he would buy next.

The same, no doubt. Roland always bought the same car, and if Jacqueline were to die he would find another one. A Nadine or a Martine maybe, but a Jacqueline even so. There are people like that, who think they can make things last for ever if they try hard enough.

For the past hour, Bernard had been driving around aimlessly, turning left here and right there, as luck or misfortune would have it. He had no idea where he was going but one thing he was sure about, he had no desire to go home, not straight away. Like a fly trapped under a glass he was looking for the way out while knowing only too well that none existed. As when he had left the station he felt burdened by the excess of freedom he was unable to use. Signposts pointed him in different directions: Lens, Liévin, Noeux-les-Mines, Béthune ... but they were traps, leading only to fields of mud crushed under the weight of the impending dark. Occasionally he passed through villages, brown brick houses set out like Lego belonging to a child devoid of imagination, blank windows hung with lace curtains depicting a pair of peacocks face-to-face or else plump cherubs in the same pose, and roofs topped with TV aerials resembling giant dragonflies. Who could possibly stop off in one of them, unless he had broken down? And yet people lived there, had their joys and sorrows no less than those who lived in picture-postcard landscapes drenched in sunlight and azure. In those parts you would stop to buy regional pottery, local honey or to visit an old Romanesque church. Here there was nothing but home-brewed beer and war memorials of a soldier pointing his bayonet towards an indifferent sky, framed by four artillery shells with chains between them.

But you can't continue going nowhere for long, especially

when night is falling, and so Bernard convinced himself he felt like eating moules-frites beside the station in Lille. It was years since he'd done that. He smiled at his own audacity. There was Yolande, it was true, but how could he let her know since she never answered the phone? In any case, she wasn't aware of the passage of time. And anyway, stuff Yolande, stuff Roland's dog, stuff it all! Illness made you self-centred, that was its greatest advantage.

He didn't order moules-frites but doughy, cheesy flamme-kueche. Inside Aux Brasseurs, once he had tucked himself away in a corner, he had felt so overwhelmed by all the noise, the belching and smoking throng – it was like something out of Breughel – that when the waiter had come to take his order he had asked for the same as the people at the next table, just to keep things simple. By now he was ruing his rashness. He hadn't even got a newspaper to read to make him look in command of the situation. This was taking ages, he'd already looked through the menu a dozen times. The clientele here were groups of friends or at least couples. Hang on, there was another man on his own. He even thought he recognised him as the travelling salesman who was cutting a swathe through the area, persuading lonely housewives to buy lingerie on credit, much to their husbands' anger. The man was eating mussels with no concern for the fact his loud slurping was getting on the other diners' nerves. He had the dispassionate and ice-cool air of a bounty hunter in a western. Or maybe it wasn't him after all. As a result of looking at people, since he had nothing else to do, Bernard ended up recognising everyone. That was odd, but not as improbable as all that. He had never left the area, and had seen a lot of people pass through the station. That said, no one recognised him. It was all an illusion, a whirl of faces seen here and there, a fug of beer and cigarette smoke. You rub shoulders with the whole world in a lifetime, but forget people again as you go along, like friends you make on holiday – you promise to keep in touch only to consign them to oblivion at once. How could it be otherwise? You'd need ten lifetimes to keep on top of all that. Besides, at the end of the day, we only need a few satellites to make up our galaxy. All stars are alike. That old pal Robert we were so fond of, who was lost in the mists of time, reappears one fine day calling himself Raoul or François or ...

'Flammekueche with lardons!'

'For me, please.'

'Another beer?'

'Umm ... all right.'

'Excuse me, Monsieur, but there's a lady on her own looking for a table, and there aren't any free. Would you mind if she shared yours?'

'Well, no, I ...'

'Thank you, Monsieur. Madame? This way, please.'

She wasn't beautiful, she wasn't ugly, she almost wasn't, full stop, and yet she was very fat, first-rate camouflage.

'Good evening, Monsieur, thank you so much. It's so crowded here that it's hard to find a table if you're on your own.'

'Don't mention it, it's fine.'

'And this way, we're not on our own any more.'

They both gave an embarrassed little laugh, which lent them a family resemblance. Not wanting to appear as if she wished to invade Bernard's privacy, the lady pulled out a pair of glasses and a theatre programme which she began to study with a frown of concentration while she waited for her food. For Bernard the situation was even more embarrassing than when he had been alone. He tackled his flammekueche in small mouthfuls, dreading that at any moment he might drop slivers of onion or lardons on his lap. In any case, by halfway through his meal he was no longer hungry. He felt torn between the desire to run away as fast as his legs would carry him or to fall deeply asleep then and there. But he could do neither. The lady had already started on her grilled ham hock and he would have to ask her to stand up if he wanted to leave the table. He was doomed to spin out his beer for as long as he could, whilst affecting the air of someone wishing to enjoy the moment to the full. It was strange, but he felt he recognised her too. It wasn't her facial features, nor her general appearance but rather something in the way she chewed, switching her food from one cheek to the other with a twist of the lips. He was convinced of it now, he had eaten with this woman before. Sensing his gaze, heavy with beer, resting on her, the lady looked up. Bernard blushed, they smiled at each other awkwardly. This happened two or three times until nothing was left of the hock but a bone picked clean.

'We've met before, haven't we?'

'I don't know, but it seems like it. I didn't like to say. It would have looked as if I was trying to take advantage of the situation.'

'I know what you mean. But no one would care, you know. If by any remote chance someone was interested in us, which I doubt, they would take us for a nice retired couple on their monthly night out.'

'Are you retired?'

'Yes, just recently. I'm getting used to it. Education. And yourself?'

'The same, but SNCF. Do you come from these parts?'

'I was born here and still have a few relatives in the area, but I live in Dijon.'

'Ah. But seriously, I do think I know you from somewhere.'

'That may be, one comes across so many people in a lifetime. Perhaps years ago, at school, or summer camp, at a dance ...'

'Possibly. No point in wondering about it. We wouldn't be the same now in any case.'

'That's true, but you can't help it, it's like a need to search for survivors around us. Other people's lives are annoying but they're also reassuring.'

'I apologise. I won't go on.'

'Don't worry. I feel the same.'

Really, it was better this way. As far as possible, Bernard avoided delving back into his youth. Not that his memories were any more painful than the next man's, it was just that his past seemed to him as cold and desolate as a deserted house.

At this point he might have left the table with a polite 'Lovely to make your acquaintance, good night, etc.'. He couldn't bring himself to do it, however. It was months since he had felt as much at ease as he did here. The lady seemed to find it agreeable as well, even though conversation had lapsed.

'Would you like another beer?'

'Yes, but somewhere else perhaps, it's so ... busy here ...'

'My name's Bernard.'

'And I'm Irène.'

They had just had two more beers in a red, velvety bistro, as snug as a fur muff. They had reached the stage of sharing experiences they had never had, those exquisite falsehoods exchanged by people whose paths have crossed and who will never see each other again.

Two insignificant lives transformed by the light filtering through the orange lampshades into unique and exotic existences, which still always brought them back in the end to: 'What now?'

Now all there was between them was two empty glasses and a skein of intertwined lives, the ends of which hung down pathetically on either side of the table. The sound system was on low, playing 'My Funny Valentine'. Chet Baker's voice comforted them in the great sorrow rising in their breast and bringing tears to their eyes.

'Not a bad choice for the closing credits.'

'Would you like me to see you back to your hotel?'

'No thanks, I'll get a taxi.'

'Why, when I've got my car outside?'

'OK, if you wish.'

The street was glistening after a slight drizzle. Irène slipped her arm through Bernard's.

'I think I'm a bit tiddly.'

Awkwardly, each one tried to adjust to the other's pace. Each step was a struggle, one step forwards and two steps back. The car was there waiting, though, as bright as a new pin. They got in. Irène's hand alighted on Bernard's as he went to start the ignition.

'Bernard, I would like you to kiss me.'

Their lips were cold, their tongues timid. There was a taste of the first time and dentures. Irène dissolved in tears on Bernard's shoulder.

'I'm sorry, it's been such a long time. I thought that was never going to happen to me again. Everything I've told you this evening is a lie. I've never travelled, I've never known great emotion, all my life I've been afraid of suffering so I've never experienced anything momentous. Nothing out of the ordinary has ever happened to me. Motorway, nothing but motorway, just grey monotony, with a few stops in lay-bys and breaks for frozen sandwiches. It'll soon be time to pay at the tollbooth and I'll have seen nothing, nothing at all. I don't want to go back to my hotel. Take me home with you, Bernard. Just for this one night – I'll leave in the morning, I promise!'

Yolande, Yolande, why must you always stand between me and the sun?

'Is that really what you want?'

'Yes. I've slept on my own almost all my life but tonight I really don't think I can face it.'

Irène was asleep by the time they reached the outskirts of Lille. Bernard was envious of her trust, how she let herself go, the unusual quality of her sleep. The dashboard lights cast a greenish glow around her profile. She slept the way children sleep, mouth slightly open, plump-lidded, unreachable.

Vimy, ten kilometres, diversion, roadworks ... Bernard set off into the depths of the night on an earth track, exuding inky dark. For several hundred metres now the headlights had picked up nothing at all. It was like the end of the earth.

The end of the earth was a building site. People had decided that it wasn't distant enough, and so they were extending it by spreading concrete over the nothingness. Bernard stopped and switched off the headlights. The absolute blackness gathered in his eyes until, little by little, he began to make out the gigantic shapes of the machines, silent gaping mouths ready to gobble up the sky once they had swallowed the earth.

He brushed Irène's soft cheek with his fingers and whispered, 'We're here.' Without waking, she moved her shoulder slightly as if to nudge a sheet back into place. Bernard could have sworn she was offering him her throat. Between his thumb and first finger, the Adam's apple went in and out, in and out, in and out ...

There wasn't much life left in the body. For a split second he saw Irène's pupil flicker then grow cloudy like that of Roland's dog. The life of one person had just passed into the body of the other. Bernard couldn't loosen his grip. He made the orgasm last until the pain went all the way up his arm to his shoulder, then to the very highest point of his crown, until it blew the top of his head off.

Then he got out of the car and fell on his knees in the mud.

'It's not my fault! I'm the only one who's dying!'

There was no echo in this place. The silence absorbed everything, like the sky, the earth, the concrete. Death mopped up life so that no trace of existence should sully the relentless onward march of the A26 autoroute.

Irène was not to have the same grave as Maryse. Despite scouring the whole of the building site, the best place Bernard could find was the cesspool covered by a small yellow corrugated-iron hut, which the workmen used as their dustbin and lavatories. Just at the moment the body sank into the cesspit, releasing appalling vapours, he remembered: Irène Lefébure. They used to have lunch sitting opposite each other in the school canteen. She wasn't an unpleasant girl but she'd repelled him a bit because of her bulimia, which meant that she used to finish everyone's leftovers. They'd called her 'the dustbin'.

As he was about to get back into the car, Bernard felt as if someone's gaze was burning into the back of his neck. The moon pierced the clouds like a cigarette hole in a blackout curtain. As with Maryse, the moon was full. Pure chance. But that wouldn't stop them talking of a serial killer, the full-moon murderer.

WOMAN'S BODY FOUND ON SITE OF A26 WORKS
Workmen on the site made the grisly discovery late on Tuesday afternoon. The police have carried out initial investigations, which are proving very difficult. There has been so much digging and compacting of the ground by machinery that the state of the corpse makes identification impossible for the moment. It will be necessary to wait for the results of the ...

Yolande was reading the newspaper, tracing the words with one finger and using another to swing her 'More than yesterday and much less than tomorrow' pendant from side to side like a pendulum. She was speaking in a singsong voice, like a child reciting a fable. Bernard kept his eyes fixed on the pendant.

...the time to complete additional investigations ...

I know, why don't I bake an angel-hair cake tonight? You know, with lots of sugar. It's ages since I did that.'

'I'm not really very hungry.'

'It doesn't matter, I feel like making a cake. It's a day for it, and besides there are a lot of ends of packets.'

'If you like. Pass me some water, please. Thanks. Help me to drink, I can't lift my head.'

Bernard was searching for the rim of the glass. His eyesight was deteriorating. A whirl of rings with wavy outlines and dark insides was dancing in front of his eyes. The two mouthfuls of water came back up, and dribbled down his chin through his beard.

'You pig!'

Yolande went back to her reading.

With the information currently available to the police and magistrates ...

(What's she going to do with my dead body? Stuff it into the bottom of the wardrobe? Bodies everywhere, in the mud of the building site, at the back of cupboards...)

It would be rash to link it to the disappearance of the young woman Maryse L ...

What's the point of me reading to you, Bernard, if you're not going to listen? Your mind's elsewhere. If you go on pretending to be dead like this, you really will die, so there. You're horrible to me, I'm going.'

Yolande was angry. He'd become a right pain with his illness, no time for anyone but himself. He'd been like that when he was little, snivelling at the slightest knock. Yolande had never been ill, ever. Let him hurry up and die, and that would be an end to it. She didn't know what it was he wanted. He could always hang himself if it was taking too long. People were always like that, complaining about their lives, going 'it's too hot' or 'it's too cold', 'I'm too young', 'I'm too old', etc. They only needed to follow her example and not like anything, that way you were never disappointed and other people got a bit of peace as well. She had nothing against her brother, mind you. All their lives the two of them had been like one and the same person, but whether you lost a tooth, a brother or an arm, there was no need to go overboard about it! In any case, it was for his benefit that she was making the angel-hair cake. It was a favourite recipe from *La Semaine de Suzette*. It was tasty, easy to make and filled you up nicely.

She trotted off into the kitchen, and poured all the ends of vermicelli packets into a salad bowl. There was an amazing amount. Pulling a saucepan out from under a heap of dirty dishes, she set off an avalanche of metalware.

'Oh shit! Filthy rotten bastards! Damn bitch of a saucepan!!!'

She kicked the floor clear. Of course, he was wallowing in bed all day, savouring each remaining drop of life, so obviously she was left to see to everything. Shaking with fury, she gave the saucepan, still coated with the remains of last night's noodles, a quick rinse under the tap.

'What've you done with the sugar? Oi, you!'

And yet the day had begun on a positive note, she'd been in a good mood when she'd got up. A shaft of light coming through a chink in the shutters had bounced off the white enamel of her bowl. That was all it had taken to bring back a whole flood of happy memories. Life was the way it was, but sometimes it gave gifts, even to people who didn't deserve them, even to wrong'uns like her. That was in the way of things. After all, life killed off plenty of fine people, through wars, road accidents or illness. It was only right that it should make up for its stupid tricks.

The day they had drowned that bitch Fernande's cat, a lovely day. The old bag was always spreading evil gossip about her, hands clutching her windowsill, with her mangy cat wedged between her huge tits.

'That Yolande's been seen leaving the dance with ...'

Yolande wouldn't have minded going with all the local boys she talked about. There hadn't been as many as all that, but it

52

still got her a tanning with the razor strop as soon as her father heard about it. Titi, that cat's name was. It stank. By promising Bernard a lollipop, she had talked him into distracting the old girl long enough for her to stuff the tomcat into a potato sack. Then they'd run to the bomb crater, the one where you could fish for frogs, and she had weighted the sack with pebbles. Inside the cloth, Titi had made a token effort at wriggling. Perhaps he thought it was a game – you could never tell, where children were concerned.

Yolande had whirled the sack round above her head before flinging it right into the middle of the pool with a loud 'ha!' The water had broken into a rippling smile before it grew perfectly impassive again, like a pool of oblivion. Bernard had clung to his sister's skirt.

'That's a crime, isn't it, Yoyo? You've committed a crime.'

'Of course not, it's only a cat. Serves it right, ugly beast.'

Yolande had lain full length on the bank, hands behind her head, serene, in the satisfaction of a job well done. Her skirt was hitched up to her thighs, letting in the soft April breeze. A flock of white clouds grazed on the blue overhead. Soon it would be Easter. She was seventeen and longing to get stuck in to all that the world had to offer. On the wireless the talk was of nothing but war, today, tomorrow, or the day after, and of Chancellor Hitler who was frightening everyone except her. If he was really such a bogeyman, that chap, then all the big noises spouting into the microphones had only to do what she'd done, stick him in a sack and throw it into a bomb crater. But oh no, they preferred to scare one another, holding up the spectre of war at arm's length like a scarecrow forming a perch for crows. War, in weather like this, it was a joke! Here, war, 1870, 1914, and earlier still, was just a part of life. All it had left behind were holes you could drown feline collaborators in and where kids fished for frogs. No need to get so worked up about it! In any case, people didn't go to

53

war when the weather was so fine. All these people needed was a good lay and they'd forget about fighting. Backside, pussy, prick, eating, sleeping, like in primitive paintings or on the walls of the toilets in the station or cafés, nothing but pleasure, then, at the end, a sack weighted with stones and a hole in the water. That was what life meant for her, and that should be enough for the whole of humanity.

The foolish young sun drying its rays above the pale-green shoots carpeting the fields seemed to agree with her. The less you thought, the more you lived, and whatever you could take was one fewer thing for the Boches to get. The Boches or someone else, stupidity didn't stop at borders. She was at this point in her reflections when Bernard had started yelling: 'Yoyo! Help, Yoyo, I'm drowning!' The sack with Titi in it was lying by the edge of the water near a long wooden rod, and in the middle of the pond her brother was flailing about as he went under. Yolande had leapt into the thick black liquid. It wasn't very deep, maybe two metres in the centre, but the little idiot had got his foot caught in some scrap metal and couldn't get it free again. She had had trouble extricating him, he was panicking and yelling at the top of his voice. Finally she'd succeeded in pulling him to the bank by his hair. They had flopped down, panting, beside the sack swollen with water, stones and Titi, now defunct. They stank of mud. Black bubbles were still bursting on the surface of the crater, letting off smells of infernal farts.

'Are you mad or something? It's full of God knows what in there. Why d'you do that?'

'I just slipped, Yoyo. I didn't want Titi to die. I thought a good ducking would be enough.'

'Well, he's dead anyway, and you could have ended up the same way, you little shit. Let's see your ankle.'

It was all swollen, bloody like raw steak. Yolande had torn a strip from her dress to use as a bandage.

'Yoyo?'

'What?'

'You stink.'

'So do you.'

They'd rolled around on the grass, laughing like things possessed. Coated in mud all over, they'd slithered into each other's arms like eels. Yolande had poked her tongue into his mouth to make him be quiet. Her brother's body had juddered between her thighs and then for one brief moment everything was still. War itself could not have divided them. The silence had something of eternity about it. Then a frog jumped into the water. Yolande sat up again, the blue of her eyes had darkened to violet. Bernard was smiling, eyes closed like a child asleep, lips slightly parted. Yolande had remembered a poem she'd read at school, about a young soldier lying dead in a verdant spot bathed in sunlight. It had ended with 'Nature, cradle him gently, he is cold' or some such.

'You'll never do that.'

'What?'

'Fight their stupid war. You'll be like me, you'll live for ever.'

With one kick, she'd consigned Titi to his ineluctable fate once more and they'd gone home. For that one day, Yolande had been treated like a queen, she had saved her little brother's life. No one had picked quarrels with her. The best thing of all had been hearing fat Fernande calling for her cat.

Now Bernard had spoilt everything. His illness had made him selfish, he had no time for her any more. At a corner of the table, Yolande was mixing vermicelli and caster sugar.

Even seen full on, Bernard was now only a profile, with a lipless black hole in place of a mouth. What life he had left was lurking there, in that well of shadows, evident only in shallow gusts of foul-smelling breath. He no longer knew whether he was awake or asleep, there was no difference, just the same state on repeat for almost a week now. Fragments of the newspaper article would come back to him: 'Grisly discovery, police, woman's body ...' Each word was so charged with meaning that a whole sentence would throw him into complete and utter confusion. He wasn't afraid for himself, the A26 was swarming with foreign workers – Spaniards, Turks, North Africans – almost 250 firms were at work on the section, 700 workers, that was where the finger of suspicion pointed. And in any case, what could they do to him? Life had already condemned him for a crime he had not committed, being born without intent. There were a lot of words ending in 'ion' in the article: 'investigations, identification, conclusions, etc'. After that he amused himself by making a string of other words ending in 'ion': circulation, ascension, passion, circumvolution. That one was a beauty, a graceful swirl. Recitation: '*La cigale ayant chanté tout l'été se trouva fort dépourvue quand la bise fut venue.*' Mademoiselle Leny, his primary school teacher, used to pronounce it 'la Biiiise!' Her eyebrows would shoot right up to the top of her forehead when she said 'la Biiise!'

Yolande had been the one to teach him how to kiss, and to masturbate, but that was later. They'd almost gone the whole way once. One Thursday afternoon, when he'd had flu. It was winter, in the last year of the war. She was cold and had lain down next to him in the bed. People were cold the whole time, coal was hard to find. He was worried that she would catch his germs, but she'd said she didn't care, she was stronger than they were. They'd been looking at a film magazine. She was deliberately lingering over the pages showing scantily dressed film stars: 'What about her, doesn't that make you feel anything when you look at her? Her legs, there ...' In a flash, one fever had been replaced by another. There were no flies on his pyjamas, the cord at his waist was cutting into him. It was Yolande who had undone it. Slowly, Bernard's hand had made its way up under his sister's skirt. He'd stopped at the first hairs, at the top of her thighs, not daring to venture further, into the unknown jungle. The elastic material of her knickers was stretched tight, a yielding shell which fitted neatly into the palm of his hand. He had lain on top of her, burning up, drenched in sweat. Yolande had opened her legs and pulled her pants out of the way, while her other hand guided Bernard into position. But at the moment of penetration, she had pushed him sharply away.

As for the rest, he no longer remembered. He must have masturbated, in all probability.

'I'm dying, and I've got a hard-on.'

Nothing else had ever happened between him and his sister.

'I find him more disgusting every day. He's drunk by ten in the morning, and every evening I get a pasting because some customer has been giving me the eye, or for any old thing. Shall I tell you what? I wish he'd die.'

'That'll happen.'

'Yes, but when?'

Jacqueline was making huge figures of eight with her cloth on the waxed tablecloth. There wasn't so much as a crumb of Bernard's lunch left, but she carried on, as if she were trying to rub off the brown and yellow floral pattern on the tablecloth or something even more stubborn, Roland's life for instance. She had her sleeves rolled up to the elbow. Bernard had always loved her arms, strong, hands reddened from washing up. It must be good to sleep in arms like those.

'You're not listening to me – where are you?'

'Yes, I am, I'm here.'

'No, you're here but you're not here. You look like a saint in a church, smiling at everything but not seeing a thing.'

'I don't know. It's as if I've been away somewhere. I recognise things and people, but it's all changed ever so slightly, like the tracing on top of a drawing that's moved by a fraction of a millimetre. I don't know how to explain it to you.'

'I've not heard from you for a whole week. Were you having a rough time?'

'That's putting it mildly. But yes, I really thought I'd had it. Death comes closer, like the sea, it hits me full in the face, a huge wave of black foam. I tell myself the time has come, in my head I've packed my bag, and then it draws away again. It'll be back.'

'Aren't you scared?'

'Not any more. When I was a kid on holiday at the beach, I used to practise walking with my eyes closed, in case I went blind some day. It's the same sort of thing.'

'You're going and then you come back – is that what you're saying?'

'If you like.'

'If it was me, I wouldn't come back.'

'You don't get to decide, you just have to go along with it.'

'What about the pain?'

'That's what keeps us alive. Without the pain or even just the fear of pain we'd all be off at the first unhappy love affair.'

'That might not be such a bad thing.'

'I don't know about that. All I know is, if you're still here, it must be for a good reason.'

'Oh well, do enlighten me then, because I can't for the life of me think what it is!'

'Yet you are here.'

'Barely …Why, Bernard, why have we spent our whole time walking alongside our own lives?'

Jacqueline's lower lip was beginning to stick out and tremble, her eyes misted over. Her face was so close to Bernard's that he could see nothing else, as if all there was in the world was this woman's face, ravaged by regret and steeped in exhaustion. It was as though he were looking at her through a magnifying glass – wrinkles, hairs, blackheads – it was hardly proper. It was life that had caused all this damage, like a river gouging out its course down a mountain, day after day, for so many days. And behind those eyes damp with tears was a little girl struggling, trying to get out of there, beating her fists against the glass walls of the jar in which she'd been suffocating for ...

'I don't know where you've gone, Bernard, but you've no right to leave me here, no right at all. One day I'm going to do something stupid, I'll get a gun and blow that bastard Roland's head off and I'll do the same to your bitch of a sister ...'

'Be quiet, Jacqueline. You're talking nonsense now. Some things can't be killed with a gun because they're dead already.'

'You're talking like a dead man. But I'm still alive. Go away, you're even worse than the rest, nothing can affect you any more.'

Jacqueline got up so abruptly that her chair toppled over backwards. She righted it again so violently it was as if she wanted to drive it into the floor. The bang echoed awhile in the empty room of the restaurant. Bernard's hand still smelt of Jacqueline's: disinfectant and floorcloth. An hour before, there had been lots of people here, eating macaroni and roast pork amid noisy laughter. No trace of them now, as if they'd been imaginary. Life was about being there when things happened, if not it was a desert. People appeared and disappeared and you never knew where they'd come from or where they were headed. Paths simply crossed.

When Bernard tried to pay for his meal, Jacqueline told him to go to hell, without even turning round.

The rat caught the full force of Yolande's slipper.

'A rat's at home anywhere. Comes from goodness knows where and never gets where it's going. The thing goes from one house to another, making tunnels for itself all over the place. No limits at all. Dirty beast! That bastard of a butcher came by just now. He sounded his horn several times. Usually Bernard puts his order in on a Tuesday. But he's not here, he's never here, even when he is here. Oh well, we won't be eating meat any more, it's as simple as that. Or else we'll have rat. If he's not in his bed pretending to be dead for days on end he's disappearing off somewhere. "I've got to keep myself busy," that's what he says. As if! He's joined the Resistance and doesn't want to tell me. The Boches have taken over his body but he's holding out against them with his mind. I've seen right through him. He must be derailing trains, that's his thing, trains. I see him come home with his conspirator's face on. As if you couldn't tell he's killing Boches! Once a fellow's killed another fellow, he's not the same any more. I remember Zep, Zep's short for Joseph, Joseph Haendel, that was the name of my Boche. One day he was in a platoon which had to kill some hostages. When I saw him the next day he wasn't the same man. You'd have thought he'd lost something precious, like an arm or a leg. He was looking all around, he seemed distracted. At night he would wake up yelling things in German that I couldn't understand: *"Nein! Nein! ..."*

drenched in sweat. He was a good country lad, Zep, a Bavarian. Pigs, hens, ducks, rabbits, he'd slit their throats by the dozen, but the hostages, that he just couldn't stomach. You can't eat people, I wonder if that was why. Always looking over his shoulder. And before him, all he could see was the Russian front. A rat in a trap, that's what my fine Zep had become. All the men became Ripolin Brothers, lined up one behind the other like in the paint adverts, but it wasn't paintbrushes they were holding, it was daggers. Row upon row, their white tunics stained with blood like that bastard of a butcher. "I kill you, you kill me." And the more they killed, the more of them sprang up again, it was truly miraculous! That's why there'll never be an end to the war – anyway, it's always been here, it's that kind of country, there's nothing else to do but go to war. The only thing that grows is white crosses. Even Bernard's not been able to keep out of it. But what the hell, let them go on tearing each other to bits. It makes sod all difference to me!'

Yolande went back to the needlework which had been interrupted by the incident with the rat. She was sewing scraps together, pieces of silk and ends of lace, on to what was left of a red dress, and humming '*Couchés dans le foin*'. She got up and stood before the wardrobe mirror, holding the extraordinary garment up in front of her, stepped back a little, primped and posed, tried out a few dance steps and burst out laughing.

'I don't give a damn about the Resistance! You're all made like rats! You've all lost!'

Whenever Bernard went out prowling around aimlessly, sooner or later he would find himself beside the railway. Sometimes he stood on the bridge above the tunnel and waited for the trains to go by. He knew them all, the 16.18, the 17.15 ... He would see them coming in the distance then being swallowed up, almost as if inside him, with a din of metal on metal that shook the handrail he was leaning on. Shutting his eyes, he would count how many seconds they took to pass right through. He had already seen himself toppling and trains running over him. He'd imagined the scene a dozen times, the engine hurtling on at top speed and cutting him in two like an earthworm. Always at the end of this dream, however, his two halves would be wriggling on either side of the track and would manage to stick themselves together again. Bernard would find himself in one piece, walking along the rails with no idea where he was going. Rails leading to more rails ... Today he was hanging around the warehouses of the disused goods station. Beneath the tall metal structure there was a raised platform where the wagons used to be loaded, with straw, or livestock, up to fifteen times a day sometimes. Dozens of men had worked here. Where were they now? The police kept an eye on the place. People said youngsters came here to get up to mischief, smash the few remaining windows, take drugs. So they said. The concrete paving slabs had burst under the pressure of irrepressible vegetation. Tons of steel and cement would never be a match for the puniest blade of grass. All that work for nothing. What if Bernard were the only survivor of some cosmic disaster? And if there were no one left in the world but him, rattling around all on his own in this deserted shed? Then, if death laid eggs in his stomach, what if he was the first man on earth and everything was going to begin all over again with him? On the walls was obscene graffiti, of erect penises, and legs spread wide, which reminded him of points on the tracks. They'd been boldly drawn in chalk, or scratched using a sharpened stone. This was Lascaux, this was the dawn of humanity, hunting scenes. Men had lived here. Even after countless centuries they still had nothing to express but the need to procreate, to have sex, over and over again. What price evolution?

'Hey, Granddad, what do you think you're doing?'

A young guy with eyes like a cat was staring at him, sniggering, sitting on a beam with his legs dangling in mid-air, two metres up.

'Nothing, just taking a walk. I used to work here a long time ago.'

'Long ago, so you're a dinosaur then?'

'I was just thinking that myself.'

'Have you got a fag?'

'No, I don't smoke.'

It was like a circus act. The young man threw himself backwards, bounced off the wall, catapulted off a heap of old planks and landed at Bernard's feet.

'You could have been killed!'

'Don't worry on my account, old man. Don't you know it's dodgy around here?'

'So they say.'

'Aren't you afraid?'

'What would I be afraid of?'

'Me.'

'Sorry, but to be honest, no, I'm not frightened of you.'

'Funny, you don't look all that tough.'

'I don't understand – what is it you're after?'

The young man sprang to one side, flicking open a knife. 'Your wallet, you old prick, or I'll fucking kill you!'

'Oh, is that all? Here you are.'

Bernard smiled and reached for his coat pocket. The young man, thrown by Bernard's attitude, moved back.

'Wait! You're weird. What are you so happy about? What've you got in your pocket, a gun?'

'Of course not, I swear.'

'Don't move!'

'I must have two or three hundred francs, take it.'

'Don't move I said!'

Bernard took a step forward and put his hand in his coat pocket. The youth shrank back in panic, his foot met with empty air, and he toppled backwards. Bernard didn't have time to catch him. He disappeared over the edge of a platform, making a strange sound like someone taking a deep breath before diving underwater. Bernard rushed forwards. There he was, a kid twisting and turning on the rusty rails, dry grass growing between them, with his own knife sticking out of his chest.

'Don't hurt me, M'sieur! Call an ambulance!'

'Of course I won't. It's an accident, don't be scared ...'

The kid's hand clutched at his sleeve. His gaze turned blue, like a newborn baby's. A bubble of blood burst at the corners of his mouth.

'Don't do this to me, kiddo!'

One last spasm and the young man was no more than a piece of rubbish, a disused shell like the shed open to the elements on all sides. On his knees beside the corpse, Bernard lifted his eyes to the rusty iron sky. He no longer dared lay a finger on anything, for fear of seeing humans, things or animals crumble to dust at his touch. He had become the instrument of death, death itself. He felt no guilt, death being a psychosomatic illness, but he was astonished by its lightning speed.

Fifteen minutes earlier, the kid hadn't existed, any more than Bernard had existed for him. Then wham! – the young man had come to life for just a matter of minutes, the lifespan of a clay pipe at a shooting gallery. As for him, in some strange way his imminent and inescapable death seemed to make him immortal. Rising in his chest was not a sob but a burst of laughter, straight from the heart, of the kind that seizes you when words fail. Bernard wondered how he was going to drag the body – by the feet? Under the arms? They say there is nothing heavier than an empty heart; the same is true of a lifeless body. It is life that holds us upright, which gives us that lightness of being. Without life the bones, the flesh weigh tons. But why go to all that trouble? He had nothing to do with it this time. What was the point of wearing himself out to plant this seed of death beneath the A26?

Force of habit. He could, he supposed, go to the police station and explain what had happened. The idea made him smile. But he was too tired to play that game. The young man would do very well where he was, lying with his cheek against these rails which led nowhere. It was the most fitting end for someone who had gone down the wrong track. Bernard turned his coat collar up. It was cold. In the sky the dark was spreading like a pool of ink. A sprinkling of stars appeared. Bernard aimed his finger and rubbed out a few. Every second, some of them died, people said. What did that matter when four times as many were born in the same time? The sky was an enormous rubbish tip.

Bernard walked off, sniffing. He could feel he was getting a cold. Once in the car, before starting the engine, he looked for a tissue in the glove compartment. There was one left, a used one. While he was wiping his nose, the beam of headlights came sweeping over the countryside and slowed as it drew level with him. Bernard turned his back. That was what was so annoying about nature – whenever you thought you were on your own some country bumpkin popped up from behind a hedge. But the car picked up speed again and disappeared, leaving a scarlet glow-worm trailing behind.

Yolande's soup consisted of some leftover cabbage, a tin of ravioli in tomato sauce, two potatoes, a chicken carcass, a handful of lentils, a vanilla pod and two or three other ingredients she couldn't quite recall. While emptying the cupboards into the large cooking pot she had said to herself that her recipe would be called 'Everything must go'.

'Is it nice?'

'It's unusual – what is it?'

'Slum-it soup. You weren't here when the butcher came. You're having what there is.'

'I'm sorry. I'll go shopping tomorrow.'

'Have you been out derailing a train again?'

'What are you talking about?'

'Do you think I'm an idiot? I know your little game, it's an open secret. To be honest, I couldn't care less, if it makes you happy. But damn, I could have murdered an escalope!'

'I'll get some tomorrow, I promise. It's not bad, this soup. A little ... exotic maybe.'

Obediently, Bernard cleaned his plate. Yolande left hers untouched, giving him her china-doll stare.

'So you'll eat any old thing and say nothing to me?'

'I said I liked it, Yoyo.'

'That's not what I'm talking about! My dress?'

'Oh yes. It's beautiful. It could almost be the one you were wearing the day ...'

'Aha, so you do ... I found it in the wardrobe. I've added a few frills and some lace round the collar.'

'Of course! It's very pretty. Stand up, turn round ... Splendid!'

A slight blush crept over Yolande's cheeks. She went back and forth, twirled around the table. Bernard turned the pendant lamp on her as a spotlight.

'If our thick bastard of a father had just let me move to Paris I'd have been another Chanel. And there's nothing to it, you know, just reusing some old bits and bobs. It can't have taken me more than a couple of hours!'

'It's a masterpiece. Really.'

'And it goes nicely with that little chain you gave me: "Less than yesterday and three times as much as tomorrow".'

'More than yesterday and much less than tomorrow.'

'Same difference. I'll have to make myself a coat to go with it. Could you give me your old SNCF one? You won't need it any more, you're going to die.'

'Of course. Yolande, shall we dance?'

'All right. I adore you.'

They couldn't really have said what they were celebrating, Yolande's amazing dress, the death of the young man, the unspeakable mush congealing on their plates or simply a moment of grace which had strayed into this place which had known so few, but they did it with all their heart. Bernard waltzed his sister around; she was laughing, head flung back and white hair flying like an ashen cloud. Round and round they whirled, heedless of the furniture they bumped into as they went past, knocking things over, raising flurries of dust and scaring a rat off its dustbin feast. The world could have stopped turning and they would still have continued their drunken waltz atop its ruins, to the accompaniment of Yolande's reedy tones as she sang softly: '*J'attendrai, le jour et la nuit, j'attendrai toujours, ton retour ...*' The swaying ceiling light was a makeshift glitter ball, multiplying their shadows on the walls. They were a whole ballroom, just the two of them. What else, who else could they ever need? Bernard surrendered to the ever faster rhythm forced on him by his sister. Eternity must be like this whirl, a gigantic food mixer, blending bodies into one paste, one wave crashing into oblivion. Bernard lost his footing, stumbled and fell full length on the floor.

'You wretch! Give up now, would you?'

Yolande took hold of him by the collar and tried to get him on his feet again. Bernard opened his mouth but couldn't make even the slightest sound. His body no longer responded to the orders issued by his brain. He was in unknown territory.

'Shift your backside, will you! Hang on, have some wine, that'll sort you out.'

He saw his sister stride over him, her legs as spindly as a chair's. He heard her uncorking a bottle. She came back and poured the wine straight from the bottle into his mouth. Bernard couldn't swallow any longer. He could understand everything, see everything, hear everything but he no longer knew what to do to live. He didn't have the instructions any more. Apart from this feeling of panic he wasn't suffering, unless he'd forgotten how to do that as well.

'Dance! You mustn't stop dancing, not ever!'

Dragging him like a broken puppet, Yolande hoisted him on to her back and walked him round the room. Bernard's gaze fixed on the corner of the table, a patch of wall, a myriad of tiny details it seemed he was seeing for the first time, pencil marks on the doorframe with the legend 'Bernard aged six, Yolande aged eight', all the things a bull must see when the horses are dragging it out of the ring. Nothing hurt, there was just the strange feeling that he'd forgotten something, like when you leave the house and wonder whether you've turned the gas off properly.

Exhausted, Yolande walked him round the table one last time before putting him down on his bed. She collapsed on to a bedside chair.

'See where your stupid tricks have got you? Everyone who plays at war ends up like you. But you won't listen to me, you will go out playing the hero. I'm going to make you a nice eggnog. There's nothing like eggnog.'

The last thing Bernard saw was a monstrous hen pecking away with the tip of its beak at an endless worm.

'A settling of scores, I don't think so!'

'And why not? There's a whole load of junkies hanging around the depot. The guy the police found was one of them. His arms were covered in needle marks, from what they're saying.'

'And the remains of the woman they found in the works on the A26, was she an addict? And the kid who's never been found, she was one too, was she?'

'There's no connection, Roland.'

'Hmm, well, I think there is, and I've got my own theory about it, what's more.'

'Out with it then!'

'I know what I mean. And when the time comes, there'll be quite a few who won't know what's hit them. Whose round is it?'

There were just three of them left propping up the bar, noses in their beer. Roland was at the pump. He couldn't wait for them to clear off. At this time of day he was as prickly as a hedgehog, everything got to him. All he wanted to do was sit down in front of the TV and stuff himself with sounds and pictures to the point of oblivion. The dog he'd bought to replace Féfé was a non-starter, he'd had to take it back to the kennels that afternoon. He'd given them a piece of his mind and no mistake. The Strasbourg–Monaco match scheduled for that evening had been postponed because of bad weather. And all these dickheads could talk about was the young man who'd been found stabbed in the disused warehouse of the old goods station. No need to get upset over him. One little shit more or less – who was counting? But on his way back from his parents' in Brissy, it was definitely Bernard's Renault 5 that he'd seen parked near the shed. Naturally he hadn't said a word to anyone. His little secret, he was hugging it close, so he could come out with it at the right moment. For years now he'd had him in his sights, that Bernard. Right family of lunatics, him and his tart of a sister. Never mind that they were local, one of these days it was all going to go up, and it would be him, Roland, who set it off. And that slut Jacqueline would have to shut her big mouth. He'd always known he was a pervert, that bloke, with his 'butter wouldn't melt' act. Even as a small child he'd been like that, doing things on the sly and hiding in his sister's skirts as soon as things went badly for him. All the things that had happened in the neighbourhood, the kid who'd vanished, the body on the building site and that little toerag the other evening, it had all started the day Bernard left his job at the station. Always prowling around in his Renault 5, or disappearing off. If someone went to the bother of digging around in that direction they'd turn up some interesting things, that was for sure! You'd only had to see him put a bullet in poor Féfé's head, hadn't so much as batted an eyelid, not a moment's hesitation, bang!

'OK, Roland, we're off now. See you tomorrow.'

'Right, see you tomorrow.'

Roland bolted the door behind them. He was about to leave the room when he met his own gaze looking back at him, that of a tall blond young man, a good head taller than the rest of the football team in a yellowing photo which had pride of place between two trophies and three pennants. Nothing got past him into the net in those days, people respected him. He could have turned professional if he'd wanted. Why hadn't he wanted? Not finding an answer to that question, he told himself it was because of Jacqueline. She had to be of use for something. Couldn't even give him kids – or do the dusting. Roland whisked the cloth from his shoulder and gave the two cups a polish. Then he turned out the lights and climbed wearily up the stairs to the flat.

There were dozens of buttons, hundreds even, scattered over the table. Tiny ones in mother-of-pearl, little half-spheres with painted flowers on them, leather buttons, wooden buttons, some in horn and others covered with fabric. Yolande's fingers caressed them, sorted through them, mixed them up, married and divorced them and began all over again, untiringly. She had boxes full. Before emptying out a new one she would plunge her hands into it, like a miser with his gold. Bernard had passed away at around one in the morning.

She had not been at his bedside. A kind of gap had opened in the silence while she was making vigorous cuts in the SNCF overcoat. She had gone into his room. He had the same over-earnest look as in his school photographs. A complete act, anything for a quiet life. It hadn't mattered what anyone thought of him just as long as they left him in peace. His watch had stopped at eleven forty-five. He must have said to himself that his train was late. He'd been looking at his watch constantly in recent days. She'd wondered momentarily where she was going to put him, before telling herself he was in as good a place as any. As for the escalopes, that was scuppered, he wouldn't be buying any more now.

The Big blue coat button family ran into the Mother-of-pearl shirt button family. 'How are you today? Shall we go for a walk? Tip-tap-tip.'

Four days of Siberian chill. Nothing was moving on the plain, the cold took even the wind's breath away. Work on the A26 site had been brought to a standstill. The silence was such that you could hear a frozen branch snap like a glass straw from a mile away. It no longer seemed like death even, more like the time before life, before life had even been thought of. Yolande spent hours face-to-face with the cooker, as rigid as the chair she was sitting on, chewing the inside of her cheeks. Four days, four years, four hundred years ... And then the chap had rung the doorbell. When no one answered, he'd knocked several times. He took a few steps back and looked upwards. All the shutters were closed. He scribbled a quick note on his knee and slipped it under the door. Yolande was watching him through the world's arsehole. She'd waited for him to disappear off in his little blue car before seizing on the note. 'Hello Bernard! Down at the station we're wondering how you are. Give us a ring or join us for a drink. See you soon, Simon.'

Yolande folded the note in two, then in four, in six, then eight, till it was no bigger than a pill and she swallowed it. Others would come. She would swallow them all. She'd swallow everything. That's what she'd do. Everything could be eaten. The rats were eating Bernard, Yolande would eat the rats. With garden peas. She had loads of them. Bernard didn't like them but he'd always got a tin when he did the week's shopping. It was a tradition. There were sardines as well, plenty of them, and tomato sauce. She had all she needed, several times over. She had the wherewithal to live two lives here, two lives sheltered from others. She could do it all herself. She needed no one else. Music, for example, on that mandolin. She knew a tune: 'Ramona ... I'll always remember the rambling rose you wore in your hair.'

'Bugger off!'

The mandolin narrowly missed the rat running across the table. The echo of the instrument made ripples on the surface of the silence. Yolande closed her eyes. The same movement in the darkness inside her head.

'Don't lean out of the window, Yoyo, you'll get your head torn off if we go through a tunnel.' It would all be going so fast that it was impossible to open your eyes or even breathe. Now and then you'd get tiny smuts in your face. The tears in the corners of your eyes would be drawn upwards and vanish into your hair, streaming backwards with the wind. It took a smack across the legs to make her come away from the window and sit quietly on the seat. The intoxication would last for quarter of an hour and then she'd be at it again, on the pretext that she felt travel sick. That's how she would have liked to go through life, eyes closed, at the window of a train hurtling onwards, at the risk of getting her head torn off in a tunnel. They'd made do with shaving it.

Yolande had thought Bernard had moved, but no, it was a rat, a big fat rat under the bedcover. She hadn't missed that one, eliminating it with one blow from the dictionary, open at the page with the D's: deride, derision, derisory, etc. Afterwards she'd dissected the animal with her little sewing scissors, ever so neatly. She'd cooked it in red wine like a rabbit, a rabbit the right size for her, a one-portion rabbit.

She was alone in the world now, surrounded by miniature rabbits, rather like Alice in Wonderland. After dinner she would play the little horse game, while she dipped biscuits into a thimbleful of red wine. She would be both Bernard and Yolande. When she was Yolande she would cheat, of course.

The dice was stuck on five. Besides the unseen presence of mice and rats, nothing moved. The pendant lamp still cast its forty watts of greyish light on the board with its tiny racecourse, now lying in ruins. Bernard had got angry with Yolande who was cheating shamelessly. In an instant, the little horses had gone flying to every corner of the table. Only one was left standing, a green one, on the square marked 7.

Yolande wasn't going to play with Bernard any more. She was asleep, chin on her chest, arms hanging by the sides of the chair and a mauve crocheted shawl round her shoulders. She had quickly tired of being Bernard and Yolande, switching from one side of the table to the other. After a short while she had lost track of who she was. Then she had played the part of Bernard in a rage, simply to have done with it.

Bernard had gone off to his room in a sulk. Yolande would have liked to play on. She hated things coming to an end. She'd always been like that. She'd never wanted to get off a merry-go-round. Later on when she'd go out partying all night, she took badly to the first glimmerings of dawn. She'd get angry with the people who left her and went off to bed. When there was a biscuit she liked, she wouldn't eat just one but ten, even if it made her sick. Nothing was ever supposed to stop.

Every night she struggled against sleep. She lost every time, but one day she'd win. She would keep her eyes open, like statues do. She might be covered in moss and pigeon droppings but she would not let her eyelids close. Generations of dribbling old men and snivelling babies would pass by and she wouldn't so much as blink.

Seeing her like this, wound in her mauve shawl like a withered bouquet, you'd never know she was made of indestructible stuff. Time had been on her side since birth. Yolande was life's great witness. Let them go and get buried in their lousy cemeteries. Their marble slabs and plastic flowers would rot before she'd lost a single tooth. There was nothing they could do to her, and that's what really got to them. She was like the sea, they could throw anything they wanted at her, even an atom bomb. *Boom!* it would go, and then the surface would grow perfectly smooth again as if nothing had happened. Scarcely a ripple. And when she'd had enough of everyone swarming around, then she would overflow, in wave upon wave from her statue body. In her sleep, Yolande parted her thighs and revelled in peeing where she sat.

Yolande had awoken with a start, a silent cry filling her mouth. Something had smashed on the floor. Her bowl half full of red wine. Some creature going past, no doubt. They were everywhere. You couldn't see them but they were there, nibbling, scrabbling, gnawing even the very shadows. She pushed the shards of her bowl under the table with the toe of her slipper. Her back hurt, the chair had been pressing into her ribs. It was a horrible day. Although it had barely begun, she could sense that from a thousand tiny details, her itching head, the cold in her bones, the way things all seemed to have moved imperceptibly from their usual places so her hand had to feel around for them. The matches that needed striking ten times before she could light the gas. Yolande set the water to boil because she had to start somewhere. She pressed up against the cooker, her hands cupped round the small blue flames. She felt stiff, as rigid as the chair on which she had spent the night. Her neck and knees cracked with every movement. The water took for ever to come to the boil. Yolande poured in half a jar of instant coffee, added four or five sugar lumps and filled a cup that was as stained as an old pipe. The first scalding mouthful made her cough. Then she busied herself, moving things about for no reason, just to avoid being paralysed by the light filtering through the world's arsehole. She made heaps, heaps of little horses, heaps of biscuit crumbs, heaps of little balls of paper, heaps upon heaps, stacked up the plates with leftover food congealed on them, donned coat upon coat, and put socks on over her slippers.

She ran from one place to another, bumping into stacks of newspapers which collapsed in her wake, raising clouds of outdated information. Everywhere she felt hunted by the pale light creeping in like smoke through the gaps in the shutters, and the keyholes. All those gaps had to be plugged with scrunched-up pages of newspaper. On one of them the distressing photo of Maryse L. crumpled and disappeared in her hands. As she went to plug one last slit in a shutter, Yolande had time to see the Germans hiding on the other side of the street and a handful of Resistance fighters springing from one dustbin to the next. They no longer had enough space outside to fight their war, now they wanted to do it in her house. In her terror she found cracks in every corner, one there, another one here! The daylight was pressing with all its might against the walls. She didn't have enough arms to battle against the pressure from outside. There was cracking and banging on all sides. It was so powerful and she was so fragile. She rushed into Bernard's room. A troop of rats fled at her approach. She began to lay into her brother with her fists.

'Bastard! How can you abandon me now?'

Shaking with fury, she grabbed the cover from the bed, put it over her head and huddled down behind the door, arms wrapped tightly, so tightly round her knees, a mass of shivers. On the mattress the exposed corpse gave a toothy grin.

It was past nine at night, yet the lights were still on in the café. This was the only light in the darkness shrouding Place de la Gare. It looked like a fish tank filled with yellow oil, inside which Roland was darting back and forth, giving things a wipe down with his cloth, a bullfighter's cape without a bull; it was lovely and idiotic at the same time, as he was alone amid the tables and chairs. A car zoomed away from behind the premises. Jacqueline was at the wheel. She hadn't even taken off her apron, just put on a big woollen jacket on top. Her hair was a mess, there was anxiety in her gestures. In the rear-view mirror she glanced at her swollen right eye.

'Lousy bastard!'

She could no longer remember what had started it, something insignificant as usual, a few centimes out on a bill, a disagreement over what to watch on TV, a word out of turn. In recent months she and Roland had been sitting on a powder keg, the tiniest spark was enough to blow it all sky high. That evening they'd reached the very end of the road. It wasn't Féfé's head Bernard should have put a bullet in, but that arsehole's.

'Just take a look at yourself, with your big fat beer belly hanging out everywhere, your furred-up tongue and your bulging eyes. What a handsome footballer!'

'You're having a go at me! Have you looked in the mirror lately? You've got tits like floppy flannels and hair like a floorcloth.

Even those piece of shit Arabs building the motorway wouldn't be turned on by you. You're ancient, old girl, you're ugly, and you smell of dishwater.'

'Maybe not to everyone.'

'All right, you bring that Bernard here, then, the poofter, and I'll show him a thing or two. I may not be perfect, but at least I don't rape young girls, kill women and murder kids!'

'What are you talking about?'

'I'm saying what I know. Young Maryse who's never been found, the murdered woman on the building site, all that started at precisely the time Monsieur Bernard began prowling about the area.'

'My poor Roland, you really should stop drinking, it's sad ...'

'We'll see about that. And what was your precious Bernard up to beside the warehouse when the kid got himself stabbed? I saw him! I was driving past and I saw him even if he did turn away when I slowed down. What's your answer to that?'

'You're talking rubbish.'

'We'll see who's talking rubbish tomorrow when I go to the police.'

'You wouldn't do that.'

'Watch me.'

'Leave him alone. You know perfectly well he's ill.'

'Ill, my arse! He's a dirty, lousy, two-faced fucking murderer! Ill or not, he'll pay for it, just like his slag of a sister did, even if she did get off too lightly!'

'Oh that's right, when it comes to dishing out justice your family are the experts. Wasn't it your father, who'd feathered his nest on the black market, that shaved her head? Right here in this room?'

'Don't you talk about my father like that, you slut. Tomorrow I'm going to the police and I'm telling them what I know!'

'You're a hero of the Resistance too, now, I suppose. You

disgust me! Anyway, you won't go, you don't have the balls.'

'So that's what you think, is it?'

His fist had caught her full in the face. She'd just had time to fling a chair at his legs before making a run for it.

'Bastard! Rotten bastard!'

And yet, though she wouldn't admit it to herself, the accusations were eating away at her like a worm in an apple. In her shocked state and at night, anything became possible, question marks dangled from the stars like fish hooks. It would be good to pull in the net and find it empty but, to be honest, Bernard had been so strange lately it was as if he had a secret, something he was keeping to himself, something which, like all secrets, was just dying to burst from his lips. But that was his illness, nothing but his illness. It was unthinkable that Roland should poison his last days by setting the police on him. That scumbag would stop at nothing. Bernard, a killer?

It's difficult to drive with only one eye, you only see half the world, the uglier half. She couldn't really remember the way to Bernard's, she'd only been there once or twice, a very long time before. A sombre, grey house – she'd had to wait outside.

'I'm sorry, Yolande's very fragile. Oh shit, my keys ... It doesn't matter, I always leave a spare set under the flowerpots.'

That had been a lovely day. Roland had gone off to Le Touquet for three days, to a café owners' meeting, something she'd got out of without even having been invited. It was a Sunday, and there hadn't been many for lunch. By three o'clock she was free. Bernard had taken her to the forbidden places of their childhood. They'd both been a little tipsy, had forgotten, for a few hours, who they were. And during those few hours they'd found they were unchanged, free of the little nicks in the skin at the corners of their eyes. They'd seen the sea tumbling pebbles on the beach, and imitated the gulls, turning their scarves into wings; they'd eaten chips though they weren't hungry, drunk beer without a thirst, like any other couple trailing their Sunday behind them like an ornamental poodle. A few hours in which they could believe they were what they never would be. Roland wouldn't be back until the next day. Like misers they counted out the hours, minutes and seconds they had left. Bernard had suggested the cinema.

'Five minutes – I'll be right back.'

She had seen him hunting around under the geranium pot which contained nothing but a spadeful of dry soil, then give three knocks on the door and disappear inside after turning the key. For the twenty minutes during which she had waited in the car, she'd wondered what Yolande would look like after so long. And what it was like in their house, and what it would have been like at Bernard and Jacqueline's if life had had other ideas. She was on to the choice of wallpaper in the bedroom when he had emerged again, gaunt and looking sad.

'I'm so sorry, Jacqueline, we're going to have to call it a day. She's not well. I'll take you home.'

'I quite understand,' she'd said, strangling her scarf on her knees.

Life had had the same lurid violet tint as this evening, and the sweep of the headlamps was powerless to soften it.

'Oh where is it? Bloody hell!'

There it was, it was coming back to her now. The disused mine shaft, and the first hovels of this dump which might indeed be called 'Bloody Hell'. Her right eye felt like a piping-hot fried egg stuck to her cheek. The only light in the windows she passed was from the bluish TV screens. One more right turn, all the way along, the very last house.

Others had sprung up in the meantime but it was easy to recognise, grey, unseeing, deaf. Jacqueline parked and switched off the engine. She hesitated then caught sight of Bernard's Renault 5 squashed up against the gate like a fag end in an ashtray.

A sliver of light came from the downstairs window.

A woman, even if she's in her pinny and wearing a black eye, always tidies her hair in the rear-view mirror. The cold was nipping at her thighs, the points of her breasts. She ran across the road the way girls run, legs going out to the sides, holding her jacket closed across her chest with both hands. Even at fifty-five and counting, a woman is still a girl. She had to push open a rotting wooden gate with a letter box nailed to it: Yolande and Bernard BONNET.

The house seemed to hate her. She would be hard put to it to say in what way, why, and how it showed this, but it hated her. Its way of puffing out its walls as she approached, and swallowing her up in its covered doorway.

Jacqueline knocked three times, louder at each turn. All she got in reply was a dull thud as if the house wasn't hollow inside, was without resonance.

'Bernard! It's me, Jacqueline! I've got to talk to you! Open up!'

The house retreated still further into itself. Jacqueline took a step backwards and flung a handful of gravel against the shutters. Nothing.

'I know someone's there. Yolande, open the door, it's important!'

Despite the bedcover over Yolande's head, the handful of gravel was like a volley of buckshot to her. Her head was still thrumming from the knocking at the door, which had dragged her from the sleep engulfing her, soft and black as soot. They were going to mount an attack, it was imminent. They would not pass by. All these years, one on top of the other, had made the walls of the house as thick as a blockhouse's. Yolande stroked her hair. They wanted to take her back to the café, to do it all over again, that was why they'd sent Jacqueline. But Bernard had made her a promise, no one could get in, no one could see. It was like Switzerland here, the war would stay outside. To ward off ill fortune she sucked the 'More than yesterday and much less than tomorrow' pendant. The gold didn't taste of anything. It wasn't worth the blood spilt for it. With a swift tug she snapped the chain and swallowed the pendant.

Jacqueline had found the key under the flowerpot. She was reluctant to use it. This house was out of bounds, but Roland would stop at nothing. He wouldn't be sober again for a week, he'd be sprawling about at the police station. She didn't believe a word of what he was saying of course, but Bernard was so weak. She wanted people to leave him in peace for what little time he had left. The key was rusty, it lay heavy in her hand like a weapon. She gave the door one last thump.

'Bernard, Yolande, I'm begging you!'

The key grated, as if unwilling to do its job. Then the door opened.

It wasn't the noise of the key in the lock that made Yolande jump but the icy draught, the breath of the outside. That shit Bernard had betrayed her. They were there! She could hear footsteps. In her head she was yelling, 'Bastard, you bastard!' She huddled still further into the corner of the room, wrapped in the bedcover, with only her eyes peeping out. She was no longer able to control the shivers rippling through her body from head to toe. Her right hand was looking for something, it didn't matter what, as long as it could be used as a weapon. A Bic biro, a Cristal, with blue ink.

Jacqueline retched as she ventured into the hall, where an infernal stench leapt out at her like a wild cat.

'Oh, good God!'

Any rubbish tip would have looked like a picnic spot compared to this house. A heap of old newspapers collapsed as she made to steady herself against the wall. A creature slipped between her legs. Stifling a cry, she felt about for a switch but thought better of it. It might look worse in the light.

'Bernard? Yolande? Don't be frightened, it's me, Jacqueline.'

She moved forward blindly, arms outstretched in front of her, towards the glimmer coming from under a door. She had only four steps to take but it seemed like several kilometres. As she moved, among the countless stale odours crowding into her nostrils, one gradually stood out, sweetish, yellow, rancid. She had never smelt it close up and yet she knew. It was in the genes. When her father had died, the same smell had filled the air outside the room she'd been forbidden to enter.

'But why can't I go in?'

'Because.'

When her father had emerged, it had been in a long box of pale oak. The wax polish had never managed to banish the smell from that room. Gingerly she pushed the door in front of her. Centimetre by centimetre her field of vision increased: the stiff bulk of a wardrobe, the corner of a chair with a cup on it, a bedside table bearing a reading lamp with its shade at an angle and ... Bernard's profile, eyes and mouth open, emaciated. Her hand flew to her mouth. Tears came into her eyes.

'No! Oh God, no!'

Her foot trod on something plastic, the lid of a pen. Bernard was staring at the ceiling with a silly grin. One of his lips seemed to have been gnawed. Bernard's elbows and knees stuck up beneath the sheet. Run away as fast as she could ... But that was impossible. All the mysteries were there, all the things you want to know about 'the Hereafter'. In any case, the orders from her head were no longer getting through to her limbs. It was horrible, monstrous, but it was fascinating. She stayed there in astonishment, faced with this life in which death had taken up residence. Her blood shot up and down in her veins like an elevator gone mad, then froze around her heart. She didn't hear the bedcover moving behind her. Once upon a time there lived Bernard and Jacqueline ...

Yolande had pounced, gripping the biro in her fist. Pulling Jacqueline's head back by the hair she had plunged the biro into her exposed throat. The blood spurted out, spattering Bernard's cheek. Gurgling noises came from Jacqueline's mouth. Her arms were flailing. But Yolande kept her grip. Several times she struck with the pen, into her neck, her eye, five times, ten, twenty! Until that tart from the café fell like a rag doll at her feet.

'Good shot! Good shot! Good shot!!!'

While she'd been kicking the body, Yolande had lost her slipper. She looked for it under the bed. There it was, she'd found it. As she drew her head out from under the bed again, she found herself eyeball to eyeball with Jacqueline whose face, streaming with blood, was still making drowning noises. Yolande planted her lips on Jacqueline's and kissed her greedily.

'There, that's for Bernard, you little trollop.'

Wiping her mouth on her sleeve, Yolande got to her feet. Never had she felt so cold. That was the outside rushing in.

The passageway was filled with darkness. The others must be lying in wait in the bushes. That air ... that air ... She went to close the door but it was as if she were charmed by the Pied Piper. In front of the immense dark, she wavered, stretching out her hand. The night had no walls, no limits. That was frightening and enticing at the same time. Silence didn't exist, or else it was made up of a thousand tiny sounds. The wind on her face was an invitation. 'Come, Yolande, come. Here's something that has no end.' The air took hold of her under the arms, gently, tenderly, like her lovers of long ago. Scenting the air, Yolande quivered with all those good things. She ventured on to the doorstep. The night slipped under her skirt. 'Come here, Yolande, the world is yours for the taking. You've earned it, haven't you?'

'Yes, yes. I'm coming, but I can't come like this. I've got to do my make-up first.'

Jean-Claude was a sales rep in ladies' lingerie. He had just laid the horny bitch of a wife of an unemployed man, after getting her to sign an order worth 1,500 francs. He was happy. He was on his way home to Douai. At the side of the road, his headlamps picked out a woman's shape, a platinum blonde. He slowed down and drew up alongside. Second helpings, maybe?

'Can I do anything for you?'

The face which appeared in his wound-down window left him open-mouthed: the McDonald's clown, with far too much rouge, false eyelashes and a layer of cracking plaster all over the cheeks.

'Darling?'

'No, nothing, thanks.'

Jean-Claude sped off. He was to be involved in an accident three kilometres further on as he joined the motorway. The last thing he saw in this life would be the leering after-image of Yolande on his retina.

Outside, it was like being in the cavity of a wall. All that darkness, on every side. Yolande never grew tired, she could go on walking for hours. In the house, she had given the rooms names, the five-step room, the three-step room and so on, but here you could go on walking until the end of time. You didn't feel the cold when walking. It was best to always be on the move. The far-off was so intoxicating. No matter where you were going, that was always where you ended up. One, two, one, two …Walking, that's what mattered. There were those hiking songs: '*Un kilomètre à pied, ça use, ça use* …' That wasn't true, it didn't wear you out, not even your toes. It was arriving that wore you out. Yolande wasn't going to arrive, ever. On leaving the house, she'd turned right, taking the road that she'd used to take to the village. It was the same, and yet not the same. There were loads of different houses which hadn't been there before, ugly, pointed bungalows with dogs howling at the gate. Often, coming home from a dance, she'd taken this road. There hadn't been all those rakes on the roofs. What did they want to go raking the sky for? To grow what? The fields hadn't changed much, with their rabbits, eyes red from the headlamps, and that fine smell of fertiliser. The soil was good, it made you want to lie down in it like a trusty old bed when you're tired.

Kneeling on the verge, Yolande grasped handfuls of earth, smearing it on her face.

She got the same pleasure from it as when she buried her nose in a hunk of freshly baked bread. She flung handfuls skywards, calling out, 'Again! Again!'

At the edge of a wood, a fox watched her go on her way singing at the top of her voice, 'Robin Hood, Robin Hood ...'

The Café de la Gare still had its lights on. Roland was asleep at a table, his head buried in his arms and his hunting rifle propped up against the imitation-leather banquette. He was having a dream about hunting. He had killed all the animals in the forest and was continuing his destruction with the trees, but they were refusing to fall down. Soon he would have run out of cartridges and there were still so many trees ...

Yolande's path could lead nowhere else. There was only one and it led inexorably to Place de la Gare. Everything had changed: the shops, most of the houses, the lines of certain streets, the in-your-face adverts in which naked girls who looked like her cavorted, new streetlights looking like strings of sorrowful moons along the paths. And yet nothing had changed. The same familiar ennui enveloped the house fronts, cocooning the threadbare dreams of those who were asleep inside. The three kilometres she'd covered had given her a momentum which no force on earth could stop. She wasn't going anywhere, she was simply on the move, she could cross walls, rivers, slag heaps, time itself. The end of the night was always further off, receding with every step she took. Each of her strides pushed the horizon back. A cat sprang across the road in front of her. He had mistaken her for a car, she was going so fast, eyes scouring the darkness for any signs of the past. It was still there, its lines faintly visible beneath the slap-dash paintwork of the present.

'Bastards! They're trying to make me believe …Well, I don't believe anything and I never have.'

The remains of shouts, of taunts still hung from the leafless branches of trees: 'Slut! Whore! Give your arse to a Boche, would you? Shave her head!' They were like the tatters of burst balloons. She had never been frightened. She'd known she'd be back one day, one day which would be like a night. She went by, waving like the Queen of England.

Set in the darkness, the Café de la Gare shone like a cheap piece of costume jewellery in a La Redoute catalogue. It was cheap, bargain basement even. Yolande pushed the door, perfectly naturally. It opened, producing a half-hearted chime. The man slumped over the table hadn't reacted at all. He was snoring. The glass in front of him shuddered every time he breathed. Yolande blinked, the neon lighting was oppressive, boring into her retina. There was too much electricity in this new world, electricity everywhere, as soon as she touched the edge of a table or the back of a chair. Current, current like during a storm, blue-green zigzags snaking all around her. This world had no place for her. She wasn't electric. She didn't have little lights that came on all over like that pinball machine which flashed 'Game over!' This world was a Christmas, and she wasn't invited. She no longer understood, everything had changed, the murals had turned into enormous photographs, undergrowth in which she couldn't keep track of herself. She would have liked to go home, shut herself up and no longer see. She had no reference points, even the teaspoon lying on the counter wasn't like the one she knew. She felt hemmed in by a crowd of objects whose uses she didn't know. Only the man sprawling at the table resembled something she might have been familiar with. Timidly she went and huddled up against him, placing the rifle between her knees. The chap groaned, and shifted the shoulder with Yolande's head resting on it.

'... don't, Jacqueline ... Jacque— Shit! What the hell???'

Roland had sat up with a start.

'But ...Who are you? What the hell are you doing here?'

'André?'

'I'm not André!'

He rubbed his eyes. The person speaking to him, who thought he was his father, didn't have a real face, but rather a mush of chalk and redcurrant juice brightened by two mint-green eyes.

'What do you want with me?'

'André??? Why haven't you got old like all the others?'

'I'm not André, I'm Roland ...'

Before he had time to say anything else, Yolande was on her feet again, pointing the gun in his face.

'Why aren't you dead, you fat bastard? Everyone else dies – why not you?'

'You're mistaken, I'm Roland. André was my father.'

Yolande cocked the gun.

'You're a stupid bastard, André, you always were.'

'Don't! Yolande, you're Yolande!'

At the front the bullet didn't do too much damage. It was at the back that it all burst out, sending a shower of brain and bone all over the undergrowth. On the shelves, the bottles had shrunk closer together. Not a table or a chair so much as breathed. Silence reigned once more.

All of a sudden Yolande felt very weary. Her shoulder still trembled from the kick of the rifle. She flopped down on to a chair opposite what was left of Roland.

'It's a cold world out there and I'm going to make sure they know it.'

Exhausted, Yolande went to sleep.

How's the Pain?

by Pascal Garnier

translated from the French by Emily Boyce

Even a broken clock is right twice a day.
Proverb

The sound coming from somewhere in the darkness was barely audible, but it was enough to shatter his sleep. The drone of the moped grew louder until it was directly beneath his window, grating on his nerves like a dentist's drill boring into a decayed tooth. Then it faded into the distance, leaving nothing behind but a long rip through the fabric of the sleeping city. He hadn't opened his eyes or moved except to twitch his mouth in annoyance at the buzzing mechanical insect. Lying flat on his back with his hands crossed over his chest, Simon could have been a recumbent tomb effigy. One at a time he opened his heavy eyelids, gummed together like the rusty shutters of an old shop. He groped for his glasses on the bedside table, but could barely see any better once he had put them on. The pale light of dawn behind the floral-patterned lace curtains bathed the room in a uniform grey. Every object and item of furniture seemed devoid of substance, as if they had been hastily sketched on the walls. The bedspread, blanket and sheets had hardly been disturbed. He had slept peacefully, without waking. If that two-stroke engine had not roared in to break the spell, he would probably still have been asleep now. His travel clock beside the lamp showed 6.11 a.m. The alarm was set for seven. No matter, he was wide awake now. Besides, time did not follow its usual course in hotel rooms; it stagnated like the dead arm of a river.

Simon glanced around at his rudimentary universe: his shoes, sitting quietly at the foot of the bed, a sock rolled up inside each one; his jacket hanging limply over the back of the chair; the little table where he had emptied out the contents of his pockets, with the car keys and documents, his wallet, notebook, a pen, a handful of coins, a few banknotes and a large envelope addressed to Bernard Ferrand. He checked its contents: his Geneva bank account number and a power of attorney for Bernard, along with a short note saying, 'Thank you and good luck.' He gazed at it for a few moments, then screwed it up with a shrug and lobbed it into the wastepaper basket. Next to the envelope sat an apple and a skipping rope, still in its colourful plastic wrapping. A poor copy of Van Gogh's *Sunflowers* hung on the olive-green wall. The bathroom light was still on. A notice on the back of the door informed guests of the fire drill, room rates, mealtimes and so on.

Was it him that creaked or the bed, as he extricated himself from the sheets? He rubbed his neck. Wretched trapped nerves. His knees were like banister knobs. His calves were dry and hairy like crab claws, his toenails hard as ancient ivory, like the claws of an aged dog. He yawned, got up and raised a corner of the curtain. The same pallid light outside as in. The clouds were low, clinging like tufts of cotton wool to the mountains encircling Vals-les-Bains, Ucel and Saint-Julien-du-Serre. It was impossible to tell what lay beyond. Between the streaks of rain running down the window, he could just about make out the muddy waters of the Volane flowing past the Béatrix-spring rotunda.

'It was too good to last. The forecast says it's going to carry on raining all week.'

'You're the one who wanted to take the waters. We'll just have to go to the pictures.'

This was a conversation Simon had overheard the previous evening, from the neighbouring table in the hotel restaurant. A retired couple: the wife shaking her head over the menu, the husband hiding behind *Le Dauphiné*. The front page was taken up with the news of the death of a well-known film producer, pictured sporting a dazzling display of dentures and a glitzy starlet on each arm.

Simon tucked into his Vichyssoise and fillets of sole and saved the apple for later, which is to say, now. He bit into it. A little floury. Disappointed, he put it down and went into the bathroom.

He had still not worked out the shower. It was a toss-up between freezing-cold or boiling-hot water. Perhaps because his body sensed that it had already been deserted, it refused to respond to his brain's orders. The glass tumbler slipped from his hands and smashed on the tiled floor. He knocked his elbow, banged his knee and cut himself shaving. All he saw in the mirror now was the outline of a blurred face seeking anonymity. A dab of aftershave and that was it, done. He changed his underwear out of respect for the people who would soon be dealing with his corpse.

Once dressed, he paced the few steps from the window to the bed, from the bed back to the window. Then he took the skipping rope out of its packaging. The brightly coloured box showed a little girl in a pink dress playing in a daisy-strewn meadow. He had bought it the day before in the souvenir shop next to the hotel, just before it closed. The shop assistant had smiled at her last, curious sale of the day. The rope was white, with red handles. He tested its strength by tugging on it sharply. 'Made in China', he read with suspicion. Then he placed the chair underneath the frosted-glass ceiling light with its stylised tulips, and clambered onto it. He carefully tied one end of the rope around the hook on the ceiling and looped the other around his neck. He was perfectly calm. He was not quite sure what to do with his hands. He clasped them behind his back and waited, wearily watching the raindrops streaking down the windowpane.

Maybe it was sleeping too long beside his mother's cold body, or else it was the permanently damp atmosphere that had made Bernard feel so out of sorts – stiff, sniffling, fuzzy-headed. What was it with these old folk, loading their dirty work onto him as if he were some mule? It was a good thing Fiona and Violette had stayed put. Still, hey ho, better get on with the job.

The lift took Bernard up to the fourth floor. The doors opened and a bell pinged. The corridor was empty. His footsteps were muffled by the brown, leaf-patterned carpet which seemed to go on for ever. 401, 402, 403 ... He sneezed and then blew his nose as quietly as he could. 404, 405, 406. He was a couple of minutes early. Monsieur Marechall was a stickler for punctuality. He waited. Water dripped off his cagoule onto his shoes. Eight o'clock on the dot. Very gently, he turned the handle of the door which opened without the slightest creak. Just as planned, Monsieur Marechall was standing on the chair, facing the window, hands behind his back like a naughty schoolboy made to stand in the corner. He hadn't flinched, though he knew Bernard had come in. Took guts.

Apart from a ripple along the curtain folds, nothing moved. It was like looking at a photograph. Snatches of conversation from the road outside, a shrill laugh, a car door slamming, an engine starting up. The last sound jolted Bernard into action. Two steps forward. He closed his eyes and kicked the chair from under Monsieur Marechall's feet. A cracking sound but no cry, just the crash of the chair on the floor and a whoosh of displaced air. Bernard remembered a wooden puppet he had had when he was little; you pulled a string and its arms and legs jigged about. He waited until all he could hear was a rhythmic creaking that grew softer and softer before he opened one eye. One of Simon's shoes had fallen off, an expensive loafer deformed by a bunion. Bernard did not dare look up. He collected the cash, keys and car documents from the table, along with the envelope, as agreed. He was hungry and bit into the half-eaten apple. Tasteless. It was hard to find a decent apple these days. He sneezed again. They were saying it would rain all week. He left the room and shut the door behind him. No point saying goodbye to a dead man. At the end of the corridor, Bernard found the lift in use. He took the stairs.

They had met a few days earlier on a park bench beside the Volane, opposite the casino. It was a Saturday, some time around 11 a.m. A bravely struggling sun made the landscape look like a naïve painting. The trees were green, the flowers pink, yellow and red, the sky blue and the shadows grey. The pathways were teeming with people, as wedding parties gathered at the foot of the grand stone steps – the perfect spot to line up the families in front of the camera. It was a little bit like paradise, with everyone dressed up, perfumed and polished like the best china, all kissing each other or crying with happiness.

'Could you all move in a bit please? And a bit more? The lady with the blue hat, could you take a step back? Thanks, that's great! Now just the bride and groom please, among the roses.'

The photographer was a true professional; he had no qualms about destroying the flowerbeds or tyrannising his models to ensure that this would truly be the most beautiful day of their lives.

'Get down on bended knee please, sir – that's it, like Prince Charming. Smile, smile! Take his hand ... Perfect!'

The fixed grimaces on the newlyweds' faces suggested either they desperately needed to pee or their new shoes were rubbing. The groom's suit looked stiff as a board, while his bride stood surrounded by masses of netting that could have been spun from a candyfloss machine. Clinging to the train like limpets, the bridesmaids twisted their ankles tottering in their first pair of heels. Mothers dabbed their eyes, fathers puffed out their chests with pride, kids played catch, sending up eddies of dust. Groups of spa visitors, recognisable from the cups in wicker holders dangling from straps slung over their shoulders, mingled with the families and took pictures, condescending to share in the simple rituals of the indigenous population.

'Isn't this lovely?'

'You think so?'

'Well, yes. Seeing all these people so happy, it's nice, isn't it?'

'How do you know they're happy?'

'You can tell.'

'You can't trust appearances. It's usually all for show. What about you, are you happy?'

'Depends ... yes, I think so.'

'Are you married?'

'No.'

'What happened to your hand?'

'An accident at work. One of the machines. Lost two fingers.'

'Nasty.'

'It hurts a bit, but it's only my little finger and fourth finger. I never used them. Plus it's my left hand and I'm right-handed.'

'Well, that's all right then. You just lost a bit of weight.'

'It was my fault. I'd had a bit to drink. I didn't use the safety guard. But my boss is a good guy and he's taking me back, in a different job ... The pay's not so good, but at least it's work. I've been lucky!'

'A real stroke of luck, I'm sure! Let me introduce myself. I'm Simon Marechall.'

'Bernard Ferrand. Are you here for the spa?'

'Are you joking? Do I look like one of those decrepit old crocks?' Simon asked, horrified. 'Just look at them with those ridiculous sunhats, the silly cups round their necks, their baggy shorts and knock-knees. Their bandy legs are like battered Louis XV chairs: it's an antiques market! They should have dust covers put over them. No, no,' he concluded, 'I'm just passing through. What about you?'

'Um, just passing through too, while my hand heals. My mother lives in Vals. We don't see each other very often so I thought I'd make the most of my time off.'

'So there are people who really live here. I thought they must be film extras. You know the area then?'

'Not very well. I live in Bron, near Lyon. I'm not from here; I just come now and then to see my mother.'

'Is there much to do?'

'There's the casino. You can go for walks, visit the Château de Cros, see the volcanic rocks. Then there's Jean Ferrat, of course.'

'Jean Ferrat, the singer?'

'Yes, he's from Antraigues. Sometimes you see him at the market on Sunday mornings.'

'That's terrific!'

'You like Jean Ferrat then?'

'Very much. Do you?'

'Not specially.'

'Bit before your time, I expect.'

'It's more that I've heard my mother singing his songs so often, it's almost like he's a friend of the family.'

Laughing, Simon took a tissue out of his pocket to wipe his sunglasses. He had grey eyes, the colour of steel: cold and hard.

'I like you very much, young man. How old are you?'

'I'll be twenty-two next month.'

'How would you like to have lunch with me?'

'I can't, I have to go back to my mother's. I'm already late and I need to pick up some bread.'

'What a shame. How about this evening?'

'Um, OK.'

'Do you know of any good restaurants?'

'Chez Mireille is supposed to be good. I think it's a bit pricey but ...'

'Don't worry about that, it'll be my treat. Tonight at seven thirty then. Come and meet me at the Grand Hôtel de Lyon. Simon Marechall, room 406.'

'OK then, thanks.'

Simon's hand was cold, dry and tense. With his black shades back on, Simon seemed to Bernard like the night glaring down, though in fact the older man was slightly shorter than him. One set off towards the hotel district, the other in the direction of the old town.

Even though the street was bathed in sunlight, Madame Ferrand's little shop remained hopelessly gloomy. It was years since she had pulled back the faded cretonne curtain across the shop window, and its dust-coated folds made it impossible for passers-by to see in. But it didn't matter, since nothing was for sale here any more. It had become Madame Ferrand's apartment. The back room was used as a kitchen-cum-bathroom and a small adjoining storeroom served as a bedroom. The 'shop' itself, as Madame Ferrand still called it, now formed the living room. It was furnished with a sagging sofa heaped with cushions, throws and blankets of dubious cleanliness; three ill-assorted chairs; a wobbly pedestal table; a dining table with flaking varnish, and a curious floor lamp in the shape of a life-sized nude Negress, wearing a raffia lampshade askew on her head. The floor was covered with a patchwork of threadbare rugs. On the walls, dog-eared adverts for long-gone brands, posters of dead singers, and tourist-office promotions for countries since ravaged by war bandaged the wounds in the peeling wallpaper. Odd remnants of shelving, racks and spotlights bore witness to the owner's many and various ventures, snuffed out one by one by stubbornly adverse fate.

Madame Ferrand had invested the sum total of her meagre savings in these modest premises twenty years earlier. She had had no hesitation in entrusting little Bernard, then aged two, to the care of her parents, leaving her free to seek her fortune in Vals-les-Bains. Why Vals-les-Bains? Perhaps because of Jean Ferrat, whose revolutionary lyrics could not fail to ignite the pure working-class heart of a mother seduced by a stockbroker from Lyon, who vanished without trace when baby Bernard was born. Unless it was something as mundane as an ad in *Le Dauphiné* that put the idea into her head one lonely evening, kindling in her the hope of escaping her unremittingly squalid fate.

She was thirty-five, feisty, determined, good with her hands and not without talent. Ignoring the derision of neighbouring shopkeepers, she worked on her hats by night and fixed the place up during the day, successfully transforming an old-fashioned haberdasher's into a stylish millinery boutique in the space of a month. Chez Anaïs opened on schedule at the end of May, just in time for the tourist season. But by October, she had to face facts: she had not found her clientele. Her extravagant headpieces certainly amused the spa visitors who came to try them on, giggling in front of the mirrors, but they never bought anything.

After a period of understandable despondency, she sold her stock to a ragman for next to nothing and, with the same enthusiasm and pugnacity as before, opened a local handicrafts shop with a young hippy by the name of Daphne. A new sign, 'Aux Herbes Tendres', went up in place of the old. They sold beeswax candles, real leather belts and bags, brass jewellery, weird preserves, strange infusions and incense sticks, a lot of incense sticks, some of which were kept tucked inside Daphne's long woollen coat. Business was going pretty well until the day Anaïs's partner ran off with the till, leaving her with nothing but her eyes to cry with, a few armfuls of lavender and bitter memories of her first Sapphic love affair. '*La femme est l'avenir de l'homme*,' crooned Jean Ferrat, so couldn't a woman be another woman's future too? She was furious with Jean Ferrat that autumn and furious with the rest of humanity too, which is what set her thinking about going into dog grooming. You rarely come across a retired couple on a spa break without one of those hideous golden poodles in tow. Of course, Anaïs knew nothing about dogs and the equipment costs would be substantial, but nothing ventured, nothing gained. This time, she was sure she was onto something. She'd had it with the human race and was putting her faith in man's best friend. Come spring, Madame Ferrand donned an immaculate white coat to welcome the first customers to her pooch parlour. But at the beginning of July, she was forced to close the doors due to an unfortunate incident. A faulty switch on a drier had turned a dachshund called Caruso into a hot dog. The sale of the equipment just about covered the legal fees.

Anaïs was by no means the only one to experience a run of bad luck. One by one, the shops along Rue Jean-Jaurès went under, turning it into a ghost town. Only those supplying life's basic essentials (namely the baker, the butcher and the tobacconist) were able to survive. This part of town, where tourists wandered aimlessly as if roaming the ruins of a lost civilisation, seemed destined for oblivion. After buying a few postcards, they would hurry back across the Volane to the reassuring shade of manicured hotel gardens.

But Anaïs was not one to throw in the towel at the first hurdle, nor the second, nor even the third. There must be a lesson to be learnt from this string of failures. One evening, as she groped for her glasses in the storeroom, her light-bulb moment came: 'That's it! Seeing!' The scent of incense wafted back to her as she recalled her former partner's mysterious revelations, secrets she had made her solemnly swear never to share.

'No way am I going to keep that to myself, you old bitch!'

True, she might have drunk a little too much rum from the bottle of Negrita she was clutching, but she was just as shrewd as the next person!

Within a month she had digested the Egyptian Book of the

Dead, that of the Tibetans and even the Popol Vuh. She mastered palm reading as easily as a shareholder learning about the stock exchange or a racegoer studying form. Finally, she saw a future ahead. Even better, the investment required was paltry: a pedestal table, a tarot set, a clock and that was it. Not to mention the fact that, in order for her to concentrate, she would need to be in complete darkness, drastically reducing her electricity bills. With the last of her money she had business cards printed to drop through letterboxes. It was cold, it was winter, she wheezed and her legs puffed up, but the Negrita kept her going. All she needed to do was wait.

Her first three clients suffered violent deaths in quick succession. One choked on a plum stone, another was hit head-on by a bus on her way to mass and the last was devoured by her own dog. Rumours spread quickly in small towns like this and nobody else took the risk of consulting her.

Anaïs took to coughing to pass the time, a hacking cough which tolled like a death knell inside her chest and which she had come to accept, like an old dog that had latched onto her.

In one last, admirable burst of optimism, she wrote a slate sign: 'Anaïs's Bric-à-Brac', which she hung in the shop window. The only remnants of her failed ventures were a few musty felt hats, some bunches of dried flowers, three or four candles which had lost their scent, a dozen cracked leather dog collars and a tarot set. Strangely enough, she sold the lot.

These days she lived off her incurable cough, which brought her a small disability allowance, along with the modest but regular parcels she received from Bernard. It was enough to buy her daily bottle of Negrita, enabling her to watch calmly as the dust settled like grey snow on a life that should not have been. 'My past is a joke, my present's a disaster, thank goodness I have no future,' she would say to console herself.

'Mother, lunch is almost ready, come and sit down!'

Walking past Béatrix ice-cream parlour down the road from his hotel, Simon gave in to a childish whim. He sat down at a table underneath the plane trees whose leaves filtered the sunlight, casting extraordinary shadows. With the defiance of a little boy, he ordered the biggest and most expensive ice cream on the menu. While he waited for it to arrive, he flicked through the spa brochure he had picked up from reception that morning. The town boasted six springs: Constantine was the best for treating weight problems, dyspepsia and gout; Précieuse was the one to go to for liver conditions and diabetes; Dominique was very effective against anaemia and fatigue; Désirée was recommended for its laxative effects; Rigolette was prescribed for colitis; Camuse, to ease digestion. These waters could only be drunk on prescription, but there were three others – Saint-Jean, Favorite and Béatrix – which could be consumed in limitless quantities. The list of the conditions they were capable of curing was both endless and disconcerting: industrial dermatitis, nasal fractures, tropical liver diseases, trigger finger, abnormally large intestines ... There were as many ailments to treat as there were ice creams on the menu. Who could claim not to suffer from a single one of them?

He glanced up. The average age of the clientele was somewhere between sixty and a hundred. Though he fell into this age bracket himself, the sight of so many pensioners in one place made him dizzy. While he had always considered his presence on earth to be a miscasting and had done his best to distance himself from his playmates from a tender age, he had never felt so trapped, in the clutches of some merciless predator. A young waitress set down in front of him the huge glass of garish ice cream studded with ridiculous cocktail umbrellas. Aside from her, he could see only three humanoids who had so far escaped the ravages of time. All of them were on wheels (bicycle, skateboard and Rollerblades) as they zipped past, intent on dodging the Zimmer frames.

Why on earth had he stopped at Vals-les-Bains? It was simply down to a pun. A Strauss waltz had been playing on France Musique as he drove towards the town. 'A last waltz ... a last Vals?' Admittedly a violent bout of sickness had also forced him to stop for an hour, leaving him feeling shaky. He was in luck, a Belgian couple had just cancelled and there was one room left at the Grand Hôtel de Lyon. He had planned to stay just one night, but when he woke up to a glimpse of spring sunshine, a coffee and some excellent croissants, something in the air had made him want to truant for the day.

He still hadn't touched his ice cream, which was beginning to resemble a jaundiced cowpat. He toyed with his spoon, looking at his reflection in its curved surfaces. What had come over him, inviting that lad to dinner? He probably took him for an old queer. What if he didn't turn up? He hadn't seemed too bright, but that was what he liked about him: his honesty, his awkwardness, and that bandaged hand he moved about like a glove puppet. There was no denying it, he had made some strange choices since his arrival, like this ice cream he had never even wanted in the first place and which was now just a mess. He tried a mouthful anyway. All the flavours had mingled together and it was impossible to identify a single one. It was just cold and sweet.

While he was fishing for change in his jacket pocket, his revolver almost fell out.

'Shit, it really is time to call it a day.'

'So why's this man invited you to dinner then? You don't think he might be a poofter?'

'Don't think so, no. He seems normal.'

'What's "normal"? Everyone seems normal, but they're not really. Anyway, you're a big boy now, you can look after yourself.'

'Don't you want any more of your chop, Mother?'

'No, it's too fatty.'

'Lamb's always a bit fatty, that's what makes it so tasty. You never eat anything.'

'Well, you can't do everything. Eat or drink, you have to make a choice.'

'You drink too much. You smoke too much as well. No wonder you're always tired.'

'I like being tired, it's relaxing. What are you doing today?'

'Not sure. It's a nice day, might go for a walk down by the river. How about I make you some vegetable soup for tonight? You like veggie soup, don't you?'

'If you like. How's your hand?'

'It's all right. I went to see Dr Garcin this morning to get the dressing changed. He asked after you.'

'And what did you say?'

'That you were fine.'

'You're a rotten liar ... just as well.'

'And what are you going to do?'

'Same as usual. A nice nap before I go to bed.'

It was a place only he knew. You went under the bridge before taking a pebbly path beside the Volane for about fifteen minutes. Then you had to jump from rock to rock, without worrying about getting your feet wet, to reach a little sandy cove shaded by gnarled willows. No one could see you. The bubbling of the water drowned out the hubbub of the town and the cars on the road above. He had discovered this spot when on holiday here at the age of ten. It was in the days when his mother was selling strange herbs with Daphne. He'd never much liked that lady. Firstly, she was ugly, with all that red hair and hippy clothes. She couldn't smile properly either; every time she tried, stroking his head, she looked like the wicked stepmother offering Snow White the poisoned apple. She smelt bad and painted her nails black like claws. If he'd been a dog, he would have bitten her.

Bernard leant against the warm rock, took off his shoes and socks and wiggled his toes in the grey sand. The pebbles formed a pool where the water could catch its breath before continuing along its course, foaming at the mouth. Dragonflies flitted across the surface and sometimes you might see a trout circling in the clear water below. They were beautiful, the dragonflies, as delicate and glittery as Tinkerbell. The trout were pretty too; so gentle, so shiny, so alive. Once he had caught one in his hand. That was a moment he would never forget. It was like holding life itself between his fingers with its golden eyes, supple body, shimmering scales and gills that pulsed like pipe valves. He stroked it for a long time, too long. It bucked one last time and all that was left in his hands was a limp, motionless object. He had tried to put it back in the water but it had instantly capsized, baring its white belly to the sky. He had buried it tearfully, right there under the willow stump. Even after washing his hands ten times, it took two days to get rid of the smell of sludge. He never did it again.

No, this Monsieur Simon Marechall was no queer. He had invited him out because he liked him, simple as that. It was spending all her time shut away in that dump of a shop that made his mother see the dark side of everything. Anyway, he had known queers who were no worse than the people who didn't like queers. All you had to do was say no. Once he had said yes, just to see what would happen. It was in the third year of secondary school and the boy's surname was Gambin or Gamblin or something. Gamblin's dick had the same effect on him as the trout between his hands. He let it go. Gamblin wanted to be a diver when he grew up. He swam like a fish. Everyone dreamt of being something then: diver, pilot, fireman or farmer. But Bernard had never found his calling.

'What do you want to do for a living?'

'Dunno.'

Having miraculously got to the end of the fourth year, borne along like a stowaway, he was advised to take the vocational route, not being academically inclined. Baking, hairdressing, mechanics, plumbing – he was happy to have a go at anything, only nothing went right. However hard he tried, however much he concentrated, nothing went in. Sometimes he thought he had understood, but he was so used to being taken for an idiot that when things seemed too straightforward, he undid everything he had done and it would all go to pot. It was only during his military service that he finally achieved something, passing his driving test first time. It was the best day of his life – well, not the whole day. That night, after celebrating with some mates, he had gone joy-riding in a Jeep and ended up inside for two weeks. It was still a good memory though. The best. In truth, he had no other memories to speak of, just little things like the trout, Gamblin's dick, random bits and pieces that resurfaced now and

114

then for him to toy with in his head, the way a baby plays with its feet. Mostly, though, each day just wiped out the day before.

A fly landed on his knee. It was young and quivering with energy. In a fraction of a second, Bernard held it captive under his hand. He could feel it batting around inside. It tickled. Slowly he spread his fingers and the insect zigzagged away. When it came to catching flies, he was unbeatable. Shame you couldn't make a career out of it.

He stood up and looked for a really flat pebble. Skimming stones was another of his talents. The pebble glanced across the surface of the water like a flying saucer, bouncing six times before reaching the opposite bank. It was a hot day. He took his clothes off and lay in the current, holding his injured hand up towards the sky like a periscope so as not to get the bandage wet. He wasn't thinking about anything now. It was just nice to dissolve into the water.

Leaning back in his chair with his head tilted back, Simon smoked a cigarette and watched Bernard tucking into his daube of beef, his nose almost in his plate. It was a fascinating sight. The young man used his fork like a dagger, stabbing it into the meat to hold it in place. Then he cut off big chunks which vanished into his mouth with mechanical regularity. As he swallowed each barely chewed mouthful, his throat and shoulders shuddered slightly before he began all over again, taking the occasional glug of water to wash it down.

'You've got quite an appetite!'

'I always do. I'll eat anything – and the food here's damned good, isn't it?'

'It is very good, yes.'

In no time at all, the plate was wiped clean, sparkling as if it had just come out of the dishwasher.

'Aren't you going to finish yours, Monsieur Marechall?'

'Help yourself!'

'I could eat beef stew out of a bin.'

Chez Mireille was one of those bijou restaurants found in all small provincial towns. The walls were painted blue and pink, with intricate gilt patterns to give a touch of class. For passers-by peering in, the cosy scene was framed by lacy curtains with satin tiebacks. Mireille, a busty blonde of a certain age, glided seamlessly from table to table checking that everything was to her customers' liking. She was like the little dancer inside a music box, spinning in time to the tinkling of a Mozart tune.

Just like the wedding parties in Parc Saint-Jean that morning, everybody in the room was clean, attractive and pleasant. They spoke little and quietly. A dropped teaspoon caused quite a stir. Here, too, the average age veered towards the top of the scale; Bernard was the odd one out. He had dressed for the occasion, which is to say he had swapped his sloppy tracksuit for a pastel shirt, a navy-blue jacket that was slightly too short in the sleeve and a pair of dark-grey trousers. He could not believe his luck, and sat beaming at everyone and everything – even the water jug and bread basket. He had passed Chez Mireille countless times but never dreamt of going in. Now here he was lapping up every second and it was a pleasure to see. Pushing away the second plate as spotless as the first, he leant back in his chair with a satisfied sigh. Watching him, Simon was riveted.

'Cigarette?'

'No, I don't smoke.'

'And you don't drink wine either?'

'No. It makes my head spin, I don't like it.'

'Very sensible. Now tell me, what did your job involve?'

'We made clamps.'

'What for?'

'I dunno, just clamps. Big ones, small ones, medium ones. You had to make a certain number in an hour and then they got packed up and sent who knows where.'

'Wasn't that rather repetitive?'

'It's a job. Once you know what you're doing it's just mindless. Pretty cushy really. What about you, what do you do?'

'Pest control. Getting rid of rats, mice, pigeons, fleas, cockroaches, that sort of thing.'

'Is it going well?'

'Very. But I'm getting on a bit. I'm thinking of selling up and retiring.'

'Lucky you, retiring! Doesn't suit everyone though. There was this old guy at the factory and for his retirement present we got him this beautiful spinning rod. He never stopped going on about all the fishing trips he was planning when he stopped work. Two weeks later, what did he do? Threw himself into the river. As for me ... well, I wish I was retired already.'

'And what would you do if you were?'

'Nothing.'

'Don't you have any interests? You wouldn't want to travel?'

'No. I'd just like to have enough money to do nothing.'

'You'd get bored.'

'I don't think I would. When you're out of work and broke, you're bored because you spend the whole time thinking about how you're going to get some money. But if you've already got it, doing nothing's easy.'

'Don't you like reading or going to the cinema?'

'I've got a problem with books. When I get to the bottom of the page, I can't remember the beginning, so it takes me ages to get through them. And I fall asleep in the dark at the cinema. So what are you going to do when you retire?'

'I don't know. I like the sea. And boats.'

Mireille brought over the cheese trolley. Bernard took a wedge of everything. Simon ordered another bottle of Cornas.

'Can you believe how many cheeses they've got? It's insane. I haven't even heard of half of them. Is that all you're having, Monsieur Marechall?'

'I had some Gruyère.'

'You're just like my mother, you eat out of your glass. So you're into boats, are you? Model ones or ones you go on?'

'Ones you go on, as you put it.'

'And where would you go, on your boat?'

'Anywhere. The best bit is setting sail.'

'I'm the opposite – the best bit for me would be getting there.

So you've been on a lot of boats then?'

'I've travelled a fair amount. What I'd like is just to sail from island to island, without following a plan.'

'Nice are they, islands?'

'Some of them are lovely, yes. In fact each one has its own charm, even the bleakest.'

'Don't you end up going round and round in circles?'

'No more than anywhere else on earth. If you think about it, our planet is nothing more than an island in space.'

'Maybe, but a pretty big one. It'd take quite a while to get around the whole thing.'

'Not all that long. Anyway once you've had enough of an island, you just set sail again and it's like starting from scratch.'

'Why would you want to start from scratch? You seem like you've done well in life. I can't seem to get off the starting line.'

Probably by association, Bernard ordered the floating island for dessert. Simon was happy just to finish off the bottle of wine. He could consume huge quantities without showing the slightest sign of inebriation; only his gaze became more intense and unsettling. He never stumbled or raised his voice. In actual fact, he couldn't stand drunks. He generally stuck to water, so as to keep a steady hand. But some days, some nights ... The strange thing about this young blockhead was that he wasn't actually stupid. He displayed a kind of guileless common sense which Simon found refreshing. It reminded him of the possibility of a simpler life. It was like coming across a spring gushing with cool water at the end of a long hot walk. Bernard's vulnerability made him invincible.

They left the restaurant and headed back up Rue Jean-Jaurès (steering clear of Bernard's mother's shop), crossed the Volane and walked down Boulevard de Vernon towards the Grand Hôtel de Lyon. It was a mild evening, almost as bright as daylight with the full moon swinging like a pendulum amid the stars. They passed only two people on their way: a man walking his dog and another leaning against the trunk of a plane tree, vomiting.

'Which countries have you been to, Monsieur Marechall?'

'Oh, I've been all over the place: Asia, the Middle East, Africa, Latin America, anywhere that's had a war. I was in the army before setting up my business.'

'Ah, I see. Being in the army takes you places. I was in Germany once; even then it was just over the border. Apart from the language it's the same as here. I went to Switzerland with school once too. It was really nice, just like the postcards. Have you been?'

'Yes. It's very pretty. It makes you want to die.'

'Why do you say that?'

'Well, because it's so quiet ... and full of flowers.'

'You're right actually. They know a whole lot about geraniums.'

'So what's this building here?'

'That's the Vals mineral water plant.'

There was something feudal about this massive structure whose shadow loomed over half the street. Its arched windows reflected the moon's pearly light. Most of the surrounding warehouses had been boarded up, making the building's long, towering walls seem even more formidable. Who could tell what dark deeds went on behind closed doors? Simon seemed entranced.

'It's like the hull of the *Queen Mary* coming in to dock ...' he muttered.

'That's a boat, isn't it? What was it called again?'

'It's more than a boat. It's a giant of the seas!'

'Only here, the water's inside rather than all around it. Thirty million bottles come out of there every year. The factory's been going over a hundred years, so that's a whole lot of water – enough to make the place float!'

'You're right. Perhaps it will sail away one day.'

'I was only joking.'

'Have you been to the sea much, Bernard?'

'No, never. The closest thing I've seen to the sea is Lake Geneva.'

'Would you like to go?'

'Yes, why not?'

They carried on walking in silence, Bernard trying to imagine a body of water greater than Lake Geneva, Simon racking his brains to think of the ultimate island.

The multicoloured lights strung among the trees outside Béatrix ice-cream parlour were still on. A waiter in shirtsleeves was clearing tables and stacking chairs. A few stragglers hung around the rotunda hoping for some excitement before returning to their hotel rooms to stuff themselves with sleeping pills. The more optimistic ones made straight for the casino whose lights could be seen flickering through the trees. It was only ten thirty, and Simon wasn't ready to go to bed.

'One last drink?'

'No, I'd better get going. I have to look after my mother. Thanks again for dinner, I really enjoyed it.'

'OK then. See you around.'

'Tomorrow's market day.'

'I'll see you there then. Good night.'

Simon ordered a pear brandy in the lounge. Two men were playing snooker, badly, but they strutted around like world champions. While waiting for his drink Simon inspected the bookshelves and lighted on an old, yellowed copy of *Treasure Island*. He settled into a cracked leather armchair and thumbed through it, hoping to recapture the pleasure he had felt when he first read it. The island had not changed, but he had.

Anaïs was snoring loudly on the sofa, a spirituality guide propped open on her chest like a little tent. The blanket had slid off and her dress had ridden up, revealing her legs splayed wide. She wasn't wearing any knickers. Her bushy pubic hair crept up over her belly. Bernard saw nothing indecent in the scene; he was just a bit surprised that that was where he came from. He put the book down, taking care to mark her page, before lifting his mother up and putting her to bed. He tucked her in, pulled the quilt up to her chin and planted a kiss on her forehead. She rolled over with a moan.

On market days, Rue Jean-Jaurès was unrecognisable. The stalls lining the pavements hid the empty windows of closed-down shops. A constant stream of people swarmed down the narrow street, their heaped baskets occasionally colliding and creating pedestrian traffic jams. The cool morning air fragrant with the smells of flowers, fruit, roast chicken and fresh fish could tempt even the most abstemious to indulge. Trestle tables sagged under the weight of mountains of cherries, transformed by sunlight into piles of shimmering rubies. Simon couldn't resist buying himself a handful, biting into them as he walked. There were no subtle shades here, only vivid kaleidoscope colours.

Market traders improvised skits to charm customers into parting with their cash. In front of a stall selling local handicrafts in the shape of goatskin drums, snake-head charms, plywood Bantu masks, glass-bead necklaces, elephants made out of tyres and an array of boiled leather hats, a German tourist was haggling over a bag that appeared to be made from reptile skin. The seller was a burly African wearing a thick overcoat despite the heat.

'*Nein! Moi acheter, mais pas vrai croco!*'

'*Si! Croco véritable!*'

'*Si croco véritable, moi pas acheter. Imitation, oui.*'

The vendor rolled his eyes, but since neither of them had much grasp of the language the transaction soon descended into farce. The poor man's prospective customer was a hardline ecowarrior, signalled by her tow-coloured hair cut in a severe bob and Birkenstock sandals. From the way she was clutching it to her chest, it was obvious she liked the bag, but the idea that it might have come from a living creature repulsed her. Still, the consummate salesman would not back down.

'*Vrai croco!* My uncle kill it with his hands! Good price for you!'

'*Nein!* Plastic, yes, animal killed, no.'

It was all getting too confusing. The trader wearily agreed to knock the price down, reluctantly admitting that the bag was indeed made of plastic, 'but good plastic!' The German woman left delighted with her purchase while the stallholder counted the banknotes, making a gesture to indicate that she must have a screw loose.

Further up, where the road opened out in front of the post office, two trucks stacked with tapes and CDs vied noisily with each other, belching out the voices of dead or obscure singers, accordion music, Algerian raï tunes, rock and local folk in a primordial cacophony. Other vehicles spewed hunting gear from their open flanks; everything from thick hand-knitted socks to deerstalkers, long johns, tartan shirts, sheepskin-lined gilets and the full range of combat trousers.

There were garments to tempt the ladies, too. Almost inconceivably large flesh-coloured knickers and bras hung from metal hoops, swaying among flirtily floral nylon blouses and other items from an era so remote that it was difficult to imagine any survivors still out shopping.

In front of one of these stalls, Simon felt a hand on his shoulder.

'Hello, Monsieur Marechall.'

'Hello, Bernard.'

'So, what do you think?'

'It's very ... colourful.'

'Ooh, look over there!'

'What?'

'The tall man with the white hair and the moustache!'

Simon's eyes followed the direction of Bernard's finger. A dignified old man in an olive-green velvet suit was filling a crate with vegetables.

'Yes?'

'It's Jean Ferrat!'

'Good heavens, you're right, it looks just like him.'

'It doesn't just look like him, it is him! You're in luck, he doesn't come every Sunday.'

'Very lucky, indeed. Now, Bernard, do you have time for a coffee?'

'Yes, I've done my shopping.'

Nobody was asking Jean Ferrat for his autograph.

They sat outside the betting café facing the church and ordered two espressos. The smell of pastis and cigarette smoke wafted out from the doorway along with the shouts of punters clustered like flies around the TV screen. Simon insisted on moving to a table where he could sit with his back to the wall, even though it meant being out of the shade of an umbrella advertising some brand of aperitif.

'You did the same thing at the restaurant last night.'

'It's a habit of mine.'

Bernard looked around smiling, his shopping basket wedged between his knees. The comings and goings of the motley crowd seemed to delight him.

'I love market days. There's a sort of holiday atmosphere. There's no one along here during the week. Apparently it was a bit livelier before.'

'Before what?'

'Before the factories shut. The pulp mills, basalt ... there were jobs, you know. Now the only places where there's any life are the spas, the hotels and casino – and that's only in high season.'

'I think I smell roast chicken, do you?'

'Oh, that's me, I bought one. My mother doesn't eat much but the smell of roast chicken always gets her mouth watering. She'll only have a wing, but it's something at least. I'll make some mash to go with it.'

'You love your mother very much, don't you?'

'Of course, she's my mother. Everyone loves their own mother.'

'But from what you've told me, she hasn't had a great deal of time for you over the years.'

'I don't blame her for that. She just wanted to make a success of things. If everything had gone to plan, she would have sent for me.'

'And how does she manage when you're not around?'

'A couple of neighbours pop in ... I send her a bit of money. It'll be harder now though; I won't be earning as much.'

'Would you like some cherries?'

'Yes, thanks. They're still expensive – this is my first of the season. I should make a wish.'

The sweetness took away the bitter taste of the coffee. Bernard puffed out his cheeks and spat out the stone which bounced off a 'No Entry' sign on the other side of the road.

'You've got a good aim.'

'I was catapult champion when I was a kid.'

'What did you wish for?' asked Simon.

'If you say it out loud, it won't come true.'

Simon lit a cigarette. The smoke coming out of his nostrils made him look like a dragon. Bernard was tying knots in the cherry stalks.

'Tell me, Bernard, do you have a driving licence?'

'Damn right I do! I passed first time when I was in the army.'

'Are you by any chance free for a couple of days?'

'To do what?'

'I have to get to Cap d'Agde for a business trip but I'm feeling rather tired. I could really use a driver. Three hundred euros a day, all expenses paid. Only we'd need to leave early tomorrow morning. How does that sound?'

'Are you saying it would be six hundred euros for two days?'

'Exactly.'

'Jesus! That sounds great ... but I'll have to talk to my mother first.'

'While I'm working, you can enjoy yourself and see the sea.'

Bernard was squirming in his chair as though sitting on an anthill. The three good digits on his left hand were drumming on the tabletop while he scratched his nose with his right hand and frowned. He wasn't used to making snap decisions.

'I'll have to talk to my mother ... The thing is, Monsieur Marechall, I don't like to say it, but she thinks you're a poof.'

'Well, why don't we go and see her together? I'm sure we can make her change her mind.'

'When?'

'How about now? Let's not beat about the bush! Why don't you invite me round for lunch? If there's enough for two there'll be enough for three. We can buy her some flowers, or a cake – or both!'

'I think she'd prefer a bottle of something.'

'I'll take care of it. Tell me where she lives and go and let her know I'm coming. Ladies don't like it when you turn up unannounced.'

There was a definite spark between Simon and the tall Negress lamp. She was just his kind of woman: her full lips made no sound and her big white glass eyes shone with total devotion. He heaved himself up from the sofa to put the raffia lampshade straight, and blew on it to clear the dust, which rose up in a little grey cloud and settled again on a nearby surface. He couldn't resist running his hands over the perfect curves, the breasts, belly and hips of this synthetic wooden body. He had known a woman like this once, in Djibouti ... Safia, yes, that was her name. Just as silent and just as radiant. He had been happy with her. He had even thought of staying. In fact, he almost did end up there for good when a riot broke out.

'You all right there, Monsieur Marechall?'

'I'm fine, yes. Take your time.'

'I just have to toss the salad and I'll be right with you. Mother will be ready in five minutes.'

Bernard's voice seemed to come from much further away than the shop's storeroom, from a distant land Simon had once known and sometimes regretted leaving. He had been to some weird and wonderful places in his time, visiting pagodas and brothels in Asia, sleeping in huts or under the stars in the African desert, but he had never come across anything like Anaïs's shop before. Time itself seemed to have deserted this nowhere land, for fear of being bored to death. He returned to the sofa, perching on the very edge; for if he had the misfortune to sink right into it, he might never make it out of the quicksand of worn velvet cushions.

Bernard had laid the table with mismatched plates and odd knives and forks. The champagne, a cake box from Baudoin and an already wilting bunch of red roses lay side by side. Bernard emerged from the kitchen, his sleeves rolled up and a tea towel over his shoulder, clutching a bowl of salad.

'Here we are, it's ready! Mother's just coming. The thing is, she likes to look good, and she doesn't have people round very often. Mother? ... Mother?'

'Coming!'

It was a strange, double-pitched voice, like the famous Mongolian singers who can hit the low and high notes at the same time. The vision that appeared afterwards was just as remarkable. Anaïs had 'done herself up', decking her shapeless frame in all her showiest finery: moth-eaten silks, faded lace, oil-stained satin, multi-string bead necklaces, clattering metal bangles, globe-sized earrings, Moroccan slippers with worn-out soles, and a frayed turban. Her face was plastered with a thick layer of make-up.

She leant against the doorframe for a moment, her cartoonish kohl-lined eyes judging the distance between herself and Simon and sizing up any obstacles to avoid on the way. Then, like a bull charging the matador, she puffed out through her nose and lunged forward with her hand held out, her face split by a smile reminiscent of a gash made by a machete in a watermelon.

'*Enchantée, cher monsieur, enchantée*! You're most welcome!'

Simon caught her just in time to stop her tripping over a fold in the rug and smoothly kissed her hand. The patchouli oil she had splashed all over herself could not disguise the lingering smell of rum.

'It's unforgivable of my son not to have warned me! So it'll just be a simple meal, I'm afraid.'

'It's my fault for turning up out of the blue.'

'Not at all, not at all! Do please sit down.'

Bernard just managed to slide a chair under his mother's buttocks in time to avert an accident. It must have been a considerable effort for her to get to the table, as she was short of breath and clutching her chest. She fluttered her false eyelashes, one of which was coming unstuck.

'Goodness me, roses! Champagne! And a Baudoin cake! You shouldn't have!'

'Honestly, it's the least I could do, turning up like this.'

'It's a wonderful surprise. Bernard, would you put these flowers in a vase for me please?'

'What vase?'

'Well, I don't know, just a vase, a jug, something!'

Bernard disappeared off to the back of the shop with the flowers, leaving Simon and Anaïs alone at the table.

Though time had not been kind to her, leaving her with sunken eyes, a mouth twisted in bitterness, slack cheeks, skin as dimpled as a peach kernel and straggly hair falling from her turban, Simon could see this woman must once have been beautiful. There were still traces of gold sparkling in the green of her eyes. But her liver-spotted hands, weighed down with jewelled rings as false as her teeth, were incapable of remaining still. They toyed with her knife and fork, folded and unfolded her napkin. Her restless hands gave away her unease at having no place in the world.

'So you're just passing through Vals?'

'That's right. I was on my way down from Paris and was getting bored with the motorway, so I took the back roads and stopped when I got tired. I ended up here by chance, really.'

'Chance, yes, what a thing ... And where are you staying?'

'The Grand Hôtel de Lyon.'

'Oh, very nice. I used to go there sometimes, way back when, for ... a cup of tea in the lounge. Do they still have the snooker table?'

'Yes, it's still there.'
'Still ...'

He was a good-looking man, this Monsieur Marechall. Handsome and smartly turned out, but a little too cool, too sure of himself, too controlled. When he looked at Anaïs it gave her a jolt, like a shard of glass being jabbed into her back. He didn't seem like a poof though ... so what did he want Bernard for?

'Are you a Scorpio?'

'No, Pisces.'

'Then you must be a Scorpio rising?'

'I have no idea. I know nothing at all about star signs.'

'Scorpio rising, without question. Haven't you ever had your birth chart read?'

'No. I'm not really interested in what the future holds.'

'It's not about the future, it's about now.'

'That doesn't mean much to me either. Your Neg— your lamp is beautiful.'

'Isn't it just? I've had it since ...' Her voice trailed off. 'It's made of ebony, you know!'

'I'm sure.'

They both turned to contemplate the exotic goddess wearing a flickering sixty-watt bulb on her head. Simon pictured himself back in the arms of Safia, the sunlight filtering through the shutters and streaking across their bodies as they lay entwined on the hemp-woven bed. The clamour of the street, the dust, the shouts of hawkers ... Anaïs was reliving the day when her erstwhile lover, Léo – a dealer in stolen goods, rather than antiques – had carried the black goddess to her on his back, in repayment for a debt. He really was handsome, Léo ... As for being ebony, the statue was in fact made of a mixture of resin and sand and had been mass-produced in Saint-Étienne. The factory's stamp was printed on the base. But what did that matter now? Even a miserable past largely compensated for a nonexistent present. Their memories were carved from real ebony. They both jumped when Bernard reappeared.

'I couldn't find a vase so I've put the roses in some water in the sink. Right, we're just about ready. Monsieur Marechall, would you mind opening the champagne? I don't know if I can manage it, with my hand.'

Simon did as he was asked, pouring the sparkling wine into the cheap supermarket glasses while Bernard put radishes, butter and salt onto the table. Anaïs pulled a face.

'Is that all you could find for a starter?'

'Radishes are lovely. They're in season. I tried one and they're not too peppery. So, what shall we drink to?'

Simon lifted his glass.

'Let's drink to your future, young man, and to our pasts, my dear.'

Anaïs contrived a sort of smile and downed her drink in one. They talked about everything and nothing, good times and bad, biting into radishes that tasted of springtime. Anaïs was not impressed with the champagne. It made her feel bloated and failed to get her sloshed quickly enough. So, on some pretext or other she took herself off to the kitchen to take a swig of rum. It was only after her third visit to the kitchen that she began to relax.

'So you want to steal my son.'

'Well, borrow his services. I don't think I'm up to driving all the way to Cap d'Agde. But if you'd rather not ...'

'I couldn't care less. So long as he gets paid ...'

'Of course! I'll even pay half up front. It'll be two days at most and he can call home each night.'

'I don't have a phone. Well, I do, but it's been cut off. Anyway, no one calls me. Bernard, give me some mash, will you, and a bit of breast too. I'm hungry today.'

'I'm glad you've got an appetite. Do you want a bit of crispy skin?'

'No, just the white meat. What exactly is it you do?'

'I have a pest-control business. Getting rid of rats, mice, insects, cockroaches and so on.'

'You must be getting plenty of work. The world's overrun with vermin!'

'Yes, business is pretty good.'

'That's what you should have learnt to do, Bernard, instead of getting your fingers chopped off by those damned machines. You know what? Machines need getting rid of too – they deprive us of our bread and butter. In the old days, everything used to be done by hand. Look at this shawl – pure wool, hand-knitted. Now it's all made in China and they crank out acres of the stuff every day! But there's no contest when it comes to quality. Feel this, go on, feel it! It's twenty years old this shawl and it's just like new!'

Simon ran his finger over the rag Anaïs was holding up to him, solemnly nodding his head in agreement.

'That wasn't made by a machine. That was crafted by human hand, an artisan from the Ardèche – or Sweden or Denmark, I can't remember. His workshop was in Antraigues, he was a pal of Jean Ferrat's. He made everything himself, hats, cardigans, mittens. I think he's dead now. Died of cold, or so I heard ... Bernard, open a bottle of red to wash down the champagne.'

'Don't you think you've—'

'No, I don't. Off you go and find a bottle, like I said.'

Anaïs was melting like a candle, her elbows sliding towards the edge of the table. Her bloodshot eyes stared dead ahead, like brake lights jammed on in the face of a hazard, a hole in the road or a gaping abyss.

'Are you sure you're not a queer?'

'Quite sure. I just need a driver. I met your son and I trust him, that's all there is to it.'

'Uh-huh ... It's just that I'm his mother, I know him. He's so ... It's like he was born yesterday.'

'That's what makes him so likeable.'

'And means he's always being taken for a ride. Couldn't you take him on in your company? He's missing a couple of fingers but he's not lazy.'

'The thing is, I'm about to sell my business and retire.'

'Ah, what a shame. You think you're in luck and then ...'

'I'm sorry, I ...'

Anaïs slumped forward with a snore, her forehead landing in her plate and her arms lolling either side of the chair. Bernard came back in holding the cake on a plate and a bottle tucked under his arm.

'This is Lou Pisadou cake, a speciality of Vals ... Mother! Christ, what's the matter with her?'

'She's asleep.'

'She's drunk too much. She's not used to it and whenever she has someone over, she drinks gallons so obviously ... I'm so sorry, Monsieur Marechall.'

'Don't worry. We should probably put her to bed. I'll help you.'

'OK, thank you.'

They laid her on her bed in a cubbyhole that seemed to Simon like a sort of crypt. After tucking her in, they went back to the table.

'Can I still cut you a slice of cake?'

'No, thank you, I'm full. It was a very good lunch.'

'A coffee then?'

'No, I think I'll head back to my hotel for a nap.'

'It's not her fault, you know. She never has company.'

'There's no need to apologise, Bernard. Your mother is a

134

lovely lady, perhaps just a little overemotional. We got along very well. Now, here's half your pay. So I'll see you tomorrow at nine o'clock, at my hotel?'

'Nine o'clock without fail, Monsieur Marechall!'

They shook hands and Simon exchanged one last glance with the Negress lamp before leaving.

'Now that's what I call a motor! There's a proper engine under that bonnet! And German too, they don't come more reliable.'

Bernard was as ecstatic as a little boy who had just been given his first pedal car. He drove well, smoothly negotiating every corner – and God knows there were enough of them on this road. The rolling hills were tinged mauve and pink in the morning light. The car was so quiet, the suspension so perfect, it felt as though they were sitting still while the countryside sped past.

Although he had taken his pills, Simon had not slept a wink all night. The pains which had abated for a while had suddenly started again. Bernard really was a godsend. Were it not for him, Simon would never have been able to get on the road today. And Bernard's youthful enthusiasm cheered him up. He was already feeling a little better. The clouds glowed with the pastel blue and pink shades of sugared almonds. Something odd had happened yesterday as he walked back to his hotel after that unusual lunch with Bernard's mother. Rue Jean-Jaurès was deserted at that time of day. As he passed the church, he heard a mobile phone ringing from inside; for some reason, the doors were wide open. The phone rang and rang, but no one picked it up. His curiosity piqued, Simon went inside. The church was empty. The phone was vibrating on a prayer stool. He picked it up and raised it to his ear. Three times he said, 'Hello?' His voice bounced off the ceiling vaults like a trapped bird, but there was no reply. He put the phone back where he had found it. The church seemed huge to him, though it was actually quite modest in size. Three rays of light – red, blue and yellow – shone through the ugly stained-glass windows, converging in a multicoloured pool at his feet. He had the strongest feeling that something had passed him by, that he had missed some important appointment. It was ridiculous but he could have sworn the phone call was meant for him. He felt abandoned and alone, surrounded by nothingness. He almost ran out of the church. Maybe that was what had kept him awake all night.

'If we keep on at this rate, we'll be there in less than two hours. Are you OK, Monsieur Marechall?'

'I'm fine, I'm fine. Where are we now?'

'Le Teil.'

'Let's stop for a minute. I need to use the toilet.'

They pulled up in front of the train station and dived into the first bar they came to.

'What would you like, Monsieur Marechall?'

'Anything, a coffee.'

Bernard watched him disappear off to the toilets. He looked pale, his brow dripping with sweat. It was a pity; Bernard was in holiday mood. Twirling the keys of the Mercedes for all to see, he casually asked for two coffees and two croissants. The waitress winked at him and smiled. The joys of having money … He stretched his legs out under the table, clasped his hands behind his head and stared up at the ceiling with its fake beams. There was only one other customer, a tall, skinny, spidery man perched on a bar stool, his gaze lost in the celestial void that filled the window. In his right hand he held a half-pint, in his left a cigarette. Spinning out the hours. He didn't bat an eyelid when a petite blonde woman carrying a baby in an orange blanket stormed in and started screaming at him.

'You fucking bastard!'

The spidery man let his left arm be shaken, but clung fast to the half-pint in his other hand.

'Give me the keys, you bastard!'

'The keys are gone.'

'What do you mean, "gone"?'

'The bailiffs came this morning. There's no flat, no keys, no nothing.'

He put an end to the discussion by downing the rest of his beer. The young woman opened and closed her mouth over and over again, without making a sound.

'But ... You told me you'd paid the rent, you said it was all sorted.'

'Well, it wasn't. So shut your mouth and piss off.'

The owner looked up from his newspaper and frowned.

The woman swivelled round, clocked Bernard, plonked the child on his lap, grabbed an ashtray and lunged at the man. It was 9.30 a.m. on a sunny day in Le Teil. The owner grudgingly came out from behind the counter armed with a cosh. His weary expression showed he had seen all this many times before.

'Right, out of here now. Sort out your domestics somewhere else! Go on! Out!'

'I haven't paid for my half!'

'It's on the house. Now fuck off before I call the police.'

A warm liquid ran onto Bernard's lap. The kid was emptying itself like a leaky hotwater bottle.

Simon pulled the chain and the toilet bowl was spotless again, all traces of the blood he had vomited wiped clean. The light coming through the window coursed through his body like fresh milk. He felt empty and hollow, but better. Sometimes the illness loosened its grip on him, like an executioner tired of delivering blows. It would be back for more, no mistake, but not right away. They were getting to know each other rather well, him and his illness.

138

Coming out of the toilets, he was astonished to find Bernard in Madonna pose, cradling a baby.

'What's all this?'

'I don't know! A couple are having a row. It's peed on me and I haven't got a change of trousers.'

The infant, swaddled in its orange blanket, looked as bewildered as Bernard.

'What on earth's going on?'

The woman was now grappling with the nineteen-stone bulk of the bar owner, who was blocking her way.

'Just let me past, dickhead! My kid, I just need to get my kid and I'll never come back to this shithole again!'

She managed to squeeze past him, cross the room and retrieve the child without a word of thanks to Bernard, then stomped out with a determined stride. The coffee had gone cold. Simon gulped his down in one go. Bernard's arms were still held in a cradling position.

'For a moment you made me think of St Christopher carrying Jesus across the river. It bodes well, since he's the patron saint of drivers.'

'I stink!'

'Come on, let's sort you out.'

Simon paid the bill.

'Sorry about that,' said the owner. 'There's more and more of that sort round here. Scroungers, living off benefits we slog to pay for. And then they go and breed, God only knows why.'

Bernard walked with his legs slightly apart. Simon steered him into a passably stylish shop – quite possibly the only one in town.

'We need a suit for this young man. Something smart but not too "old".'

Bernard stared at Simon in amazement.

'A suit?'

'Well, you'll need one sooner or later. Anyway it's for my benefit, not yours. We can't have you driving a Mercedes dressed like that. People will think you've stolen it.'

The jacket was a perfect fit, but it felt to Bernard as rigid as a suit of armour. He squirmed his way into the driving seat, trying not to crumple it.

'I've never worn any of this formal stuff before, you know?'

'It'll be fine, just try not to think about it. Now tell me, what are you going to do when we get to the sea?'

'Well ... sit down and look at it, I suppose.'

'Good idea. I envy you, seeing the sea for the first time.'

The plane trees lining the road broke up the light. The air coming in through the windows smelt of distant shores. Bernard drove one-handed, his head cocked slightly to the left.

'Monsieur Marechall, can I ask you something?'

'Yes, what is it?'

'Were you unwell earlier?'

'I was just a little light-headed. Remembering Africa, times gone by ... old age ... Hang on, what do you think you're doing? Why are we stopping?'

Bernard had pulled up on the verge and twisted in his seat.

'Back there, behind the red car! It's the girl from the café with her baby. The tall guy's hitting her!'

'So?'

'So we should do something.'

'Don't get involved. It's none of your business. Now drive.'

'I can't, Monsieur Marechall. The kid peed on me, it's like we're family.'

'Family? For God's sake! No, you stay there behind the wheel and keep the engine running. I'll go, it'll be quicker.'

He was right, it did not take long. Everything was played out in the rear-view mirror: Monsieur Marechall walking calmly towards the red car, hands in the pockets of his raincoat. Reaching the scene of the argument, he says a couple of words to the girl who begins running towards the Mercedes, hugging her child to her chest. The tall guy lifts his arm and Monsieur Marechall takes something out of his pocket. The tall guy lifts his other arm and disappears into the ditch as if by magic. The girl with the baby scrambles into the car, her face beetroot red, hair dishevelled, panting, wild-eyed; Monsieur Marechall walks back just as calmly, gets into the car and does up his seat belt with a sigh.

'Well, what are you waiting for? Go!' He turned to the woman in the back. 'Where shall we drop you, Madame?'

'I ... I don't know, down the road.'

Shortly after Montélimar they had to stop at a service station, the little girl's ear-splitting cries signalling she was hungry. While the young mother took her baby off to the toilets, Simon leant against the car door, smoking a cigarette, and Bernard kicked around a battered Orangina can. Simon stubbed his cigarette out under his foot and turned up his collar.

'Let's drop them at Nîmes.'

'Why Nîmes?'

'Because we're not going to have them trail along with us all the way to China. And Nîmes is very nice.'

'But what if they don't know anybody in Nîmes?'

'It's not my problem. We helped them out – what more do you want? I've got work to do and we've already wasted a lot of time.'

'You're right, Monsieur Marechall. Got to get to work.'

Bernard adroitly struck the can on the volley, sending it into a bush. He threw his arms up.

'Goal! ... Monsieur Marechall?'

'Yes?'

'How did you handle that guy?'

'Which guy?'

'The one who was hitting her. He looked a lot stronger than you.'

'I don't know. He must have seen I had no time to mess around. Right, what the hell's taking them so long?'

'He didn't get back out of the ditch ...'

'He must have landed awkwardly. Ah, here they are! Let's go.'

Babies are like open-ended tubes, filled up at the top and emptied at the bottom. Since this baby had just been filled up at the service station, it emptied itself around Avignon. Even with the windows open, the smell was overpowering. Simon knew the stench of shit, blood and rot all too well; it was the smell of war, and he was used to it. But something about this poo, mingled with wafts of sour milk, was getting to him. It was not a horrible smell, exactly; it was a farmyard odour, the whiff of the compost heap, a primeval human memory that aroused a certain nostalgia. But these two impromptu passengers were really beginning to try his patience. They had not been planned for and Simon hated surprises.

'Will you stop shaking her around? It's making her give off even more gas.'

'I'm not shaking her, I'm rocking her. She'll cry if I don't.'

'That's all we need.'

Bernard had said nothing but could feel the tension rising.

'What's the baby's name?' he asked.

'Violette.'

'Oh, that's a pretty name!'

Simon shrugged his shoulders and ground his teeth.

'Doesn't smell like violets, that's for sure!'

'Well, she's a baby, Monsieur Marechall, it's only natural.'

'Only natural? What about death cap mushrooms, they're

natural too, and hemlock, and a lot of other poisons besides! The world's full of natural children. Three-quarters of them should never have seen the light of day.'

'How can you say that?'

'Because it's true. Half the planet's dying of hunger. The poor should just eat their offspring. I mean, it's protein, isn't it? That's the way to cure starvation.'

'That's a bit much, Monsieur Marechall. People eating their own children!'

'Well, why not?'

Wriggling about in her dirty nappy, Violette began to screech. Her mother, Fiona, held her more tightly.

'That's a horrible thing to say. She heard everything ... Don't worry, poppet, Mummy will never eat you ... She needs changing but I've run out of nappies.'

Simon clapped his hand to his forehead and took deep breaths to calm his nerves.

'Here's what we're going to do. In a quarter of an hour we'll be in Avignon. We're going to drop you off at a chemist's, or a supermarket, wherever, and we're going to say goodbye. We all go our separate ways. Understood?'

'I don't know anybody in Avignon ... What am I going to do with the baby?'

'Do what you like! You're young, you're not bad-looking, you'll find another man like the last one and so it'll go on. Bernard, stop as soon as you can; we've already wasted too much time.'

'Right, Monsieur Marechall.'

On the back seat, the child had fallen asleep, her body floppy and mouth wide open. Fiona was snivelling quietly, tears glistening on her cheeks. Bernard kept glancing back at her in the rear-view mirror. It hurt him to see her like that. She reminded him of that girl ... Liliane, who had only stayed at the factory a few days. Long enough for him to fall in love with her. Nothing had really happened between them other than sharing a lunchbox once and grabbing a coffee at the bar of Le Penalty. Even so, it had been a love affair. Fiona had that same vacant look in her eyes, the same sickly skin that bruised easily, the aloofness of those who are just passing through.

Ma môme, ell' joue pas les starlettes/ Ell' met pas des lunettes/ De soleil/ Ell' pos' pas pour les magazines/ Ell' travaille en usine/ A Créteil.

My girl don't put on airs and graces/ She don't wear sunglasses/ In the shade/ She don't pose for no magazines/ She works in a factory/ in Créteil.

Good old Jean Ferrat. He knew how to talk about that stuff.

'Bernard, we just went right past a chemist's. Why didn't you stop?'

'I didn't see it until too late. There's a lorry on my tail.'

They could have been anywhere. The outskirts of towns look the same in every part of the world. Uncertain places, business parks and shopping centres, *terra incognita*, no man's lands cluttered with neon signs promising eternal happiness to whoever buys this or that product. You know you're alive when you're buying stuff. Judging from the rows of parked cars lined up with military precision, heaven could wait. Here, it was possible to live and die just like in real life, in a fraction of the time.

'Park up, Bernard. They have everything here. Well, goodbye, Fiona. Good luck.'

Fiona's gaze seemed to fall elsewhere, a place where nobody ever looked. Her hair was piled messily on top of her head. She played with a loose strand, twisting it around her finger.

'I haven't got any money.'

Simon puffed out loudly through his nostrils like a buffalo, scrunching up his eyes.

'Bernard, here's fifty euros. Give it to her and take them to die somewhere else, OK?'

'OK, Monsieur Marechall. I'll walk them to the entrance.'

'Fine.'

Through the windscreen, he watched them walking towards Auchan. They looked like a happy little family pushing their trolley along. The sun was shining into his lap. He leant back against the headrest and rubbed his temples.

'One day I came into the world ... and then what?'

He felt a sudden sense of emptiness coupled with an awareness of the sheer incongruity of the situation. What the hell was he doing sitting in the middle of nowhere, waiting for some gangling halfwit to come back? He had a contract to carry out and he had never to this day failed to do the job. He was feeling much better; he did not need anybody else. Those three were all of the same ilk. They would get by just fine without him.

Simon slid behind the wheel and started the engine. Where the hell was the exit? There were arrows pointing in every direction, but they never seemed to lead anywhere. Driving round in circles, he inevitably, fatally, ended up back at square one. Bernard was standing with Fiona and Violette, holding a huge pack of nappies under his arm and watching unfazed and entirely unquestioningly as Simon pulled up alongside them.

'I was going to fill up but there's a queue. You get back behind the wheel, Bernard. Get in then.'

The motorway carved its way through a moonscape of scrub-land and dry rock. It was eleven o'clock and the sun was beating down relentlessly.

'... and while you're working, I'll find them a place to stay, somewhere nice but not too expensive. What do you think, Monsieur Marechall?'

'I don't give a damn, I just want them out of my hair.'

'Don't worry, Monsieur Marechall. I'll pay for it out of my wages.'

In the back, Fiona was shaking her head as the arid hillsides flashed past.

'Can we put some music on? It'll help send Violette to sleep.'

'Do you mind, Monsieur Marechall?'

On Radio Nostalgie, Dalida was belting out her tear-jerking classic, 'Ciao Amore' ... Simon was asleep before the baby.

'Time to wake up, Monsieur Marechall. We're nearly there.'

Simon opened one eye and closed it again almost immediately, assailed by the sunlight daubing the windscreen with a lurid carousel of colours. Past a certain age, sleep becomes a rare luxury, given up reluctantly. His mind had been empty of dreams or nightmares, which seemed to him like the most perfect state of grace, as though he had never existed at all. But now he was forced to re-inhabit his pitiful skin that sagged over tired muscles and stuck to creaking bones; to regain his basic thoughts and functions, which at that moment meant nothing to him.

'Where to now?'

'Le Grau d'Agde. Go right, along the River Hérault.'

'Oh yes, it's signposted ... Ah, look. Isn't that sweet?'

'What?'

'The two of them sleeping in the back. It's like a First Communion picture.'

'Do you remember what I said? I don't want to see them again. You're going to find us a decent place to stay. We're moving on tomorrow.'

'Don't worry, Monsieur Marechall. No probs. Here we are, this is Le Grau whatsitsname.'

'Right then, drop me off here. We'll meet at ... four o'clock sharp, at the aquarium, OK?'

'I'll be there, without fail. Oh, Monsieur Marechall, I meant to say ... I'm just so happy to be here, thank you.'

'The sea's straight on, at the end of the road. Four o'clock.'

The car drove off, leaving Simon standing slightly disorientated on the pavement, pounded by the force of the sun. For a fraction of a second he wished he could change places with the big schmuck who thought he was on holiday, even if it meant having two fingers missing. He only stepped back into his shady world once he had put his dark glasses on.

He bought thirteen red roses at the first florist's he came to.

'Thirteen? People usually buy a dozen.'

'Not me.'

While the florist – a pretty enough girl, despite her repaired harelip – made up the bouquet, the shop's warm, humid atmosphere and exotic fragrances transported Simon back to the Indonesian forests he had so loved. He could have stayed there for ever, too ... He could have lived anywhere but here, in fact. Funny how things turned out.

'That'll be twenty-six euros, please.'

Outside the shop, he looked at his map. Impasse du Lavandin was only a few streets away. He did not pass a single person on his way. The theme tune of a German soap opera floated from open windows, a daily dose to numb the tired brains of the local retirees. They lived in big houses and apartment blocks with fragrant-sounding names like Les Acacias, Les Mimosas and Les Pins. In reality it smelt more like a cemetery, with hints of barbecue smoke and sulphur ointment used for hernia bandages.

Number 4, Impasse du Lavandin was a detached house built in no discernible style, a sort of 1960s shoebox with a disproportionately large neo-classical terrace tacked on to it. It was surrounded by a high wall topped with shards of coloured glass set into the concrete. Beside the gate, above a letterbox marked 'J.-P. Bornay', an intercom invited callers to buzz and give their name or else beware of the dog. Said dog was depicted on a ceramic tile, tongue lolling, eager fangs bared. Simon pressed the red button. A crackly voice answered, drowned out by wild yapping.

'Who is it?'

'Monsieur Marechall. I'm a colleague of your husband Jean-Pierre's. He asked me to give you something.'

'What is it?'

'Flowers, I think.'

'Flowers? Are you joking?'

'If you wouldn't mind letting me in, I'll just drop them off. I'm in a bit of a hurry.'

She, on the other hand, seemed in no hurry at all, making Simon wait a good five minutes before the gate was buzzed open.

Asymmetrical flagstones formed a hopscotch path across the freshly mown lawn, dotted with clumps of spiky succulents and a random assortment of newly planted flowers. Behind a metal grille, the frosted, probably bulletproof door was ajar, letting out the jabbering of a television along with a hyperactive Yorkshire terrier. The flaccid face of a woman appeared in the shadow of the doorway, the bags under her eyes betraying her worries. Simon proffered his bouquet with a smile. She did not take it straight away, eyeing him with suspicion, her nostrils twitching.

'Isn't there a card with them?'

'Oh, yes, there is! I'm so sorry, it's in my pocket. Do you mind?'

She gingerly took the flowers, while Simon took out of his pocket Jean-Pierre Bornay's last message to his wife: a bullet between the eyes. She toppled backwards into the dark hallway, her body strewn with thirteen red roses. The dog chased around in circles a few times, trying to understand the rules of this strange game, then stopped to cover his mistress's face in long tongue strokes. Simon knelt down, snapped a rose from its stem, slipped it into his buttonhole – a little tradition of his – and stood back up, wincing. With the butt of his gun he knocked out the dog, which had started to claw at his trouser leg. So there it was, Jean-Pierre Bornay was free to be joined in holy matrimony with his secretary. Another job well done. Simon could bow out honourably.

The further he got from this geriatric neighbourhood, whose residents generally died of their own accord, the livelier the streets became. Car horns beeped and people hurried by, jostling, cursing or paying no attention to each other. All was right with the world.

Simon could not find a single telephone box in working order, now they had been superseded by mobile phones. He went into a café to call the man who had hired him.

'It's done. Meet me at five o'clock at the aquarium ... What do you mean, you can't? ... I'm not happy about this ... As soon as it opens tomorrow, nine thirty, and no messing about!'

Though considerably annoyed by this setback, Simon nevertheless sat down at a table and ordered a glass of Suze. This, along with the thirteen red roses, was an essential element of an unbending ritual. He got it from his father, a miner from Doullens, who had taught him always to do his best and shown him the satisfaction of a job well done. It was a kind of tribute to this worthy man, snatched from him when he was just twelve, his lungs destroyed by silicosis. If his father had not expressly forbidden him from following in his footsteps, down into the bowels of the earth, Simon might have been a mining engineer now, or dead, or on the dole. As a child, Simon had lapped up the mysterious tales of subterranean life his father told him, coughing up coal dust into his handkerchief. The firedamp explosions, the sense of brotherhood, the strikes – it was like something out of Zola or Jules Verne. It must have been a wish to experience something similar that had prompted Simon to join the army at the age of eighteen. Everyone had been disappointed because he was a star pupil, destined for great things. But what kind of adult would he be if he did not fulfil his childhood dreams?

Though he moved quickly up the ranks, he soon realised that opportunities for real adventure were few and far between. Although he had the chance to do some digging, it was not to find buried treasure but to bury rigid corpses, bundled up by the dozen like human firewood. It was no more glamorous than working at an undertaker's.

The Suze seemed more bitter than usual, the noises around him more acute, the colours more vivid. Everything was too strong for him, including the relentless waves of hot and cold sweeping over him. It was coming on again. Staring into the pure white porcelain urinal calmed him briefly, as he stood emptying his bladder next to a man in a blue tracksuit.

'Lieutenant?'

'I'm sorry?'

'Aren't you Lieutenant Marechall?'

'No, I'm afraid you're mistaken.'

'I'm sorry. I thought for a moment ...'

'It's fine, these things happen. Goodbye.'

Picot. He had just pissed next to that arsehole Picot, a play-it-safe mercenary and small-time killer Simon had nevertheless pulled out of a swamp in Burma. There was no denying it: the world was closing in on Simon and soon even he would be surplus to it.

The shark was drowning its sorrows inside its glass cage. It turned this way and that for no apparent reason, taking no notice of the opaline jellyfish and shoals of multicoloured fish swimming out from clumps of soft seaweed. There was not much to choose between aquatic life and life on earth; either could be equally boring. The proof was in the amphibians which had dithered between the two for thousands of years without ever making their minds up, or the Valium-drugged crocodiles whose sleepy eyes peeked above the surface of muddy pools. Like Simon, who stood watching them, all these creatures seemed to be on standby, waiting for something that was always just out of reach. Over-excited kids pressed their noses against the glass, banging their horrid chubby little hands against the walls of the tanks. Their shrieks ruined the silence of this other world. From the looks on the faces of their harassed parents, it was clear many would gladly throw their offspring to the piranhas. The world might well end in the same murky green waters that spawned humanity.

'Are you OK, Monsieur Marechall? You don't look too good.'

'It's the lighting in here; it makes everyone look washed out. Have you found a hotel?'

'Even better! Shall we go now?'

The shock of stepping from the gloom into bright daylight made Simon burn up. He staggered back to the car.

'You'll see, Monsieur Marechall, it's a dream spot!'

'I have no interest in dreaming, I just want to go to sleep. I'm tired.'

'No probs! You'll be in paradise in no time.'

They drove for no more than quarter of an hour. Simon had closed his eyes, opening them again only when he felt the car slowing down.

'What the hell is this? A campsite?'

'Not just any campsite, Monsieur Marechall, a three-star campsite. And don't worry, we're not going to be sleeping under canvas.'

Beneath towering pine trees lined up like soldiers, they passed an array of caravans, from the tiniest to the most palatial, before pulling up outside a mobile home as warm and inviting as a fridge.

'Is this supposed to be a joke?'

'Just wait until you see it all, Monsieur Marechall. The sea's just behind us, fifty yards away. It's got all mod cons and it's way cheaper than a hotel.'

'I don't give a damn how much it costs! I asked you to book a hotel!'

'Don't get cross, Monsieur Marechall. If you don't like it, we can go. But just come and have a look. It's better than a hotel – it's got a kitchen and a shower, just like home.'

Simon did not have the strength to put up a fight. Tangled up in the threads that were just about holding him together, he trailed behind Bernard.

'So here's the kitchen. It's got a hotplate, microwave, fridge, hot and cold running water. Bathroom, with towels and everything. That's your room there. Just pull the screen across and you've got it all to yourself. I'll sleep in the hall, there's a fold-out sofa bed. Isn't it great? Have a look out the window – you can see the beach and the sea ... You were right – it's really something, all that water, it's amazing!'

Simon sank onto the bed, his arms outstretched. Resistance was futile.

'You're not very well, are you, Monsieur Marechall? I'll leave you to rest. I'll sort everything out. I went to check out the shops – what do you think about having mussels for supper? ... Take your time. I'm just going down to the beach to see Fiona and the baby and then I'll get some food in.'

'They're here too?'

'Not in the same caravan – I'm not stupid! I've rented one for them just next door. Now you lie back and relax, you'll be snug as a bug in a jug.'

'In a rug.'

'Yes, if you like. Happy?'

'Delirious. Now bugger off.'

'OK, rest up, Monsieur Marechall, see you later. You know, I just can't thank you enough for all this, the sea, this whole adventure ...'

'Get out.'

The bed was hard and, even with the bottle-green chenille blanket over him, Simon was cold. The pillow was as comfortable as cardboard. None of it mattered now; Simon's sole desire was to escape from his body, which he managed to do after swallowing a handful of pills that shut off his brain with a watertight seal. Really it was no worse being here than anywhere else. He did not feel bad or good; he felt nothing at all. The lingering stench of cleaning products, used to scrub away all traces of the previous occupants, left Simon with a curious feeling of virginity.

Simon did not really sleep. It was a kind of semi-slumber, bobbing just beneath the surface, which left him wishing he could grow scales and inhabit the aquarium. The light of the setting sun made the room blush girlishly. His watch gave the time as 6.12 p.m., and he accepted it.

Outside, the breeze carried the tang of pine and salt water. When Simon reached the beach he did as everyone does; he took off his shoes and socks, rolled up his trousers and made for the water.

There it was, waiting faithfully. The sea glimmered with copper shards of sun, dribbling white foam and babbling the time away with idle chatter. Standing upright in a world without vertical lines, Simon dropped down on the sand and laid his shoes out next to him as though waiting for Father Christmas to fill them. A red ball bounced close by. A little boy and his father came running after it. They looked happy – the ball especially. With a burst of imagination, the sun had turned a hopelessly clear sky into an engaging spectacle, taking the lonely little cloud no storm had wanted and trimming it with gold.

'All right?'

Fiona loomed behind him in silhouette like a harbinger of doom, hunchbacked under her daughter's grip.

'What do you care? Where's Bernard?'

'Gone shopping. Can I sit down?'

'It's a beach, it's public property.'

She was wearing a red T-shirt and white shorts. She had nice legs. The little girl was staring at the horizon as solemnly as a child can contemplate such things. The sky and sea were coming together like the two edges of a bloody wound.

'Bernard's nice, isn't he?'

Simon made no comment.

'Are you related?'

'No.'

'Oh, I thought you were. It must be because he looks up to you. He walks the way you do, has the same frown ... You end up looking like the people you're fond of, don't you think?'

Simon was studying his feet, which were so pale they were

practically blue, with a bunion on the left big toe and calloused nails. His ankles were ringed with the imprint of his sock elastic. He buried them in the still-warm sand. If he had been alone, he might have interred himself up to the neck.

'Why don't you like me?'

'Why should I? I have no interest in you.'

'Why did you get me out of that fix then?'

'Because of Bernard. He would have made a pig's ear of it. I didn't have time to waste. Now, would you mind leaving me the hell alone?'

'Fine! You were right to hide your feet, they're disgusting.'

Fiona's buttocks left two perfectly round craters in the grey sand beside him.

On the dot of eight o'clock, the TV news signature tune spread like a powder trail down the row of caravans, the newsreader's chubby face replicated endlessly. It was a mild evening and most of the holidaymakers were eating outdoors. Bernard was at the stove, Fiona was laying the table and Simon was trying to outstare Violette, who was propped up with cushions on a camping chair. All around them, corks were popping, ripples of laughter broke out and cooking smells mingled in the evening air. The whole situation was so bizarre that Simon had not even tried to protest when Bernard told him there would be three and a half of them for dinner. There was nothing to be said, nothing to be done except sulk. He felt like a serious stage actor who had wandered onto the set of a slushy movie. He could not follow the plot, but it was too late to back out now. The mischievous director had already called, 'Action!'

Bernard brought over the mussels and doled out generous portions. He and Fiona were like an old married couple, sharing habits, exchanging knowing winks and making thoughtful gestures, with Fiona helping him as he struggled to open the mussels with his bandaged hand. Simon swallowed three or four and drank half the bottle of white wine by himself. His forehead creased in a frown, he sat wondering what casting error had landed him here, a stranger in paradise. By odd coincidence, it had just been announced on the news that Gloria Lasso had died.

Her biggest hit was none other than 'Étrangère au Paradis', the soundtrack to the four years he had spent in the Aurès mountains of Algeria, hunting down *fellagha* militants. The song had been on wherever he went – in the barracks, in tents and in brothels, trickling from the transistor radios glued to every soldier's ear, their stomachs heavy with nostalgia and warm beer.

'Who was Gloria Lasso?' asked Fiona.

'Dunno. More mussels?'

It all seemed so distant that Simon began to wonder if it had really happened. Most likely it had, since that was where he had learnt to kill. Everything was going so fast, even the present day had to be glimpsed through a rear-view mirror.

'Aren't you going to finish your mussels, Monsieur Marechall?'

'I'm too tired. I'm going to bed. Don't forget, eight o'clock tomorrow morning!'

'Without fail, Monsieur Marechall. Good night.'

He had barely made it into the caravan when Bernard and Fiona heard him coughing and throwing up in the bathroom.

'Do you think it was my mussels?'

'No, they're lovely. It's him – he's not well, your Monsieur Marechall.'

'What's wrong with him?'

'Death, that's his disease. You can see it on his face and it's nothing new. That man has never had feelings for anyone.'

'I think you're wrong there. I think he likes me a lot.'

'Maybe ... Maybe he loved someone once but she turned him down and he never got over it. Watch out. A drowning man never wants to go down alone.'

The sea and the sky, vying with each other in their vastness, traded handfuls of stars.

'I'm a bit chilly. Violette's asleep; I think I'll head indoors.'

'I'll walk you back.'

A few TVs still hummed, but most had been turned off. With

the little girl in his arms, Bernard felt he could go anywhere, do anything. He took strength from the warm, squidgy human ball of dough he held against him – and the sight of Fiona's moonlike buttocks strutting in her tight white shorts.

'You can come in if you want.'

'That would be nice, but I can't. It's not that I don't want to, it's just I'm a bit worried about Monsieur Marechall. He might need me. See you tomorrow then?'

'See you tomorrow.'

Fiona's lips …

Monsieur Marechall was sprawled across the dishevelled bed wearing only his boxers, open-mouthed and scrawny as a giant skinned rabbit. Just as he was used to doing for his mother, Bernard put him straight, slid a pillow under his head and pulled the blanket up to his chin. Bernard wasn't sleepy. If life was as kind to him every day as it had been today, he would never sleep again. Excitement bubbled through his veins like champagne. It was even better than the day he'd passed his driving test, because this time the only thing he was drunk on was pure, unalloyed happiness.

Once he had made sure everything was in order, Bernard went back down to the beach. The sand was crisscrossed with the footprints of thousands of children, adults and dogs, which seemed almost to come alive in the moonlight. It was as moving a sight as the red clay handprints discovered on the walls of prehistoric caves. Not as ancient, of course, but renewed and immortalised with each passing day. A white plastic bag was lifted high on a gust of wind like a miniature hot-air balloon, and then disappeared behind a bush. This thing with Fiona could turn into something, a relationship. And what was more, she already had a baby he had not even needed to have a hand in making. Things with Monsieur Marechall were not so rosy, though. He was worried about him. What was this 'death' disease Fiona had talked about? Something he had picked up through his job? The truth was, he was really quite attached to the old grouch. Without a father of his own, he had to find a substitute, and Monsieur Marechall fitted the bill.

Bernard lay down on the sand, which moulded snugly around his body. The waves were lapping, the stars whispering. Everything was as it should be, perfectly still, until he caught sight of a stupid green satellite flashing in the distance, reminding him that time was passing. Monsieur Marechall had an important meeting in the morning, at nine thirty on the dot, and then ... then it would be time to say goodbye to Fiona and Violette and he would be back to square one, in Vals-les-Bains. He didn't fancy the prospect of going back to his humdrum existence one bit. Except ... he could drive Monsieur Marechall back to Vals and maybe, if he had done a good job, he might even get a bonus, in which case there was nothing to stop him coming back here. Fiona's caravan was booked for three weeks. If he set his mind to it, he could make a lot of headway in three weeks ...

The moon grinned down on him as he built up his little Lego bricks of hope.

'And have you ever been to the bottom of the sea, Monsieur Marechall?'

'I went diving in the Red Sea once.'

'Ooh ... is it really red?'

'No.'

'What's it like then?'

'Just like where we're going now.'

'The aquarium, OK ... The reason I asked is because I had this dream last night that I was down there, at the bottom of the sea. I could breathe just like normal. Everything was slow, quiet and warm, like being inside someone's tummy. There were other creatures down there and weird wavy seaweed. We all swam around, brushing past each other and saying hello. It was so calm, so – I dunno – peaceful. Then suddenly I was being pulled to the surface. I was flapping around but there was nothing I could do to stop it. My mouth was full of bubbles when WHAM! I hit the surface of the water which must have been frozen or something; it was smooth and hard like a mirror. I was banging my hands against it but it was no use – there was no way up or down.'

'So then what?'

'Nothing. I woke up.'

'Dreams are so stupid.'

'You're right, Monsieur Marechall, they are. Why do we have them?'

'Because real life isn't enough. Park over there, just in front, and leave the engine running. If I'm not back in ten minutes, come down and find me.'

'The same place as yesterday, in front of the shark?'

'The same place.'

'Are you sure you don't want me to come with you? You don't look very well.'

'Ten minutes, OK?'

Only the thickness of the windscreen stood between dream and reality. It might have been a hangover from Bernard's dream, but people, objects and animals seemed to be moving in slow motion before him. No sooner had the guard opened the gate to the aquarium than Monsieur Marechall disappeared inside.

There is nothing as boring as someone telling you their dreams. Simon screwed the silencer onto the barrel of his gun and waited, concealed in a dark corner. The shark continued its endless circling, indifferent to everything including its own existence. The minutes dripped by, like water from clothes on a washing line. On laundry days, Simon used to sit and watch his mother hanging out the washing in the yard. Her apron pocket was filled with wooden pegs; she always kept one between her teeth. Shirts, overalls, long johns and faded woollens flapped like the flags of a ship in distress – or rather a rudimentary raft. There was not a single item that had not been darned or patched. He was ashamed to see their pitiful, intimate garments aired in public. Yet the same show was being staged in every back garden along the terrace of small brick houses. Scrub as they might, the hard-working housewives could never get their laundry clean under that soot-filled sky.

A figure appeared at the top of the stairs. It was not Jean-

Pierre Bornay. He was too tall and thin. Simon gripped his gun and took a step forward. The man noticed him and stopped in his tracks, like a heron that has spotted a fish.

'Marechall?'

'Where's Bornay?'

'Couldn't make it. Sent me instead.'

Simon allowed the stand-in to come within a metre of him. Looking at him straight on was like seeing a face in profile; only one eye was visible, as round and cold as that of the shark.

'Have you got the envelope?'

'Yes, here.'

He held it out to Simon with his left hand, but his right remained out of sight.

'Open it.'

The stranger's eye grew even rounder and his mouth twitched nervously. Simon deflected the gun pointing at him and simultaneously fired through his pocket. The stray bullet struck the piranha tank, which shattered like a star and finally burst, spewing out an almost solid wave of seaweed, roots, shards of glass and flailing fish. The man clutched his stomach and fell first to his knees, then onto his side. Simon leant down to pick up the sodden envelope. As he straightened up, he saw Bernard on the third step, rooted to the spot with horror at the scene before him. There was a man squirming at Monsieur Marechall's feet, soaked in red water and surrounded by funny little fish, all jagged-toothed mouths and tails flapping around in the darkness. An alarm began ringing. Monsieur Marechall grabbed Bernard by the elbow and pulled him away.

'Move, now!'

As they barged up the stairs, they passed the dazed guard who stammered, 'What's going on? What's happened?'

The shock of stepping from the gloom into bright daylight

made them both teeter. They groped their way back to the car like blind men and clambered inside.

'Drive, damn it! Go!'

Bernard stalled twice before the car joined the flow of traffic.

'Where to, Monsieur Marechall? Where to now?'

'To the campsite. Go back to the campsite.'

Simon was breathing heavily through his nose and speaking through his teeth, his jaws clamped shut.

The town had not seen or heard anything. People were passing, dogs pissing, trees growing.

Back at the caravan, Simon sat at the table with his head in his hands, glaring at the contents of the envelope: a soggy bundle of Monopoly money.

'The bastard. The fucking bastard.'

Standing beside him with his arms dangling, Bernard was nodding in agreement, despite the fact he had no idea what to make of the morning's events. It was as though last night's dream had carried on in some jumbled way, as mysterious and unfathomable as the deep sea. There was a knock at the door. Bernard halted his mechanical head movement and went to answer it. The faces of Fiona and Violette appeared, haloed in the late-morning sunlight.

'Morning! Did you sleep well?'

Bernard made a face that could have passed for a smile. Simon did not look up.

'I was thinking, if you're still around at lunchtime we could have a barbecue. We've got everything we need in the caravan, even the charcoal,' said Fiona.

Bernard turned nervously to Simon and addressed his hunched back.

'Monsieur Marechall?'

'Piss off, the lot of you.'

'OK, Monsieur Marechall. I'll be right next door if you need me.'

'Get lost!'

*

This was not the first time he had been screwed over, but because this contract was to be the last of his long career, it left an especially bitter taste in his mouth. And it was all down to that pathetic little insurance salesman wanting to pull a fast one. He squeezed the stack of notes and a few drops of greenish liquid oozed out. No one really went out with a bang. No one. But to end up on a campsite in Cap d'Agde, escorted by a simpleton whose only wish was to play happy families, barbecuing sausages on the beach? It was a complete joke. He was going to make J.-P. Bornay swallow this Monopoly money; he would shove the whole lot down his throat!

Yet all his rage and wounded pride could not propel his spent body into action. It was all he could do to heave his leaden arse off his chair and collapse on the bed, arms outstretched. 'Poor old thing. You're worn out, like your dad's old pants. You've got plenty of money put away. As for Bornay, you win some, you lose some – what the hell does it matter? Let it go. You've had a hectic life, it's time to calm down and enjoy a peaceful old age.'

Simon clamped his hands over his ears, closed his eyes and clenched his teeth.

The face of Negrita rum, a laughing West Indian woman, came in and out of view as the bottle rolled across the floor. Once it had come to a stop against the skirting board, only her gold hoop earring was visible on the label. The last dregs of rum ran back and forth from the bottom of the bottle to the neck. Lying sprawled on the sofa, Anaïs followed the liquid's ebb and flow with bleary eyes. The bottle had slipped from her hands as she raised it to her mouth.

'Who cares, I've got another one.'

The trouble was that in order to fetch it, Anaïs would have had to get up, go into the kitchen and bend down to open the cupboard under the sink, which was all too much for her now. Everything seemed out of reach. The world was shrinking a little further from her each day. She might not have a phone, but that dolt Bernard could still get in touch. He knew how to get hold of her; he just had to give her neighbour, Fanny, a ring ... But no! He would leave his poor mother to die like a dog while he had a ball with that fancy friend of his! Well, they could all go to hell, the whole damn lot of them!

'What do you think you're looking at with those dead eyes, you stupid cow?'

The Negress went on stoically shining her sixty-watt light beneath the dusty raffia shade. She had seen all this many times before – around seven o'clock most evenings in fact.

'One day I'll drop dead and then you'll all be sorry! "Ooh, where's Anaïs? Where is she?" Well, Anaïs won't be around any more. So long, suckers! No one left to give a shit about your stupid games and dirty tricks! I'll be up there, on high, in the great big empty hole where the Good Lord's supposed to be, and I'll sit there on that old bastard's throne and I'll be the one in charge – God knows I couldn't do a worse job than him! I'll be the one laughing then, when I'm pulling all the strings, ha! No, actually, actually I'll drop everything. I'll make feathered hats for the angels and if they won't wear them, I'll send them to hell and roast them like chickens! Round and round I'll turn that spit, round and round ...'

She was rotating her right arm so enthusiastically that she fell off the sofa.

'Shit, I've hurt myself!'

An unfamiliar crowd of microscopic creatures gathered around her body, like the Lilliputians surrounding Gulliver, a motley crew of nature's embryonic creatures and freakish prototypes, too insignificant to be named. All seemed as taken aback as she was at the encounter.

'It's funny, you think you're on your own, and then ...'

Anaïs fell asleep, a beached whale snoring in a miniature world known only to alcoholics and saints.

The merguez were curling up on the barbecue, oozing a rust-coloured oil that made the coals flare up. Fiona was turning the sausages with a long-handled fork, leaning back and shielding her eyes from the smoke.

'You know, that Monsieur Marechall of yours doesn't only kill cockroaches.'

Bernard was absently bouncing Violette up and down on his knee. He had not touched the glass of rosé Fiona had just poured him. It had been difficult to give her a chronological account of the morning's events. Everything was so mixed up, his dream, the aquarium, the man dying amid the piranhas, the Monopoly money ... He could not make head nor tail of any of it. In the space of forty-eight hours he had been catapulted into another universe in which only Violette and Fiona seemed real. He clung to them like a shipwrecked man to a life raft.

'Cut some bread, will you? The guy's a professional, a hit man, like in the movies. Except this isn't a movie,' added Fiona.

Bernard could not take his eyes off the sharp knife Fiona was using to slice the tomatoes into perfectly even rounds. He had never imagined life could be so fraught with danger. He held Violette tightly. Her vulnerability made him feel safe and he never wanted to let her go. She was his shield, his lucky charm.

Violette wriggled about in her nappy, her eyes, mouth, nose, ears and every pore of her skin wide open to each new sensation, which she recorded like a human computer. She was not thinking about anything, imagining anything or asking herself any questions and consequently did not waste time looking for answers. She was happy just to wave her arms and legs about like a beetle on its back. Staying alive was all that mattered. There was the sky, the sun and the sea, and that was enough. Her avid pupils took in all the essential details. She also knew how to shit and piss, which she duly demonstrated to stop the knee she was sitting on from jiggling.

'Fiona? I think she needs changing.'

'Again? Can you watch the merguez?'

Mother and child disappeared inside the caravan.

Bernard turned over some of the sausages, which were already burnt to a cinder. The wind had picked up enough to make two or three multicoloured kites twirl gently in the sky. A black dog ran after them, barking. Between the sky and the water, the horizon stretched wide as a taut rubber band.

'One of these days it's going to snap.'

'Bernard!'

'Ah, Monsieur Marechall, are you feeling better?'

He looked like a scorched tree rooted in the sand, against a clear blue sky of the type usually found only in travel brochures.

'We're going.'

Bernard finished swallowing his mouthful of merguez sandwich.

'Are you sure you don't want something to eat before—'

'We're going.'

'OK, Monsieur Marechall, I just have to grab my jacket.'

Fiona was looking daggers at Simon. Violette was asleep on her chest, her mouth hanging open.

'It's not nice, what you're doing. Not nice at all.'

'No one asked your opinion.'

'Well, I'm giving it anyway! You'll be dead soon but you're too shit scared to go on your own. Why can't you just leave Bernard be?'

Simon did not answer. He was gazing at the sea. There was no land in sight, not even the tiniest island. Bernard came running out, putting his jacket on as he went. He looked like a kind of cormorant, clumsily gearing up for its first flight.

The interior of the car smelt of sand, salt, curdled milk and baby wee.

'You stink of piss.'

'I know, it was Violette. Shall I wind down the window? Oh, and where are we going?'

'I'll tell you.'

The traffic was moving easily as they drove along roads with curious names: Gingembre, Estragon, Genièvre, Cannelle, Place du Volcan, Passage du Thym and Passage de l'Origan, Rue des Anciens-Combattants-de-l'Afrique, Rue de la Marne, Rue du Chemin-des-Dames and finally, after Carrefour du Souvenir-Français, Rue du Rêve.

'Stop here.'

Outside number 12, a nondescript-looking man was loading suitcases into the boot of a dark-blue Audi. A tall, horsey blonde woman stood perched on her high heels, craning her neck anxiously about her.

'Now, Bernard, you're going to get out and ask them the way to Rue Jean-Mermoz.'

'Rue Jean-Mermoz, OK. Then what?'

'Then you leave me to do the rest. That's it.'

'That's it?'

'Go on, then. Take the map – make it look as though you're lost.'

The closer Bernard got to the couple, the more it felt as if he was walking the wrong way up an escalator. The short distance between them seemed to go on for ever.

'Excuse me, I'm lost. I'm looking for Rue Jean-Mermoz.'

The man was sweating. There were dark patches under the arms of his short-sleeved shirt and his balding head shone like a polished banister knob.

'Don't know it. Haven't got time.'

'But it's somewhere near here, if you look on the map ...'

The man examined the map with eyes like round marbles. The tall, horsey woman trotted over.

'I know where it is. Go back the way you came, then take—'

She didn't manage to finish her sentence. The barrel, fitted with a silencer, made a little *plop!* sound and she fell to the ground like a tree trunk sawn off at the base. Simon aimed his gun at the domed forehead of the short moustachioed man.

'On your knees. Open your mouth.'

J.-P. Bornay obeyed – or rather, his body did, and a tiny bit of his brain. As for the rest, the lights were out and there was nobody home. Everything had happened so quickly, he was beyond fear. Simon took a handful of Monopoly money out of his pocket and stuffed the notes between Bornay's teeth.

'Eat them! I said eat them!'

He began chewing slowly, wild-eyed. The map slipped from Bernard's hands and came to rest against the railings of a large house.

'You're a fool, Bornay.'

Plop! A dark hole opened up in the brow of the kneeling man and his eyes glazed over with the vague stare of a newborn baby. As he fell forwards, Simon kicked him back.

'It's done. Let's get out of here.'

Bernard would have liked nothing better than to get out of there, but his feet seemed to have sunk into the tarmac.

'Are you coming or what?'

'Monsieur Marechall ... I've shat myself ...'

'Fiona will sort it out.'

Simon got behind the wheel, since Bernard was not in a fit state. He drove cautiously, obeying stop signs and red lights.

'I feel like a glass of Suze. Do you?'

'No.'

'Wait for me out here then.'

Bernard did not feel like anything. He was as numb as a slab of frozen fish. His soiled underpants were stuck to his buttocks but he felt neither shame nor discomfort. He could have stayed like this for hours, days, years, thinking of nothing at all, oblivious to everyday life marching by on the other side of the windscreen, left, right, left, right …

Simon downed his Suze at the counter of Bar de l'Espoir. The bar's name made him think: What was the use of hope, anyway? It served no more purpose than what he had just done, but that was simply the way it was and you had to live with it. Every time he ran out of arguments, as happened often, his father would hurl this maxim at him. It was straightforward, no-nonsense, to the point; a kind of magic formula.

The sandcastle Fiona had built for Violette was quite special, with four turrets, a curved doorway and a winding road leading up to it. But the waves had already started to gnaw away at its foundations. Just her luck: clever Mummy, she'll put it back together again. The sea is mean. It draws you in, withdraws and then, as soon as you turn your back to it, comes and snatches back everything it just gave you. So much for Mother Nature. Fiona's mother, on the other hand, had been more straight with her; all she had ever given her was a childhood in care and her first name. It wasn't so bad, her name. Everyone had called her 'Fion' when she was a kid. When she turned eighteen, she had tried to find her mother but it was complicated; there was a ton of paperwork to fill in. She gave up. She thought about going on one of those TV shows that reunites long-lost relatives, but what would have been the point? What would they have had to say to each other? And so she'd got pregnant with Violette by the first guy who had happened along. All that mattered now was the two of them together, four arms, four legs, two heads. As long as they had each other, they had twice the chances of getting by. Battered by the waves with their lace of foam, one of the turrets collapsed.

The only sun on Violette was a single ray which scorched the

176

end of her nose, in spite of the hat Fiona had made her out of the newspaper. If Violette had been able to read the article hanging over her left eye, she would have learnt that the man known as 'The Butcher of the Ardèche' had just been arrested. Though come to think of it, she probably would not have cared a jot. The only things she was interested in were her wiggly toes. When she could finally reach them, she would be a big girl.

'Anaïs, can you hear me? Georges, I think we should get her to hospital.'

The word 'hospital' was banned under Anaïs's roof, a taboo subject never to be mentioned. No sound came out of her mouth but she began rolling her eyes wildly while wringing Fanny's wrist. She was no longer averse to the idea of kicking the bucket, but it had to be in her own home. It was ashes to ashes, dust to dust – and there was no shortage of that here. The feather duster would just have to wait.

'At least go and get the doctor! Don't just stand there!'

Georges had made love to Anaïs once, a long, long time ago. Back then, Anaïs was what was known as 'a fine specimen of a woman'. This was in the days between the dirty ginger dyke running off and the dogs coming along. Fanny had gone to stay with her sister in Montélimar for a couple of days, he couldn't remember what for – a new baby, was it? Or a funeral? Anaïs had read his fortune with tarot cards ... No, actually it was some Chinese thing, I Ching. She used these wooden sticks and read baffling stuff out of a fat yellow book, like 'to retire is favourable'. In those days, retirement was the last thing on his mind: he only had eyes for those two big breasts resting on the open book, which he wanted to grab with both hands and bury his face between. The future mattered to him only when placing bets. He had opened another bottle of wine and they had rolled about on the sofa, which squeaked even then. It was over quickly, but it was good. They parted on friendly terms and it never happened again.

'What the hell are you waiting for, Georges? Can't you see she's gone blue?!'

Georges left the house. He passed Jean Ferrat outside the bakery.

By the time Fiona had taken care of his clothes, Bernard had stepped back into his old skin, but not his old life. Nothing would ever be the same again. While Monsieur Marechall slept in the caravan, Bernard went for a walk on the beach with Violette nestling against his shoulder. He walked a certain distance before turning round and going back, over and over again. It was not the same sky above him now, nor the same sea. Everything had changed, but no one else had noticed. It all had the whiff of an illusion, an artful fake. Nothing was certain any more. The rocks could be made of cardboard, the pine trees out of balsa wood; Violette might be nothing but an inflatable toy, the sun a spotlight and himself just another walk-on actor. Life had lost its substance. All it had taken was a little *plop!* for everything to vanish, without explanation.

There was a small souvenir shop selling postcards next to the campsite reception. Having promised to send one to his mother, Bernard paid it a visit. The postcard he chose depicted a sunset so dazzling he almost needed sunglasses to look at it. He sat at a table in the adjoining bar and ordered a mint cordial. Violette was still asleep, glued to him like a leech. He could not think what to write, so he began with the address, chewing the cap of his pen while he waited for inspiration. 'Dear Mother ... [Was she really that dear to him?] I'm down at Cap d'Agde which is ... an up-and-down sort of place. ['Up-and-down sort of place' didn't really mean anything, and yet it summed it up perfectly. You could go from heaven to hell here and not even notice.] The weather is good. It's nice to see the sea, which is bigger than Lake Geneva.'

Bernard put down his pen and drank half his glass of mint cordial. The ice cubes had melted to the size of cufflinks. The sight of the green syrup took him back to the aquarium and made him gag. The little girl started to wriggle, dribbling into the neck of his T-shirt. Instinctively he jiggled her up and down, which made his writing wobbly. 'The sea isn't green here, same as the Red Sea isn't red. Monsieur Marechall told me that, because he's been there. It just shows you shouldn't believe everything you hear.' Bernard drained the last drops of his drink. The ice had completely melted. He had nothing else to say so he rounded off with: 'I'm fine and hope you are too. Lots of love, your son Bernard.'

A rush of sadness surged from his chest to his eyes. He would have liked to send his mother a message in a bottle, saying: 'Come and get me, Mummy, it's too grown-up here!' But it would never arrive. He stuck on a stamp and slipped the postcard into the back pocket of his jeans.

'What a lovely baby! Is it a little boy or a little girl?'

'A little girl.'

Sitting at the next table was a podgy woman, with a mass of curly hair like a panful of macaroni. She looked like a cartoon fairy godmother.

'What's her name?'

'Violette.'

'Violette! It's good luck to be named after a flower, you know. My name's Rose.'

And she really was rosy, everything from her skin to her clothes, but not her eyes, which were periwinkle blue. She looked well over fifty and was drinking a strawberry milkshake.

'Are you here on holiday?' she asked.

'Yes and no, a bit of both.'

'I've been coming for years, same weeks, same bungalow. I'm a creature of habit. I'm from Namur, in Belgium. And you?'

'Lyon.'

'Thank heavens for that! I'm not keen on Parisians, they're so snooty! Are you having a nice time?'

'It's OK.'

'You must be here with your wife?'

'Um ... yes, but my boss as well. My wife's at the dry cleaner's and my boss is having a lie-down.'

'I see ... You must think me awfully nosy, but what do you do for a living?'

'Driver.'

'How wonderful! You must travel a lot. I'm a taxidermist. Well, I'm retired now, I just do it for fun.'

'Taxi— So a bit like me, then?'

'Oh, no! I'm a taxidermist, I preserve dead animals.'

'Ah, you stuff things?'

'That's it. I used to work for museums, now I have private clients, mostly old ladies who can't bear to be parted from dead pets – dogs, cats, parrots, all sorts. Last time it was a boa constrictor!'

'A boa, really ... My boss works in a similar field, although he doesn't do preserving. He's a pest controller; he gets rid of cockroaches, bugs, mice, rats ...'

'I've done rats too! How fascinating, I'd like to meet him!'

'We're leaving tomorrow.'

'Oh, what a shame! Well, how about this evening? Come for a drink at my bungalow. It's the last one, over there, under the big pine tree.'

'I'll have to ask him ...'

'Yes, of course. I'm sure he'll agree to it. I'll expect you around seven.'

Rose was barely taller standing than she was sitting down. She called over the waiter.

'Gégé, put these two drinks on my tab, would you? So I'll see you this evening, Monsieur ...?'

'Bernard.'

She stroked Violette's cheek with her chubby little finger.

'Isn't she pretty? What lovely soft skin! And those great big eyelashes, they're like butterfly wings! You just don't want them to grow up, do you?'

She bounced off down the road like a tennis ball, the net of darkness already closing in around the trees.

Simon was well practised in taking his gun apart and putting it back together with his eyes shut. But this time he had dropped a spring and could not find it anywhere, even with his glasses on.

'Have you lost something, Monsieur Marechall?'

Bernard was standing in the hallway, his suit hanging over his arm in its plastic bag like a sheath of dead skin.

'No, I'm looking for four-leafed clover. One of the springs fell out, a stupid little spring!'

Bernard crouched down next to him and held up the missing piece.

'This one?'

'Where on earth have you been?'

'Just hanging around, waiting for Fiona to bring back my clothes.'

'We're leaving tomorrow.'

'I thought so. We haven't been here long.'

'Long enough. Help me up.'

Once he had settled back into his chair, Simon continued putting together the pieces of his deadly jigsaw puzzle. One by one he got the action working, loaded another round of bullets and secured the safety catch. His hands were shaking uncontrollably, governed by a force stronger than his own will. He clasped them tightly together, interlocking his fingers until they turned white. Bernard sat down opposite him at the table.

'I know what you really do for a living now.'

'So?'

'So nothing. It's not exactly your average nine to five.'

'The job needs doing, as long as there's a demand for it.'

'Even so, I'd have rather you just got rid of rats.'

'Rats, people – they're all the same. They breed just as quickly.'

Bernard was staring at the pistol on the table. It was hard to believe such an ordinary-looking object could do so much damage.

'Why the woman? She hadn't done anything to you.'

'No witnesses. Never leave any witnesses.'

'What about me?'

'You? Well, you're working for me, which makes you my accomplice.'

'Don't worry, I won't say a thing. I'd forget the whole thing ever happened if I could.'

'That's exactly what you have to do. Tomorrow's another day, after all.'

'Yes, and it's when we're leaving ... Oh, I met a woman earlier who does a similar sort of job to you.'

'What woman? What does she do?'

'Hang on, let me think ... Taxi-something ... She stuffs things.'

'Taxidermist?'

'That's the one! She stuffs dogs, cats, boa constrictors, all kinds of dead animals. She's Belgian and she's retired. She invited us to pop round for a drink this evening.'

Simon stood up, rubbing his back. He had to stop himself laughing. This young imbecile was really too much – first the teenage mother, now a Belgian taxidermist!

'Where on earth do you find them?'

'I didn't go out looking for her! She was the one who started talking to me. I was writing a postcard to my mother in the bar by reception. I had Violette on my lap; she was cooing over her and started chatting to me. She's here on holiday, staying in the last bungalow along the main path. Rose, her name is. She's getting on but she's got all her bits in the right places. She's expecting us at seven, but I can call it off if you'd rather.'

Simon could not help but admire Bernard's ability to adapt to the most bizarre situations. That great twerp had a born gift for resilience.

'Well, why not?'

'I was worried you'd be angry. Right, I'd better go and tell Fiona – I didn't want to say anything before talking to you ... Oh and by the way, she thinks Fiona and I are married and Violette's our daughter. I couldn't put her straight, it would have got too complicated.'

'And I'm the granddad, am I?'

'No! You're my boss, I'm your driver.'

'Well, that's all right then. OK, off you go, back to your little family.'

Simon could not remember the last time he had been in such a good mood. He smiled as he weighed the gun in his hand, the steel gradually warming in his palm. It was nothing but a memento now, like the tools retired labourers hold on to as a reminder of times gone by. They had come a long way together, he and his gun, but neither seemed fit for much any more. He slid it under his pillow out of habit, but something told him he would not be using it again and he felt a huge weight lifting.

Rose had everything she could possibly need in her bungalow, with glasses for every type of drink and a crocheted coaster to go under each one. Olives, peanuts, cocktail sausages and homemade crisps were piled high in cut-glass dishes. The hostess twirled around the table in a flimsy lilac chiffon negligee like a moth dancing in the light of the scented anti-mosquito lamp. She had a kind word for everyone, especially Violette, whose cheek she stroked each time she went past. Simon and Fiona were on the pastis, Rose on beer, Bernard on mint cordial and Violette on her bottle, staring up at Venus in the night sky. Unlike her neighbours, Rose had personalised her bungalow, decorating it with fairy lights, frilly curtains and pots of brightly coloured geraniums.

'It's another place to call my own. I've been coming here for so long, the same weeks every year. Francis, the manager, gets everything ready for me before I arrive. It's like having a second home, I suppose. I like to feel at home wherever I am. The world belongs to all of us, doesn't it?'

'Absolutely!'

'Namur is a pretty little town but the winter goes on for ever! Do you know Namur, Monsieur Marechall?'

'Yes. I'm from the north, so Belgium's just across ... We used to go over to buy beer and tobacco. But I haven't been back in a long time.'

'It's pretty much the same. The north will never change. And what about you, Madame Fiona, where are you from?'

'From a care home. Don't s'pose it's changed much there either. My mother was Italian, I think, or maybe it was my dad ... You have to make these things up, when you don't know the truth.'

'Of course you do, my poor darling ... Well, you have your own family now. All that matters is the here and now.'

'That's right. Excuse me for a moment, I need to go and change the baby.'

'Be my guest!'

'Will you give me a hand, Bernard?' Simon and Rose watched the young couple and their baby disappearing into the shadows. The image was almost biblical.

'How wonderful to be young!'

'Indeed!'

'Can I get you another?'

'Just a drop.' There was a bit of peanut stuck between Simon's teeth. He tried to dislodge it with the tip of his tongue, but there was no shifting it. Soon he could concentrate on nothing else.

'So you get rid of rodents, I hear?'

'Not just rodents, all kinds of pests. But I've just sold my company to take retirement.'

'You'll never look back! To begin with you won't know what to do with yourself, but really you won't have a care in the world ... unless you worry about how long you've got left.'

'I don't think about it.'

'Oh, I do. I don't have a problem with dying, it's eternity I'm worried about. The first animal I preserved was a squirrel. Poor little thing! If you'd seen the state he was in ... a truck had run him over. But now he's fresh as the day he was born! You'll think me ridiculous, but I feel like ... like I'm giving the Creator a helping hand, fixing His mistakes. Plus I enjoy needlework.'

'Nothing wrong with that. I've got nothing against eternity, but personally I think I'd die of boredom.'

'Ah, come on, you'd get used to it eventually!'

Rose looked like a Chinese lantern. Her chubby face bobbed from side to side and her wide smile revealed all her teeth, no doubt just as false as the pearls she wore around her neck. Was falseness really the enemy of truth? Rose reminded him of the Hanoi madam who was just as happy to pocket fake dollars as real ones. Their hands were lying on the table millimetres apart. She was not wearing a wedding ring, and neither was he.

'It's getting chilly, I think I'll put a shawl on.'

Simon lit a cigarette. Without meaning to, he blew a smoke ring that settled around his head like a halo. Meanwhile, in her largest saucepan, the Great Bear was cooking up a fricassee of stars.

'Didn't you see the way she was touching her?'

'She likes children.'

'Of course she does, she's a witch! She can do what she likes with her stuffed goats, but I don't want her coming anywhere near Violette.'

'Fiona! You're going a bit far, she's just a little old lady—'

'I don't like old people! They stink, that's why they put on so much perfume. They're all at death's door, just like your precious Monsieur Marechall!'

The nappy spread with innocent shit fell into the bin with a dull thud. Violette was lying on her back, squirming and whimpering.

'You don't think you're being a teensy bit paranoid?'

'Of course I am! That's the reason I'm still alive today. Your boss is a hit man, Rose is a monster, and you ... you're just a stupid idiot!'

She threw herself into Bernard's arms, sobbing and pounding his back with her fists.

'Let's get out of here, you, me and Violette. I don't want us to be tainted by them. We have a right to live our lives, damn it!'

Fiona was wearing a new face. The tears streaming down it gave it the appearance of an unfinished watercolour, an island emerging from the mist.

'Make love to me.'

'What here? Now?'

'Yes.'

Not easy, no, it was not easy at all, but when Violette's right hand managed to grab her left big toe, she was over the moon. She had finally caught the stupid thing and now she was going to stuff it in her mouth. That was it: she was a big girl now.

'We need to get you to hospital, Anaïs. Believe me, I know what I'm talking about. This is a matter of life or death.'

'Who the hell do you think you are? Already dead, are you? Know all about it, huh? No? Well then, shut your trap.'

She did not actually say this to the doctor since her jaws refused to come unstuck, but by God she had thought it. A needle had just pricked her arm, spreading its welcome venom through her body. Fanny and the doctor were talking in hushed tones in the corner. From time to time, Fanny lifted her arms and let them drop again in a symbol of helplessness, like a fledgling bird afraid to fly the nest. Georges stood with his hands clasped behind his back, in conversation with the Negress lamp. Why couldn't they all just go away and leave her alone? ... Things were going just as well for Anaïs as for the rest of them, better even, since she did not intend to carry on any longer. She just had to wait for them to get fed up and piss off. She was used to waiting, she had been doing it all her life – hanging around for buses, love, success, a phone call ... Strangely, the less time she had left, the less the waiting bothered her.

The doctor was the first to leave the scene, carrying his little bag filled with needles, rubber tubes, pills and bottles. Then it was the turn of Georges, whose lumbering uselessness was beginning to get on his wife's nerves. He did not wait to be told twice. Death, like birth, was not a sight he was madly keen to see.

He was happy enough to stick where he was, somewhere between the two. Fanny, on the other hand, settled into the armchair next to the sofa where Anaïs lay, determined to watch over her, offering her puny body as a shield against all harm. It was a laudable stance, but within quarter of an hour she was snoring, her chin resting on her bony chest. Anaïs coughed and shifted until she was sure her neighbour's nasal symphony was in full swing, before sitting herself up. It was a struggle, but she made it. Her head was spinning, but what did it matter? She had got her sea legs years ago. The pains running from shoulder to hip did not bother her any more. She had adopted them and tamed them, like mangy stray cats. Having reached the edge of the sofa, she attempted to stand, only to discover this was a risky enterprise. Crawling on all fours, she moved towards the kitchen. It was a tricky business, but more stable than relying on her hind legs. Besides, this was how everyone took their first steps and learnt to be independent. She just had to throw herself back in time, to the days of discovering the world from the ground up. Right arm ... Left knee ... Left arm ... Right knee.

Once again, the parallel world of miniature creatures shyly gathered to spur her on. She knew she could trust the little monsters, because they were cute. They bent over backwards to help her push open the kitchen door. The floor was icy cold, each tile a territory to be conquered. With the effort of crossing it, she blew powerful gusts from her nose and mouth which scattered the flocks of grey fluff and whipped up crumbs, like an elephant stomping through the undergrowth. Anaïs came to a halt in front of the cupboard under the sink, where normal people keep their cleaning products and alcoholics keep their bottles. The last bottle of Negrita was definitely in there somewhere, but where ...?

It was pitch black inside the cupboard. Anaïs groped about blindly, picking out various plastic and glass containers by touch.

But danger was lurking in the absurd habit she had picked up from her mother — a house-proud woman of strict morals — of pouring the last drops of detergents, bleach and the like into empty bottles to save space. Since at Anaïs's house the only empties were Negrita bottles, and on top of that she could not see a thing, the whole operation was very likely to end in disaster. But she was so thirsty! All around her the little creatures held their breath.

'Now let's see if God exists!'

She grabbed the first bottle at random and took a long swig.

Simon pushed away the flabby thigh resting on top of his and freed himself from the tangle of sheets. He felt sick. The heady smell of Rose's perfume was overpowering. Unless it was something else, a deeper disgust at an entire existence, which rose in his throat, mingled with the aftertaste of pastis. Walking on tiptoe, he gathered his belongings and left the bungalow. The cool night air did him good but not enough to stop him emptying his stomach, clutching the rough trunk of a pine tree with both hands. He got dressed, shivering from head to foot. He had not been able to do it. 'It doesn't matter,' she had whispered in his ear, 'at our age ...' Apart from a window at reception and a few street lamps along the main path, there were no lights on. It was like a graveyard. The regular ebb and flow of the waves made the dreary walk seem to go on for ever. When he finally reached his caravan, the car that should have been parked next to it was gone.

'The little bastard!'

Bernard's bed had not been slept in. Simon ran back out to Fiona's caravan. Deserted. He was seized with a strange panic, as though he had died and no one had thought to tell him. Even solitude, his only companion for as many years as he could remember, seemed to have let go of his hand. The darkness was becoming denser around him, invading his nose, mouth and ears like the soot of his childhood. He staggered back to his caravan, turned on all the lights and searched under his pillow. The gun was there, warmed by the cushions but utterly useless. He sat on the edge of the bed, the weapon dangling between his thighs like a flaccid penis, staring past the half-open door into a picture of crushing emptiness. He had been scared many times before, but never like this. This was a childlike, uncontrollable fear that was slowly shutting him down like an anaesthetic. 'Be still my beating heart.' He felt neither hate nor anger, he just could not understand.

'Why have you done this to me, kid? Why?'

A chemical precipitation, caused by a complex mixture of conflicting emotions, made a warm, salty liquid spring from the corner of his eyes, a liquid he had not tasted for what seemed like centuries. The teardrop trickled through the network of lines on his cheek to the corner of his mouth, and from his lips to his chin. It felt as good and sweet as an endless ejaculation. For once, his heart was doing more than pumping blood around his body. He raised himself up painlessly, walked towards the beach, crossed the strip of grey sand and immersed himself up to the waist in the black waters. And there, swinging his arm like a farmer sowing seeds, he tossed the gun as far as he could throw it. The weapon went to join the pile of junk that carpets the seabed, just another thing among all the others, just as Simon was only one among many humans.

'Don't you think we might be doing something really, really stupid?'

'What are you talking about? Surely you don't actually think your Monsieur Marechall's going to shop us to the police?'

'No, not that ...'

'Well, what then? Where do you think you were going with him? Straight into a brick wall, that's where, or else going inside. And as for that old hag, she'd have had Violette off me and stuffed her, no question.'

'That's total rubbish! What the hell are we going to do in Spain? I can't speak a word of Spanish.'

'It's no harder than Italian. In Italian, you put an "i" on the end of every word and in Spanish you put an "o". Also Spain's really close and I've got friends in Barcelona.'

'Really?'

'Well, acquaintances, but that'll do, right? We deserve another shot at life. You have to take your chances where you find them.'

'I suppose ...'

Fiona was sitting in the back, with Violette sprawled across her lap. Looking at her in the rear-view mirror, Bernard saw the face of a stubborn little girl, closed like a fist. How could people change so quickly? Last night, in the half-light of the caravan, she had seemed so gentle, or at least so calm, like Violette after a feed. They had made love with the lightness of two butterflies, simply, without haste or hunger. She had fallen asleep, or perhaps just closed her eyes. She was breathing in time with the child asleep in the Moses basket, following the rhythm of the night. The beauty spot on her left breast was the centre of a world in which pain, fear and sadness were no more. Bernard held his breath, for fear of bursting the fragile bubble in which they were floating. Never before had he felt so complete, a man in perfect harmony with his life. He was exactly where he should be. Then she had opened her eyes so suddenly, he was startled.

'Let's get out of here, Bernard!'

'Uh, where to?'

'Spain.'

'Spain? When?'

'Straight away, right now, this minute.'

Even the sky looked different today. Milky clouds trailed across a sun as ill-disposed as Bernard to starting the new day. The landscape seemed dull and flat, patches of land blistered with characterless houses.

'I'll have to stop and get petrol.'

'OK, I'll sort Violette out.'

They stopped at a service station selling any old rubbish at any price to anyone who would buy it. As he paid for his tank of petrol, Bernard noted bitterly that they were getting through money like there was no tomorrow. They were running low already and by the time they got to Barcelona there would be nothing left. Spain, for goodness' sake! The petrol station was already trying to flog plastic bulls, castanets and models of gleaming toreadors and flouncy flamenco dancers. They had not yet crossed the border and already he felt homesick. But what was troubling him most was the dirty trick they had played on Monsieur Marechall. OK, he was a hit man, a criminal, but he was much more than that. Monsieur Marechall had always been straight down the line with him and had put his trust in Bernard. He had taught him things like ... that the Red Sea isn't red, for one. He had treated him like a man, like a son almost, and he, eight-fingered Bernard, had behaved like the lowest of the low, nothing but a common thief. His reflection in the window disgusted him. He would never be able to look himself in the eye again. He was worth less than a cigarette butt in an ashtray.

Fiona reappeared, spruced up. She had caught the sun on her nose and cheeks, which made her look like a shiny little toffee apple.

'They're selling car seats for babies in there – what do you think? It would make things a lot easier. I've had enough of sitting there with Violette plonked in my lap. What's the matter? What's that face for?'

'Listen, I'm not going any further, Fiona. Here, take what's left of the money and you go to Barcelona, but I'm taking the car back to Monsieur Marechall.'

'Are you out of your mind? We're almost at the border – we'll be in Barcelona by this evening!'

'I couldn't care less about Spain. I've never cheated anybody and I can't do it, I just can't do it.'

One big, tight ball of words was stuck in Fiona's throat, which she could not spit out or swallow. She was choking and looking helplessly about her. All around people were getting into their cars, munching snack bars and holding paper cups. Others were getting out, stretching their legs with hands on hips, walking their dogs or scolding snivelling kids ... Normal people.

'Christ, Bernard! Look around you. Don't you want to be happy? Don't you want an easy life like all these people have? You and me, we met each other and that means something. We can have a life of our own, just us, like we've never had before. We have a right to that, damn it! We deserve it!'

'I want that too, Fiona, it's all I want. But I can't do it by going behind someone's back. I couldn't look at myself in the mirror again.'

'But he doesn't give a shit about you, your Monsieur Marechall! He's using you, and once he's got what he wants from you he'll put a bullet through your head.'

'I don't think so, Fiona, I don't believe that. Listen, here's what we're going to do. You take the money and go to Barcelona to stay with your friends. I'll take the car back and then I'll come and meet you there. I promise you, I swear.'

'I don't know if you're just stupid or completely naïve, or both. You're leaving us here in a fucking service station car park to go back to a murdering old bastard, and you're telling me you can't bear to let somebody down? What kind of an idiot do you take me for? It would be funny if it wasn't so pathetic!'

Fiona sat down on a low concrete wall, her eyes brimming with tears. Violette started to whimper, then cry.

'Oh, don't you start!'

'Calm down, Fiona. Don't talk to her like that. Give her to me.'

'NO! Don't you touch her! Go on, fuck off! Get out of here! I don't want your fucking loot! I'm telling you, get the hell away from me!'

People were turning to look at them. Bernard crouched down in front of the girls with his head in his hands and his back bent. Why did life have to give with one hand and take away with the other?

'They seemed like such a nice couple as well. Are you going to report them?'

'I don't think so.'

'They looked as though butter wouldn't melt though, didn't they? It makes you wonder if you can trust anyone ... You know, I saw that man on the news the other day, the one who killed the three English girls, being taken into court by two policemen. Believe it or not, they were the ones who looked dodgy. The killer just looked like your average man in the street, like you or me.'

Simon was stroking the sand with the flat of his hand, making figures of eight, building little heaps and watching the grains running through his fingers. He had not moved since sunrise, having stayed up all night waiting for it. Rose had passed him on her morning jog and sat down next to him. She had not stopped to draw breath, eagerly filling every silence the way people do when visiting sick relatives. It did not bother him; she was just another part of the scenery. The sky had clouded over and an easterly wind ruffled the crests of the waves, threw up swirls of sand and tossed light objects about.

'It's going to rain later.'

'Maybe.'

'Do you think they'll come back?'

'I don't know.'

'What will you do?'

'I haven't thought about it.'

It was true. He had not come to any decisions. He was just there, as he always had been, wherever he was in the world. He was an island.

'Don't worry, it'll sort itself out. Young people mess about but in the end ... Listen. How about I take you out for lunch?'

'That's very kind of you.'

'Great! I'll go and get changed. Come and meet me at the bungalow.'

'Will do.'

Rose bounced off along the shore like a beach ball. An injured seagull was batting one wing and emitting piercing squawks. All the other seagulls had abandoned it to its fate. Tired of flapping around, it sat on a rock and waited for a miracle that would never come. In which part of Africa was it that people greeted each other every morning with the question 'How's the pain?' Simon could no longer remember.

'No, Marike, he's not a toy boy, he's the real deal, our sort of age. But he's a good-looking man, not an ounce of fat on him, smartly dressed, very proper ... You bet I'd like to take him back to Namur ...! He's selling his business, he's retiring ... What's he like in bed?! There's more to life than that, you know ... Very affectionate, yes ... I couldn't tell you if he's been married before, I only met him yesterday ... Right, I must go, I've got to get ready, I'm taking him out for lunch. The poor thing, he had his car stolen ... That's right, Marike, I'll tell you all about it. Speak soon.'

In the bedroom of the bungalow, the mirror had given up trying to follow Rose's hour-long dance of the seven veils. A dozen dresses, each lacier than the last, were piled up on the bed. Rain began to hammer down on the roof. Rose glanced up, wincing.

Simon was sorry to leave the beach. The sand seemed to bristle with buckshot. The seagull hid its head under its good wing.

'It's the best fish restaurant in town. I can recommend the squid *à la sétoise*, it's delicious!'

After ordering, Rose slipped off to the toilet. Simon reached over to the next table and picked up the newspaper. Smiling shots of Bornay, his mistress and his wife filled the front page: 'Crime of passion or cold-blooded murder?' He skimmed the article. The three victims had been killed with the same weapon. Strangely enough, the same calibre of pistol had also been used in the aquarium shooting of a man with a murky past. The guard had seen two men fleeing the scene but had been unable to give detailed descriptions. It was dark, everything had happened very quickly. There was no apparent link between the two incidents.

Simon folded up the newspaper, indifferent. As far as he was concerned, it was nothing to do with him. He had always wiped the slate clean at the end of every contract, so that remorse and regret had no chance of rearing their heads. Simon was a pro, a sort of bailiff who did what he was told, no questions asked. He took lives the way others removed furniture.

The squid *à la sétoise* was indeed excellent. Rose was talking passionately about her craft, the art of preserving the appearance of life. It was a constant struggle against time, as flesh is fragile and, even treated, deteriorates quickly.

'But you can do amazing things these days! Especially with the eyes – I've got drawers full of them: dogs' eyes, cats' eyes, all kinds of birds' eyes. It's what I put on last, the cherry on the cake, if you will. The eyes are where all the life is. Take you, for example. You come across as rather hard, almost severe, but your eyes are full of tenderness, with a hint of melancholy. It's very touching. I suspect that's why you rarely take off those dark glasses, to hide any sign of weakness. Forgive me, I'm prying.'

'Nonsense!'

'I can't help myself. I just can't resist peering into people's hearts, because that's where all the mystery is, don't you think? Right there, at the heart of the heart.'

'Absolutely. But remember if you peer over too far, you might fall.'

'At my age, there's not much left to lose. You could just as easily fall in love as into a coma ...'

When Rose blushed, she glowed like hot metal. Simon felt like throwing a bucket of water over her to cool her down. She fanned herself with her napkin. They had been the first to arrive and now that they had reached dessert, the restaurant was heaving.

'It's boiling in here! Do you fancy going for a stroll? It's stopped raining.'

'I'd like that very much.'

This is what he was planning to say: 'Monsieur Marechall, I'm very sorry for what I did but, as you can see, I've brought your car back. I don't want you to think I'm some petty thief. I don't know what came over me – maybe I'm in love. Maybe I was scared, too. You have to admit you do a funny sort of job. But I do respect it, and you've always been straight with me. So if you want, I'll carry on with the job and take you back to Vals, even if you don't give me the rest of the money. You know, I just want a quiet life with Fiona and Violette, earning enough to get by. You see, I'm an honest person and I'll always have good memories of you, even if you don't want anything more to do with me. It's up to you.'

Fiona was sleeping on the back seat, or pretending to. It had been no easy matter, winning her over, but at the end of the day she had probably had enough of being shunted from pillar to post. On top of that it was raining and maybe, just maybe, she did have feelings for him, even if she had never said as much.

'He'll put a bullet through that thick head of yours.'

He had bought the car seat to console her. It was tricky to fit, with all its straps, buckles and hooks. The baby was bright red, strapped into the seat with her arms sticking out like two little wings. But she did not cry. Her big round eyes stared at the treetops, the roofs and the telegraph wires flashing past, outlined against the grey, rain-streaked sky. She had nothing against the car but preferred the beach because it was bigger and the things around her stayed still. When she grew up she would be a civil servant, with an office all to herself and everything neatly arranged. Every day would be like the day before. This dream of stability made her so happy that she pooed and wet herself all at once, and then blissfully wallowed in the warm, soft mulch.

God existed, but He did not look like the pissed-off Father Christmas character people usually imagined. For starters, He was a She, and She was black. She wore a madras cotton turban, two big hoop earrings, and a huge smile. She had created rum in her own image and the little creatures rejoiced at this revelation, breaking out in a frenzied Caribbean *biguine* around Anaïs.

She stood up almost effortlessly. Now if that wasn't a miracle! She took another good swig to buck herself up for her first steps into this brave new world. Then she screwed the lid back on tightly and placed the bottle on the draining board; that way she no longer ran the risk of confusing God with a common cleaning product. Thinking of cleaning, she frowned, taking in just how filthy her kitchen had become; two weeks' washing up was stacked in a perilous pyramid, the cooker was caked with grease and the lino stuck to the soles of her slippers.

Feeling in great shape, she armed herself with a scourer and a floor cloth and rolled up her sleeves.

The clattering of pans roused Fanny from her sleep. She rubbed her eyes. Anaïs was not on the sofa.

'Anaïs ...? What on earth are you doing?'

'The housework, obviously. Don't come in, I'm washing the floor!'

'But what about the doctor?'

'Yes, what about the doctor?'

'You were ...'

'Well, I'm not any more – I'm on top of the world! And it's not down to that stupid so-and-so, it's thanks to God. I've just seen Him, clear as I see you now. That's right, dear, it doesn't just happen at Lourdes, you know. Now listen, Fanny, I'm very grateful for everything you've done but, as you can see, I've got my work cut out here. It's getting late and I know Georges doesn't like to be on his own at night, so please, go back and keep him company.'

'Are you sure ...?'

'Positive. Off you go.'

Fanny took herself off, shaking her head, and Anaïs turned on the radio. As luck would have it, Jean Ferrat was singing 'La Montagne'.

The kitchen was now gleaming but Anaïs wasn't done yet. She tackled the bedroom next, then the sitting room. Untouched for decades, the vacuum cleaner seemed to be enjoying its own second wind, sucking up so much dust she had to change the bag three times. She saved the Negress lamp until last, polishing every nook and cranny with a soft cloth.

'Oh, Negrita, dearest Negrita! We should bow down before you!'

It was two in the morning when Anaïs finally sank back onto the sofa, basking in the glow of her hard work.

'My God, I'm hungry. I could eat a raw elephant!'

Anaïs unearthed a tin of sardines and began devouring them, mopping up the sauce with a crust of stale bread. She had patched things up with life now; the last mouthful of rum sealed the deal. Afterwards she let out a loud burp, a delicate combination of oily fish and alcohol. She scrupulously washed her plate, glass and cutlery, brushed her teeth and went to her room, put on a pair of Japanese pyjamas she had never worn before, and slipped between the clean sheets of the freshly made bed. She was not ready to sleep, not with this feeling of serenity bathing her like amniotic fluid. In the warm glow of the bedside lamp, whose shade was draped in a pink scarf, she lay with her hands behind her head and closed her eyes, smiling like a baby.

'Now all I need is a project I can get my teeth into ...'

The pavement of Boulevard du Front-de-Mer was drying in patches. The sky looked off-colour and the sea was the shade of a dodgy oyster. The wind was doing its utmost to get inside the shawl wrapped tightly around Rose's chest.

'It's almost like being back home. The weather's always like this in Belgium, even on a good day. We're used to it, but you still get sick of it sometimes. You've travelled a lot, haven't you, Simon?'

'A fair amount.'

'To hot countries?'

'Yes. You can get sick of blue sky too.'

'What are you going to do, now you're retired?'

'Nothing, like everyone else.'

'Oh, you mustn't! You need to make plans. You could come and see me in Namur?'

'Why not ...'

Yes, why not? Rose's house was bound to be cosy. He could sit warming his feet in front of the stove, flicking through an atlas in search of an imaginary island. Rose would cook him chicory *à la cassonade* or *au jambon*. And then he'd die and she would stuff him, putting glass eyes in his empty sockets to make him look alive. That was as good a plan as any. He was smiling to himself at the thought of it when a searing pain shot through him like a bolt of lightning. It took his breath away. All he could see

208

were streaks and bubbles, like film melting under the heat of a projector.

'Are you OK, Simon? ... Simon!'

Luckily since the promenade was used mainly by the elderly, there was a bench every five metres. Rose sat him down, patting his hand and cheeks and saying words he could not understand.

'I'm going to get my car. We'll go back to the bungalow and I'll call a doctor. Stay where you are, I'll be right back.'

The pain had gone, leaving nothing behind but the tail of a comet thrashing in empty space. 'I'm sitting on a bench ... I'm sitting on a bench ...' was all he managed to think.

'So what does your mother sell in her shop?'

'Uh, nothing. She's had a go at selling loads of things but it never worked out. Now she just lives there, if you can call it a life. Have you seen this? Violette loves ketchup!'

The baby was greedily suckling Bernard's sauce-covered finger.

'Well done, you've got it all over her. She looks like Dracula or something.'

The snack bar where they had stopped for sausage and chips was empty apart from the owner and a guy clinging to the bar like a mussel to its bed.

'What's the point in a shop that doesn't sell anything?'

'There isn't one.'

'What's Vals like?'

'Small. It's quite smart on one side of the Volane, with the baths, casino, hotels and gardens for the old and rich. It's completely dead across the river, where the old and skint live.'

'Sounds like paradise ... you really know how to treat a girl!'

'I never said we had to stay there. It's where my mother lives, that's all.'

'Have you never thought of doing something with the shop?'

'No, like what?'

'Well, I don't know ... But in a touristy town like that, you can always sell something. Tourists get bored, so they buy stuff.'

'Hmm ... if that was true, my mother would be a millionaire by now.'

'Maybe she just hasn't found the right thing yet.'

'Maybe.'

On the other side of the steamed-up window, cars were driving up and down the road like grey ghosts. On their plates, the few leftover crooked chips were returning to the frozen state the cook had briefly released them from, floating in a swamp of ketchup. Fiona was puffing on a cigarette and daydreaming, resting her cheek on her hand. Bernard was cradling the little monster snoring through her wrinkled-up nose.

'How big's this shop?'

'About half the size of this place, I'd say, maybe a bit smaller. And it's a bit of a mess. Well, it's falling apart.'

'But you said it's on the main road, didn't you?'

'Yes, but in the poor bit, so it might as well be a dead end. Every day except market day, it's: "Move along, nothing to see here!" Don't start getting ideas, that's what wrecked my mother's life. We can go back to Bron; there's a job waiting for me up there. The streets aren't exactly paved in gold, but it's steady money.'

'I'm not getting ideas. I'm just interested, that's all.'

'Anyway, once you've seen it you'll know exactly what I mean. Shall we get going?'

Violette agreed to be strapped in without protest, one eye open, the other shut, her lips pursed in resignation. Fiona joined Bernard in the front, which made him happy. Once he had put a bit of money aside, he would buy himself a car. Nothing as flashy as Monsieur Marechall's, but his own set of wheels all the same. He already had the child seat, which was a start. Fiona put her hand on his thigh and turned on the radio. Before setting off, they kissed like kids, their mouths tasting of warm Coke and ketchup.

'Men are always the first to go, whether they run off with a tart or kick the bucket,' thought Rose. 'Marike's right, you have to get them young, at least then you have a chance of holding on to them. Not that she has it much better herself; she's still a widow with gold-diggers sniffing around her. "Stormy weather, brightening up later on," they said on the radio this morning. Fat chance!'

She was absently plaiting together the tassels of her shawl, sitting on the edge of the bed where Simon lay fully clothed but for his shoes. He had categorically refused to let her call a doctor. A handful of pills and he had fallen asleep, ashen-faced with two great purple bags under his eyes. Rose had never been married, at first because she did not believe in it – or to avoid being ditched like her mother was – and later out of habit. It was only in the last four or five years that she had begun to think about ending her days with someone – with a man, that is. She was healthy, comfortably off, had plenty to keep herself busy, but she was unable to shake off a growing sense of sadness. She had even thought about taking out a lonely hearts ad or signing up to a dating agency, but her pride had stopped her; she wanted a real love affair, the kind that comes along when you least expect it. In a sense she was already in love, but did not yet know with whom. Then this Simon chap had turned up out of nowhere! Despite having known him only twenty-four hours, she had realised straight away he was the one. And seeing him like this now, lying stiff with his hands crossed over his stomach, his nostrils pinched and skin waxy – it was too much to take in. The tricks life plays on us ...

'Shoot, Simon! Just shoot, damn it! It hurts too much, I'm finished ...'

The weapon trembled in Simon's hand, the barrel pointing at his friend Antoine's forehead. Simon had killed men before, but on the battlefield you were never quite sure – the enemy was too far away, hidden by branches and rocks. This time it was different, standing inches away from his friend's pain-racked face.

'We're all born to die ... Shoot, please!'

Simon had shut his eyes. He was a little boy, crawling under the table where his mother was shelling peas and chatting with her friends. It was dark underneath their dresses. His finger had pulled the trigger. Not him, his finger. Ever since, each time he killed a man, he saw himself back under that table, amid a forest of grey woollen-stockinged legs.

What was Rose doing? It looked like she was knitting. Those podgy little hands ... He held out his open palm. Rose turned to him, the lashes of her owl-like eyes caked in lumpy mascara, a weak smile on her lips.

'How are you feeling?'

'So, what did he say?'

'Nothing. He didn't even seem surprised. He just looked at me.'

After dropping Fiona and Violette at their caravan, Bernard had parked the car outside Monsieur Marechall's. He was out. Bernard had immediately thought of Rose. All the way to her bungalow, he kept running over the speech he had prepared in the car. But he got muddled, jumbling his words. By the time he knocked at the door, his mind was utterly blank. Rose let him in. Her make-up was smeared, but she was smiling. Monsieur Marechall was sitting on the edge of the bed, his hands cupping a mug of hot tea. His shoelaces were undone, his skin sallow and almost translucent, the rim of his eyes the dull pink of ham that's past its best. He looked like one of those antique Chinese ivory figurines. There was no movement to his face, no trace of emotion in his expression. Bernard felt dizzy looking at him. Eventually he managed to prise his tongue from his palate and speak.

'It's me, Monsieur Marechall. I came back. I brought the car ...'

No reaction. Total silence.

'I'm sorry, I ...'

Rose came to his rescue, placing her hand on his shoulder.

'It's OK, Bernard, leave it. Simon had a funny turn earlier on, but he's a lot better now. Don't worry. Are Fiona and the baby with you?'

'Yes.'

'Good, good. Go back and see them. I'll be along in a little while.'

As he allowed himself to be ushered out, Bernard thought he saw a smile hovering over Monsieur Marechall's lips, but perhaps that was just what he wanted to see.

'He didn't say anything at all? He didn't even call you an idiot?'

'Not a word, I swear. He was just staring at me, but at the same time I'm not sure he really saw me at all.'

'He must have been seriously shaken. I once saw a guy get an electric shock while he was fixing a meter. Christ, he looked like he'd come back from the dead! What if he pops his clogs tonight, or tomorrow? What'll we do then?'

'I don't know. Let's not think about it.'

'You really hit the jackpot with that one, I'm telling you. Anyway, we're out of milk for Violette – do you want to go and get some?'

'Anaïs? You're up?'

'Of course I am. I'm not exactly going to do my shopping on all fours!'

'I heard you were ill ...'

'Well, you heard wrong. Where's the grated Gruyère?'

'At the back, in the dairy section.'

Anaïs's bulk filled the narrow aisles as she moved up and down the shelves of the Petit Casino. Her wellingtons squeaked and her umbrella dripped, leaving a snail trail on the tiled floor. She had such good memories of the previous evening's sardines that she picked up three cans, followed by pasta, rice, flour, chocolate, biscuits, peas, eggs ... Other than the three bottles of Negrita, she grabbed products at random, not even bothering to look at what she was throwing into her basket. The truth was she couldn't care less. She just wanted to fill her cupboards, as though preparing for a siege. She only stopped stuffing things into her basket when the handle began to dig into her arm. She barely managed to haul it up to the till. After putting through all her purchases, the grocer looked less than pleased to be told she would pay him tomorrow.

'Don't you believe me?'

'Yes, but—'

'Bernard's coming back this evening, or tomorrow. He'll drop by and settle the bill.'

*

It was still raining, the water glazing the road and fringing the gutters. Faceless, stooped figures scurried along, keeping close to the walls. It was this rotten weather that had made Anaïs stock up, because it was going to carry on like this for ages, perhaps even until the end of the world. It made no difference to her since she was already dead, but eternity was a long time and she needed to be ready for it.

Back home, she put down her umbrella and took off her raincoat with a sigh and swapped the oversized wellington boots for her good old slippers.

'The sky can fall in if it wants. We've got everything we need, haven't we, princess?'

The Negress lamp smiled back at her. She went into the kitchen to put away her supplies, poured herself a good glass of rum and stood back to admire the cans lined up like ornaments on the shelves.

'Now, give me one good reason why I should go out. Just one!'

She started to laugh, the same laugh as the woman on the Negrita bottle.

By now Rose was treating Bernard almost as a son, asking after Fiona and the baby. She had said, 'Simon had a funny turn earlier on,' talking as though they were all part of the same family, of which he, Simon, was the head. There was something both comical and touching about it. What on earth did they have in common? When Bernard had walked in like a great sheepish oaf, Simon could not help but see in him not a physical resemblance, but a kind of unexpected extension of himself. That was why he had looked at him without speaking. It was strange. It was as if they had all been shipwrecked and fate had thrown them together on a desert island. The situation they found themselves in was so out of the ordinary it was as if their pasts no longer existed, but had gone down with the rest of humanity. They were all flailing, naked, towards one another, each seeking some comfort, some reason for their survival.

Thinking him asleep, Rose had tiptoed out, probably to go and see Fiona and the baby. Simon was still feeling weak but he could not stay in the bungalow any longer, suffocated by Rose's cloying perfume. He needed fresh air. It was hard going, walking through the wet sand. It clung to his soles like clay. As a child, he would go out and gather potatoes from the muddy fields and come home with his feet caked in muck. Sometimes you would be in it up to your knees. Every step you took, the slippery earth sucked you in further with a disgusting slurp. In Indonesia, he had seen men sink into the swamps. Once their head had disappeared, a big bubble formed on the surface of the bog, then it burst and it was all over. It would probably be his turn to go under soon. The idea itself was not so hard to stomach; what bothered him was not knowing when or where. Until now, he had always been the one to decide such things. Except with Antoine ... He remembered it like a baptism, but the other way round. That was how he wanted to go, the way Antoine had: at the hands of a friend. Simon had been around Bernard's age at the time ...

'Did you never have kids because you couldn't, Rose?'

'No. I just never found the right man.'

'But you must have been pretty once. You're not bad-looking now!'

'Thanks. I had plenty of offers, but I didn't want to be tied down. I was anxious to keep my freedom.'

'That doesn't have to stop you! Freedom means a lot to me too. But I wanted a kid of my own. So I went with the first half-decent-looking guy who came along.'

'It was a bit different in my day. And what about Bernard?'

'It's different this time. I already have Violette, for one thing. We've only just met. We'll see. If things go well with us, maybe we'll have another one together.'

Rose was tickling Violette gently. The little girl appeared to enjoy this, smiling and gurgling. Chubby girls understand each other. Fiona draped a babygro over the radiator to dry.

'You know, Rose, don't be offended, but I was scared of you at first. You have to admit you do a funny sort of job!'

'Don't worry about it.'

'And I was scared of Monsieur Marechall too. You don't often come across people in his line of work either!'

'Thank goodness for people like him, though! Rats and rodents do all kinds of damage ...'

'Rats! Right, yes, of course ... Anyway, he's quite harmless now.'

'I'm worried about him. If you'd seen him earlier ... I really thought he ...'

'Now now, Rose, don't cry. The docs can work miracles these days.'

'Let's hope so, oh, let's ... I'm sorry, it's just this is the first time for me!'

'For what?'

'Well, love at first sight, just like in books! At my age, it's hardly likely to happen again!'

'Now come on, he's not dead, he's just old ... Look! Here he comes now, with Bernard.'

Rose rushed to the window, half smothering Violette between her breasts.

'He really shouldn't be walking about like that after what he put me through today. It's not right ...'

Bernard was shuttling the milk carton from one hand to the other, trying to appear composed, while slowing his steps to keep pace with Simon. He was sure he was going to come out with something stupid, but faced with Monsieur Marechall's inscrutable silence, he bit the bullet and blurted out, 'Monsieur Marechall, I wanted to say—'

'Don't say anything.'

'OK, I won't. But you can still count on me. I'll finish the job, just like I said.'

'We're leaving tomorrow. You and me, that's it.'

'OK, Monsieur Marechall, OK. It's just I thought that Fiona and—'

'Just you and me!'

Monsieur Marechall had stopped walking and was clutching Bernard's arm with more strength than he looked capable of:

an eagle's grip. Despite his frail state, with the wind ruffling his tufts of white goose-down hair, there was still a glint of steely determination in his eyes.

'Tomorrow, you'll take me back to the hotel in Vals, and you'll do exactly as I say, from start to finish. After that ... do what you want, I don't care.'

Simon let go of his arm and started walking again, slowly placing one foot in front of the other, head bowed, shoulders hunched.

Anaïs had spent the day eating and drinking, drinking and eating, until she made herself sick. Then, after vomiting, she started all over again, mixing cassoulet, chocolate and sardines on the same plate. Strictly speaking, all the supplies she had bought that morning were supposed to keep her going through the afterlife, but since Anaïs felt that journey might be a bit on the long side, she told herself that by devouring the lot in record time, eternity would somehow be speeded up. The logic of this was debatable, but there must have been something to it, because several hours had passed without her noticing. It was dark outside.

'Shit, eleven o'clock already! What shall I have for supper? Soup!'

The little creatures thought this a splendid idea, clapping with both hands (and sometimes even more hands than that, as some of the little monsters had four or even six of them). A nice soup for dinner, an eleven o'clock broth.

Soup is a universal dish, eaten everywhere in the world. All you need is water and anything else you can find to chuck in.

The first bottle of Negrita was empty, of course. The liquid in the second bottle came up to the chin of the woman on the label or, turned upside down, to the level of her madras cotton turban. Anaïs tipped it back and forth several times, pondering the passing of time the way others do with an hourglass. There was no question: time definitely went by more quickly in liquid form.

Anaïs poured herself a glass to celebrate her astute observation. She could have been a researcher, a great scientist like Marie Curie, with a bit of help. But no one ever had helped her. What a waste! Only the people who discovered things got rewarded for it, but, hell, you had to look for things before discovering them! The fact that liquid time passed more quickly than mineral time, that was quite a revelation, wasn't it? ... Well, it was their loss. She would keep that one to herself and it would be centuries before they understood this irrefutable natural law for themselves.

The kitchen had gradually started to look like an upturned dustbin again. The spiders were spinning webs in the corners once more; the grease-coated lino was slippery underfoot just like in the good old days, and the fluff balls had gathered again like sheep quietly grazing along the skirting boards.

'So what? You don't care about me; well, I don't care about you either.'

Standing with her legs wide apart, wobbling on her rocker soles, Anaïs filled a big stockpot with water and threw in a handful of pasta, another of rice, a tin of peas, a packet of lardons, a sprinkling of grated Gruyère, a few tears ...

'He could at least have sent me a postcard. A stupid sunset or something ...'

The little creatures moaned along with her. Anaïs chased them off with a whack of the tea towel.

'Get the hell out of here! Can't you see you're getting on my nerves? You're always under my feet! ... Now where on earth have I put the matches?'

She could not see clearly, or else she saw too clearly, as though looking through a magnifying glass. Every object appeared ridiculously large. Failing to judge distances, she kept knocking things over like skittles, until in the end she no longer dared touch anything and stood, panting and puffing like a whale, both hands flat on the table. A whistling sound came out of nowhere, boring into her eardrums, while a sickening smell turned her stomach and dulled her mind. She sank to her knees, bringing with her the oilcloth and everything on top of it.

'What a godawful mess ...'

She slumped forward, flat on her face. The life drained out of her body like oil from a drum.

'Do you think you will actually visit Rose in Belgium?'

He did not respond.

'She'll be waiting for you.'

'Better to be waiting for someone than for nothing at all.'

'The reason I'm asking is I really like Rose. I'm glad she gets on well with Fiona and Violette. It means they're not on their own any more. It's like we're a little family.'

'Will you stop going on about your "little family"?'

'Ah, come on, you say that but what about you and Rose?'

'Would you mind your own business? You'll see your girls again in two days. In the meantime, just let it drop, OK?'

'All right, Monsieur Marechall, I won't mention them again. It's just that when you're happy you want to shout about it, don't you?'

Simon refrained from making a snide comment. There was no point. Bernard wore his new-found happiness like a shining suit of armour. The stupid fool couldn't help smiling at everything: the other cars cutting him up; the leaden sky just waiting for a sign before erupting; the dingy, humdrum buildings that lined the road; the police cars lying in wait behind the plane trees. Simon could almost hear the needles clicking away inside his head, knitting together a bright little future with a little job, a little house, a little wife, a little daughter ...

'Will you stop thinking!'

'I'm not thinking, Monsieur Marechall, I'm watching the road. Drat, there are road works; there'll be traffic jams. Here comes the rain!'

Flashing signs forced the cars to slow down and get into one lane. The windscreen wipers swept the raindrops away, leaving fleeting fan shapes on the glass. Only one thing threatened to mar Bernard's constant bliss, which was the task Simon planned to entrust him with. The slowing of the traffic seemed like an invitation to test the water.

'What will you do after you go back to Fiona and the baby?'

'We're heading back up to Bron. My hand's almost better so I can go back to my job. We'll just have to find a bigger flat because my bedsit ... well, when you put the key in the door you pretty much break the window, if you see what I mean. Rents are steep in town, but we'll manage somehow. Fiona's smart, she'll find herself a little job.'

'A little job, a little flat! Never been tempted to think big?'

'Very funny ... We get by as best we can! I wasn't born with a silver spoon in my mouth. You've seen my mother ... I need to look after her as well. It won't be easy, but love gives you strength. And the other half of my pay from you will be a good start.'

'You won't get very far with that.'

'As far as Bron. Don't you worry, I only lost two fingers, I've still got both arms!'

And he smiled, just as he had when Simon first met him on the bench and he had said: 'It's only my little finger and fourth finger. I never used them.' The kid had a talent for survival, like newborn babies found alive in dustbins.

'Listen, Bernard. Apart from yesterday's escapade, which we'll pass over, I've been very pleased with you. You've always delivered, even in, shall we say ... "delicate" situations. So if you wanted—'

'No, Monsieur Marechall, I'll have to say no straight out. I like you very much, but your job, well, it's just not for me. I'm sure it pays well, and maybe I'm just a pathetic person with pathetic dreams, but at least I can look at myself in the mirror every morning and not feel ashamed. I'm not criticising you, I know deep down you're not such a bad person, but I don't want to end up sad and lonely like you. Each to his own, Monsieur Marechall, each to his own.'

'Hang on a minute, I'm not offering you a job! I was about to ask a favour.'

'Oh. What kind of favour?'

'The kind of favour you can only ask of a friend.'

The little Playmobile people were waving flags to direct the traffic. The cars gradually got back up to cruising speed.

They arrived in Vals-les-Bains late in the afternoon. It was still raining, not heavily, but persistently. Bernard found a parking space right outside the Grand Hôtel de Lyon. He was not smiling now. He kept his hands on the wheel and stared straight ahead.

'OK, Bernard, so eight o'clock tomorrow morning? Right, Bernard?'

'Yes! Eight o'clock tomorrow morning. You really are messed-up though, Monsieur Marechall.'

'Let's shake hands.'

Before getting out of the car, they both noticed the child seat still strapped to the back seat. Simon shook his head, smiling.

'Handy, those things.'

They parted on the pavement, one stepping into the hotel lobby, the other heading towards the old town. Neither looked back.

The Panda Theory

by Pascal Garnier

translated from the French by Gallic Books

He was sitting alone at the end of a bench on a deserted railway platform. Above him, a tangle of metal girders merged into the gloom. It was the station of a small Breton town on a Sunday in October – a completely nondescript town, but certainly Brittany, the interior anyway. The sea was far away, its presence unimaginable. There was nothing picturesque here. A faint odour of manure hung in the air. The clock said 17.18. Head bowed, his elbows on his knees, he examined his palms. Hands always get dirty on trains, he thought. Not dirty exactly, but sticky, especially under the nails, with that grey grime that comes from others who have touched the handles, armrests and tables before you. He raised his head again, and, as if spurred by the surrounding stillness, stood up, grabbed his bag, walked a few metres back up the platform and took the underpass to the exit. No one crossed his path.

He used his teeth to tear open the plastic wrapper of the tiny tablet of soap then washed his hands thoroughly. The washbasin had two taps, which meant that he had to switch between the freezing water from the left and the scalding water from the right. He didn't intend to look in the mirror but couldn't help catching sight of himself as if he were an anonymous passer-by in the street. The waffle towel, staple of cheap hotels, was little bigger than a handkerchief. He looked around the room as he dried his hands. A table, a chair, a bed and a wardrobe containing a pillow, a moss-green tartan blanket and three clothes hangers. All made of the same imitation wood, MDF with a rosewood veneer. He flung the towel onto the brown patterned bedspread. The room was stifling. The radiator had just two settings, on and off. He had once disposed of a litter of kittens by shutting them in a shoebox lined with cotton wool soaked in ether. The miaowing and scratching had not lasted long. His bag sat at the foot of the bed like an exhausted dog, the handles flopping by its sides, the zip tongue hanging out. He yanked the curtain back and flung open the window. Still that manure smell. A streetlamp cast a pale glow over half a dozen lock-up garages with corrugated-iron doors of the same indefinable colour. Above it all, the sky, of course.

And, of course, the bed was soft. The frosted-glass lampshade overhead, clumsily suggesting some sort of flower in bloom, failed to brighten up the room. He switched it off.

'Do you know anywhere round here to have dinner?'

'On a Sunday evening? Try the Faro. It's the second left as you go down the boulevard. I don't know if they're open though. Do you want the door code in case you come back after midnight?'

'No need. I'll be back before then.'

The receptionist was called Madeleine, or so the pendant round her neck informed him. She wasn't beautiful, but not ugly either. Somewhere between the two. And very dark-haired; there was a hint of a moustache on her upper lip.

A few dark shops, like empty fish tanks, lined the street. A car passed in one direction, two in the other. There was no one on the street. The Faro was more of a bistro than a restaurant. Apart from the owner, sitting behind the counter with a pen in his mouth, engrossed in some calculation, it was empty.

'Good evening. Are you open for dinner?'

'Not tonight.'

'Ah, well, in that case I'll have a Coke. Actually, no, a beer.'

Off his stool, the man barely measured five foot four. Stocky with bushy hair, he resembled a wild boar but with doe eyes and long curling lashes. The man pulled a beer, gave the counter an automatic wipe, and placed the drink on the bar.

'I usually do food, but not tonight.'

'Too bad.'

The owner stood awkwardly for a moment, his eyes lowered, busying himself with his cloth, and then returned abruptly to his stool behind the till.

Other than the four brass lamps illuminating the bar, the rest of the bistro was in total darkness. Probably because there weren't any other customers. You could just make out the tables and chairs and, in the back room, children's toys: a pedal tractor, building blocks, Lego, an open book, sheets of paper and scattered felt tip pens.

He didn't touch his beer. Perhaps he didn't really want it.

'Were you after food?'

'Yes.'

'My wife does the cooking. But she's in hospital.'

'I'm sorry to hear that.'

For a moment, the only sound in the bar was the fizzing of the beer's froth.

'Do you like salt cod stew?'

'Yes, I think so.'

'I was about to close. There's some left, though, if you like.'

'That sounds great.'

'Well, take a seat. No, not here, come through.'

The back room erupted suddenly in a blaze of lemon-yellow fluorescent light. The two men picked their way over the pedal tractor, the building blocks, the Lego bricks and the brightly coloured children's drawings.

'You can sit there.'

He sat down at a table covered with a daisy-patterned apple-green oilcloth, facing a huge television.

'I won't be a sec,' said the owner. Before leaving the room he pressed a button on the remote. The TV screen spewed a stream of incoherent images and gurgling sounds, like blood bubbling from a slit throat.

... BUT THE FINAL DEATH TOLL IS NOT YET KNOWN. IN NORTHERN IRELAND ...

'*Bacalao!*'

The owner placed two plates heaped with salt cod, potatoes, peppers and tomatoes on the table along with a bottle of *vinho verde*.

'*Bon appétit!*'

'Thank you.'

... THE PARENTS HAVE ISSUED A MESSAGE TO THE KIDNAPPERS. INTERVIEWED EARLIER ...

'My wife, Marie, makes it, but I'm the one who taught her. I'm Portuguese, she's Breton. All she could cook was pancakes. She still makes them. You've got to make crêpes in Brittany! Are you a Breton?'

'No.'

'I thought not.'

'Why?'

'A Breton downs his glass in one. But you haven't.'

'Is it serious?'

'What? Not being a Breton?'

'No, your wife.'

'No, it's a cyst. She's tough. She's never been ill before. I drove her to the hospital this morning. The kids are at their grandmother's. It's best for them.'

... NO ONE WAS KILLED IN THE ACCIDENT. FROM OUR CORRESPONDENT IN CAIRO, LAURENT PÉCHU ...

'How many do you have?'

'Two, a boy and a girl, Gaël and Maria, seven and five.'

... IT COULD JUST BE HUMAN ERROR ...

'How about you? Do you have any children?'

'No.'

'Are you a sailor?'

'No.'

'I only ask because of your reefer jacket.'

'It's practical.'

... AT HALF-TIME, THE SCORE WAS 3–2 ...

The salt cod hadn't been soaked for long enough. He didn't like the *vinho verde*. He would have preferred water, but there wasn't any on the table. He only had to ask. The owner would have given him some, like the beer he had not drunk. Stupid.

'Do you know Portugal?'

'I've been to Lisbon.'

'What a beautiful city! It's huge! I'm from Faro myself. It's also pretty, but smaller. I came to France in seventy seven, to Saint-Étienne, as a builder. And then ...'

... TRIUMPH AT THE OLYMPIA. LET'S HEAR WHAT THE FANS ARE SAYING ...

'... I left the building trade to open the restaurant with Marie. Would you like coffee?'

'No, thank you.'

'Okay.'

... OVERCAST BUT WITH SUNNY SPELLS IN THE LATE AFTERNOON ...

'That was very tasty. How much do I owe you?'

'Ten euros? I won't charge for the beer.'

'Thank you.'

... WONDERFUL EVENING AND STAY WITH US HERE ON CHANNEL ONE ...

'I thought I'd be eating alone tonight. I'm José by the way. And you are?'

'Gabriel. See you tomorrow.'

'Yes, tomorrow, but as long as Marie is in hospital I'm not opening the restaurant.'

'That's fine.'

'Do you have a fridge?'

'Er, yes.'

'Could you put this in it until tonight?'

'What is it?'

'Meat.'

'Of course, that will be fine.'

'Thank you.'

The hint of moustache on Madeleine's lip was effaced by her warm smile as she took the five hundred grams of boned lamb shoulder. Anyone watching would have found the scene somewhat biblical. Today, Madeleine looked beautiful.

The flimsy wire hanger was designed for summer outfits and it sagged pitifully under the weight of the wet reefer jacket. It had been raining since early morning, a light rain that was perfectly in keeping with the town and gave it a certain elegance, a veneer of respectability. Gabriel had delighted in it from the moment he had opened his eyes; it was like a kind of salutary grief, an unobtrusive companion, an intimate presence.

There were people about, mothers taking their children to school and housewives weighed down by bulging shopping baskets. Mainly women. The men were digging holes in the road and replacing the rotten, rust-eaten pipes with new grey plastic ones. They seemed to revel in making a lot of noise and wheeling their big orange diggers in and out of the pus-yellow mud. It was a typical Monday. The shops showed off their best wares with the clumsy vanity of a girl getting ready for her first dance: bread, flowers, fish, funeral urns, medicines, sports equipment, houses for rent or sale, every kind of insurance, furniture, light fittings, shoes and so on.

He had tried on a pair of shoes just because the shop assistant seemed bored all alone in her pristine shop. But he had not bought them. He had apologised, saying that he was going to think about it. Not a sale, but a glimmer of hope at least. It didn't take much to make people happy.

After that he had stopped at a café for a hot chocolate and found himself sitting next to two young men in ill-fitting suits who talked business with the seriousness of a pair of children playing at being grown-ups. From what he could gather, their problem was how to get rid of two hundred pallets of babies' bottles and as many unfortunately incompatible teats.

'Africa. It's the only way ...'

On leaving the café he had found himself outside the butcher's gazing longingly at a rolled shoulder of lamb garnished with a cute sprig of parsley. It made him think of baby Jesus.

The radiator continued to pump out a suffocating heat. He felt overcome by a kind of tropical fever. The bed morphed into a hammock and a mangrove swamp of memories closed in on him, incoherent, tangled.

There had been toys scattered about the empty house there as well.

'You can see, can't you, Gabriel, she had everything. EVERY-THING!'

His friend Roland made a sweeping gesture that encompassed the vacant space. It still smelt of fresh paint.

'You can't tell me we wouldn't have been happy here!'

Gabriel had not been able to think of a response. He had merely shaken his head. It was sadder to see it like this, virtually unlived in, than it would have been if a bomb had hit it. Nadine, Roland's wife, had left with the kids barely a week after moving in. Everything was achingly new. Most of the furniture was still wrapped in plastic.

"'I don't like chickens." That was her only explanation! Christ! She could have said earlier! I could have kept pigs. Or something else. You've seen the sheds, haven't you? They're a long way from the house. You can't smell them. Or hear them. A farm with two thousand chickens, the very best, state of the art! I'd have paid it all off in ten years! You've seen it, Gabriel; it's impressive, isn't it?'

He had seen it. Roland had shown him around. It was awful. He couldn't help but be reminded of a concentration camp. Two thousand albino chickens under ten metres of corrugated-iron roofing, fluorescent lights glaring day and night, the birds clucking and tapping their beaks like demented toys. And an appalling sickly smell, which the ambient heat only made worse. He had hurried out to stop himself from throwing up. For a long time after, his eyes burnt with the apocalyptic scene.

Roland wept softly, fists clenched, his forehead pressed up against the window.

'They delivered the frame for the swing this morning. If you only knew how many times I've dreamt of the kids playing on the swing. Their laughter ... Why didn't she tell me sooner that she didn't like chickens?'

The Loiret can be pretty in the spring. The tubular structure of the swing frame stood stiffly between two clumps of hydrangeas. Gabriel had cooked a comforting blanquette de veau *for Roland. But his friend had barely touched it. He had downed glass after glass, mumbling, 'Why? Why?' over and over again.*

Two days later he heard that Roland had hanged himself from the swing frame.

Yes, there had been toys scattered there as well ...

'Do you want your meat back?'

'Yes, please.'

'Hold on, I'll go and get it.'

239

Two large suitcases cluttered the lobby. Someone had either just arrived or was about to leave.

'Here you are. What kind of meat is it?'

'Shoulder of lamb.'

'For a roast or stew?'

'A roast – just with onions, garlic and thyme.'

'That's the way I like it as well. Are you doing the cooking?'

'Yes, it's something I enjoy. It's for some friends.'

'You'll have to cook for me one day!'

'Yes, why not?'

'Okay then. Have a nice evening and make sure you take the door code this time. Dinners always go on till late.'

'If you say so. Goodnight, Madeleine.'

'What's that?'

'A shoulder of lamb.'

'Why are you bringing me a shoulder of lamb?'

'I was thinking of cooking it for the two of us, here, tonight.'

José's eyes widened as he looked from the bloodstained parcel of meat to the unblinking expression of his customer standing at the bar.

'That's a strange idea.'

'Is it? It's just ... As I passed the butcher's this morning the meat looked good. But perhaps your wife's back from hospital?'

'No, a few more days yet.'

José seemed on edge. At the other end of the bar, two regulars had interrupted their dice game to watch them curiously.

'Do you want something to drink?'

'The usual please, a beer.'

José poured the beer then excused himself and went over to the two men by the till. They exchanged a few words in hushed voices. The men nodded their heads knowingly and resumed their game while José headed back to Gabriel, the tea towel slung over his shoulder.

'All right then.'

'Can you show me where the kitchen is?'

'Follow me.'

It was small but well equipped and very clean.

'The pots and pans are in this cupboard, the cutlery in this drawer.'

'I'll manage.'

'I'll leave you to it then.'

'No problem. It'll be ready in about half an hour. Would you prefer potatoes or beans?'

'It's up to you. Tell me, why are you doing this?'

'I don't know. It just seemed natural. You're on your own, and so am I. You don't mind, do you?'

'Not at all. It's just a bit unusual.'

The lamb had fulfilled its promise: juicy, cooked medium so it was still pink in the middle, with a crispy skin. All that was left on their plates at the end were the bits of string. The deliciously tender potato gratin had also been polished off. As he had carried the steaming, sizzling dish through from the kitchen, Gabriel had seen José sitting awkwardly at the table like an uncomfortable house guest, staring at his own puzzled reflection in the black screen of the television which he had not dared to turn on.

'Relax, make yourself at home,' Gabriel had wanted to say.

They had wolfed down their food, their grunts of satisfaction punctuated by timid smiles.

When he was full, José had leant back in his chair, his cheeks flushed.

'Now that was quite something. Bravo! You'll have to give me the recipe for Marie.'

'It's not difficult; the key thing is the quality of the ingredients.'

'Even so ... Are you a chef?'

'No, but I like cooking from time to time. I enjoy it.'

'You've got a talent for it. Do you like port, by the way? I've got some vintage, the real thing. My brother-in-law sent it to me from back home. You can't buy anything like it here. They make all kinds of rubbish out of cider or *chouchen*. Tell me what you think of this.'

The toys had gone. He had not noticed before. He felt lost all of a sudden, somehow disappointed that the scattered toys were no longer there and the television silent. He felt as though he had narrowly missed something. A train perhaps? His heart was hammering in his chest as though he had been running.

'Here you go, try this!'

José poured the syrupy ruby liquid into two small glasses. It looked like blood. From the first mouthful, Gabriel felt his insides become coated in crimson velvet.

'What do you say to a bit of fado? Have you heard any Amália Rodrigues?'

'I'm not sure.'

'She's divine! Hold on ...'

José leapt up and waddled bow-leggedly into the living room. A cassette player clicked into action and the heartrending sound of a voice dripping with tears rose through the gloom.

'It's wonderful, isn't it? I think it's the most beautiful sound in the world. Do you ever get homesick?'

'I don't know. I suppose so.'

'Where are you actually from?'

'I move around.'

'But you must have been born somewhere.'

'Naturally.'

Not getting anywhere, José poured himself another drink. 'It's none of my business really. I'm only asking because those are the kind of questions you ask when you're getting to know somebody.'

'True enough. What's she singing about?'

'The usual stuff: broken hearts, one person leaving, the other left behind. You know, life.'

'Do you miss your wife?'

'Yes. It's the first time we've been apart since we were married. I find it hard to sleep on my own. I couldn't last night. I cleaned the house from top to bottom, as if I was looking for her underneath the furniture. Stupid, isn't it?'

'No, not at all.'

'I went to see her this morning at the hospital, but she was asleep. The doctors told me the operation went well.'

'That's good.'

'Yes, only another two or three days to go. It was raining this morning. It always rains here, for days and weeks at a time.'

Amália Rodrigues fell silent and, as if to confirm what José was saying, they heard raindrops pattering on the zinc roof over the courtyard at the back.

'Have you ever thought about moving back to Portugal?'

'Yes, but Marie's a Breton. To her, Portugal is a place you go on holiday. Nothing more.'

'And what about you, here in Brittany? Is it a holiday?'

'No, it's for life. The kids were born here. You know how it is.'

A car passed by in the street, like a wave sweeping through the silence.

'You're not drinking?'

'No, thank you, I'm fine. Anyway, I'd better be off.'

'It's not that late ...'

'I get up early.'

'Ah, well. It's been good fun. Are you coming back tomorrow?'

'I think so.'

'I told my friends earlier, the ones playing dice, that you were one of Marie's cousins. It would have been complicated to explain.'

'Good idea.'

'So I'll see you tomorrow. And I'll cook!'

It was a cave, a modern-day gloomy concrete cave at the back of an underground car park. Many had lived there, some still did, leaving evidence of their squalid existence painted on the walls: smears of shit, obscene graffiti, markings daubed in wine, piss and vomit. Burst mattresses and soiled blankets were piled up like animal skins in a rotting heap, teeming with so many lice, crab lice and fleas that they appeared to be coming to life. The place stank, though it was worse outside, except that it was so cold there you didn't notice it. Simon's squatting silhouette stood out from the shadows like a figure in a Flemish painting. In front of him, meths fumes rose from an empty pea tin which was precariously balanced on a small gas stove. Wearing frayed mittens, he held the stove steady with one hand; with the other, he dangled a chicken over the flames by its neck.

'Couldn't the old bitch have given you a cooked one?'

'She was on her way out of the supermarket. She'd got two for one. It was still kind of her.'

'The road to hell is paved with good intentions. Do they think we've got all mod cons here? Pass me the wine.'

Beneath the scarf wrapped round his head, Simon's swollen eye was watering. He raised the bottle to his cracked lips and toothless mouth and took a long swig while keeping his eyes on the chicken that had started to char over the flames.

'It's burning.'

'Only the skin. We'll scrape it off. I'll turn it over.'

Simon grabbed the chicken by its feet and flipped it over, causing its comb to catch alight. He quickly blew it out.

"'Et la tête, et la tête, alouette, alouette ...'" Light me a ciggy, will you? This is going to take for ever.'

Gabriel lit a crooked Gitane and passed it over. He was starting to warm up, more because of the fire's glow than its heat. He took off his leaking trainers and rubbed his feet. He had lost nearly all feeling in them from all the walking he was doing. When there is nowhere to go you spend a lot of time on your feet. He swigged the wine and from beneath his layers of worn clothes he pulled out the crumpled pages of a newspaper that had been wrapped around his chest.

'What's the news?'

'They're going to ban cigarette smoking in public places.'

'Must have been a cigar smoker who dreamt that one up!'

You could never tell if Simon was crying or laughing. Either way, a dry cough shook him like a half-empty bag.

'Oh, it's all for our own good, isn't it? Talk about a bloody nanny state! No smoking, no drinking, no fat, no sugar, no sex. It's as if they don't want us to die. How nice of them! What else does it say?'

'An inventor has just come up with an indestructible fabric. It's cold- and heat-resistant and even bulletproof. The Vatican has ordered some for the Pope.'

'Gone off the idea of heaven, has he? He's only trying to save his own skin, like any old moron. Here, can you hold the chicken a second? My hands are full.'

The bird was now black at either end. The skin was peeling off like flecks of paint from the lead pipes in the squat they had been thrown out of three days earlier.

'Apparently lead isn't too good for you either.'

'I know! I once saw a guy riddled with it in Marseille. It took five men to carry him!'

A fresh coughing fit made Simon double over. But this time he was laughing at his joke about the lead.

'Life's a killer. Especially for the poor. To live a long and healthy life you've got to live in a villa on the Riviera and be served by a white-gloved waiter. Yeah, but the sun gives you skin cancer! Turn it over or it won't cook on that side. Shit, not like that! You're going to fuck it up ... Jesus, man, leave it, I'll do it.'

The stuffy air was thick with smoke, and the smell of alcohol, charred meat and stale cigarettes. Both of them were hunched over, like monkeys in a cage. Everything was blurred, shapeless. The men weren't men and the chicken wasn't a chicken. Nothing but rough sketches gone wrong, crumpled into a ball and thrown into this stinking hole. Simon held the bird by its head and feet as if holding the handlebars of a motorbike heading straight into the wall.

'Joan of Arc.'

'What about her?'

'She's the only woman I've ever loved.'

'What made you think of her? The chicken?'

'Maybe. Or the Pope, I don't know. I used to carry a picture of her around when I was a kid. I'd wank off over it in the toilets, looking at her in that tight, shiny armour with her tidy little page-boy haircut and her flag blowing in the wind. What I'd have given for a can-opener to get inside that ...! Pass me the bottle and I'll tell you.'

Simon finished off the bottle and started to sway to and fro with a fixed stare, his hands wrapped round his chicken handlebars, full speed ahead.

'I once went to Rouen. Not Mecca or Lourdes like some people, but Rouen. I went and begged in the square where they burnt her at the stake. It was the most dough I'd ever made in my life – people were throwing their money at me! I got absolutely trashed that night – it was insane! Later on I was having a piss up against a wall when I saw her in front of me, stark naked, smiling at me with her arms and legs wide open. She said: "It's about time, Simon!" and I screwed her. I screwed her like I've never screwed before. Up against the fucking wall. And you can believe it or not, but the wall started swelling as *if I'd knocked it up, and just when I was about to shoot my load the wall fell in on me. But it didn't hurt, not one bit. And behind the wall, behind the wall, there was—'*

Gesticulating wildly as he relived the scene, Simon's elbow smashed into the gas stove. The alcohol spilt over him and he was engulfed in flames like a living torch, while the chicken took the first flight of its short life and landed on Gabriel's knees. Simon stood howling and banging his arms against his sides as if in the throes of a laughing fit. The fire took hold of him in a dazzling display of power, like a volcanic eruption.

Gabriel froze, numbed by the wine, awestruck. Simon threw himself onto the pile of mattresses and covers and rolled about until he disappeared under a thick plume of smoke. Gabriel grabbed his bag, trainers and the chicken and ran as fast as he could. When he stopped to catch his breath by the banks of the Seine, he tore away at the half-cooked chicken and wondered what could have been behind that fucking wall.

Gabriel ripped shreds off the candyfloss and let them melt slowly in his mouth.

We should eat nothing but clouds, he thought.

In front of him a merry-go-round whirled round: as it sped up an elephant, a fire engine, a white swan and a motorbike all dissolved into a kaleidoscope of colour and bright lights, punctuated by the piercing shrieks of the children above the heady music of the barrel organ. He had never seen Simon again. Had he melted away as well? He had almost forgotten what had happened in that underground car park it was so long ago. He remembered the chicken, the taste of charcoal and raw meat. His fingers felt sticky. He didn't have a handkerchief so he wiped them on the underside of the bench. The smell of chip fat and hot sugar hung in the air. Even the rain was sweet. Nobody seemed to realise. People came and went as if the sun were out, as if they were happy. As if. It was a tiny funfair with just a merry-go-round, a tombola, a shooting gallery and a sweet stall. He had stumbled upon it after crossing the bridge that straddled the river. This was the furthest he had been in the town and he felt as though he had crossed into another town entirely. When on foot you always travel further than you expect. You only realise how far you have gone when it's time to go back. Because you always have to go back.

'Romain, sit up straight! And hold on!'

The small boy wasn't listening to his mother. Not any more.

He was laughing, on the brink of hysteria, and bouncing up and down on his elephant, which was charging furiously forward, driven by its own massive weight. It trampled everything in its path: the fire engine, the white swan, the screeching mother with her hands cupped around her mouth, the town hall, the post office, the station, the whole town. Its dreary revolving existence had driven the elephant mad. The child and the elephant were one, a single ball of pure energy, out of control, hurtling through space, destroying everything in their path without remorse. They knew that this moment of freedom would be brief and so they made the most of it. Nothing could stop them while they were in orbit. It was at moments like this that you could kill somebody. You could kill somebody over nothing at all, because nothing was stopping you and you were too high to think about humanity.

The merry-go-round slowed to a stop. It was over quickly. Gabriel stood up as he had got up from the bench at the station a few days earlier, with sticky hands.

'Five shots, five balloons, the prize is yours.'

The butt of the rifle was as cool and soft as Joan of Arc's skin. It was easy; all you had to do was empty your mind. Kept aloft by an electric fan, the five dancing coloured balloons exploded one by one. Load, aim, fire ... load, aim, fire. It was all over in less than three minutes.

'Well done. You're a fine shot, sir!'

The stall holder resembled a badly restored china doll with her cracked make-up, bottle-blonde hair with dark roots, and thick red lipstick that had smeared onto her false teeth. Her glazed eyes, which had seen too much, were as lifeless as those of the hideous toy panda which she placed on the counter.

'Your prize!'

At the sight of the black and white animal with its outstretched arms and beaming smile, Gabriel took a step back.

'No, no thank you. It's fine.'

'Go on! You've won it, you have to take it.'

'No, I ...'

'When you win something, it's yours. Give it to your children.'

'I don't have any.'

'Well, you'd better get busy! Take it, go on. What am I supposed to do with it? I'm no thief. C'mon now, stop making a fuss.'

'Well, okay then. Thank you.'

It wasn't that it was heavy – it was just difficult to carry. He didn't know how to hold it. By the ear? By the paw? Or by wrapping his arms round the whole thing? As he walked past, people turned to stare, some smiling and others laughing outright. The cuddly toy didn't care. It continued to gaze wide-eyed at its surroundings with the same fixed happy smile, regardless of which way up it was carried. And so Gabriel arrived at the Faro encumbered by his unwanted progeny. The metal shutter was pulled down, but he could see a light on inside. He knocked several times, the panda perched on his shoulders. Finally José appeared, unsteady on his feet and looking anxious.

'Oh, it's you. I forgot, I'm sorry. In you come.'

The shutter rolled up slowly with the grating sound of rusty metal. It ground to a halt halfway up, exhausted, and Gabriel had to squeeze underneath. José looked as worn-out as Gabriel.

'Is everything okay, José?'

'Not really. What's that?'

'A panda. I won it at a shooting gallery. I thought the kids might like it.'

'That's kind of you. Come on in.'

On the table in the back room the bottle of port stood next to an empty glass. Gabriel tossed the grinning panda onto a chair as José slumped on another. Though one was in a state of bliss and the other in despair, Gabriel couldn't help but notice a resemblance between the two of them. He sat down and waited silently while José covered his face with his hands, rubbing his eyes and stubbly cheeks.

'Do you want a drink? Shit, it's empty. I'll get another.'

José didn't move though. It was as if he was stuck to his chair, which was in turn welded to the floor. The room was silent except for José's laboured nasal breathing, drawn up from the depths of his chest. Beside him, the panda, like a happy guest, sat waiting for dinner. The only thing it lacked was a napkin round its neck and a knife and fork in either paw. It was exactly the same size as José.

'How's Marie?'

'Well, you know ... It's not a cyst. They don't know what it is. She was sleeping. I mean ... she's in a coma. She looks so different, all yellow, her nose all pinched, and purple around her eyes. She's got no mouth, just a small slit with a tube coming out. And all the machines in her room make noises like televisions that haven't been tuned properly. They either don't know what's wrong with her or they just won't tell me. I didn't recognise her at first. I thought I'd got the wrong room.'

His eyes filled with tears and his nose began to run. He was drowning from the inside. Gabriel lowered his head and traced the outline of a daisy on the tablecloth with his finger. She loves me, she loves me not ...

'Have you eaten?' Gabriel asked.

'No, I'm sorry, I completely forgot about you.'

'Don't worry. You need to eat something though.'

'I'm not hungry.'

'I could rustle something up. I know where everything is. Let me help.'

'If you want. Thank you for coming. I don't really know what I'm doing at the moment. There are some bottles under the sink. Let's have a drink.'

'I'll go and get you one.'

Pasta, tomatoes, tuna, onions and olives. Gabriel worked like a surgeon, his actions neat and precise. It was like being back at the shooting gallery. No need to think, just act. In the space of fifteen minutes the pasta bake was in the oven, he had laid the table and filled the glasses with wine. José had already emptied his twice and was staring mournfully at the panda.

'What kind of animal is it? A bear?'

'A panda.'

'It's big.'

'Yes.'

'The children love anything that's big. It reassures them. I didn't have the heart to go and see them after the hospital. I phoned them and said that everything was okay and that the four of us would be together again soon.'

'You did the right thing.'

'They didn't believe me. "Papa, your voice is all funny," they said. You can't hide anything from kids. They're cleverer than us. When I was a kid, I knew everything, well, most things. But now I don't understand a thing. What's the point of growing up? It's stupid.'

'I'll get the pasta.'

With his elbows on the table, José hoovered up his meal. The tomato sauce ran from the corners of his mouth, to his chin and down his neck. Like an ogre. Once finished, he pushed the empty plate away and burped, then wiped his mouth on his cuff.

'Jesus, that was good! You're hired. I'm not kidding. You're hired, seeing as Marie ...'

José thumped the table. The bottle and glasses went flying. The panda slumped on its shoulder. José grabbed the stuffed animal and threw his head back. All you could see was his uvula going up and down like a yo-yo.

'For God's sake, *why*?!'

He pounded the tablecloth with his fists. The panda rolled onto the floor. José collapsed forward, his forehead on the table, his arms dangling by his sides. His back began to shudder. Gabriel picked up the bottle and glasses.

'We had everything we needed to be happy. *Everything*.'

'I know.'

José looked up and wiped his nose on his sleeve. He was frowning, his mouth twisted in an ugly grimace.

'What do you know?'

'Pain.'

José screwed one eye shut and focused the other on Gabriel. He was dribbling. He was ugly. He was hurting.

'Who are you? I don't give a shit about your pain. Why aren't you telling me she's going to be okay, that everything is going to be fine, like it was before? Why are you looking at me with those doe eyes and not saying anything?'

'Because I don't know.'

'*You don't know?*'

Furious, José leapt up, his eyes bloodshot, and knocked the table over. The veins in his neck bulged, his muscles tensed. He stood there, shoulders hunched and fists clenched, ready to pounce. Gabriel didn't flinch.

'You don't know anything. You don't know anything at all! All you know is how to cook. Get lost. Fuck off. You and your fucking bear. Beat it. I never want to see you here again. Never, ever!'

The pavement gleamed as if covered with shiny sealskin. The night skies of cities are always yellow, rain or no rain. Gabriel picked up the panda and laid it on the lid of a dustbin. It sat there, confident, radiant, offering its open arms to whoever wanted to take it home.

'When they die, cats purr. Yes, it's true, I'm telling you! When I had to have mine put down she was purring ... Hang on a second ... Monsieur Gabriel, can I talk to you a moment?'

'Of course.'

Madeleine said her goodbyes to the Sonia on the other end of the phone and hung up. She was wearing a low-cut pink T-shirt, which emphasised her chest, especially when she leant forward. Her little nameplate necklace bounced from one breast to the other.

'Are you thinking of staying for much longer?'

'I don't know, perhaps a bit longer, yes.'

'It's just that your room is reserved for someone else from the fourth to the seventh. Would you mind changing rooms?'

'No, not at all. What day is it today?'

'Actually, it's the fourth.'

'Ah, well, in that case I'll go and get my things.'

'Thank you. The rooms are practically the same, you know.'

'It's no problem at all.'

'I'm putting you in number 22. It's on the next floor up.'

'Great. I'll go and get my bag.'

'One more thing. I wanted to ask you what you were doing today.'

'Nothing really. Why?'

'I'm off this afternoon and I wondered, well, whether you fancied going for a walk? It's not raining.'

Her cheeks flushed red. She should blush more often. It suited her.

'Is that too forward?'

'No, not at all. It's a great idea. Of course, I'd be glad to.'

'I finish at noon.'

'Perfect. I'll see you later then.'

It was the first time he had seen her outside work, in her entirety, standing up and not behind the desk. She was tall, as tall as he was, maybe even taller. It was a little intimidating. Even so, it was she who lowered her eyes and clutched her bag with the awkward charm of a young girl caught stepping out of the bath.

'Okay, shall we go?'

'After you.'

She opened the door as if about to plunge into the unknown and strode off down the road on her long legs in a sort of blind charge, the tail of her raincoat flapping in the wind. She talked as fast as she walked.

'I know a great Vietnamese restaurant, or Italian if you prefer. There's a very interesting models museum and a cinema, but I don't know what's on. It's a small town. There's not a lot to do, but it is pretty, especially by the banks of the—'

'I've got some calves' liver.'

'Sorry?' Madeleine stopped in her tracks. Her dark eyebrows arched so high they almost touched the roots of her hair.

'Calves' liver. I could cook it for you if you want. I have all the ingredients. Do you like calves' liver?'

'Yes, yes, I love it, but—'

'At your place. I could cook it there.'

Madeleine looked bewildered, as if she'd been plonked down

in the middle of nowhere at a crossroads of identical streets. She burst out laughing.

'You're quite something, aren't you! Why not? I live nearby.'

They walked side by side at a slower pace. Madeleine didn't say a word, but shot Gabriel the occasional curious glance, followed by a disbelieving shake of her head.

'You know,' Gabriel said, 'I often end up wandering around unfamiliar towns. I like it, but it's nice to have somewhere to go.'

'Do you travel around because of your work?'

'It's not exactly work – it's a service I provide.'

'What sort of service?'

'It depends.'

'And does it take you all over?'

'Yes, all over.'

'Here we are. I live on the third floor. The one with the geranium at the window.'

The stairwell was unremarkable. It was typical of a modest 1960s building, clean, with a succession of dark-red doors distinguished from one another by nameplates and colourful doormats. Madeleine Chotard's – that's what was written on the copper nameplate: M. Chotard – was in the shape of a curled-up cat.

Cats were everywhere in the two-bed flat in all sorts of varied guises: a lamp stand, wallpaper, cushions. There were figurines in wood, bronze and porcelain of cats jumping, sleeping, arching their backs, stretching ...

'The kitchen is on your left if you want to put your stuff down.'

Even more cats in the kitchen: cat salt and pepper mills, cat jugs ... Gabriel put the food on the worktop next to the hob and went back into the living room to join Madeleine. The room was small, but bright and very clean. Not a single cat's hair in sight.

'Make yourself at home. Do you want a drink before you start?'

'I'd love one.'

Being at home obviously freed Madeleine from the demeanour required at work. She was comfortable with her body, most probably sporty, natural – what's known as a fine specimen. The strip of flesh visible between the bottom of her T-shirt and the belt of her skirt when she bent over to take a bottle from the cupboard was smooth and flat, not an ounce of fat.

'I haven't got a great choice. To be honest, I hardly ever drink aperitifs – I just keep some for friends. Do you fancy a Martini?'

'Perfect!'

It was as if there were a second world underneath the smoked glass of the low coffee table, an almost aquatic parallel universe where the reflection of the hands dipping into the bowl of peanuts merged with the floral carpet.

'It's funny seeing you here,' she said.

'It was you who invited me, the other day. You suggested I cook for you.'

'I was joking.'

'Well, I took it seriously. Would you rather go to a restaurant?'

'No! It's just that it's surprising, that's all. Normally you get to know people in a public place like a café or a club ...'

'A neutral place, yes. But why do you want to get to know me?'

'I don't know. Maybe because you always look a bit sad and bored.'

'You must get a lot of people like that at the hotel, travelling salesmen, loners, people passing through ...'

'This is the first time! Don't think—'

'I didn't mean anything like that, believe me. I'm happy to be here. Are you hungry?'

'A little, yes.'

'Okay then, I'll get started.'

'Do you want me to show you ...?'

'No, it's fine, thanks. I'll manage.'

It was as he had expected. Luckily, he'd thought of everything. It was a typical singleton's kitchen. The fridge was practically bare and contained just a few fat-free yogurts, half an apple wrapped in cling film, some leftover rice, a half-frozen lettuce stuck to the back of the vegetable drawer and a jar of Nutella for those nights when she needed comfort. It was touching.

The new potatoes were soon bobbing up and down in the boiling water, the shallots slowly caramelising in the pan to which he added the two good-sized pieces of calves' liver drizzling them with balsamic vinegar and sprinkling a pinch of finely chopped parsley. The surrounding white ceramic tiles, unused to such aromas, blushed with pleasure. Madeleine's face appeared in the doorway, her nostrils twitching.

'Mmm, it smells nice.'

'You can sit down if you like. It's almost ready.'

The liver was cooked to perfection, the onions melted in the mouth and the potatoes, glistening with butter, were as soft as a spring morning.

'It's been a very long time since I've had calves' liver. I never think to buy it. It's delicious. And the shallots ...!'

I am cooking for you because I like you. I am going to feed you. We barely know each other and yet here we are, just inches apart, where together we're going to drool over, chew and swallow the meat, vegetables and bread. Our bodies are going to share the same pleasures. The same blood will flow in our veins. Your tongue will be my tongue; your belly, my belly. It's an ancient, universal, unchanging ritual.

'... and that's why she was worried.'

'Who was?'

'My grandmother, of course.'

'Ah, yes, sorry.'

'It was just a bit of anaemia. It often happens to kids who grow too quickly. I hated that.'

'What?'

'Minced horse meat cooked in stock. I just told you. Weren't you listening?'

'Yes, yes, of course. Minced horse meat cooked in stock. It's true. It can't have been that appetising for a little girl.'

'You said it. But she thought she was doing the right thing. I was very fond of her. I'll have a bit more wine, please. Thanks, that's enough! I think I'm a little bit tipsy.'

'Did she die?'

'Yes, five years ago.'

'And your cat as well?'

'Yes. How did you know?'

'I accidentally overheard you mention it on the phone this morning.'

'It's true. Last year. She was called Mitsouko, after my perfume. She lived to be fourteen.'

'And you haven't replaced her?'

'No, but I often think about it.'

'When you have your Nutella nights?'

'Nutella nights? What do you mean?'

'Nothing. I don't know why I said that.'

'Would you like coffee?'

'Yes, please.'

The flat had already changed. It was now filled with the smell of cooking, rather than the smell of nothing at all. Things had been moved around and the sofa cushions were creased. There was another person there. Madeleine must have been aware of it when she heard him moving around in the kitchen. Gabriel walked over to the window and raised the net curtain. It was a small, anonymous street, the sort of street you go down on the way to somewhere else. How many times had Madeleine

260

stood by the window cuddling her cat, waiting for something to happen down below? And how many times had she drawn the curtains without witnessing anything but the slow flowering of her picture-postcard red geranium?

'Sugar?'

'No, thanks.'

'The street isn't exactly lively, is it?'

'It's a street.'

'I sometimes think it's more of a dead end. The rent is cheap, though, and it's quiet.'

'I once lived on a street like this. One day I saw a Chinese man fall from a sixth-floor window.'

'That's awful!'

'It took me a moment to realise that it was the Chinese man from the sixth floor. He flashed past. It was a beautiful day; the window was open. I didn't see what happened, but I felt it, like a large bird or a shadow passing over. And then I heard shouts. I leant out of the window to have a look and saw something lying in the middle of the road in the shape of a swastika. There was an elderly couple across the street. The woman was screaming. All the other windows opened at once. Someone yelled, "It's the Chinese man from the sixth floor!"'

'What did you do?'

'I think I closed the window. I didn't know him that well. We'd met a few times on the stairs. A neighbour told me later that he was a bit unstable and part of a cult, something like that.'

'It must have been a weird feeling.'

'You feel a bit of a voyeur, even if it's unintentional. All day it felt as though I had something in my eye I couldn't get out, a kind of indelible subliminal image. It was quite annoying. I don't know why I'm telling you this – it's stupid.'

Gabriel regretted telling the story. The room now teemed with falling Chinese men. Madeleine was hunched over, staring into her cup, her brow furrowed. Would she ever dare open her window again? Would she let her geranium die of thirst? What if she was indeed sporty and her hobby was parachuting? He was an idiot.

'Do you do much sport, Madeleine?'

'Yes, I like swimming. I go to the pool three or four times a week. I love it. How about you?'

'Sometimes. I like swimming in lakes. It's peaceful and relaxing.'

'I'll swim anywhere, in lakes, rivers or the sea. Ever since I was little I've loved the sea. I was never scared of it. To be honest I feel more at home in the sea than on dry land. I went scuba diving in Guadeloupe a few years ago. It was incredible. Have you been to Guadeloupe?'

'Unfortunately not.'

'It's like paradise. Would you like to see some photos?'

'I'd love to!'

Madeleine's happy memories were stored in a little imitation-leather album labelled 'Holiday 2002'. She sat down next to Gabriel and opened her bible on her knees. Every photo showed white sand, coconut palms, rolling waves, a riot of flowers, a blindingly blue sky above a turquoise sea, all framing Madeleine's perfect body, sitting, lying, standing, swimming or frolicking with the clown fish. A celebration of Madeleine as God had made her.

'If you only knew how beautiful it is over there. Everything smells great, everything feels soft, everything tastes sweet ...'

'Even the sea?'

'Even the sea. Here, hold this. All I have to do is close my eyes and I'm there. Close your eyes. Can you hear the sea?'

As the album slipped onto the floor, Madeleine leant against Gabriel who shrank back into the sofa.

'I don't think it would be a good idea, Madeleine.'

'Don't you like me?'

'Yes, I do. You're very beautiful.'

'Do you think I'm a nympho?'

'Not at all. Anyway, there's nothing wrong with that.'

'Do you prefer men?'

'No, it's not that.'

'Are you ill?'

'No, not that either.'

'So why not then?'

'I don't know what to say. But what does it matter? I cooked for you.'

'So?'

'So nothing. It's just how it is. There's nothing to understand. Don't be offended. I like you a lot.'

Carefully, Gabriel extricated himself, got up and smoothed down his hair. He was as pale as a plaster saint, haggard, tired of a life that was bringing him down.

'I'm sorry. I would have liked to make you happy. Don't hold it against me; it's not your fault.'

Madeleine stared at him from the depths of the couch like a discarded rag doll, her legs and arms splayed.

'You're weird. Really weird.'

'See you tomorrow, Madeleine.'

The wardrobe took up most of the shop window. It was a beautiful piece and the owner of Obsolete Antiques must have been proud of it to display it so prominently that it overshadowed everything around it. Made of blond wood with a shiny satin finish, it was the perfect size, a classic, devoid of cumbersome ornate embellishments. Gabriel's reflection in the shop window fitted it perfectly. It was as if it had been made for him. The wardrobe's door was invitingly ajar. The perfect sarcophagus. The journey into the afterlife would be a cruise.

'Eight hundred euros you say?'

'It's solid birch. And well built. Dovetail joints. No nails or screws.'

'Edible then?'

'I'm sorry?'

'It's edible. There's no metal in it.'

'I don't understand.'

'Forget it. It's very beautiful. Thank you.'

It was a shame that Mathieu was dead. He would have liked to buy it for him. Mathieu had already eaten one, the one in which his wife had died. She had locked herself in by accident, the door closing on her, and had suffocated amongst her own furs. Mathieu had been infatuated with his wife and the grief had driven him mad. He had blamed the wardrobe and vowed to eat every last bit of it. It took him years. But bit by bit, splinter by splinter, he had eaten the entire thing. Each morning, using a penknife, he had sliced a piece off and chewed it with the single-mindedness of which only a spurned lover is capable. It had been a mahogany Louis-Philippe wardrobe. He took barely two years to finish one door.

'You know what, Gabriel, it's the fittings that are the problem. The wood itself is fine. It's the fittings that slow me down. That's what's annoying about a Louis-Philippe.'

But Mathieu's appetite for revenge eventually diminished, and even though he was loath to admit it, his hatred for the wardrobe had turned into the same all-consuming love he had felt towards his wife. He savoured the object of his resentment with a gourmet's relish.

'I boiled a corner piece in water yesterday and you know what? It tasted just like veal!'

One night Mathieu called Gabriel in tears.

'Gabriel, come over. I've finished.'

He lay on his bed, emaciated because, ever since his fatal promise, he had stopped eating anything other than mahogany, which is hardly nourishing. The only thing left of the wardrobe was the imprint of its feet on the dusty floor and the huge oblong of darker wallpaper.

'It tasted good, you know ...'

Those had been his last words. His gaunt hand, lying clenched on his chest, had unfurled like a flower and a key had fallen from his palm.

It was just about the only thing that Gabriel had kept from his former life – a key that would never open, or close, another door. He always kept it on him, deep in his pocket. It matched his body temperature: burning or freezing. He told himself that one day he would give it away or even lose it and that somebody else would find it, as that is what happened to things. They passed from person to person.

It wasn't far to the Faro, the same short distance as from Madeleine's house to the antique shop. The town was so small. The café was open. José was reading the newspaper. Behind him, wedged in a corner among some bottles, was the panda, its arms outstretched. A couple sat at one of the tables. José looked up. Because of the cigarette clamped in his mouth, you couldn't tell if he was smiling or grimacing. Perhaps both. He sighed, blinked, stubbed out his cigarette and dragged himself wearily over to the counter. He hesitated then shook Gabriel's outstretched hand, holding on to it for longer than normal.

'The usual?'

'A beer, thanks.'

José's beard had grown. Apart from the panda's determined grin, the two still looked uncannily alike.

'Well, I couldn't leave it out there for the dustmen to take away, could I? It's not doing any harm in the corner there, is it?'

'No, it's very welcoming.'

'Yes, it'll cheer up customers. It hasn't had any effect on those two though.'

José jerked his heavily stubbled chin towards the couple.

'They look half drowned. And it's not even raining.'

The man and woman sat opposite one another with their arms folded. They leant over two empty coffee cups, their foreheads nearly touching, looking like two bookends on an empty bookshelf. The man was well into his forties. His face was angular and gaunt with deep-set eyes, hollow cheeks and nostrils. His greasy hair was swept back off his face and curled on his coat collar. The woman had her back to Gabriel, but he could see a little of her face in the mirror. She looked disreputable; a dusting of white powder coated her blotches, spots and wrinkles. She resembled a cake that had been left for too long in a shop window. She seemed roughly the same age as her companion. They both had the same mouth. Fleshy, sensual blood-red bee-stung lips. They must have kissed a lot. They weren't talking. They were just watching and absorbing one another, oblivious to the world. At the man's feet sat a dented instrument case. A saxophone, perhaps?

José gave the counter a quick wipe and snapped the cloth.

'They've been here for an hour. They're not even talking to each other. Listen, I'm sorry about last night. I was drunk.'

'Don't worry about it. How's Marie?'

'The same. A green line going up and down on a screen. Oh, by the way ...' José paused.

'What?'

'I'm going to see the kids tomorrow. Do you want to come along with me? I don't feel like going on my own.'

'Of course, I'd be happy to.'

'Thanks. I don't know what to say to them. They're only little. I should buy them a present as well ... excuse me. Yes, what can I get you?'

The man was sitting up, his hand raised like a schoolchild's.

'Do you have any peanuts?'

'No, I don't.'

'Oh ... shame.'

Gabriel took a packet out of his pocket. He had bought two bags from a corner shop after leaving Madeleine's flat. The peanuts he'd had at hers had given him a taste for them. You should always carry a packet of peanuts around with you.

'I've got some. Here.'

'That's kind, thanks. How much do I owe you?'

'Nothing.'

'No, really, come on.'

'I've got some more, it's fine. What's in your case?'

'A saxophone.'

'Do you play?'

'No. I'm selling it.'

'Can I have a look?'

'Of course.'

The man's hands were very long and thin, like two big white spiders. His dirty fingernails fumbled at the clasp. Inside, coiled like a snake on dark-red velvet, gleaming under the bar's lights, lay an engraved golden saxophone.

'It's a Selmer. A real one!' said the man.

'How much do you want for it?'

'Five hundred? Four fifty? Four hundred?'

'Five hundred then. I'll take it.'

The couple stared at Gabriel as he opened his wallet and spread the notes out on the table.

'There you go. Five hundred. Good evening.'

The man's Adam's apple rippled up and down his neck. He gulped like a fish out of water.

'It used to belong to my father. You've got a good deal.'

'I wouldn't know. I'm no expert.'

Gabriel went back to the bar and placed the small coffin on the counter. Behind him, out of view, the couple grasped each other's hands, basking in their good fortune. José, his elbow on the counter and the tea towel on his shoulder, rubbed his cheeks.

'Can you play the saxophone?'

'No. Do you think your children would like it?'

José didn't answer. He lit a cigarette and took a few short puffs, squinting through the smoke.

'Maybe you're just mad?'

No matter how hard he tried, his key wouldn't turn in the lock. Through the door he heard hurrying footsteps. 'Who is it?'

Gabriel took a step back. Room 12.

'Sorry, I ...'

As the door opened, the man from the café was revealed, silhouetted against a yellow glow.

'Oh, it's you! Have you changed your mind about the saxophone?'

'No, no. It's just that this used to be my room. It was habit. I made a mistake, I'm sorry.'

The man stood there in his underpants, dishevelled, a cigarette hanging from his mouth. He seemed confused by Gabriel's presence. The corridor's timer light clicked off.

'Which room are you in?' the man asked.

'Number 22 on the next floor. I'm sorry—'

'Do you want a drink?'

'No, I'm fine, thanks.'

'Come on in. We owe you one. Rita? It's the man from the café, the one who bought the saxophone. He's in the same hotel as us.' The man leant forward towards Gabriel. 'She's a bit of all right, isn't she?'

The room, his room, stank of alcohol, cigarettes and medication. The window was closed and the radiator was on full. The woman sprawled on the bed wearing very little, her legs spread and her hands behind her head, shamelessly showing off her hairy armpits. She resembled a piece of meat lying on a cloth ready to be sliced up, Gabriel thought. Sleepily, the woman looked up at Gabriel. She seemed almost as bleary-eyed as her partner.

'Well, shit, it's a small world, isn't it?' she said. 'Sit down. We don't do standing up.'

Gabriel sat down at the foot of the bed on the room's only chair while the man poured him a mouthful of gin in a toothglass.

'Apparently, when you drink from someone else's glass you see their thoughts. Bad luck for you!'

'Thank you.'

The man rejoined the woman on the bed, his back propped against the wall. He was obviously not used to making pleasantries, but he said, 'It's not everyone who would do what you did! You really got us out of a hole, you know.'

'No, I didn't know. But I'm happy to have been of some help.'

'We were broke.'

'It happens sometimes.'

'More often than we'd like! What brings you here? Are you passing through?'

'Yes.'

'Lucky you. I spent my entire childhood here. The only good thing about this shitty town is it encourages you to move on as soon as possible!'

'But you're back.'

'Forced to come back. My father. Family stuff. Money, you know.'

The man emptied his glass and handed it to Rita, who, with what looked like a huge effort, extricated herself with a sigh from the tangle of sheets and went to fill it up again. Her hip brushed Gabriel's shoulder on her way past. It was she who gave off that smell of medication, sweat and disease. She drank half the glass and then slumped back down next to the man. She kept scratching herself, on her nose and her arms. Her nails left long red scratch marks on her pale skin. Gabriel felt as though he was on a hospital visit. Just to be polite, he took a tiny sip of gin. It was lukewarm and tasted medicinal. He set it down on the table and tried to work out the best way to leave as soon as possible. But the man started up again, more for his sake than his visitor's.

'A sodding saxophone. That's all I could get out of the old bastard. This time I really thought he was done for, no fucking chance though! He's like a tick hanging on to his shitty life. A bag of decaying organs, that's all he is. But with a heart like a Swiss watch, indestructible. Tick tock, tick tock. The old fucker. He knows full well I'm up to my neck in shit and that all he has to do is sign a rotten piece of paper to get me out of it. But no! He enjoys having me on a leash like this. It's the only thing which gives him a hard-on,' the man said. 'Do you have any family?'

'No.'

'Well, you don't know how lucky you are! All my life, he's been a pain in the neck! You can smell how this town stinks, but, I tell you, it's not the manure, it's him! Yeah, him! Jesus Christ, I'm not going to settle for just the sax! No way! I don't know what the hell it was doing there. I'd never seen it before. It was in front of the door next to the umbrella stand. So I just took it. Sometimes you do things without knowing why. So as not to leave with nothing ...'

Somewhere in the far distance a clock struck eleven, the noise muffled by the dark of the night. Gabriel stood up.

'Well, it's late. I'll be on my way. Thanks for the drink.'

'I'll see you out.'

Before opening the door, the man whispered to Gabriel, 'What do you think of Rita?'

'Well, uh ... I hardly know her.'

'Physically?'

'She's, erm, well endowed.'

'Well endowed?'

'Attractive then.'

'Because I could always ... if you want ... I could go for a wander. You know what I'm saying?'

'That's kind but no. I'm up early tomorrow.'

'Ah, another time then perhaps?'

'Perhaps. Goodnight.'

José's car smelt of wet blankets, grease and stale cigarettes. As Gabriel got in, José asked him to ignore the mess; he meant the used tissues, crumpled sweet wrappers, oily rags, old chewed pens, screws, bolts, springs, the greying remains of the stuffed toy rabbit and the set of tattered road maps.

'I haven't had time.'

With every jolt, the saxophone on the back seat knocked against a big gift-wrapped box. On either side of the road, fields of mud stretched towards the hazy horizon. The landscape felt unreal. Did Gabriel believe in it? Even the presence of a few crows failed to convince him. Gabriel had felt this way all morning. He had gone through the motions, but felt nothing. Madeleine had been in her usual place, behind reception, encased in a tight-fitting grey suit, like soft armour. She had said 'good morning', asked him if he had slept well, if he liked his new room, without ever referring to the previous afternoon. They had wished each other a good day. The pavement under his feet might as well have been a rolling walkway transporting him from his hotel to the Faro. José had shaved, combed his hair and put on a clean shirt.

'What's in the box?'

'A little kitchen on wheels for Maria. Where did you eat last night?'

'Nowhere. I went for a walk and had a few peanuts before going back to the hotel. How about you?'

'I wasn't hungry. I watched TV.'

'Watch anything good?'

'I don't know. I can't remember. I went and slept in the children's bedroom. I can't sleep in our room any more.'

'Any news from the hospital?'

'No. I'll call later. It's good that you're here. I have to speak to Marie's mother, Françoise. Would you look after the kids while I talk to her?'

'Of course.'

'She's a good woman, Françoise. And brave. She lost her husband just before Marie was born. She's always managed by herself.'

Françoise stood on her doorstep flanked by the two children. Had they been replaced by weapons then she would have made a magnificent war memorial: a Grandmother Courage draped in a charcoal-grey shawl, her chin raised high, her wiry hair tamed in a tight bun and her steely eyes challenging the futility of the human condition. How long had they been standing there in front of the door? The children timidly returned José's wave as he parked the car in front of the gate.

Everything here was strangely symmetrical. Identical squares of lawn lay either side of the gravelled driveway next to identical fruit trees and identical hydrangea bushes, which grew in front of identical grey-green stone walls. You could have folded the scene in half along a vertical line starting at the point of the roof and everything on the left would have corresponded exactly with everything on the right, square of lawn on square of lawn, tree on tree, hydrangea bush on hydrangea bush, brother on sister, half of the grandmother on the other half. The grandmother now opened her hands and released the children, who ran over and wrapped themselves round their father's legs. Gabriel followed behind, smiling at the scene – the daddy bear playing with his cubs.

'All right now, kids, careful!'

'Papa, Papa! Presents!'

Gaël, a stocky little creature with curly black hair, took after his father, while Maria, with her blonde hair, pale skin and her grandmother's bright blue eyes, had obviously inherited her looks from the maternal side. They were handsome children, clean and fresh and full of life.

'Presents! Presents!'

'Say hello to my friend Gabriel first.'

The two children went over to Gabriel and planted sugary kisses on his cheeks before falling on the presents.

'Françoise, this is my friend Gabriel.'

A firm but welcoming handshake. She had instantly assessed her son-in-law's friend. She seemed satisfied.

'Your garden is beautiful,' Gabriel said.

'It never looks its best at this time of year. It's just work, that's all. It grows all the time, especially the weeds. Come in.'

Despite her slightly brusque response, Françoise didn't mean to be unfriendly. Order and discipline were what kept her going. It was the only thing she had found to support her through a life punctuated by hurt and suffering. She wore her resignation as a retired soldier wears his medals. A brave, worthy woman, she didn't ask anything of anybody.

Roast chicken, mashed potato and an apple tart. A simple and filling meal. Throughout lunch, José did his best to appear cheerful in front of the children, but each time one of them mentioned their mother his fork trembled in his hand, and his eyes, red through lack of sleep, would appeal to Françoise and Gabriel for help.

'Okay, children. I have to speak to your grandmother. Gabriel, if you wouldn't mind ...'

It was ages since he had spent time with children. He had

forgotten how to speak to them. He felt awkward and clumsy, oversized ... Like poor old Gulliver.

'Can you show us how to play the saxophone?'

'I think you have to blow into it and press the keys.'

Gabriel took a deep breath and blew into the saxophone, but only managed a sound like breaking wind, which sent the children into fits of giggles.

'You farted! You farted!'

They all had a go on the instrument. Gaël blew with all his might, turning bright red, but with little success. Maria, on the other hand, managed to produce three clean notes on her first go. Gaël and Gabriel couldn't believe it and were a little put out.

'I didn't know I could play! It's easy!'

She started again. Once, twice, three times. She was good. Her brother's mood darkened.

'Okay, that's enough!' he said. 'You're playing the same thing over and over. Shall we play with the kitchen now?'

Children's disagreements, unlike those between adults, were always over in a flash. The brother and sister were soon happy organising a tea party. Gaël seemed to take a real interest, sorting out all the pieces and putting them in their proper place.

'Right, what are we going to cook?'

'Snails!'

'Okay then. Gabriel, you sit there. You're the customer. What would you like to eat?'

'Snails, please. And then a steak and chips!'

'We've run out. But we've got chicken with noodles and Gruyère.'

'That'll do nicely.'

Juliette had been the same age. Gabriel had bought a live lobster and was preparing to grill it on the barbecue. His daughter peered at the crustacean waving its pincers and wiggling its tail in the smoky air, her chin just level with the table. She looked like an elf with her little upturned nose, cherry-red mouth and almond green eyes hidden behind strands of sun-kissed and sea-sprayed hair. Both of them were in their swimsuits. It was hot, very hot. The terrace shimmered in the heat.

'Are we going to eat it?'

'Yes, it's very good.'

'It's moving.'

'When it's cooked, it'll stop moving. Careful now, I have to cut it in two.'

'Will it hurt?'

'No. It'll be so quick that it won't feel a thing.'

'How do you know?'

'I just do. Watch out now.'

He split the lobster lengthwise with a sharp decisive crack. Thick liquid trickled from the white flesh onto the chopping board. The lobster's pincers stayed open as if seizing the moment. Juliette had watched the whole thing. Clinging to the table with both hands, she hadn't blinked.

'Well done!'

And then she had danced round the hot white terrace singing at the top of her voice, 'Well done, well done, well done!'

He had given her the biggest piece.

'Here are your snails, sir. Watch out, they're hot.'

Gabriel pretended to taste the blobs of playdough on the small yellow plate handed to him by Gaël.

'Mmm, they're delicious! My compliments to the chef!'

'That's me, not her.'

'Well done to you both.'

Gaël shifted from foot to foot with a tea towel over his shoulder. He looked just like his father behind the counter at the Faro. He sat down cross-legged in front of Gabriel and looked

277

him straight in the eyes.

'Why do we only eat dead things?'

'Because ... because they cook better.'

'So when Maman dies, are we going to cook her?'

Maria had picked up the saxophone again. A fourth note rose from under her fingers. She looked astonished.

'What are you talking about, Gaël?'

'Nothing. I just wanted to know. Do you want your chicken now?'

'The doctor told me he was going to try something. I didn't really understand what. Apparently, it sometimes works.'

José unthinkingly tapped the image of the Virgin Mary stuck to the dashboard, as others might touch wood. The windscreen wipers did their job, but without enthusiasm. Here it was always the rain that won.

'Your kids are very nice.'

'Yes, they're very nice. And Françoise too. And you. And Marie. Jesus! Why!'

José smashed his fist against the steering wheel. The car swerved. A red lorry coming the other way veered out of their path in a cacophony of beeping. José pulled over and collapsed over the steering wheel, his back shaking with sobs. A tidal wave of tears. What could mop up so much sorrow? Gabriel put his hand on José's shoulder. It was all he could do. He thought back to the red lorry that had been heading straight for them. He hadn't been scared. He was ready. He had been ready for a long time.

'I'm sorry, Gabriel. I almost ran us off the road back there.'

'It's okay. It's okay.'

We've already spun off the road, floundering and sinking, endlessly bailing out water.

'Would you like me to drive?'

'Yes, please. I'm a wreck.'

The town unfolded before them through the rain like a Japanese paper flower. It shone, unfurling into the most unlikely shapes, spreading out like an ink stain on a sheet of blotting paper.

For the panda everything was for the best in the best of all possible worlds. It was as happy to see the two men return as it had been to see them leave. It's only trick was to keep its arms open. It held nothing and retained nothing. Take it or leave it, it was all the same to him.

'I don't think I'm going to open.'

'Best not. Anyway, it's already late. Do you want me to make you something to eat?'

'No.'

'How about a little soup? Something small. You could have it in front of the TV.'

'Okay then.'

Leek and potato soup was the best thing for any man who was close to the edge.

'All you have to do is heat it up. I've put some butter in it.'

'Thank you.'

On the television, two football teams, the reds and the blues, battled it out. José had sunk so low on the couch he had become part of it.

'Who are you supporting?'

'I don't care. Whoever's winning.'

'Do you want me to stay?'

'No. I'd rather be by myself. Don't be offended.'

'Of course not. I understand. I'll see you tomorrow.'

'Yes, tomorrow.' Gabriel shook José's hand. It weighed the same as a large steak.

'I was afraid you'd left.'

'I was about to.' Madeleine looked exactly as she had done that morning, as though she had spent all day under glass, waiting for evening to come.

'What are you doing tonight? Would you like to go for a bite to eat?'

'Where? At mine?'

'No, I haven't had the time to ... What about the Chinese? Or the Italian?'

'Let's try the Chinese.'

They unconsciously fell into step together, arm in arm, left, right, left, right. They looked like an old couple. The rain fell like musical notes onto Madeleine's umbrella.

'How was your day?' she asked.

'Very strange. Do you like children?'

'Of course, well, you know, like everyone does. Why do you ask?'

'I was playing with some children today, a little boy and girl. They reminded me of stowaways on a ship. They make the most of their size and stay out of sight, but I think they want to take us over. They're clever, so very clever! When you play with them, you unwittingly collude in your own downfall. They want to take our place. I saw them the other day at the fair with their elephants, trampling everything in their way.'

'Gabriel! You can't say that! You were that age once as well.'

'But not like them. I never picked up a saxophone and played it just like that when I was five.'

'I don't understand.'

'It doesn't matter. Sorry. Ah, is this it?'

Chinese restaurants in provincial towns are always empty. The Golden Lotus was no different. There were funny rumours about what they put in their food. There were so many spelling mistakes on the menu that they used numbers to help identify what was what. Gabriel put his money on numbers 4, 22 and 16 while Madeleine went for 5, 27 and 12. The Chinese are gamblers by nature, and smile for a living.

'Tea or rosé?'

'Let's have both.'

Behind Madeleine, an illuminated waterfall flowed freely between two fluorescent pagodas to striking effect. A voice, thick with a sweet and sour accent, belonging to someone in the back of the restaurant, made Gabriel want to wave a fly swatter about. It made him think of that well-worn line from adventure films: 'It's too quiet – something's up.' Madeleine leant over the table, her chin cupped in her hand.

'It was nice of you to take me out.'

'Making you happy makes me happy. How was your day?'

'One more. Or one less. Depending on your viewpoint.'

'After I left yesterday, I wondered why you don't look for work in Guadeloupe. I'm sure there's no lack of hotels over there. And what with your experience ...'

'I've thought about it. I know I could find something. It's just that I was there on holiday. And I always want to be on holiday.'

'You'd only get bored.'

'I don't think so. Some people always need to be doing something. Not me. I just want to be.'

'Like pandas.'

'Sorry?'

'I said pandas, but I might as well have said lizards, or anything.'

'Exactly. I know I'm not that intelligent. You've seen, the few books I own are just there to fill the space. It doesn't bother me. I could spend whole days lying on a beach in the sun and not thinking of anything, not even dreaming or making the effort to live. I'm a big lazy so and so.'

When she laughed, you wanted to climb inside her mouth and never get out.

'How is your Peking duck?'

'A bit dry, but it's okay.'

The usual cup of rice wine, on the house, with a pair of buttocks painted on the bottom, rounded the dinner off. No other customers had come in. It was like being at home, just the two of them. They could have grabbed each other, there and then, on the dirty tablecloth covered in soy and chilli sauce stains and gone at it. The staff wouldn't have minded. Madeleine would certainly have been keen. There, on the table. Without thinking. Without dreaming. Without making the effort to live ...

'Would you like me to walk you home?'

The rain had stopped, exhausted. The sky was completely drained. A few streetlights stood sleeping like blind sentries.

'Here we are then. See you tomorrow, Madeleine.'

'You're a tease!' she said as her mouth crushed Gabriel's.

Building C, stairwell 3, the rubbish storeroom. It was there, in the creeping darkness, that big Babeth introduced generations of kids to their first French kiss. Her tongue plunged into Gabriel's mouth with demonic force. It wrapped around his tongue like the boa constrictor that had captured Tarzan in the comic he had read the day before. It wasn't a tongue but an enormous muscle, a tensed, turning bicep which filled his mouth, burrowing ever deeper and suffocating him.

The only way out was to bite down on the piece of wriggling meat.
Babeth howled out in pain, throwing punches and pulling his hair.
He let go and ran off through the dark labyrinthine cellars, the taste
of blood in his mouth, the beast screaming insults and spitting curses
from deep within her lair. Two of his friends were waiting their turn
at the top of the stairs.

'Well, how was ... Fuck! You're covered in blood!'

The three of them ran off as fast as their legs could carry them.
Gabriel was twelve.

'I'm sorry, Madeleine. I'd rather not.'

'Am I so disgusting?'

In the glow of a streetlight Madeleine's face began to dissolve
in a whirlpool of doubt. Gabriel hugged her and patted her
gently on the shoulder. He had done the same for José after the
experience with the red lorry.

'Not at all, Madeleine. I promise you. You're very desirable.
It's just that I'd rather not.'

Like José, she was sobbing. Then, suddenly pulling away
from him, she spat out the word 'Arsehole' before slamming the
door in his face.

Gabriel thought that when the world ended it wouldn't make a
sound. A little moan, at most.

'"You're not leaving the table until you finish your food!" I didn't like soup so what did he expect? I didn't care – I had all the time in the world. I would've waited there until my plate was full of maggots. An hour later, he chucked me out. I was left out on the doorstep with my plate on my knees, all because he needed the table for his stupid jigsaw puzzles. The local cats all knew the routine. In five minutes my plate was empty and I was allowed back in. In, out, in, out ... That's what I've done all my life, always between two doors. But now he's gone for good I don't know what side I'm on. You know, Gabriel, it's a strange feeling. It's as if I've nowhere to go, as if I have to get out myself. Rita! You're making a pig of yourself. This isn't some dump, you know.'

It was the most expensive restaurant in town. Two stars and on the cusp of a third. Opulent. Someone had knocked on Gabriel's door that morning. It was the saxophone guy, Marc, with a smile that stretched from ear to ear.

'That's it! He's dead, stone-cold dead! We've won the lottery! Rita and I want to take you out for a meal, to pay you back for the peanuts.'

His father had passed away during the night. He had fallen out of bed – a bit surprising according to the nurse, who said the old man hadn't been able to move in ages. But considering the amount of medicine they shovelled into old people these days, anything was possible. The solicitor had called Marc at 8 a.m.

'And that's not all! With the house and garden in the middle of town alone I've got enough to last me two, maybe three, lifetimes. But the old bastard had investments all over the place too! I'm seeing the solicitor about everything later. Rita, don't you think two plates of snails as a starter are enough?'

Gabriel had only eaten one portion. The food was excellent, especially the chopped morels. His breath heavy with alcohol, Marc whispered in Gabriel's ear, 'I'm doing a runner tonight. I can't have her cramping my new lifestyle.'

Rita smiled at him as she wiped her plate clean with a large hunk of bread. She certainly hadn't heard Marc, but she was no fool and she didn't care. They loved each other, or, rather, the complicity that had united them had over time come to resemble love. They could kill each other and not hold it against each other. That's life though, isn't it? As a result of travelling in the same carriage stinking of feet, you manage to find your little corner of intimacy; you understand each other. You get used to each other's smells and tricky ways; you take on the habits of the other. Familiarity is everything, no need to think or choose; you feel as at ease with the other person as you do with yourself. The tatty old slippers, the bed hair, the hair left in the comb, scenes from life which surprise us each morning. Yes, it isn't always a pretty sight looking in the mirror. It's true that there are days when you just want to smash it, but you don't because, if you did, you'd be left staring at the wall, and the wall is even uglier than you are.

'How are your sweetbreads?' asked Marc.

'Delicious!'

'I can't stand offal. It smells too much of insides and the thing with insides—'

'Insides?'

'You don't know what's in them. So when are you leaving?'

'I don't know. It depends which way the wind's blowing.'

Marc frowned, taken aback, trying to fathom the hidden meaning in Gabriel's ambiguous response. Unable to find it, he shrugged his shoulders, emptied his glass and held the bottle up to the maître d'.

'Another,' he shouted.

Rita was playing with her napkin, having polished off her stuffed quail.

'I used to be able to fold all sort of things, like fans or cones. It's weird – I can't do it any more. I think it's the wrong kind of material.'

'Come off it!' Marc laughed. 'The material? Why don't you go and wash your hands and mouth. It looks like a dog's arse.'

Rita didn't know whether to laugh or cry as she looked at Marc with her cowlike eyes. She picked up the napkin, folding it into a small triangle, and held it under her nose, humming 'How Much is that Doggie in the Window'. She stood up, knocking over her chair, which a waiter rushed to pick up.

'You're right, Marco. I need to go and powder my nose.'

Rita zigzagged unsteadily between the tables towards the door that led to the toilets. Marc pulled two huge cigars out of his pocket and offered one to Gabriel, who declined. He bit the end off one and spat it onto his plate. He didn't know how to blow smoke rings, only shapeless clouds.

'What are you going to do now that you're rich?' asked Gabriel.

'Lounge about like a rich person! I've lived enough as a poor person. It won't make much of a difference, except that I'll be able to eat when I'm hungry and be warm when it's cold. You have to make use of what you've got, don't you?'

'Absolutely.'

'The only thing I'll miss, to start with, will be Rita.'

'So why leave her?'

'That's the way it is. The poor with the poor, the rich with the rich. Otherwise, what would happen? Everyone has to stick to their own kind as my dad used to say. It's not my fault if I'm now rich! This cigar is disgusting. It must be as old as Methuselah; it's as ancient and dry as his heart. You know what he used to do?'

'No, what?'

'He used to get a hard-on when they bathed him. A hard-on! The old bastard! Standing to attention! No joke. Crazy, eh ...!'

Rita was coming towards them, her face plastered with make-up. She looked like something out of a Greek tragedy. She was trembling from head to toe.

'Marco, I don't feel very well. I want to go back to the hotel.'

It was Marc's turn to go white. He got up, leaving a handful of notes on the table, and took Rita by the shoulder.

'Stupid bitch. Not here, shit, not here. Hold it together. Sorry about this, Gabriel. We'll see you later.'

On the walls of the church, the saints sagged. They looked unwell – haggard, gaunt, unshaven with greasy hair, overburdened, their eyes heavy with mystical worry. Even the haloes which glowed above their heads failed to brighten them up. They were exhausted. Evidently, the Last Supper menu hadn't been that appealing. That was why, no doubt, they were all eyeing up the baby Jesus resting in the arms of the Virgin Mary like a suckling pig, plump and sweetie pink. 'This is my body ...' You shouldn't tempt the devil that lurks at the bottom of your stomach. The smell of incense that permeated these places was reminiscent of the smell of meat that clings to bad Greek restaurants. With a little more effort, the pale light glinting through the stained glass could have brought a psychedelic touch to the emptiness, but it was happy to go where directed. It shone like a little celestial pee-pee. After Marc and Rita had left the restaurant in a hurry, Gabriel had gone off in search of somewhere to digest his food in peace. He had thought about going to the cinema and taking a seat in the dark, but the problem with the cinema was that the films were usually quite loud, with stories which were more annoying than real life. The church seemed like a better idea. The straw-seated chairs were perhaps a little less comfortable than those in a cinema but entry was free and he wouldn't have to put up with any popcorn eaters.

He must have nodded off for a bit because when he opened his eyes again he became aware of an elderly woman sitting next to him grinding her badly fitting dentures between her thin lips. The impression was of an elderly bird that had fallen out of a nest, its beak flattened by an unsuccessful landing. An impression heightened by thinning blue-rinsed hair rising in a quiff above a wrinkled forehead, a protruding chin, prominent cheekbones and a neck with folds of soft skin over an unswallowable Adam's apple.

'You were snoring,' the old woman said.

'Forgive me.'

'That's not up to me. It's up to the Lord God Almighty,' she said. 'You know what?'

'What?'

'My dog was poisoned this morning.'

'Your dog?'

'That's what I said.'

'I'm sorry.'

'I've just lodged a complaint at the police station because I know who did it!'

'That's the right thing to do.'

'Between you and me, I didn't really like the dog. I only went to the police on principle.'

'I see.'

'He was horrible. He barked all the time and was bad-tempered as well! He belonged to my former husband, a real mongrel.'

The old woman hadn't yet turned to look at Gabriel. She kept her gaze fixed straight ahead on the altar, munching on her false teeth, gripping the handbag that sat on her bony knees.

'It was a black and white mongrel called Georges. They used to go hunting and fishing together.'

'Your dog was called Georges?'

'Yes, like my husband. It was his idea. "That way, if I get lost," he said, "all I have to do is call out my own name!" It used to make him laugh. He died a nasty death.'

'Your husband?'

'No, the dog. It wasn't a pretty sight, believe me. It was terrible. My husband's death was much quicker. He decapitated himself with his chainsaw when he was out pruning the cherry trees. He didn't suffer. Well, that's what the doctor said. But what does he know? He's never been decapitated!'

'And your dog?'

'Poisoned meat. Rat poison. You know, those little red pellets. His vomit was full of them.'

'That's terrible.'

'Yes, terrible. His eyes bulged and his tongue was hanging out as if trying to escape his mouth. Animals are stupid, especially dogs. Perhaps it's the effect of the people they spend time with. They only think of themselves. They're not like us, they don't have a soul.'

With a crooked finger, she made the sign of the cross so rapidly it looked like an aeroplane propeller.

'Are you waiting for Father Mauro?'

'No.'

'He's always late. He's a drinker.'

'Ah.'

'Yes, he's a drinker. And he masturbates in front of St Rita as well. I've seen him do it. Everyone has their flaws, I suppose.'

'That's true.'

'I've only come for confession. I've got an appointment at the hairdresser's at four o'clock and it's already twenty to. I won't be long. I've just got to tell him that I was the one who killed Georges but that I've blamed it on my neighbour. Speak of the devil, here he is now ... Have a nice day.'

'And you.'

The old lady got up and scurried shakily down the aisle to meet a jovial-looking priest of the sort you'd find on a cheese packet. God had no need to worry, business was good.

The street swarmed with extras but there was no audience, or director. And there was probably no script either. Everybody wandered around without aim or purpose, hesitant and unable to find their place. Perhaps that was the intention. It wasn't unusual to bump into the same person in different parts of the town; grim-faced, lost in thought and waiting, in the absence of a revelation, for some sort of sign. The entire town seemed on standby. The sky was equally unsettled, with threatening clouds, light rain and intermittent flashes of lightning. Swarms of minuscule gnats, impervious to swiping hands, buzzed overhead. Nothing made sense. If being alive was just a hobby then how could you be sure that there would be a tomorrow? Just as there was no guarantee there had been a yesterday. It was a day to kill someone for no reason.

Gabriel had bought himself a frying pan, a pot and a camping stove. He was going to eat alone in his hotel room tonight. Ham, mashed potato and chestnut purée. He'd had enough of them. He didn't want to see them or listen to their whining. And yet, without realising, he found himself in front of the Faro. The bar was crowded, like a teeming fish tank. Noticing him outside, José waved his cloth in Gabriel's direction, inviting him inside. Now the panda and José looked so alike it was hard to distinguish them; they both grinned like Cheshire cats. As Gabriel didn't move, José dashed out from behind the counter and opened the door wide.

'What on earth are you doing? Come on in!'

'It's fine, I—'

'She's opened her eyes, Gabriel! She spoke to me!'

'What did she say?'

'Joke.'

'Joke?'

'Joke, or poke, or folk, I didn't really understand. She wasn't quite with it but she said it three times, with her eyes wide open! The doctors were completely baffled. Come on in! You know, Gabriel, you and me. Now it's going to be ...'

José crossed his fingers; his eyes welled up with tears. He slapped Gabriel on the shoulder and pushed him inside. Where had this spontaneous generation of carefree youth who laughed, sang, told jokes and emptied glass after glass come from? All it took was a little watering for them to pop up like mushrooms from between the slats in the floorboards. What use is a miracle if there is no one there to witness it?

'No, not beer. It's champagne time!' José exclaimed.

'By the way, I tried to call you at your hotel to tell you the good news but you weren't there. The girl on reception said she'd let you know. I thought I'd invite her along. I hope you don't mind?'

'No, not at all. Here's to the end of your worries, José. I'm very happy for you.'

'You'll see. You're going to get on really well with Marie. Everything will be like before, but even better.'

'I'm sure it will.'

The searing rays of sunlight which set the terrace ablaze were diffused as they struck the motionless beaded curtain, so that all that passed into the living room was speckles of light, instantly swallowed up in blue shadow. Blandine was asleep on the couch, her mouth slightly open, her brow misted with the perspiration of sleep. One arm was folded under her head and the other hung by her side, her fingers brushing the coir mat. The cats lay at her feet, breathing in sync. Somewhere in the distance, a long way away, someone played a piano. The same passage of music, over and over. A newborn baby cried, a boat came into port, a fly landed on the ceiling. The house creaked, whispering gossip. The smell of the barbecue, dried herbs, charcoal and melon skin lingered in the air. On the first floor, in a hammock that Gabriel had fitted the day before, Juliette rocked back and forth while sucking her thumb and dreaming of unexplored futures. Gabriel closed his book. Every page seemed like a closed shutter. Focusing on anything else but the sweetness of this magical moment seemed inappropriate, even rude. Yet despite his best efforts he wasn't able to let go, to surrender to sleep, to experience the same feeling as the others: his wife, his daughter, the cats, the fly. He felt excluded from everybody's bliss, from all the innocence. But he didn't know why. It was as if he had committed a crime of which he had no memory. A surge of injustice mixed with guilty despair rose within him and threatened to suffocate him. He bit into his closed fist to stop himself from screaming out as tears rolled down his cheeks. He should never have taken the plane the day after.

'Gabriel?'

Madeleine's face appeared through a fog of cigarette smoke. She had changed her hair, which was now held back on either side with combs. It suited her, made her look younger. Just behind her stood Rita, her badly lipsticked lips stretched in a crooked, timid smile.

'You look like you've seen a ghost. Shall we get a table? The bar's too busy.'

Rita instinctively headed over to the same table that she had shared with Marc two days earlier. Force of habit. The three of them sat down and José served each of them a glass of champagne.

'It's on the house! And there's more where that came from. Gabriel's like a brother to me. Just tell him whatever you want and I'll be right over.'

The women sat side by side, the curly little hairs on the back of their necks visible in the mirror behind them. Madeleine raised her glass.

'I'm not sure what we're celebrating, but cheers!'

They clinked glasses. People are fragile. Hard and fragile, like glass.

'For someone who doesn't know anyone round here ...'

'It's all down to chance. José was the first person I met. Well, apart from you. Do you remember, when I first arrived, I asked you if you could recommend a restaurant?'

'And Rita? You know each other, don't you?'

'That's by chance as well.'

'So that's how you live, by chance?'

'That's right, yes, just like everybody else. And what about you, Rita? What brings you here, if you don't mind me asking?'

'Me? My chance is called Marco!'

She smiled bitterly and downed her drink in one. Some people wore their misfortune with elegance. Rita was one of them. Her heart, hammered by a thousand blows, echoed like a gong, a bronze shield on which fate could make no dent.

'He's buggered off. I was stuffed when I got back to the hotel after lunch. I collapsed and when I woke up he'd vanished.'

'He'll be back, I'm sure. Didn't he have a meeting with his solicitor?'

'You don't take your toothbrush to the solicitor. Gone, with his suitcase, without leaving me a penny and without settling the room, the bastard. Can I get another?'

'Of course. José, do you mind?'

'Thanks. Excuse me while I nip to the loo.'

José refilled the glasses and whispered in Gabriel's ear, loud enough for Madeleine to hear.

'So then, you rascal. You don't hang around, do you? Two at a time!'

Madeleine covered her mouth to stifle a laugh, then said seriously, 'Poor soul. I think she's hooked on drugs. Have you seen her pupils? They're pinpricks! When she came down from her room earlier she was in a right state, her eyes smeared with make-up. She looked a total wreck. I saw this Marco leave, but as she was upstairs I didn't think anything of it. What a bastard! I'd just got off the phone to your friend José. I felt sorry for her and she told me you knew each other so I suggested she come along. Is that all right?'

'Yes, of course it's all right, Madeleine.'

'Where did you meet them?'

'Here. I gave them some peanuts.'

'Peanuts?'

'Yes. They had a saxophone for sale. I bought it to give to José's kids.'

'A saxophone? You do some strange things!'

'Do I?'

'Yes. You've only been here four or five days and already you know so many people. It's amazing how you've become part of their lives. You make yourself at home wherever you go, don't you?'

'I don't mean to. I swear it's not my fault. Do you think it's wrong?'

'I didn't say it was wrong! You just make my head spin a bit. You're nowhere and everywhere at the same time. I don't know what to do with this poor girl. And I don't know what I'm going to say to my boss – he's not the sympathetic type.'

'I'll pay her bill, don't worry.'

'That's kind of you. What's going to happen to her though?'

'I don't know.'

'You don't think she'd commit suicide, do you?'

'No, she's not that type. She wants more from life.'

'Here she is now.'

The men standing at the bar turned and nudged each other as Rita walked past. She wasn't beautiful, but she had something about her and knew how to flaunt it. She crossed the room nonchalantly, rolling her hips, revelling in the lusty stares of the men.

'Men! Well, you have to have them. Lots of them though, not one! I've finished with that!'

She knew how to laugh. It was a hearty laugh, intelligent and frank. She didn't hold back. Madeleine looked on admiringly, with a touch of envy.

'I feel good with you two. If I had the cash, I'd take you both out for something to eat. I'm starving!'

Rita had an urge for red meat and chips. The only thing now remaining on her plate was the bone from her steak and a smear of mustard. She had been to the toilet twice and had downed three bottles of beer. She was like a time bomb; you never knew exactly when it might go off. Madeleine had taken them to a Western-themed restaurant. It suited the situation perfectly. Beefy blokes came here to eat beef and drink beer, which clouded their gaze with a mixture of guilt and greed.

'Have you ever seen a white poppy?' Rita asked.

'No.'

'I found one once. I was young, about eight years old. It was a Sunday in spring. I used to live in a little village called Subligny, near Sens. I was at a picnic with my cousins, uncles and aunts. We made posies of wild flowers: daisies and cornflowers. The weather was gorgeous. It had been a long, long winter. The grass came up to my chin. The sky was a picture-postcard blue. We laughed and chased each other while the men opened bottles and the women laid out the tablecloths, pâté, ham and salad. It was a wonderful day. And then I found it, there on its own, a white poppy. White! I fell down in front of it as though it were the Virgin Mary. It swayed in the wind, which swept through the field. There were others next to it, normal red ones that didn't care about being picked or trodden on, just normal poppies, you know. I plucked it at its base and ran with it, holding it up in the air like a flag, to show my family. They were all amazed at my albino poppy. They took my photo. I was as pleased as punch. Here, look, I've got the photo.'

Rita rummaged around in her miniature handbag, the bag that contained her whole life, and pulled out a shiny purse from which she picked out a yellowing photograph with curled corners and scalloped edges like a *petit beurre* biscuit. It showed a laughing, chubby little girl, with a Joan of Arc haircut, brandishing a skinny flower in both hands above her head. Behind her, against the backdrop of a milky sky, stood the blurred image of a small scowling boy. Rita, the queen of an unforgettable day.

'You can tell it's me, can't you? I pressed it between two paper plates so I wouldn't forget it. But after, because everybody was drunk, it got lost, probably thrown in the bin or something. It wasn't a big deal. Whether they're red or white, poppies don't last.'

The photo passed from Gabriel to Madeleine.

'It's funny, I've got similar photos of me when I was a kid, this age with the same haircut and the same outfit. I used to wear these awful glasses. God, I was so ugly! You don't look so bad, Rita. So what are you going to do now?'

'I don't know. I can't decide. I've always been like that. I don't like deciding things. My only options are nothing or anything. What would you choose? I've spent my life following different people to different places. That's why Marco was good for me. He always knew where he was going. As often as not it was straight into a wall but at least it was something, right? Why did that bastard have to leave me? I'd better not go anywhere. I don't know much, but I've got this gut feeling. He's going to need me – I'd stake my life on it. You're a man, Gabriel. What do you think?'

'I don't know. Yes, maybe wait a while.'

'Yes, I'll do that. The only problem is I'm completely broke.'

'I'll take care of that. I'll settle your room.'

'That's very kind. We could share the same room if you want. That would save money.'

'I'm not sure that's such a good idea.'

'Ah, okay. Oh, I'm sorry, Madeleine. You know what it's like when you get wrapped up in your own problems; you don't think about anybody else. I'm stupid.'

The two women turned to one another and looked into each other's eyes as if staring into a mirror. Madeleine took Rita's hand.

'There's nothing going on between me and Gabriel. Isn't that right, Gabriel?'

Gabriel didn't answer. He stared at his hands, which were flat on the table, as though dealt out in a card game. He was thinking about the ham and mashed potato he had planned for himself that evening.

Madeleine pulled herself up like a ship's figurehead, her sumptuous chest thrust forth against the wind and tide, heading for distant lands. 'You can stay at mine for a bit, Rita. We'll work something out.'

'Why would you do that for me? We hardly know each other.'

'I don't know. Ask Gabriel. He must know. He knows everything.'

Love me tender, love me sweet, never let me go. The music at the end of the film. The restaurant's lights went out one by one. The bill paid, it was time to digest the steak and chips, to sleep off the beer wherever they could. Tomorrow was another day.

They soon forgot about the rain. It coursed from the rooftops and down the gutters as naturally as blood through veins. Madeleine's umbrella was too small for the three of them so, depending on the size of the pavement, Gabriel walked behind, in front or to the side.

'Well then, goodnight.'

The two women stood glued to the umbrella handle, watching Gabriel dripping under the streetlight.

'You can't just leave us like that! Come upstairs for a drink. You've got something to drink, haven't you, Madeleine?'

'Yes, but he doesn't want to.'

'Another time. I have to get up early tomorrow. Goodnight.'

The women watched him turn and walk away, hopping over puddles, hunched over like a question mark.

'He's one of a kind that one. Do you have a crush on him?' asked Rita.

'Maybe,' said Madeleine.

'He reminds me of a priest sometimes. But he is a man after all and you never know with men. What about women, Madeleine? Do you like women?'

The sound of their laughter matched the rippling noise of the rain on their umbrella. They looked like a two-headed bat. The town yawned, the rooftops overflowed.

The only thing left in the freezer compartment was a huge calf's tongue studded with ice crystals. It was otherwise empty, just like the apartment. Gabriel had spent the day waiting for it to defrost on the chopping board. A whole day watching the mute tongue's slow thaw. He didn't have anything else to do. At about seven o'clock he threw the tongue into a pot of simmering stock and made a punchy sauce with tomatoes, gherkins and shallots. There was enough to feed an army. He ate it all though, the tongue that said nothing, out on the terrace, until it made him sick. All that remained were fragments of bone and cartilage. The telephone had rung as he vomited, his head over the toilet bowl, his hands gripping the porcelain sides. It didn't matter. He didn't have anything to say to anybody. Wrapped in the cats' tartan rug, he made his way back out onto the terrace. It was warm but he shivered as he looked up at the sickle moon scything the stars. Usually, at this time, Juliette would have been asleep, sucking her thumb, and Blandine would have been drawing at her workbench with the cats running around. But he had just vomited a whole calf's tongue and had run out of words to describe the night and the sea and what he was still doing alive.

'What are you thinking about?'

'A calf's tongue.'

'You're unbelievable. All you think about is food. So how did it go with the girls last night?'

301

'Good. We went out for a meal and then I went home.'

'Alone?'

'Alone.'

'I don't get you. They were all over you, especially the tall one, the one from the hotel. What's her name again?'

'Madeleine.'

'Man, all you need to do is click your fingers. She's a good-looking girl. And the other one isn't bad either. She's a different type. So you didn't do either of them?'

'They're friends, just friends.'

'Well, it's your business. But it's a waste, all the same. Anyway, what do you think of my flowers?'

'Very nice.'

'They're orchids. They come from some island or something. Have a look in the back again to see if they're still okay, will you? I bought them early this morning.'

Gabriel leant over the back seat. Orchids were ugly. They looked like photos of venereal diseases in medical books.

'They look fine.'

'Good. Look at that idiot in front. Overtaking again and again. Look, there he is, stopped at the traffic lights. It serves him right! After the hospital I'm going to call the children to tell them to be very good when their mother comes back. She's been through a lot and it'll take her time to get back on her feet. Or we could go and see them, if you've got nothing else to do, of course.

'If you want.'

'Here we are then. I think I'm going to take my tie off; I'm going to explode.'

It was white as far as the eye could see. The waiting room was as sterile as an iceberg. Hidden behind the enormous bouquet of flowers, José looked like a small, solitary tree.

'Right, so I'll see you here later then?'

'Yup, I'll be here. Off you go.'

Gabriel sat down on a plastic chair and leafed through magazines filled with smiling movie stars, politicians and television personalities. They were all tanned with white teeth and blue eyes. They weren't allowed to be unhappy. They had been hoisted onto a pedestal, doomed to never-ending happiness. By contrast, for the ordinary mortal, unhappiness was almost a duty. Drips, Zimmer frames, wheelchairs, he could have any misfortune he wanted. Dragging himself around, shuffling in his slippers, wrapped in an oversized dressing gown, smoking a cigarette, drinking weak cups of coffee, waiting for family or ogling those of others, an ashen complexion, a vacant eye, hollow cheeks, always waiting. Waiting and living off simple platitudes like 'good luck', 'keep strong' and 'see you later'. Obviously little people could only have little thoughts. They apologised for everything they did. 'Sorry, do you mind if I take a look at that magazine?', 'Excuse me, which floor are you going to?', 'Excuse me, do you have the time?', 'I'm sorry for still being here, all repulsive and ill.' Nurses laughed as they pushed trolleys stacked with lunch trays, wafting the smells of hospital food, lukewarm and flavourless. Their shoes clicked on the floor tiles. Remembering a Brassens tune about a horse dutifully pulling its cart through rain and mud, Gabriel hummed, '*C'était un petit cheval blanc, tous derrière, tous derrière ...*'

The doors of lift B opened. José walked out. He looked like a rain-drenched panda. He passed Gabriel without registering him.

'José? José?'

José turned round. His face was empty of emotion, a mirror with nobody standing in front of it.

'Are you okay?'

'She's not dead, but she's never going to wake up. She's sleeping. That's it, she's sleeping. I'm tired, Gabriel. I want to go home. I want to go to sleep as well.'

The croissant didn't taste very nice. He had only wanted one after being lured in by the artificial baking scent pumped out by the shop. The smell had reminded him of his childhood. He hadn't really needed either a croissant or memories of his childhood. His sense of smell had fooled him. He sat on a bench and made crumbs, which he threw to the pigeons. One by one they came and belligerently tapped their beaks like mechanical tools. It wasn't a beautiful sight, but it grew on him.

'You shouldn't feed the bastards.'

The voice came from a man sitting at the other end of the bench. He looked curiously like a pigeon himself. Slightly fat, with googly eyes and a pointed nose, he was wrapped in a grey waterproof.

'Why not?'

'They shit on my window. They shit on my car. They shit on the church statues. They shit everywhere. As if there isn't enough shit in the world!'

'They're birds.'

'Exactly! They've got all the fields and woods to do it in. But no, they come and shit on us, thanks to people like you who feed them. And, besides, they aren't birds. They're rats. Flying rats. The souls of dead rats taking revenge on sewer workers. To them, we're all sewer workers. In a way, they're right, but we still have to watch out! Look at them scratching themselves. They're full of disease. Completely inedible.'

'Have you tried them?'

'Of course. I trapped them with birdlime. They're much tougher than crows. Crows are useful though. They're cleaners; they only feed on dead things. Imagine a battlefield without crows. It'd be a real rubbish dump! Apart from carrying a message from one trench to the other, what has a pigeon ever done on a battlefield? And what do we use them for now? We've got other communication methods now ... and, well, that's a topic for another day. Because they used to hang out with soldiers, because they think they're heroes, saviours of France, pigeons have got too big for their boots. They're so full of themselves. And that's why they shit on us. Humanity will end up swimming in the shit of diseased pigeons. They're all diseased. They come and go and pick up every germ there is. It's awful. It's like a modern-day Pompeii!'

'But what can we do about it?'

'Kill as many as we can and send the others back home.'

'Back home?'

'They come from somewhere, don't they? St Mark's Square in Venice, for example. We could kill two birds with one stone. They'd infect all the Japanese, American, Swedish and Bulgarian tourists. There's bound to be a pigeon loft there somewhere. Either way, if we don't give them anything to eat, then they'll go away. And, anyway, you're feeding them junk. Where did you buy your croissant?'

'The snack bar on the main road.'

'I knew it! Can you imagine what kind of shit they'll be dropping on us now?'

'You're right. I hadn't thought.'

The man shrugged his shoulders and scratched his head vigorously. Dandruff fell from his greasy hair and quickly covered his collar. He got rid of it by flapping his jacket, his elbows bent, as he stretched out his neck and cleared his throat.

'Seagulls aren't much better, you know. I once spent a night in a hotel in Cancale. My room overlooked the restaurant's rubbish bins. I didn't sleep a wink. And swallows? You think they herald the spring? Spring doesn't exist any more! I hate birds, all birds. The skies are too full. It's our rubbish bins which attract them, our monstrous rubbish bins. I leave nothing for them, young man. I finish everything. I don't leave them a crumb! I'm even going to leave my body to science. There'll be nothing left of François Dacis, nothing! As if I hadn't existed. And of that I'm proud!'

'That's all very admirable.'

'You don't need to tell me. Here, between you and me, I don't even trust angels.'

'Angels?'

'Yes, angels. They fly around with all the dirty birds and so they're infected as well! Bird flu and the rest, I tell you! Angels used to have nice plump faces like well-fed toddlers blowing on their trumpets. But today, young man, they all look like junkies. They just hover around not giving a fuck about anything.'

He scratched his head furiously again, shaking the dandruff off while clearing his throat with a cooing sound. There was a feverish look in his eye.

'The apocalypse will come from above. Like at Hiroshima. Since the big boss copped it, anarchy has ruled the clouds. It's time to go underground, young man, I'm telling you!'

The old man pulled a crumpled piece of paper from his pocket and smoothed it out on his knees with his forearm. It was some kind of blueprint.

'Bomb shelter, fallout shelter. Anti-pigeon, anti-everything. Ten metres square with four-metre-thick reinforced Swedish concrete walls, buried fifty metres below good old Breton soil.

I've thought of everything. The heating is provided by the toilet waste and the water is triple filtered. The living room is there, with a sofa, TV, radio and bar. All mod cons. Here is where the stockpiles are kept, next to the kitchen: wheat, rice, corn, pasta and tinned food. And the armoury. You never know! And the medicine area: aspirin, antiseptic, dressings. And the best bit, a cellar! Ten metres further down with everything you'd ever need. It could last me sixty years, maybe more! I'll die there, but at least it'll be of natural causes. What do you think? Great, eh?'

'Magnificent. Where is it?'

The man narrowed his eyes and tapped the side of his head.

'Top secret, my friend. It's all up here.'

He rolled up his sleeve and stared at his watchless wrist.

'Good God, I'd better go. How about ten euros?'

'Ten euros? For what?'

'My survival plan. You can have it for ten euros. Five for something to eat and then five for a wash.'

'Okay then.'

'You've got yourself a good deal there. But no more feeding the pigeons. You promise?'

'Yes, I promise.'

'Well, good evening, young man. It's getting dark; the weather's turning. You'd better go home. It's been a pleasure.'

The old man got up. He rolled his shoulders, puffed out his chest and stuck his nose in the air. He opened his waterproof and strode determinedly off, scattering the pigeons as he went.

On another bench, two teenagers sat not kissing. The boy was looking down at his enormous new trainers, size 12 perhaps. The young girl was twisting a strand of hair between her fingers and holding it up to her lips as a moustache. They both looked extremely bored. It suited them. The sky was the colour of frogspawn absorbing joy and sorrow with the same indifference. Gabriel rubbed his hands together. He had washed them ten times that day but still they smelt of the hospital. José had insisted on sleeping in one of his children's beds. The three sleeping tablets he had taken would do him until tomorrow, his big boar head resting on a Mickey Mouse pillowcase.

Rita and I waited for you until eight o'clock. Come and join us at my place if you want — Madeleine.

The note had been slipped under the door. Gabriel didn't know whether or not to go. The ravioli simmered on the camping stove in front of the open window. A church bell struck nine as if testing the density of the air. He hadn't eaten ravioli out of a tin since he was a child. He used to eat them all the time. He used to love them. Now though, even when they were covered in Parmesan, he found them disgusting, like eating spoonfuls of vomit. Yet, perhaps out of respect for his childhood, he finished them all. Afterwards, he cleaned the pan in the washbasin. The water, reddened by the tomato sauce, slowly swirled down the plughole with a revolting gurgle. He looked at himself in the mirror and saw he had sauce around his mouth. Like blood, it was difficult to get rid of tomato sauce completely. There was always some left behind. Months after ... the accident he kept finding tiny flecks on the sole of a shoe or on a button. He ended up seeing them everywhere, like strewn confetti after a carnival. He closed his eyes for a moment. The darkness enveloped him. Only the searing glow of the strip light on which he was resting his forehead remained. He left the bathroom in a hurry, threw on his jacket and slammed the door behind him. He raced down the stairs and flung himself into the street. On the pavement, he lifted his nose to the sky, took a deep breath and filled his lungs with as much of the manure-rich night air as he could. Slowly the scorching of the fluorescent tube faded away, much like a white-hot knife plunged into a tub of cold water. He strode determinedly off like an old steam engine. He reached out his hand and touched everything he passed: the freezing metal pole of a one-way sign, the corners of a tattered poster, a rough brick wall. He had to feel everything around him, dry, wet, hot and cold, to convince himself it was real. He wasn't sure of anything. He moved faster as if trying to escape from a predator – his shadow perhaps? Or the past, which was swiftly catching up with him? He could feel its icy breath on his neck. Around him the town was falling apart like a boat in a storm. The tar was rising up, the sky falling down. He was a panting wreck by the time he reached Madeleine's flat.

'Ah, Gabriel! We were wondering if you were coming. What's wrong? You look like you've seen a ghost!'

'No, I'm fine. I was running because of the rain.'

'But it isn't raining.'

'Exactly. I wanted to get here before it started raining.'

The door closed behind him, leaving the monster on the other side. Indoors, there was only the comfort of the here and now. Rita was sprawled on the couch wearing a tracksuit and slippers which slopped off her feet, probably borrowed from Madeleine. It hadn't taken her long to become part of the furniture.

'Look who it is! We didn't think you'd come.'

Rita sat up and patted the cushion next to her in invitation. Gabriel sat down and caught his breath. The room was soft, warm and sweet. Madeleine sat opposite the sofa on a pouffe. As she poured Gabriel a glass of cognac, her dressing gown hung forward to reveal the curve of her breast. She must have just come out of the bathroom. Her hair was wet and she smelt of soap, dewy and clean. Gabriel finished his glass in one. Slowly, his whole body began to relax. He should have come sooner. The two women glanced at each other. Rita poured herself a large drink.

'We thought you might make us a bit of supper.'

'Haven't you eaten?'

'Yes, of course, don't worry. We had a little tea party. Is everything okay? Do you want another drink?'

'Yes, please.'

Madeleine put her hand on Gabriel's knee.

'Is it José's wife?'

'No. Well, yes. Maybe. She's fallen into another coma. No one's sure when she'll wake up. Perhaps never. It could last weeks or months. Even years.'

'And what about José?'

'I took him back to his place. He's asleep now. I gave him some sleeping tablets. We'll see how he is tomorrow.'

Rita stood up, emptied her glass and put on a CD. It was a tango dance track, the kind radio stations usually played. She sat back down, practically in Gabriel's lap.

'I could never stand "Sleeping Beauty" stories.'

'Rita!'

'What? It's true. Even when I was little I never liked stupid fairy tales. They were either so scary I couldn't understand how adults could read them to kids or they were unbelievably soppy and annoying. It's no surprise that the world is as daft as it is if we're telling stories like that to our kids.'

'I loved "The Little Mermaid".'

'Jesus, that's another one. A bimbo who goes to the trouble of getting legs that hurt like hell for a guy who ends up dumping her for somebody else. That's morally okay, is it? You've got to be twisted to write something like that. And, anyway, it's always the women who pay the price in the end in those stories. "The Little Match Girl"? Dies of cold. "Little Thumbling"? Who ends up being eaten? The ogre's daughters, of course. Aren't I right, Gabriel? You know everything.'

'I saw the Little Mermaid in Copenhagen.'

'And what was she like?'

'Small.'

'Of course she was! They didn't haggle over the size of the statues for Stalin, de Gaulle or Émile Zola, did they? But for the Little Mermaid! Women are on the bottom rung of society; we're like a school of sardines surrounded by sharks.'

Madeleine smiled. The sea was at low tide. She looked like she didn't care about the status of women. She was daydreaming, floating in the sea somewhere off the coast of Guadeloupe.

'You should never leave the water,' Madeleine said. 'Men or women. Everything is weightless in the water. We glide and brush up against each other, bob up and down. There's no noise. Everything is quiet, the mind clear.'

She must have been a bit drunk. She stood up and spun round on her toes, her eyes closed, her body in thrall to the music, her dressing gown flaring out.

'There was nothing before, there'll be nothing after and we don't give a damn about what goes on in between. Why? Why?'

Rita reached over to the lamp beside the couch and turned it off, plunging the room into darkness. The only light came from the streetlamp. The room resembled a fish tank. Rita sidled up to Gabriel.

'She's beautiful, isn't she?'

'Yes, she is. Very.'

'Do you fancy her?'

He had bought a fish tank for Juliette on her fourth birthday, but she hadn't wanted to put fish in it. She just liked the plastic algae and the little toy diver that knelt in front of the treasure chest, with air bubbles escaping to the top like live pearls. She would fall asleep in front of it, sucking her thumb. Her bedroom was never dark. She was so very afraid of the dark.

'Do you want me to suck you off?'

'No, thank you, Rita. It's kind, but no.'

'With Madeleine then?'

'Not her either. You're both very charming, but no. Let's leave it at that.'

'Well, at least look at us then. That's the least you can do.'

'Okay.'

'It's not that Marco doesn't like women, it's just that he was one once, so he has a chip on his shoulder.'

'*What?*'

'I'll tell you the story. He must have been seventeen or eighteen. He was with three mates in a car going off to a party in some godforsaken corner of Auvergne. All the guys had to dress up as girls, and the girls as guys. Some stupid teenage game, you know. So they go off in their old banger, completely stoned, dressed up to the nines in wigs, miniskirts, high heels, bras and suspenders – the perfect male fantasy. They were having the time of their lives, taking coke and passing around joints. Everything was going great until about nine o'clock, when the car broke down in the middle of nowhere. It was pitch black. There was a little village a couple of miles away and so Marco and one of his friends decided to go and call for help or get a tow. The thing was, they'd forgotten to take a change of clothes, normal clothes, with them. But they had no choice so off they went, hobbling along in their heels, completely off their heads. They arrived at the village only to find that everything was closed – apart from a transport café. Well, what do you think happened? Two drag queens in a room full of tanked-up knuckleheads, with tattoos like toilet-door graffiti. It was no party, I can tell you. He never really got over it.

313

Something like that must have happened to Gabriel. Everyone's got baggage. Mine is so full I can't even close it.'

'You're still thinking about him, after everything he's done?'

'Of course! When you sleep with one man for so long, even if he's the scum of the earth, at some point you will have seen him hanging on to your breast as if it were a lifebelt, looking so small, fragile and vulnerable. I know it's stupid, but it's things like that that make you forgive and forget everything. Has that never happened to you?'

'No. I've had the odd fling, but nothing serious. I haven't found The One yet, that's for sure.'

'I'm not talking about finding your one true love. Just love, full stop, the kind that everyone enjoys.'

'No, I don't think I've ever found that either.'

The two women thought he was asleep, curled up on the couch. Madeleine had covered him with a blanket. He had pretended to drift off when they started dancing together and feeling each other up. It was awkward, touching and a little sad. And now they were whispering, one sitting on the pouffe stroking the hair of the other, whose head rested in her lap. A woman's soul is like the Lascaux caves, only older and deeper, so deep that you need a torch, wandering endlessly, leaving handprints, hugging the walls to find your way. Once you enter, there's no way out. You give yourself entirely, getting under her skin to the point that two become one. Madeleine's blanket smelt of her perfume. He would love to drift away down the river, to not exist any more.

'Gabriel? Are you awake? Are you crying?'

A soft hand touched his shoulder, a soft hand heavy with life.

'I was dreaming. What time is it?'

'Does it matter?'

'No, that's just what you say when you wake up, isn't it? Is it morning?'

'Not yet. Do you want a coffee?'

'Yes, please.'

The lovely Madeleine. Her face was as blank as an unwritten letter. Rita was skimming through a book, the sound of the pages passing through her fingers like the fluttering wings of a bird. She stopped at a page and began to read out loud in a voice that wasn't hers: "'I will rise now, and go about the city in the streets, and in the broad ways I will seek him whom my soul loveth: I sought him, but I found him not. The watchmen that go about the city found me: to whom I said, Saw ye him whom my soul loveth?'" Rita closed the book and turned towards the window. Maybe it was the new morning's light on her cheeks, but it looked as though she were crying.

'Isn't it funny – books can really speak to you sometimes. Gabriel, will you help me find Marco?'

You can follow footprints in snow and sand but not in town. The pavements are etched with footsteps, the tarmac is blistered, swollen, dented by them. They come, they go, they leave, they return, walk about, slow down, drag. And then, when their number's up, after a moment's hesitation, they disappear for ever, somewhere, up there.

'We've got to find him, Gabriel! We've got to find him!'

'It's too early, Rita. We can't go and wake the solicitor up now.'

'Why not? Solicitors always get up early; they don't want to miss out on a case.'

'We'll find Marco, but not like this. Not by searching for him. I've got to go and see José.'

'José? What about me?'

'One thing at a time. Go back to Madeleine's, please. You didn't sleep at all last night.'

'Don't talk to me like I'm a kid. You promised me.'

'Rita. I told you I'd help you find Marco and I will. But not now. Later, okay?'

'You're a false saint, Gabriel! That's all you are. You pick us up and then drop us whenever it suits you.'

'Rita! I never said I was a saint! I'm only a man.'

'You're worse than a man. You're an angel – you've got no balls.' Rita aimed a kick at a rubbish bin. Her lizardskin bag swung on the end of her arm like a hammer. She stamped her feet on the pavement; two large tears filled her eyes. Her mouth twisted with rage. She was a balloon ready to burst. 'A miracle? Shit, it's not much to ask, is it?'

And with that she turned on her heel and raced off down the street like a bowling ball. Luckily there was no one in her way.

'Excuse me, sir ...'

'Yes?'

'I'd like to open my shop. You're leaning on my shutters.'

'Oh, I'm sorry.'

The man was small and sepia-toned from head to foot. He looked as if he had been born old; or, rather, he was ageless. A mist of a man. For the one thousand and first time he opened the padlock and lifted the shutters just enough to slip into the shop. He reappeared almost immediately armed with a long hooked pole, which he used to push the shutters up fully. Cachoudas Cobblers. The shop's window was decked out with an array of cork-bottomed sandals, sheepskin boots, jars of cream, cans of shoe polish and heels of all sizes; anything and everything to do with feet. A strong smell of glue, leather and rubber drifted through the open door. The cobbler came back into the doorway, buttoning up his overall and taking in one final breath of fresh air. Gabriel was still standing there.

'Were you waiting for me to open? Do you need anything?'

'Yes, some laces.'

'Laces? Come in.'

The shop was so cramped that Gabriel felt the need to shrink in on himself, half dazed by the fumes of glue, sweat and sagging leather. The walls were lined with shelves crammed with boots, ankle boots, loafers, pumps, brogues, ballet slippers and sandals of varying conditions and sizes. They looked like a defeated army. The area behind the counter must have been raised as the small man now towered over Gabriel by a good head. Well, maybe not such a good head. In the light of his anglepoise work lamp, the cobbler's face appeared like that of a severe judge, coldly scrutinising his client.

'Shoelaces. Right then, what kind of shoelaces? There are are all sorts of laces. Short? Long? Rounded? Squared? Thick? Thin? Black? Brown? Red? You've got to give me some idea of the type you're after.'

'Of course. Long ones, please. Round and red.'

'For walking boots?'

'Yes, exactly. For walking boots.'

The man's face lit up. He spread his arms, and the front of his overall gaped between the buttonholes to reveal a brown, clearly hand-knitted jumper beneath.

'Okay then, now we're getting somewhere. Why didn't you say straight away? I've got some Italian ones, virtually in-des-truc-tible. They're here somewhere … hang on.'

Quick as a flash the cobbler disappeared behind his counter and Gabriel remembered that the thing he liked most about puppet shows was the puppeteer. After a good deal of muttering the man reappeared, his face beaming at having found a pair of twisted red laces wrapped in plastic. He held them between thumb and forefinger like a fisherman with his prize catch.

'They're top quality, two-tone but predominantly red. Fifty per cent cotton, fifty per cent silk, resistant to five hundred kilos, and seventy centimetres long. How many do you want?'

'Two of course. I'll take two, a pair.'

'I'd take two pairs if I were you.'

Ah, but you said they were indestructible.'

'Yes, but you never know. A manufacturing mistake or human error and *bang!* Can you imagine being stuck on a sheer rock face up in the Alps, a shoe falling into the abyss, into a rushing torrent? Night is closing in. You're all alone. You'll regret it.'

'Who said anything about being on a sheer rock face in the Alps at dusk?!'

'Well, everyone ends up there at some time in their life. Believe me, I know! So two pairs then? They're the last ones too. The factory in Modane where they make them is closing down.'

'Oh, really?'

'Yes, it's all nylon and plastic nowadays. It's sad, but that's life. You'll never be able to buy laces like this again.'

'Okay then. I'll take two pairs.'

'Good decision. Are they for somebody special?'

'No.'

'Well, let me wrap them up anyway – they're worth it.'

While the cobbler took his time wrapping the laces in sheets of tissue paper, Gabriel became lost in thought, staring at the dozens of shoes and their dangling labels.

Are we nearly there yet? He marched them up to the top of the hill and he marched them down again. One for the road. Three steps forward, two steps back. Left, right, left, right. These boots were made for walking. Where were they going? Where had they been? Where did they come from?

'Are you looking for someone?'

'Yes, he's a bit of a drifter.'

'What shoe size is he?'

'I don't know. A man, in his forties ...'

'Well dressed?'

'Not really. He's a drifter, like I said.'

'Well, in that case he'll definitely drift in here. They all come by at one time or another. There are the straight-laced types in well-fitting boots. Then there are the ones who squeeze their feet into fashionable heels. Even the monks who suffer like martyrs in their new sandals. I've seen them all. It's a bit like a lost-property office for wayward travellers here – the kind who are away with the fairies. What was his name?'

'Marco.'

'Marco, no, I don't recognise the name. I've had a Marcus, Marcus Malte. He made me stick patches on the side of his trainers. You know the kind, an artist! But as for a Marco, no, he's not been in. That'll be €24.40, please.'

Gabriel rummaged through his pockets and pulled out the exact amount.

'Excellent, thank you. The cobbler, you know, is the last stop-off before the desert. If I find your Marco, I'll let you know. Have a good day, sir.'

The doorbell chimed two notes, a *fa* and a *so*.

No, José hadn't hanged himself in the night. He was polishing the counter and serving espressos with the cloth over his shoulder, in the steam of the coffee machine. He had shaved, brushed his hair and was as spotless as a show house. His eyes were dry, too dry.

'Hi there, Gabriel. Surely not a beer at this time in the morning?'

'No, thanks. A coffee.'

José was meticulous in his preparation, mechanical. He was on autopilot, but without a plane.

'Are you okay, José?'

'I'm all right. I slept for eighteen hours straight last night. No dreams, no nightmares, just real life, I suppose. How about you?'

'Fine, thanks.'

'Right then, let's go.'

Above the counter, the panda's continued presence demonstrated its ability to be happy everywhere and anywhere.

'I think I'm going to bring her back here.'

'Marie?'

'Yes. She should sleep in her own bed. And, anyway, it'll give me something to do. I need something to do. I feel empty, like there's an echoing cave inside me. I've got to fill it, that's it, I've got to fill it.'

'What about the kids?'

'I'll bring them back as well. It'll be strange for them to start off with, having a mother who sleeps all the time, but they'll be fine. You get used to everything in the end, kids especially. Everything will be nice and peaceful.'

'Being peaceful is good.'

'Yes, it's restful. Hey, I forgot, that guy who sold you the saxophone was in this morning. He was looking for you. He wanted to see you, here, at noon.'

'Ah, thank you. I'll be here. See you later.'

It looked as though the sun had fallen from the sky and shattered like a chandelier on the ground. In the glare, his eyes were whitewashed like the terrace. And then there was the smell, of shit and rotten meat. And the silence, which the buzzing flies served only to accentuate. He clung to the railing with both hands and struggled to breathe. His lungs were tight, gasping for air. His eyes refused to register what they had seen. The space inside his head was filled with the flapping of wings, like tiny black lace fans. Juliette and Blandine lying there, ghostly pale, their faces smeared with dried blood, scribbled over with bluebottles, their blind eyes searching for an answer from the ceiling rose. No, he couldn't believe it. If he did, he could never believe in anything ever again.

The fly sat in the sunbeam as if under a spotlight. It was struggling in a sticky patch on the marble table. It looked like a circus trick gone wrong.

'Thank you for coming, Gabriel.'

Marco held his hand out. It was as cold and slimy as a dead fish.

'Do you want another drink?'

'Yes, please.'

'Waiter, two more coffees. Thanks again for coming. How's Rita?'

'She's looking for you.'

'Ah ...'

Marco leant forward to take a sip, revealing a small bald patch like a monk's on the top of his head. There was a little scar on his scalp in the shape of a half-moon. A childhood accident no doubt, nothing too serious. Marco looked like he'd spent the night on the streets under his raincoat. His pockets were full of tissues and he hadn't shaved. His eyes were bloodshot and his hands were red. There was dirt under his fingernails.

'What have you been up to?'

'I slept in a skip. Do I smell?'

'Not much.'

'How's she doing?'

'She's worried and a bit shaky. But she's being well looked after.'

'She's at 104 rue Montéléger, third floor on the left, isn't she?'

'How do you know?'

'I followed you. Are you fucking them both?'

'No, neither of them.'

'I don't mind. I'm not jealous. I'm in the shit, Gabriel.'

'What about your inheritance?'

'My inheritance?! I can't get it. My father didn't exactly die of natural causes. I ... how would you say ... helped him along. Do you remember that night when you came to our room? Well, after you left, I went out. I was off my face on coke, up to my eyeballs; I couldn't sleep. I knew that the old bastard kept some cash at his place. There's no way I was going to settle for just the saxophone. The nurse was sleeping downstairs. I forced open the window and climbed the stairs. I was suffocating in a hat and scarf I'd wrapped round my face. I opened the door to his room. He was stirring in his sleep and snoring like an old locomotive. I didn't think twice about it. I grabbed him by the throat and started hitting him round the head until he told me where he was hiding his loot. I couldn't understand a word he was saying. All that came out of his arsehole of a mouth were disgusting bubbles of spit. I looked for his false teeth, but by the time I'd grabbed them to put in his mouth he'd slipped out of my hands and banged his head on the edge of the bed. Stone-cold dead. Well, just about. He curled into a ball with his fist in his mouth, his knees tucked under his chin. He was naked as the day he was born. He looked like a foetus. He looked like me. I didn't mean to kill him. You've got to understand that, Gabriel. I just wanted to make him talk. I couldn't breathe. I sat on the edge of the bed and cried.'

Marco drank the rest of his coffee in one go and turned the cup round in his hands. He saw no future in the coffee grounds.

'I'd thought about killing him a million times, but I never thought it would turn out like this. I felt completely empty. I had no one left to hate. I was like a boxer, alone in the ring, with just myself to fight against. I felt like an idiot. I rummaged under the mattress and found two bundles of cash. There must have been more but I didn't have the heart to look for them. I gave him one last kick before I left. Yet again, he'd won. And then I went back to the hotel. Rita was fast asleep, snoring. I huddled up against her. I wanted to tell her what had happened but I didn't want to wake her. The next day, well, you know what happened, we went to the restaurant. It was all an act. Rita had too much. I actually thought she was going to overdose on me. I'd had enough of dead people. I packed my bags and took them to the lockers at the station. I wanted to go and see the solicitor and then leave town. On my way over I thought to myself that people might not believe my father had died of natural causes. There was a black car parked outside the solicitor's with four guys inside. I turned round and ran straight ahead, for a long time. This fucking town though, it's tiny. I found myself back where I'd started, the station. It seemed like everywhere I looked there were police. I only had one gram of coke left. I snorted half of it in the toilets. I read everything that people had written on the door. Cries for help. The world's in trouble, serious trouble. My memory gets a bit fuzzy after that. It was as if I was a cocktail shaker in the hands of an epileptic barman. Time flew by like a film on fast forward, an old black and white Charlie Chaplin film. I hung around the hotel and saw you come back and then go out again. I followed you.'

'You should have come up.'

'I thought about it, but didn't dare. I saw your silhouettes in the window. What should I do now?'

'I ... I don't know.'

'Please, help me.'

Marco grabbed Gabriel's wrist. It felt like an ice-cold handcuff. He looked desperately sad and unwell. Gabriel pulled his hand back.

'I think Rita would be very pleased to see you.'

'Yes. I need her. You understand, don't you? She is what she is and I can only be me. We understand each other. Can you get her to meet me? At the station café, perhaps? At about five o'clock?'

'I'll ask her.'

'Thank you. You're a good guy. I'm going to sort myself out. I can't turn up in this state. Okay then, the station café at five it is!'

'Good luck.'

Gabriel munched the rolled-up slice of ham as he walked down the road. It was wrapped, without bread, in a sheet of paper like a crêpe. He hadn't been able to make up his mind in the shop between an egg in aspic, some roast pork and a meat pie. But when the butcher had asked him what he wanted, Gabriel had chosen a slice of ham. It seemed like the easiest thing, neither a good nor bad choice, something in the middle, as bland as blotting paper. They used to give away sheets of blotting paper decorated with Loire Valley châteaux in packets of biscuits. At school, they had learnt to write with a pen dipped in ink, practising upstrokes, downstrokes and blotting the excess. It was strange to think he had once been a child. Of course he remembered, but in the way that you remember an old film: particular sequences in no particular order, insignificant details, a sound, a smell, a quality of light. He remembered the name of a classmate, Brice Soulas. What had happened to Brice Soulas? And the others, the hundreds, the thousands of others, with whom he had shared a bit of his life. They couldn't all be dead! It wasn't that long ago that he had shaken their hands, hugged them, cried with them, laughed with them and then, suddenly, they'd gone missing in action. Where were they now? Unconsciously, Gabriel began to stare at the passers-by in the absurd hope of discovering a familiar face. After a while he felt as though he knew the people walking past, so much so that when he nodded hello to them they responded. Where were they going?

'Not before the end of the month. Okay. You're welcome.'

Madeleine hung up the phone. She had bags under her eyes, but she was smiling. With her hair tied back and a black silk blouse embroidered with dragons fastened high round her neck, she looked like a madam in 1930s Indochina.

'How are you, Gabriel?'

'Fine, thanks. A bit tired. I'm going to lie down for a while.'

'Let me know if you want anything. It's quiet at the moment.'

'I will, thank you. Oh, by the way, I found Marco. Or, rather, he found me.'

'Marco? Rita's guy?'

'Yes. He wants to see her. He suggested meeting at the station café at five o'clock.'

'He's got some nerve, that one. After dumping her like he did! What does he want to do now? Leave her crying on the station platform? Have you told Rita?'

'No, I thought we could call her. Is she still at yours?'

'I don't like this one bit. He's a dirtbag.'

'That's a bit much. He needs her.'

'Yes, to pimp her out or something! I like Rita a lot; she's a nice girl. She's got the right to a second chance, another life. Marco's no good for her. He's dodgy as hell.'

'José said the same thing and he doesn't even know him.'

'Well, there you go, it's blindingly obvious. He's a bastard, a small-town pimp, a dealer who'd kill his own parents for a hit. AND ... sorry, hang on. Good afternoon, Hôtel de la Gare ... The ninth? Next month? Yes, we've got availability. What's the name? Winter? Like the season? Ah, "tour", okay. Goodbye, Mr Wintour.'

Madeleine hung up and rubbed her temples.

'Where were we? Oh yes. Do we have to tell her? He'll only treat her like shit.'

'It wouldn't be right. Rita's entitled to her say, don't you think?'

'Well, I don't know. How about we go with her to the station? I finish at four o'clock today.'

'I think we should ask her first.'

'I'll call her.'

'Okay, I'm going up. I'll see you later.'

'Blandine? Blandine? Yes, it's me. I can hardly hear you, darling. Yes, I'm fine. How are you? And Juliette? Good, good. Listen, I've missed my plane and there isn't another flight back until tomorrow. A stupid accident on the way to the airport with the taxi. No, nothing serious, but I missed my plane. No, I know, there's nothing I can do. Is it hot out on the terrace? Yes, same here. I can't wait to see you again. I miss you as well, and Juliette. I'll see you tomorrow. I love you.'

He took a room in the first hotel he saw, next to the airport. It was horrible and expensive, but he couldn't be bothered going back into town. Staying near the airport made him feel closer to home. If it hadn't been for that bloody lorry he would have been home already, on the terrace with a glass of chilled wine in his hand, with his wife, daughter and cats. The neighbour learning the piano would be murdering 'Für Elise', the baby on the other side wailing. Away in the distance he'd watch boats coming and going, their lights reflecting on the port's murky water. The smell of barbecues would linger in the air. They drove like maniacs in this country.

He went down to dinner very early, to get it over with. The restaurant was empty. A row of stressed businessmen hung around the bar, drowning their boredom. They boasted about their successes, winking pathetically at the waitress, who completely ignored them. They looked like a bunch of midgets standing on tiptoes to reach the bar.

Gabriel chewed his mezze absent-mindedly while thinking about the market that he planned to go to with Blandine and Juliette the following Saturday. A haughty woman in her forties came to sit at a nearby table, looking disdainfully about her. She had barely ordered her food before she pulled out a pair of severe-looking glasses and immersed herself in a thick pile of papers. She sat making notes while nibbling at her food, taking small mouthfuls of her fish without looking at what she was eating. All of a sudden, she dropped her fork and pen and began to groan and whimper. She spat into her napkin and clutched her throat. Her cheeks immediately flushed beetroot red. She gulped down half a jug of water to no avail. The fishbone was stuck. She was choking. With no one around to help, Gabriel rushed to her side.

'Eat some bread, not water, some bread.'

The woman was turning a shade of purple, morphing into something unrecognisable. Her bulging eyes, filled with fear as if she were drowning, settled on Gabriel, who was moulding a piece of bread into a small ball. Gurgling noises emerged from her wide-open mouth. Gabriel put the ball of bread in her mouth and indicated to the poor woman that she should try to swallow it. Two more balls of bread were required before she succeeded. Gradually, the woman's panic subsided.

'Is that better?'

'I'm OK, thank you,' she said in English.

Her voice was a bit hoarse, but she had regained her composure. The euphoria of her narrow escape was short-lived. At the sight of her immaculate white shirt now covered in tomato sauce and bits of food she leapt up and grabbed her pile of papers before storming over to the restaurant's entrance where she began to berate the manager in a language he didn't understand.

In the lift back up to his room, Gabriel chuckled to himself, promising to tell the story to Blandine. She loved that kind of thing.

*

Gabriel didn't tell the story to anyone. He kept it to himself. Now and again he imagined telling Blandine and hearing her laugh.

'I knew you'd find him. You're a really nice guy.'

'It was him who found me. Don't thank me.'

Despite the fact that she was on her third coffee, Rita could barely keep her eyes open. Gabriel and Madeleine had found her asleep on the living-room couch, her mouth open, nostrils quivering, clutching an empty bottle of wine.

'All the same, you're a good guy. Do I look awful?'

Gabriel avoided the question with a vague wave of his hand. He didn't want to tell her she looked as battered and creased as the pillow she had collapsed on. Madeleine paced up and down the room, her arms crossed, failing to contain her fury.

'You look shocking, just like you did when that bastard left you on your own at the hotel!'

'Have I got time to take a shower?'

'Yes, you've got time, but, Rita, listen to me, that man will be the death of you! I'm sorry, but I can't stand seeing you go running after him as soon as he reappears. You're a woman; you've got your dignity.'

'Dignity? Madeleine, you've got to understand that Marco needs me. He's the only person who has always needed me. It's important to feel useful, you know, even if it is to somebody like Marco. I'm not stupid, I know what he's like.'

'Go and take your shower. We're coming with you though. Are you still okay with that?'

'Of course. I'd like you to be there. You can both be my witnesses. It's crazy – I'm as excited as a bride on her wedding day!'

Madeleine shrugged her shoulders and rolled her eyes as Rita scurried off to the bathroom humming *La Vie en Rose*. It was like being on the set of a farce: doors opened, doors closed. Gabriel made the most of the interval to have a look out at the street. It must lead somewhere, mustn't it? On to another street, leading on to another street, leading on ...

'Witnesses! To a duel, in fact! What do you think, Gabriel?'

'Witnesses are important. They're not just bit-parts. You need them.'

'I'm not talking about that! I'm thinking of Rita. He's going to take advantage of her! And we're just going to stand there. You're not just going to let her go off with that—'

'I think I am. They love each other.'

'You call that *love*? I call it "failure to render assistance to a person in danger". It'll end in disaster.'

'And?'

'What do you mean "and"? You can't just let people kill themselves without trying to do something!'

'Why not?'

'Because you just can't; it's wrong.'

'You're jealous of her, aren't you?'

'*Me?* Absolutely not! I feel sorry for her.'

'You shouldn't do. She's worth much more than that. Tell me, the road outside your house, which street does it lead on to?'

'Rue Chaptal. Why?'

'I've not been down there yet. I should take a look.'

Rita charged ahead like a Russian tank, fuelled by vodka and driven by an irrepressible urge to conquer the void. She had the bodywork as well: leather and jeans festooned with zips, carefully spiked hair, pointy breasts, and crêpe-soled shoes like tyre treads.

'Of course I won't, Madeleine. I won't throw myself at him. I want an apology first. After that, we'll see.'

'Gabriel and I aren't going to let you out of our sight. Let us know if you want us to step in.'

'It'll be fine. How do I look? Do I look rough?'

Gabriel brought up the rear. The two women in front of him were an invincible team, like breakers sweeping forward. Soon they were at the station with its disappointing view. The small panes of its windows strained to reflect the dull light of a cracked sky at the end of a gloomy day. The square was now no more than an enormous hole surrounded by wire fences, at the bottom of which diggers churned up the earth while little men in yellow hard hats attempted to create, out of the chaos, the world's greatest car park. It looked like a dig in Egypt. The café modestly offered its humble purgatory to all passing waifs and strays ... Rita peered in through the window.

'There he is. He looks depressed.'

'You go in first. Gabriel and I will sit near the entrance. Don't let him walk all over you.'

From where they were sitting, Madeleine and Gabriel had a pretty good view of them, Rita from the back and Marco from the side. Even shaved and wearing clean clothes, Marco looked in the same sad state as he had done that morning. Rita shunned Marco's outstretched hand with a simple shake of her head. Crushed, Marco stared at his spurned hand. He looked as if he wanted to wrench his arm off and throw it over his shoulder. Gabriel and Madeleine couldn't hear what they were saying, but Marco's body language, his head shrunk back in his jacket collar, showed that he was ready to take the blame, to accept his fate. He would just have to wait for it to pass. And it did pass. Now it was Rita who took his hands and held them in hers. He smiled and Rita leant towards him.

'Here we go! I don't know what she sees in him. He's ugly as sin. Personally, I—'

A gust of air hit them as two strapping men entered and made straight for the row of tables where Marco and Rita were sitting. Marco turned ashen, his eyes widened and his mouth dropped open at the sight of the pair of heavies who wore official red armbands. They appeared to be going for Marco, but, instead, laid their paws on the shoulders of another man sitting at the table behind. The whole episode was over in just a few seconds. The two policemen hauled the man off his seat and dragged him out of the café, while the stunned customers looked on. Marco's hand went to his chest and he collapsed forward onto the table. Rita leapt up and started screaming.

'Marco! Marco!'

A large moustachioed man, for some reason dressed in lederhosen, rushed over.

'I'm a doctor.'

There was mayhem. People were getting out of their seats, rushing to the toilets or taking advantage of the confusion to slip off without paying. Others crowded around Rita and Marco.

The doctor loosened Marco's tie and took his pulse, while Rita watched, distraught.

'Is he dead?'

'No, but he's had a heart attack. We need to call an ambulance.'

The waiters waved white flags. The war was over.

'Jesus, really? Where is he?'

'In intensive care. They think he'll pull through.'

'Well, at least it proves he's got a heart.'

José stared at the counter he had just finished wiping. A barely visible mark had caught his attention. He scrubbed it with the corner of the cloth.

'Damned thing won't budge!'

'What is it?'

'Glue, I think.'

'You can't really see it.'

'I can. Anyway, I'm going to go and pick up the kids tomorrow. Françoise is going to live with us for a bit, so she can help out.'

'And Marie?'

'When everything is ready, at the end of the week, then maybe. I can't be by myself any more. I'm sick of my own company. What on earth *is* this?'

José couldn't stand it any longer. He took a penknife from his pocket and started scratching at the tiny translucent mark.

'There we go. It looks like a contact lens.'

José balanced the shiny item on the end of his finger like a hat and held it out to Gabriel.

'Yes, definitely a contact lens.'

'Weird thing to find on a bar. I'll put it to one side in case the owner comes back for it.'

Under the benevolent eye of the panda, watching over the world with constant cheer, José rummaged through a drawer in search of a matchbox in which to store the lens. Gabriel noted that whenever José passed close to the toy he made sure to touch its paw, tummy or nose. St Panda?

'What are you doing tonight, José?'

'Nothing, obviously.'

'I'm cooking at Madeleine's. Rita needs cheering up. Would you like to come along?'

'No, thanks. I'm not really in the mood.'

'You're allowed to enjoy yourself, once in a while.'

'I know, but ... Is Rita really unhappy then?'

'Pretty unhappy, yes.'

'Ah.'

José rubbed his stubbled cheeks, staring at the panda. Unhappy people had to stick together.

'Okay then. Where does she live?'

'Just round the corner, 104 rue Montéléger, third floor on the left. By the way, do you know if there's an Italian deli round here?'

'There's the Stromboli. It's a restaurant, but you can buy things to take away. It's on rue Chaptal.'

Rue Chaptal was a dead end in more ways than one. The scars of long-gone shops ran along its length: hardware shops, a horse-meat butcher's, a haberdashery now reduced to rusty signs with letters missing. Apart from the string of multicoloured light bulbs around the Stromboli's window, the street was in darkness.

'We're not open for dinner yet.'

'I was just after a few bits and pieces, fresh pasta, that kind of thing.'

With a show of regret the woman, who had a strong German accent, put a bookmark in her copy of *Also Sprach Zarathustra*, and rose to her full six feet. Her bobbed platinum hair was like a helmet, the fringe finishing just above her steel-blue eyes.

'What kind of pasta?'

'Tagliatelle.'

'For how many people?'

'Four.'

The woman put on a pair of latex gloves and filled a small bag with the pasta. Between her powerful fingers, the ribbons looked peculiarly like sauerkraut.

'Anything else?'

'Some Parma ham, please. Twenty or so slices, very thin.'

The leg of ham was almost whole, but looked weightless in the woman's hands. The meat slicer buzzed unnervingly as the twenty slivers piled up on one another.

'Anything else?'

'A tub of pesto, a packet of breadsticks and I could do with some antipasti, some artichokes in oil, roasted peppers. I'm sorry, but I go a bit mad when I'm in an Italian deli. I just want to take everything.'

'I know. I was like that ten years ago.'

The woman got Gabriel to try everything before packing it into tubs. She told him her story.

'I was on an architecture field trip to Florence. There was a little shop right next door to my hotel. It was dirty, dark and reeked of faraway spices, cheese and cured meat. It smelt of men. It took me four days to pluck up the courage and give in to temptation. The man who cut me five slices of coppa was called Adamo and naturally he was gorgeous. Like mine, his father was dead, and had been a fascist. We were made for each other. Adamo wanted to travel and I had some money saved up. The rest is history. Will that be all?'

'Have you got any Lacryma Christi?'

'Yes.'

'I'll take two bottles then, please. That's a great story. So what made you choose to set up shop here?'

'We wanted to go far away. This was the perfect place.'

'Do you like it here?'

'No, but "what doesn't kill me makes me stronger" as Nietzsche once said.'

'That's true. My compliments to the chef – the antipasti are delicious.'

Gabriel had barely finished speaking before the woman pressed a button and a distant-sounding voice crackled out of a loudspeaker.

'*Prego*?'

'Adamo, a customer wants to pass on his compliments for the antipasti.'

'*Grazie! Grazie mille, grazie tanti, grazie mille, graz—*'

'Okay, okay. Have a nice evening, sir.'

'You too.'

Gabriel left the shop, convinced that the voice coming out of the loudspeaker was a broken record, stuck on '*Grazie! Grazie mille.*'

It wouldn't come, no matter how much he needed to go. Piss, just piss. It wasn't rocket science. Even a newborn baby knew instinctively how to piss. But it just wouldn't come. This appendage hanging out of his flies would end up useless. It didn't look bad, not too long, not too short, silky smooth, good girth, nice shape, no spots or shrivelling. The toilet he was standing in front of looked like a pelican made of white china, its beak open, waiting patiently for his thing to recover from its momentary bout of amnesia. The sound of clinking cutlery, soft background music and the hubbub of conversation drifted through from the other side of the closed door. Life could obviously go on without him. At that exact moment, only the sunfish in the postcard pinned to the wall above the cistern could vouch for his existence. And it wasn't helping. The fully inflated creature, bristling with spikes, reminded him of his bladder.

'Come on then – are you or aren't you?'

Annoyed, he waved it around in every direction, but soon came to the conclusion that violence never got you anywhere. The more you want something, the further you push it away.

Okay then, he thought to himself, let's pretend we're here to do something else: to study the sunfish's morphology perhaps, or even to test the quality of the toilet paper. It's a good brand, thick and soft. Count the tiles on the floor. Twenty, two with bevelled corners. The journey into the afterlife promised to be thrilling.

'Right, come on. I've had enough,' he muttered to himself.

Disappointed, he tucked himself back in and, out of principle, flushed the toilet. The sound of the rushing water aroused something in his abdomen. Suddenly, he felt an urgent need and everything started all over again.

'Are you all right in there, Gabriel?'

'Fine, thanks. I'll be out in a second.'

There was not an olive nor a morsel of pasta left on their plates. Despite the grief and the sorrow, they had been hungry. The two bottles of Lacryma Christi had been drunk. Thankfully, José had brought another two bottles of wine. Rita and he were getting on well. They were all taking comfort from each other. Unhappy people were part of the same big happy family. Rita had shown José the photo of her white poppy and he had shown her a photo of his family in happier times.

Madeleine watched them tenderly, her head resting on her hand, her elbow on her knee. Which sea was she daydreaming about? How deep was she swimming?

Everything should stop here, now, when everything was perfect. It should be like this for ever. Gabriel wanted to be able to persuade them to stay as they were, not to move a muscle, not to say another word. Because he knew. He knew. He had been here once before, that day on the terrace, the heat, the closed shutters, Blandine enjoying a siesta, the cats at her feet, a fly buzzing, Juliette in her hammock, the piano playing, the baby wailing, the ferry's whistle, the smell of the barbecue and the melon skin. That day he hadn't known. He should never have left the next day. The first one to move would break the charm. Their bubble would burst.

'Hey, Gabriel. Gabriel. Are you with us? I was just telling them the story of the panda.'

'Ah, yes, the panda.'

They already had memories in common, some good and some

bad. Rita looked younger; there was something childlike about her, as if she had cried herself clean.

'It's funny. It's as though you've known each other since school.'

'If it wasn't for the couple of hundred miles between us, then maybe. Having said that, when the two of you came to my restaurant the other night, I thought you and Madeleine were sisters.'

'No, I could never stand my brothers and sisters. Anyway, that doesn't matter. We're here now, together. You get the family you deserve.'

Gabriel blinked; on, off, on, off. Anyone can feel like family in the end; you just have to replace the smiling faces in the identikit photo.

The thing that had struck Gabriel was how young they were. One was sixteen and the other seventeen. They had stood there, like bored schoolchildren, half listening to a lecture on discipline. They were probably thinking about the football match that the judge was making them miss. They had confessed to everything on their arrest. A fuck-up. It wasn't their fault if someone had told them to burgle the wrong flat. They had got the wrong door. Shit happens. They were stoned and it was late. They'd panicked when the woman and child started screaming – you know how it is. They were sorry. They would never do it again. They promised. They swore. Their past had been lousy; all they cared about now was the telly and the football score between Les Bleus and Italy. They agreed to pay the price for their youthful error. Fifteen years, five suspended, ten years in prison. They would still be young when they got out. Whether they spent those years on the inside or out made little difference. With their shaved heads, sticking-out ears, brand-new tracksuits and trainers, they looked like young sportsmen apologising after an unfortunate defeat: 'We'll do better next time.'

As hard as he tried, Gabriel couldn't bring himself to hate them. Even before meeting them, even before knowing who had done it, the enormity of the crime had stripped bare his sense of good and evil. It was like a natural disaster, a volcanic eruption, a tsunami, an earthquake, something beyond all comprehension. His lawyer and family were surprised, if not dismayed, by his lack of fighting spirit. They wanted him to show hate, a thirst for vengeance, but Gabriel had none. He had tried to imagine gouging out the eyes of his wife and child's torturers, but he couldn't manage it. Curiously, he felt he had more in common with the guilty pair than with his friends as, like him, the two boys failed to feel the difference between good and evil. He would rather watch the final with them. Like them, he had nothing left to say for himself. The guilty one, the real one, was still on the run. The one without name or form that humanity invoked every day. He would never be troubled.

They heard a roar from outside the courtroom. France were leading 1–0. Lawyers, murderers, victims and judges joined in a silent cheer.

José had drunk a fair amount and, although he struggled to get up off the couch, he managed to stand up without swaying.

'I have to go. I'm getting up early tomorrow.'

Tomorrow ... Madeleine resurfaced from her reverie. Rita rubbed her eyes and Gabriel looked down.

Rita poured the last dregs of wine into her glass and finished it in one.

'So then, it's all over.'

José blushed as if caught out. His eyes searched in vain for something to hold on to. He felt guilty. It wasn't easy playing Judas. He stared down at his feet as if they were made of lead.

'All good things must come to an end.'

'Why?'

'Because if they don't then you won't realise how good they've been. That's just the way it is, can't be helped.'

Rita fell back onto the couch with a sigh, her arm held over her eyes. Madeleine started to clear the table. Gabriel got up and offered his hand to José, who grabbed it as one would a lifebelt.

'Well, that's life, isn't it?'

'*C'est la vie*. Goodnight, José. By the way, can I come along with you tomorrow?'

'If you want. We'll all squeeze in.'

Madeleine offered him her spineless sunfish cheek. Rita didn't move from the couch. She was sleeping, or at least pretending to. José hesitated as he leant over to kiss her goodnight. He pulled back.

'So then, I'll see you tomorrow.'

'Goodnight, José.'

Madeleine emptied the ashtrays full of dreams while Gabriel opened a window. The party spirit swirled out and dissolved in the rectangle of velvety darkness like fine drizzle evaporating. Madeleine joined Gabriel at the window.

'I've drunk too much.'

They both leant against the windowsill, as though holding on to a ship's rail as it pulled out of harbour. The street was quiet.

'Have you ever been happy, Gabriel?'

'Yes, once. It frightened me.'

'Why?'

'Because it was the last time.'

'I don't know if I should envy you or feel sorry for you.'

'Neither.'

'You're going to leave, aren't you?'

'Of course, like everybody else.'

'To go where?'

'I don't know. Somewhere like this probably.'

'So why don't you stay?'

'It's not up to me.'

Below, on the opposite pavement, a blind man walked by. He

would have passed by unnoticed if it hadn't been for the tippy-tappy sound of his white stick. The sound of a shadow.

'What about him? Do you think he knows where he's going?'

'Definitely. A blind man's at home in darkness.'

'This evening, everybody was happy — José, Rita. But you weren't. What's stopping you from being happy?'

'I'm not unhappy.'

'I love you, Gabriel. It's stupid, but it's true.'

The blind man turned a corner. The sound of his stick gradually faded away before disappearing completely. The town lay still, bathing in dreams in which everybody was a hero. He had to sleep. Sleep.

'I'm going back to the hotel, Madeleine. It's late.'

She'd never been as beautiful as she was then. Much more beautiful than her geranium.

'That's a nice gun you've got there, Françoise.'

'It belonged to my husband. He was a great hunter. I clean it regularly. It's in perfect condition, like when he was alive.'

The little girl resembled a wild strawberry trampled by an elephant. Her small hand still gripped the saxophone with which she had just played a flawless, if slightly fast, rendition of *Au Clair de la Lune* for Gabriel. Beside her, as if asleep, her brother sat leaning against the wall, his arms slack by his sides, his legs extended, his chin resting on his chest, in the middle of which the buckshot had left a hole the size of an orange. Françoise lay in the hallway, a few feet from the door. She was faceless, as if a mask had been ripped violently off her. José was at the foot of the stairs on his back, his arms outstretched, his mouth wide open and his eyes burning with shock. The echo of the last gunshot still rang in the stairwell. José had been halfway up the stairs when he saw Gabriel on the landing with the gun in his hand.

'Gabriel? What on earth—'

The force of the gunshot blew him away. Gabriel stepped over José's body, put the gun on the kitchen table and filled a large glass with tap water. The smell of gunpowder had dried his mouth. Everything had happened so quickly, two minutes at most.

Happiness is a calamity you can never recover from. As soon as you catch a glimpse of it, the door slams shut and you spend the rest of your life bitterly regretting what is no more. There is no worse purgatory and no one knew that better than Gabriel. The Westminster clock struck eleven, immortalising the moment for ever. He felt vacant and hollow, his bones and arteries empty, as if all the blood that had been spilt had been his own. He was hungry and wanted a beer. That was what the two kids had done after they had torn his family apart. They had gone and plundered his fridge and drunk some beers. That must be the normal reaction. His path back to the car was strewn with abandoned luggage.

It was always like that with the horizon: you never knew where it really ended. There had to be a hole in it, that was it, an unending chasm. And the sky. It has to break into day, but you sense that it doesn't really want to. It's a sky that would rather go back to bed.

Gabriel parked the car on the roadside. He had a pressing urge. His jet of urine swept over the wild grass and unnamed indestructible plants. Once a year they blossomed, producing scrawny and charmless flowers as well as seeds, which allowed them to reproduce. All for nothing. They weren't edible and would never look good in a bouquet. Like humanity, a lot of creation is totally pointless. And yet it is this kind of landscape that is the most resistant. You could piss on it for ever.

As he closed his flies, Gabriel's gaze was drawn to the clump of brambles opposite. Despite its apparent chaos, there seemed to him to be a deep-rooted architectural logic to this tangle of barbed branches. It wasn't just coincidence that one stalk had wound itself round another three times. Nothing was left to chance. Everything happened for a reason. It was fascinating. The icy wind blew its foul breath in his face. Gabriel felt tired. He climbed back into the car, tipped the seat back and turned on the radio. The presenter was telling a stupid joke but it made him laugh. A man walks into a bar ...

The space outside the Faro where José had been parked that

morning was still empty. Gabriel pulled up, cut the engine and closed his eyes. He remembered the big brasserie at the end of the street where the two young businessmen had argued over the babies' bottles and their mismatched teats. Sauerkraut, that's what he wanted. A good plate of sauerkraut.

'What are you doing, Rita?'

'I'm cooking an egg, can't you see?'

Her face was swollen. She wore a baggy tracksuit and dirty slippers. With her arms folded in front of the stove, she stared into the pan of boiling water, watching the egg dance from side to side. Everything seemed too big for her, her skin, her clothes, her life. The little girl with the white poppy was once again forgotten in the purse at the bottom of the bag. She had the same air of resignation as José had had that morning when picking up his kids, his neck stretched out to take the yoke of a life already written and planned in advance. A look that said every day was like a Monday morning.

'José lent me his car. I was thinking, I could take you to the hospital if you want.'

'Um, yeah, I guess so. Only if you want.'

'It is today you're going, isn't it?'

'Yes, yes. I'll eat my egg and then we can go. The coffee's still hot if you want some.'

The dishes from the night before had been washed and stacked precariously in the drainer. Opposite Gabriel, Rita carefully peeled the shell off her egg. Once finished, she took her time looking at the egg before taking a bite. The coffee was lukewarm.

'What time is it?'

'Twenty past three.'

'I didn't sleep a wink last night. How are José and the kids? And their grandmother?'

'They're fine.'

'Good. He's nice, José, not complicated, not needy. He doesn't ask for much.'

'Have you heard anything from Marco?'

'I called the hospital this morning. They didn't want to give me any details. He's not dead though. Right, I'll put some clothes on and then we can go.'

'You've got a bit of egg yolk in the corner of your mouth.'

'Ah, thank you.'

Warehouses and retail parks selling all sorts of useless tat sprouted on the edge of town, amid the turn-offs and roundabouts. They were all overburdened with signs, logos and giant arrows shouting 'Come on in! This is where it's at!' But actually finding the entrance was always a nightmare. A windscreen wiper squeaked annoyingly.

'Pull over at that café there. I have to get a drink before the hospital.'

The supermarket café was full of people coming and going. But they could all have been the same person, more or less successfully disguised, with moustaches, glasses, wigs or shaved heads. Rita was already on her third beer. She wasn't talking, preferring instead to smoke and chew her fingernails, her gaze drifting towards the car park full of puddles.

'Are you worried, Rita?'

'No, it's not that. I'm fed up with going nowhere. I feel like I've been pedalling just to stay still my entire life. José's got his kids, a family ...'

'You've got Marco.'

'Yes, or maybe he has me. I've been a whore for him and now I can be his nurse! When happiness doesn't come, there's nothing you can do about it. Last night was good though, wasn't it?'

'Yes, it was good.'

'At least that's something. Let's go.'

The hospital wasn't that different from the shopping centre. It was also a cube-shaped block, probably dreamt up by the same architect, but with stretchers instead of shopping trolleys, humans instead of groceries. Here, as at the supermarket, business was good. Gabriel struggled to find a place to park. Rita fidgeted in her seat.

'Gabriel, let's get out of here.'

'Hold on, it's fine, I'll find a space. Look, there's one over there.'

'Let's go, I said! I don't want to go inside. Let's get out of here!'

'If that's what you want. Where do you want to go?'

'Anywhere, I don't care. Let's go.'

Rita's cheeks were red and glazed with tears, which she let run down her face without wiping them away. She sniffled, her lower lip sticking out dejectedly. Gabriel drove around aimlessly, a left turn here, a right turn there. They drove through a small estate full of new houses, all identical, reproduced ad infinitum. Past that, they travelled through fields, all flat except for the odd cluster of bare trees. Rita's tears had dried up. Her breathing was back to normal. She dabbed her eyes and blew her nose.

'I'm sorry, Gabriel, but I just couldn't.'

'You don't need to apologise.'

'Can you pull up here by the trees? I need to pee. Those beers ...'

Gabriel turned off down a rutted dirt track and cut the engine. Rita jumped out of the car. Through the wet windscreen he could see her scrambling through the undergrowth and then suddenly disappearing into a thicket. One day, he had taken Juliette to the mountains to see the marmots. Every time he had pointed one out to her, the animal had disappeared down a hole before she had managed to see it. They returned home with Juliette convinced that it had all been one big joke. As far as she was concerned, marmots didn't exist.

Without thinking, Gabriel started playing with one of the laces he had bought at the cobbler's. He wound it round his hand and tested its resistance by pulling on it. The rain started hammering on the roof. Rita ran back to the car and jumped in, her hair flattened by the rain.

'Fucking mud! My shoes got bloody stuck in it. I've got mud up to my knees. I hate the countryside.'

Rita brushed her hair back, slumped into the seat, closed her eyes and sighed.

'My God, it feels good to take a piss when you really need one. It's nice hearing the rain, when you're under cover ...'

Rita wasn't as heavy as he had thought. But these brambles catching at his clothes, and the slippery mud ... He got to the spot where he thought he had seen her crouch. Her face was calm, peaceful. The rain washed away her tear-smudged make-up. She hadn't struggled when Gabriel had leant in. Maybe she thought he wanted to kiss her. It was only by reflex that she had stretched her legs and arms out as the lace tightened round her neck.

'... I never left the apartment. I didn't answer the phone, pick up my mail or answer the doorbell. I spent my days lying on the terrace looking at the sky. It was still just as blue, the kind of blue you can get lost in. And then one day I got up from my deckchair and shut the door behind me. I took only what I could carry on my back. I think I caught a ferry or a train, I can't remember. Once the door had shut I started to forget. The days and nights merged into one. I slept wherever and whenever I could. With each day that passed, I forgot a little more of myself. I wandered around Paris for a bit. I could have chosen anywhere, but I chose Paris. Perhaps because I was born there and wanted to go back to where it had all started, or perhaps it was just to disappear into the crowd. It was cold. When I was so drunk I couldn't sleep, I would walk until I started to hallucinate. It was like that every day. Always the same. I couldn't feel anything, except the weight of my tiredness, and that's all I wanted. One night I got picked up half frozen off a pavement. I woke up in hospital. I don't know how but my friends found out. I asked them to sell everything I owned, the house, the car, everything, and then not to come searching for me ever again. I never wanted to go back, ever. After I left the hospital I went into a convalescent home. I stayed there for weeks, months, until one day I felt a sudden urge to see the sea. I needed something to look at other than the walls of my room. I felt trapped. I needed space, to be far away. I got the first train to Brest. Don't ask me why – I couldn't tell you. I was suffocating in the train carriage. I needed air. That's the whole story.'

The headlights from the cars travelling in the opposite direction flashed across Madeleine's face. Since Gabriel had started telling his story, she had gone rigid, as milky-white and transparent as an alabaster statue.

'Why are you telling me this now?'

'Because we're alone in a car at night. Let me know if you want to stop to eat or drink something.'

'No. I can't take it all in. Rita, José, you ... You've all been through so much. And I'm just floating through it all, oblivious ...'

'I'm sorry, I shouldn't have said anything.'

'Of course you should. It's always good to talk.'

'I don't know. I've never spoken about it to anyone. My suffering has stopped though. It's just the pain of others which hurts me. I always want to help them.'

'You're very good at it. You've been great to José, and Rita as well.'

'But not you?'

'Oh, you can forget about me. I've never been too happy or too sad, just bored. You get used to it. I'm so happy to have met you and to be here with you now in this car, tonight.'

'It's lucky you were able to get away for a couple of days.'

'My boss owed me! I had so much holiday to take. What else was I going to do with it? It was fine. It was kind of José to lend you his car.'

'It was him who suggested it. He said, "You're looking after me and Rita too much and you're neglecting Madeleine. Borrow the car and take her to the sea."'

'What a great idea! It's just that I'm a bit worried about Rita.'

'Don't be. When she reads your note, she'll understand. She was fine, really, when I dropped her off at the hospital.'

'So we've got clear consciences then?'

'Absolutely. What time is it?'

'It's just gone quarter past eight.'

'We'll be at Roscoff in half an hour. I hope there'll be a restaurant still open.'

'There's bound to be a crêperie.'

'I hope so. I'm hungry. Here we are at Morlaix.'

Road signs lit up by their headlights flashed by: Saint-Martin-des-Champs, Sainte-Sève, Taulé, Saint-Pol-de-Léon ... They were just signposts, that was all. Nothing was there to prove that these places actually existed. The night dissolved these villages like sugar in coffee. You passed them by without seeing them and forgot them almost as quickly: a high street, a war memorial, a town hall, a post office, a church, a graveyard and it was over. You moved on to the next one.

'Why did you choose the Île de Batz, Gabriel?'

'Because you can walk all the way round it in a morning.'

'Gabriel, look at this shell – it's huge!'

Blandine was running over to him holding something in her hand that looked from a distance like a skull. Her yellow raincoat was the only splash of colour in an otherwise pearly-grey landscape. He was scared she would slip on the green and brown algae-covered rocks. The wind carried his voice away, so he signalled to her to be careful. But she took no notice. She leapt over rock pools in the oversized wellington boots they had borrowed from the hotel. Her momentum carried her into Gabriel's arms and the two of them fell onto the sand. She smelt of salt and of the breeze. The shell looked like a big ear. She put it up to her ear, then up to Gabriel's and then held it against her already round stomach.

'Listen to that, Juliette. It's the Breton sea. Your mummy and

daddy are there right now. Do you want to say something? I'll pass you over.'

The sea grunted. It was grumpy that day. The drizzle made their mouths slippery.

'Darling, build us an island in the sun!'

And he did.

It was still dark when they left the hotel. Apart from the wind whistling, the streets were empty. There were only a few lights on, one at the baker's where they had bought croissants, and a neon sign belonging to the bar by the pier where they sought shelter from the rain lashing against the austere facades of the blank houses. Madeleine stirred her hot chocolate in a daydream, smiling like the panda. Gabriel chewed his croissant while watching the raindrops slide down the dark pane of glass. Besides the owner, there were two other people in the bar: a tall red-haired man with a moustache who was speaking English, and an old woman dressed in tweed and fur-lined boots, who looked very dignified, her white hair pulled back into a tight bun. The old woman sipped a cup of tea and stared absent-mindedly at the row of bottles above the bar. From time to time he made chit-chat about the weather or unknown people with John, the owner. There was a smell of stuffy bedrooms, cosy duvets and morning coffees in the air.

'Gabriel?'

'Yes?'

'Nothing. I feel good.' Madeleine placed her hand on Gabriel's. She had said it without smiling, as if it was something serious, something solemn.

'Me too,' he replied.

'Do you regret it?'

'What?'

'Us two, last night?'

'Not at all – the opposite actually. Was I okay? It's been such a long time.'

'It would have been great even if we hadn't done it.'

After eating some excellent seafood pancakes at the crêperie they had gone back to the hotel. They had taken turns in the shower and then lain on the bed watching TV, enjoying a mindless game show. Looking at them, you would have thought they had spent their lives together. In the end, they had turned the light off and made love simply and quickly with all the awkwardness of first-timers.

'There's the boat.'

John pointed to the squat outline of a boat arriving from Île de Batz in the first light of dawn, walnut-sized on the horizon. The old woman got up and put on a long green raincoat and a rain hat. She wasn't particularly tall, but with her fixed gaze she seemed to dominate everything around her, like a lighthouse.

It was hard to stay upright walking along the jetty, with the wind charging at them like a battering ram. The old lady walked in front of them, head straight, indifferent. Two men helped them onto the boat. The three passengers went and sat inside on wooden benches. It was like being back at school, packed in, their arms crossed. The waves rocked them from side to side, shoulder to shoulder.

Under the lowering sky, the Île de Batz appeared, a naked shoulder emerging from the sea. The crossing had only taken fifteen minutes but long after they had set foot on land the boat's pitching remained in their legs.

'Which way, left or right?'

'It doesn't matter. An island is like a beret – there's no right way.'

'Let's go left then.'

'Why?'

'We write from left to right and for me today is a blank page.'

They weren't really villages, just clusters of houses and place names – Kenekaou, Porz Kloz – separated from one another by creeks, dunes, moors and fields. It took them just half an hour to reach the island's easterly tip and a botanical garden. It was an island within an island, an exotic oasis where palm trees grew as if back home under sunnier climes. A ray of sunlight breaking through the clouds shone like a spotlight on the leaves of the rubber, yucca and other plants with unpronounceable names. A tern landed on a palm tree in front of Madeleine.

'It's unbelievable. This is paradise. That's what it is, paradise!'

'I know. Are you coming?'

Blandine had said exactly the same thing, in exactly the same place, ten years earlier.

Side by side, stooping into the wind, they followed the smugglers' path, the sea on their right shaking its petticoat tails in a breathtaking can-can.

'Let's sit down here for a moment.'

Down below, pink granite boulders were jumbled on top of each other, making the shapes of bizarre animals in the process of transformation.

'See that one? It looks like a tortoise. And that one over there looks like a sad dog. And over there—'

'You know what this place is called?'

'No.'

'The Snake's Hole. Legend has it that it was here that St Pol killed a dragon which was terrorising the island's inhabitants. If you lean over the side and listen carefully to the waves, it sounds like laughter. Listen.'

Madeleine inched tentatively forward. 'It must be terrifying here when there's a storm.'

'Terrifying.'

'But with you I'm not scared of anything. If you only knew how happy I am, to be here with you between the sea and the sky. You can't get any happier than this.' She paused. 'Gabriel, what's wrong?'

At the foot of the hole the water whirled, lapping hungrily against the rocks. *You can't get any happier than this*.

'Gabriel? What are you doing?'

They were high up, very high. All it would take was one small dancing step, the half-turn of a waltz, and Madeleine, like José, like Rita, like the others, would be happy ever after.

'Gabriel, you're holding me too tight; you're hurting me.'

And the waves below applauded. They applauded.

'And what would you like to drink with the crab? A white wine perhaps?'

'Yes, please.'

'And a jug of water, please.'

'Of course, Madame.'

The romantic Bernique was the only restaurant that was open on the island. They had a choice of crab or ... crab. They were enormous, the size of tanks. Madeleine fiddled with the surgical tools to extract the white meat from the creature lying open in front of her, claws hanging off the plate. Gabriel, his eyes half closed, watched her through the swirling smoke of his cigarette.

'They're enormous! I don't know where to start.'

'Do you want me to crack the claws for you?'

'Yes, please.'

Gabriel got to work using a nutcracker-like tool, itself in the form of a crab claw.

'You know, earlier, at the Snake's Hole, it's stupid but I thought you were going to push me in.'

'Really? Why would I have done that?'

'I don't know. You were holding on to me so hard and we were so close to the edge. Your eyes were empty, like the drop behind me.'

Gabriel hadn't been able to. Madeleine had reached the peak of her happiness, and would never make it up there again. Anything else would only be a slow and tedious decline. To finish her at the height of her happiness and in water, her favourite element, too, seemed like a no-brainer. But he couldn't do it. His hands had relinquished their grip on her shoulders and fallen limply by his side. His head was ringing with the roar of the sea from the hole, that swirl of foaming green jelly, indignant that it had been refused its ration. Madeleine had quickly taken two steps forward and rubbed her shoulders, staring ahead, open-mouthed.

'Let's go, Gabriel.'

'Yes ... yes, of course. Are you hungry?'

They had reached the restaurant without having said a word to each other.

Four locals, their caps pulled down low over their eyes, were playing cards at a table near the entrance. Depending on how the game was going, they let out onomatopoeic grunts and groans. It was impossible to hold a conversation, even a boring one, and shell a crab at the same time. Like the belote players, Gabriel and Madeleine spoke only in sucking noises, chewing sounds and the occasional sharp crack. Their tray was now littered with shell shrapnel and crumpled balls of lemon-scented hand wipes.

'What time's the boat?'

'Five, I think.'

'And then what?'

'What do you mean?'

'Once we get to the other side?'

'And then ...'

The boat had barely set sail and already the island had faded in the distance. Only a few twinkling lights remained on the skyline. They hadn't noticed it getting dark. It was difficult to keep your balance, even gripping the handrail, as the round-bottomed boat was thrown about by the waves. Even so, Madeleine was determined to stay on deck. It smelt of salt and tar.

'It feels like the island only existed today, for us. I'm never going back.'

She said this without sadness or regret. It was what it was ... 'I'm never going back.'

'Excuse me, could you please return below deck? It's too dangerous out here in this weather.'

José's car was waiting for them on the quayside. Loyal. Resigned.

'Do you want to get a hot drink before we hit the road?'

'No, let's head off straight away.'

The names of the towns and villages flashed by once more in the glare of the headlights, but this time in reverse order, like a film being rewound. Sometimes, at the youth club, Gabriel used to help the priest pack away the projection equipment. It was magical to see Charlie Chaplin step backwards onto a roof from which he had fallen only fifteen minutes earlier. Of course it was a film, but in his heart of hearts Gabriel thought it possible to do something similar in real life: to crank back the camera and, hey presto, wipe the slate clean and start again.

'Gabriel, you know, I think I'm going to take your advice.'

'What do you mean?'

'Go to an island in the sun. I'm going to find a job in a little hotel and perhaps, maybe, a husband. And I'm going to spend my days swimming, not thinking of anything.'

'That's a very good idea, Madeleine.'

Yes, I think so too. Can you stop at that service station? I want a coffee. Could you go and get me one?'

'Of course.'

A gust of wind blew into the car as Gabriel opened the door. It was as if someone was pushing from the other side, preventing him from getting out.

'Would you like sugar?'

'Yes, please.'

Just before he stepped out Madeleine grasped his hand.

'Gabriel?'

'Yes?'

'Thank you.'

An elderly woman was having trouble with the vending machine. Her feeble fingers pressed all the buttons in vain.

'Would you like me to try?'

With the palm of his hand Gabriel hit the side of the machine, which immediately delivered a cup and jerkily filled it with brownish liquid.

'Thank you, you're very kind.'

'My pleasure.'

Using the same method, Gabriel filled his own soft plastic cup with the same indiscriminate liquid.

Outside, the car was gone. In its place lay his bag, abandoned on the asphalt. There were only three or four cars parked on the forecourt and José's car wasn't one of them. Gabriel immediately realised what had happened. Madeleine was a good woman. She had done what she had to do. He picked up his bag, threw the cup in a bin and crossed the forecourt.

The harsh neon light created petrol rainbows in the iridescent shimmering puddles of water. There was no need to look up at the sky to admire the stars. They were all there, fallen on the ground. You could walk on them and splash them. A car engine growled. It was a small Austin. It looked like a toy car. Gabriel knocked on the window.

'Excuse me, madame, but would you mind giving me a lift to the nearest train station?'

'I'm going to Morlaix. Ah, you're the one who helped with the coffee machine. Come on, get in.'

The car was small, no bigger than a family-size box of matches. With his bag on his knees Gabriel climbed in as best he could. It smelt of mints.

'Thank you very much.'

'I don't normally take hitchhikers, but seeing as you helped me with the coffee machine it's the least I can do. We already know each other a bit. And, anyway, Morlaix isn't far. You wouldn't have the time to do away with me!'

The woman gave a tinkling laugh. Gabriel's laugh was a little forced. The woman drove in fits and starts with her nose up close to the steering wheel and her forehead almost touching the front windscreen.

'You know, I complained at the checkout about their coffee machine, but they didn't care! And I followed all the instructions properly!'

'I'm sure you did.'

'I'll tell you something. I don't for a moment believe in their progress. It's like the telephone. My children bought me a mobile phone because it reassures them. Well, believe it or not, the thing doesn't work. And it's always my fault. I'm never in the right place, or I didn't recharge the batteries, or I pressed the wrong button, goodness knows what else! There's always something that makes it my fault. They bought me a computer as well, to be closer to me, apparently. And so now I only see my grandchildren in photos and I don't get postcards any more. It's a young person's world, full of buttons. That's how it is. Anyway, no offence, but aren't you a bit too old to be hitchhiking?'

'It's a long story. I was supposed to meet somebody.'

'Where are you heading?'

'The south.'

'The south is a good place to grow old. Cannes is nice. What on earth is going on up ahead?'

A maelstrom of flashing blue lights filled the sky as a policeman dressed in a fluorescent jacket signalled to the oncoming cars to slow down. Driving up to him, the woman wound down her window.

'What's going on?'

'There's been an accident.'

'Is it serious?'

'Someone's been killed. A woman. If she had wanted to kill herself, she couldn't have done a better job. It's a straight road. either that or she fell asleep at the wheel. Could you move on, please? There are people behind you.'

José's car sat smoking, crumpled up against a wall as firemen in shiny helmets covered it in dry ice.

'People drive like idiots. They drive at top speed and to go where?'

'To an island.'

'Sorry?

'Nothing, I was just saying.'

The railway platform was deserted. Above him, a tangle of metal girders merged into the gloom.